PRAISE FO

MIDNIGHT

"A dark, dramatic, and erotic tone . . . Fans of Charlaine Harris and Jim Butcher may enjoy." —*Library Journal*

"An exciting, high-tension horror thriller with enough unresolved trust and family issues to make it credible, a hint of romance for spice, and a bit of black humor to lighten up the often dark tone, this is a nicely conceived modern vampire tale that will keep readers guessing." —*Monsters and Critics*

"Green writes a complex story featuring well-defined characters and more than enough noir mystery to keep readers enthralled." —*School Library Journal*

"An intriguing world that becomes more complex with every turn of the page . . . kick-butt action." —*Huntress Book Reviews*

"Green has given her fans an inside look at the Underground culture and social class system, from the powerful Elite, bitten by the Master, to the lowly Guards, bitten by the Groupies . . . [a] fun urban fantasy mystery." —*Alternative Worlds*

"A fast-moving urban fantasy filled with murder, mystery, and a large dose of the supernatural. The vivid characterization and danger at every turn will keep readers engaged." —*Darque Reviews*

"A dark, edgy, and complex series." —*Romantic Times*

"A dark and thrilling paranormal tale . . . a gritty and suspenseful ride." —*Romance Reviews Today*

continued . . .

PRAISE FOR

Night Rising

"A book to die for! Dark, mysterious, and edged with humor, this book rocks on every level!"

—Gena Showalter, author of *The Vampire's Bride*

"If you like your fantasy with an edge, then you've struck gold. There is a ring of truth to the biting—no pun intended—allegory. This is a fantastic start to a new series." —*The Eternal Night*

"Chris Marie Green does a wonderful job of bringing this gritty, dark novel to life . . . I can't wait to see where [she] takes the rest of the books." —*The Best Reviews*

"An exciting, action-packed vampire thriller . . . a fantastic tale that . . . provides book lovers with plenty of adventure and a touch of romance." —*Midwest Book Review*

"Dawn makes a spunky vampire slayer." —*Publishers Weekly*

"An interesting take on the vampire world . . . well written and exciting. I look forward to the next book."

—*The Romance Readers Connection*

"A killer mystery . . . Bring on book two!"

—Kelley Armstrong, author of *Men of the Otherworld*

Ace Books by Chris Marie Green

NIGHT RISING

MIDNIGHT REIGN

BREAK OF DAWN

A DROP OF RED

THE PATH OF RAZORS

Anthologies

FIRST BLOOD

(with Susan Sizemore, Erin McCarthy, and Meljean Brook)

The Path of Razors

VAMPIRE BABYLON
BOOK FIVE

Chris Marie Green

THE BERKLEY PUBLISHING GROUP
Published by the Penguin Group
Penguin Group (USA) Inc.
375 Hudson Street, New York, New York 10014, USA
Penguin Group (Canada), 90 Eglinton Avenue East, Suite 700, Toronto, Ontario M4P 2Y3, Canada
(a division of Pearson Penguin Canada Inc.)
Penguin Books Ltd., 80 Strand, London WC2R 0RL, England
Penguin Group Ireland, 25 St. Stephen's Green, Dublin 2, Ireland (a division of Penguin Books Ltd.)
Penguin Group (Australia), 250 Camberwell Road, Camberwell, Victoria 3124, Australia
(a division of Pearson Australia Group Pty. Ltd.)
Penguin Books India Pvt. Ltd., 11 Community Centre, Panchsheel Park, New Delhi—110 017, India
Penguin Group (NZ), 67 Apollo Drive, Rosedale, North Shore 0632, New Zealand
(a division of Pearson New Zealand Ltd.)
Penguin Books (South Africa) (Pty.) Ltd., 24 Sturdee Avenue, Rosebank, Johannesburg 2196,
South Africa

Penguin Books Ltd., Registered Offices: 80 Strand, London WC2R 0RL, England

This is an original publication of The Berkley Publishing Group.

Cover art by Larry Rostant.
Cover design by Judith Lagerman.

PRINTING HISTORY
Ace trade paperback edition / August 2009

Library of Congress Cataloging-in-Publication Data

Green, Chris Marie.
The path of razors / Chris Marie Green.—Ace trade pbk. ed.
p. cm.—(Vampire babylon ; bk. 5)
ISBN 978-0-441-01720-1
1. Madison, Dawn (Fictitious character)—Fiction. 2. Vampires—Fiction. 3. Americans—England—Fiction. 4. London (England)—Fiction. I. Title.
PS3607.R4326P38 2009
813'.6—dc22

2009015589

PRINTED IN THE UNITED STATES OF AMERICA

10 9 8 7 6 5 4 3 2 1

To Kaela and both Marias—
thank you, thank you, and thank you! In your own ways,
you've each pushed me onward.

Once more, thank you to everyone listed in *A Drop of Red* for the information that shaped the opening of this trilogy and influenced this installment. And again, a nod goes out to "C.S." because Queenshill remains on what is probably your land.

Additional mentions also to Jack Zipes for editing *The Trials & Tribulations of Little Red Riding Hood*, and Ginjer Buchanan, Cameron Dufty, and the wonderful staff at Ace. As always, everyone at the Knight Agency gets my thanks for all their support, as well as Judy Duarte and Sheree Whitefeather for their continued input and encouragement.

And, like last time, I've taken advantage of fictional license regarding some locations and historical details for the benefit of telling this story. All errors are my own.

Enjoy the continuation of the London hunt. . . .

ONE

Once Upon a Shadow

THE London night was giving way to a hint of morning as the shadow eased open the seventh-story window of the hotel room just enough to slip inside, roll to the carpet, and come to a crouch.

After scanning the area, the shadow flipped up a pair of night-vision goggles and rose to a stand, revealing the streamlined figure of an Underground caretaker who aided in keeping the community of vampires secure.

This was the newest *custode*, just activated a week past, due to the death of a previous keeper.

Body and mind becoming more attuned to the job with each passing hour, the caretaker now blended with the angles of darkness in the modest hotel room while extracting a strange, black, weblike instrument from a belt compartment. Then the *custode* crept over to the sleeping schoolgirl lying on the bed next to another binge-resting female vampire.

Della, the keeper thought, attaching the instrument—the tuner—to the young female's temples.

The caretaker donned the connecting end of the tuner, concentrating, eyes closed for the few moments it would take to transfer the information.

The vision/tales.

A flock of subconscious nightmares.

Minutes later, the *custode* disconnected, tucking both ends of the tuner back into the belt compartment.

Yet before departing, the caretaker leaned over to the still-resting Della and whispered into her ear, taking care not to disturb the other three schoolgirls who binge rested in the hotel room, which served as the vampires' temporary haven.

"Do you know what's in store for *you*, little girl?"

The *custode* lightly tweaked Della's baby-fat cheek.

Then, quiet as a black spider, the keeper backed away from the bed, lowering the night goggles in preparation to depart.

Sliding out the window, the caretaker kept in mind that Mrs. Jones—or Claudia, as Mihas called her—had stationed her vampire self on the rooftop. Yet the keepers went through a lot of trouble to render themselves scentless, soundless.

The *custode* flicked on the night-vision goggles then, catching the air, grabbed the stone of a balcony on the way down, repeating the graceful process by swinging on more balconies, lower and lower, until reaching the ground.

Time to go back to tracking the attackers who had breached the Queenshill School for Girls last night.

The *custode* grinned before blending with the less dangerous, more natural shadows outside.

Time to get back to the relatively safer stuff.

TWO

London Babylon, Inside the Temporary Haven

DELLA started out of her binge rest to find the curtains stirring in a breeze from the opened window, and before her next disconcerted breath, she sprang off the bed to the restless drapery, which she shoved aside.

Someone had just been in the room. But who?

What?

Yet when she peered out the window, nothing was there. Nothing at all. Not even a smell to be detected by her sharpened senses.

Only a timid, chill breeze peeling away the layers of a mid-November morning. Only the slumberous city street below the business hotel in Islington where the girls' superior, Mrs. Jones, had taken them a few hours ago for safekeeping after the attack on Queenshill by those . . .

Della wasn't so certain what they had been. Another vampire family headed by a preternatural named Frank?

Or something much worse, as Della feared?

As she let the curtain drop back into place, her skin prickled. She was only allowing her imagination to get the best of her, but she couldn't help recalling one of last night's attackers—a much meaner, leaner vampire who'd joined his violent chums in the middle of the Queenshill melee. The school had always kept the girls hidden and secure, until last night, when her and her classmates' secret lifestyle had been challenged by those attackers, who had been minus the mean vampire at first. But when he had joined them, he had ripped apart the dogs Della had called to defend against the trespassers who had crept onto the school grounds for inexplicable reasons.

Her blood curdled as she remembered barely escaping the bad vampire and his clear thirst for destruction.

As a precaution, Mrs. Jones—or "Claudia," as Wolfie, the master, had affectionately called her last night—had gathered the girls and relocated them here, in this hotel. She had also said that she would watch for any trouble from the hotel's rooftop, guarding for signs of Frank and his band, should the group decide to pursue them beyond school grounds.

However, Mrs. Jones hadn't seemed to believe that this scenario would come to fruition; she was even confident that Wolfie's main Underground at Highgate, which housed his larger community of young female vampires, would stay secure. Naturally, Wolfie had stayed away from the Underground for the time being, just as Della and her friends had been removed from the site of the attack itself—the girls' sub-Underground at Queenshill, where Della and her small class had been training to become a part of Wolfie's community after promotion.

There was just something arrogant about Mrs. Jones's faith, and it was an arrogance Della didn't quite trust.

Still, she took a bit of comfort from their housematron's insistence that last night's odd intruders be identified as soon as possible by the contractors who worked for the Underground—even though the girls had to stay away from their beloved sub-Underground until all trouble was rectified.

Della wandered back to the bed, but didn't have it in her to rest again.

Too anxious.

A niggle kept at her, but she tried not to dwell on how the girls had been so naughty last night in engaging—*encouraging*—those intruders on school grounds because it had amused the leader of Della's pack, Violet.

Yet how could Della not think about it when, at any moment, their housematron might mete out punishment for their lack of common sense?

With a contained tremble, Della lowered herself into a chair by the curtains.

But then something like a whisper, buried in her head, struck at her.

Do you know what's in store for you, *little girl?*

Shivers crackled over her skin as she wondered where the words had come from. . . .

Glancing at the other three girls who were still deep at rest on the two beds, Della tried to swallow past the sudden choke in her throat.

She sniffed, inspected the rest of the darkened room with her keen eyesight.

No one.

Nothing.

Perhaps it was merely her instincts trying to warn her, as they had been doing all along, and they had only now been sharpened to a level she couldn't ignore. Before last night—before she had taken a stand against the rest of the girls who had always treated her as the lowest of the low—Della had left her instincts to rot.

But no longer, she thought. No more—

Out of nowhere, a vision attacked: A violent stain of red on a cottage wall. A strike of bloodied white ribbon trailing to the floor and resting on the fair hair of a young girl . . .

Do you know what's in store for you, *little girl?*

This time, Della didn't merely shiver—she shuddered, just as if a thousand freezing blades were knifing her nerves.

Even the sound of gliding footsteps coming down the hallway didn't shake her out of the vision, so she stayed in the chair and squeezed her hands against her temples, as if that would help to expel the jarring pictures.

By the time the housematron unlocked the door, Della had tamed her thoughts, but even so, she cleared her mind, her expression, lest Mrs. Jones think something amiss.

Do you know what's in store . . . ?

Della swallowed as Mrs. Jones breezed into the room.

The elder vampire was in humanlike form, and although she had taken care to dress in the clothing she usually wore in her guise as a Queenshill campus dorm overseer, there was something different. A new confidence that Della had only pinpointed because of last night, when she had seen Mrs. Jones looking like a queen, her skin glowing with a breathtaking freshness that she normally didn't possess while masquerading as a human aboveground.

The change was enthralling, and even now, Della could not keep her eyes off the elder vampire, even if she was hiding that excruciating beauty under her aboveground disguise.

When Mrs. Jones came to the foot of the beds, her presence seemed to rouse the three other vampire girls.

Polly and Noreen rubbed their eyes and sat up. Violet, who still carried the almost-healed scars from last night's personal confrontation with Della after they'd escaped the attackers, only stared at the ceiling.

She was bitter about having been challenged and bested, and Della held back a satisfied smile.

However, guilt immediately set upon her, and she checked herself.

"Up and about already, Della?" Mrs. Jones asked in a husky voice that always seemed to be scraped by a cold.

Della thought it might be wise to offer something close to an honest answer. It might explain any remnants of fear.

"I heard a noise outside," she said. "So I opened the window and checked."

Mrs. Jones raised a brow. "From my rooftop view, the streets were all but empty, and I didn't catch any alarming scents so close to your room—not at this hour."

Della didn't say a word. She had been trained better.

Mrs. Jones swept out a hand, dismissing Della's report. "Perhaps it was a caretaker who came by to monitor you with one of their modern, fancy machines. I believe they have items that can even catch sight of you through a slit in the window curtain. Who knows? They do take care to cover their presence as much as possible, even when it comes to giving off a scent."

A *custode*?

Once, Della had seen the consultants during a trip to the main Underground, in a forbidden area where she had accidentally found herself among such darkness. Oppression.

Yet she hadn't felt any of that here in the hotel at all.

Mrs. Jones glided to a vanity mirror, glancing this way and that, then smiled as she ran her hand over a high cheekbone.

"The *custode* was no doubt in the midst of tracking last night's intruders," she said. "Before your Wolfie left to hide himself in one of his flats around the city for the time being, he suggested that perhaps all of us might attempt to hunt the attackers with our own predatory senses. But I reminded him that it might be best to play it safe at the moment. After all, Frank the vampire and his group did best you girls once, and I'd rather you and Wolfie were tucked in neat and tidy until the *custode*s can find the scoundrels and enlighten us as to their purposes. Besides, our contracted associates have their own means of effective searching, so it's hardly worth worrying about their success."

Della knew that the mysterious *custode*s worked on their own, wandering the fringes of the Underground and taking care of any troubles that arose outside, and when she imagined that one of them might've been so close, every hair on her arms stood on end.

From the far bed, Polly spoke. Next to her, Violet remained staring at the ceiling.

"What do you mean by '*custode*,' Mrs. Jones?"

The older vampire smoothed her brown hair back into its bun, then turned away from the mirror. "Perhaps Della would be kind enough to give you the details she learned last night. I'm off to see to Mihas . . . *Wolfie*"—she amended almost sharply—"and there, I'll tie up the loose ends that your absences at Queenshill will cause."

Noreen the Curious sleepily asked, "How will you go about explaining that, Mrs. Jones?"

The housematron gave the redhead a smile, although Della noticed it was laced with something she thought to be poisonous.

"As far as the school knows, you four have left campus on a scholarly trip."

"Shall we call our parents to tell them where we'll be?" Noreen added.

Polly made a disparaging sound. "Not likely they'll care."

Noreen's sagging shoulders confirmed that. None of their parents cared, and that had led to the decision to become part of the Underground, where they belonged and were appreciated by Wolfie.

Mrs. Jones's smile turned into one of sympathy for Noreen. "I'll contact your parents about your 'field trip' and take care of every other detail. I've whipped up a story about a most beneficial jaunt to study the cathedral in Durham. You've all decided to work there with me on an in-depth study for a few days, for the yearly project Queenshill requires of its students."

"And when shall *we* see Wolfie again?" Noreen asked.

Mrs. Jones raised her chin, her gaze flaring, and it made Della recall how she had stumbled upon their housematron and Wolfie kissing last night.

"As soon as these motley attackers are seen to," Mrs. Jones said, her voice tight, "life as we know it shall resume."

Motley was putting it mildly. Besides the vampires, there had been human servants, including a hard female who had got Della in some manner of a mental hold.

"Mrs. Jones," Della ventured. "It seems as if our territories are rather unguarded. What if the intruders are affiliated with bad vampires . . . ?"

They had all been taught not to talk of Undergrounds or other blood brothers—who had a rumored tendency to overtake other communities—in the open.

Mrs. Jones sighed, clearly spent by Della's continued fretting.

"I'm eager to return home, myself," the housematron said. "Wolfie's place"—she meant the main Underground at Highgate—"is being watched by a *custode* even as we speak."

Clearly finished with the conversation, Mrs. Jones began heading toward the door. "While I unsnarl matters, perhaps you ladies will study your French? Mademoiselle would be terribly upset with me if I didn't see to your tutoring on our 'trip.' "

Polly rolled off her mattress, her bobbed strawberry blond hair askew from her rest. She went to her overnight bag and sifted through it. "Books here and accounted for. I'm only hoping that Noreen didn't pack that awful perfume, too."

"Perfume?" Noreen asked.

"That jasmine stink."

"I don't wear perfume, much less a fragrance more suited to my grandmum."

While Polly shot Noreen a doubtful glance, Mrs. Jones narrowed her eyes, then took a deep breath, as if testing the air in the room.

Della did the same. She had noticed much earlier that the jasmine scent that had been so abundant lately was absent, yet she didn't know what to make of the fact.

With no further remark, Mrs. Jones smiled indulgently at her charges, then swanned the rest of the way to the door. As she turned the handle, she aimed one last glance back at Della.

A sharp glint lit through the dimness, and Della grabbed the armrests of her chair.

Mrs. Jones had looked at her in such a way last night. A visual cut. A never-ending reminder that she would be watching whenever Della least expected it.

As the elder vampire exited, Noreen hopped down from her own bed. Violet stayed lying on her back on the other, her gaze all but boring a hole in the ceiling.

"You'd think," Polly said as she continued tearing through her duffel, "that in our haste to leave Queenshill, we could've at least left the bloody books behind. I could've done without the load while Mrs. Jones forced us to make double time here."

"We never did gallop so fast," Noreen said, fetching her books from her bag. "But, mind that as long as we obey, we'll be cared for. It's the golden rule."

Della rose from her chair, and both Polly and Noreen stood straight, clutching their books. There was a new respect in the way they looked at Della now, and she couldn't help wrapping herself in it.

Violet clearly noticed the change in atmosphere, because when she finally spoke, her tone sliced.

"All hail to Della."

Noreen lowered her head and drifted closer to Polly, who looked as if she were trying valiantly not to glance at Violet, her best friend.

Yet Della was done with always bowing to Violet. "We can carry on one of two ways, Vi. We can be civil about our situation and make life easier in this small room. Or we can make this place a lot more crowded by going at each other once more."

Violet turned her burning purplish gaze to Della. "Pity there's a lack of tree branches here for you to impale me."

"Pity that branch didn't go through your heart when I slammed you into it."

The room seemed sucked of air. Noreen and Polly stood closer to each other, inching away from Violet's bed now.

Their former leader sat up, her sable hair spilling over the shoulder that Polly and Noreen had been forced to heal last night after that branch had run through it.

Now her voice came out as a warning hiss. "I wonder if your words would be so brave, Della, if Mrs. Jones were still in the room. If *Wolfie* were here."

"Both of them know what happened between us." Della took a breath, exhaled, almost not wanting to say what came out of her mouth next. "And neither of them rebuked me. In fact, they seemed quite pleased that I stopped taking your rubbish and fought back."

She didn't add that Wolfie had even appeared proud, that he had even mentioned that Della would make a fine soldier for the dragon—the ultimate master who would one day rise and lead all the Undergrounds in a battle to dominate the world.

Violet was shaking her head. "You don't truly believe that Wolfie will stand for your behavior, do you, Della? Mrs. Jones is going to come back, and she's going to punish you for what you did." Her voice had grown thick. "She's going to have such grand fun chaining you and making you a good girl. She's only waiting . . . only drawing out her pleasure."

Although Della thought this might be true, she would not allow the fear to consume her. She would not allow Violet or the other girls to see the panic in her mind, either, so she kept her thoughts closed.

Della tilted her head, coming off braver than she had ever dreamed. "Wolfie doesn't care, Violet. No matter how much you adore him or need him to love you back, he won't."

"That's crap."

Della shrugged, as if extending this argument would only sap her of precious energy. Then she turned her attention to fetching her French book from her own bag as Polly and Noreen lingered in anxious silence. Hunger was beginning to growl within her, and her skin, which had pores that could open to suck in blood if she wished to go that route, tingled.

She had not eaten in a while. . . .

Violet sensed Polly's and Noreen's discomfort. "You two. Are you just going to stand there like dolts? Are you going to tolerate her cheek?"

Della slid them a glance, and she didn't even have to remind them, mind-to-mind, of who had won the face-off between her and Violet last night.

Noreen stepped away from Polly and toward Della, coming to stand behind her.

Violet went even paler than her normal shade.

Then she fixed her gaze on her best friend.

"Polly?" she asked in a threatening hiss—the sort of sound that had sawed at Della in the past, excising a vital part of her own being and leaving her to search for what was missing.

Vampire or not, that was how girls such as Violet operated. That was how they fed and grew and ruled.

Polly looked from Violet to Della. From Della to Violet.

And when she held her book over her chest and quickly moved over to the table near Noreen and Della, Violet grasped the duvet on her bed, her nails growing into sharp curves.

"You're all going to regret this," she said.

Then she sent Della a lowered look of such rancor that Della decided to sit in a chair near the wall so her back would not be facing the other girl.

But she couldn't dismiss what she had seen on her classmate's face. A decision that Della couldn't quite read.

A terrible judgment that they all might have to pay for.

Pinches of caution swept up and down her flesh, yet she acted as if Violet were nothing.

Instead, she opened her French text and began running through verb tenses with Polly and Noreen.

Not too long afterward, Violet rose from the bed and went to the loo, where she slammed the door behind her. Water from the tap ran like a tumble of furious curses, but Della shut down her senses and ignored all the agitated sounds.

Yet, five minutes later, she noticed that the water was still running.

Be right back, she mind-thought to Polly and Noreen.

They remained in their chairs while Della went to check on Violet.

When she reached the loo, she found the door locked, so without much fuss, she busted it open, only to find the tiled room empty save for a heating vent's grill that was unscrewed and leaning against a wall, as if quietly coaxed off.

Her nerves jittered as she glanced at the open vent.

Do you know what's in store for you, *little girl?*

Would Mrs. Jones blame Della and the others for allowing Violet outside when it was forbidden? And what might happen if Violet was caught by the intruders before the *custode*s could catch *them*?

She used her mind to see if she could find Mrs. Jones or even Wolfie nearby, but both were out of range.

No fear, Della. No fear.

Anger took the place of all the empty, horrified places within Della, and she calmly shut off the water tap, knowing what she must do now, even without being told.

How dare Violet put them all at risk.

How dare she continue to try to hurt all of them.

Believing that Wolfie and Mrs. Jones could not possibly blame her for taking this situation in hand, Della walked into the main room, where Polly and Noreen watched her. Then she went to the window, where she threw open the curtains to the coming dawn, which would bring a sun that didn't hurt her kind unless the privilege of facing it was abused.

All the while, rage kept the fear at bay: fear of punishment, fear of having this vampire life taken away when it was all she really had.

Then Della closed her eyes and used an ability inherited from her creators.

She thought about ravens, calling every bird within distance to her aid.

THREE

The Vampire Hunters

Also Just Before Sunrise

WHEN Costin punched the wall downstairs in the lab room of headquarters, he did it with a yell of rage that barely covered the crunch of his knuckles and the crash of plaster turning to dust.

But the sound of his frustration was nothing next to the yell that pushed out of Dawn.

"Costin!" She was near raw, pissed-off tears—she could feel them rising up—and that made her even angrier.

She broke out of her shadowed corner, where she'd managed to find a slice of peace while the team debriefed about last night's trip to Queenshill. As they'd traded observations and theories about the schoolgirl vampires who may or may not have been involved with a new Underground, Costin had gained enough strength to come out of his exhausted rest and emerge from the bedroom.

When he'd entered the lab, he'd barely been restraining his

agitation, but Dawn had seen the simmer under the ice-cool way he'd come to lean against the wall.

She'd asked how he was doing, and he'd confessed that he'd been upstairs trying to expel Jonah, the entity he shared his body with. When that hadn't worked, he'd attempted to escape his host altogether, even though he knew it wouldn't be of any use because the days when he could leave this body to use his full powers were gone.

As he'd relayed that, Costin had lost his composure, going for the wall before Dawn could even react.

But now, after it was too late—and wasn't that always the case?—she went to Costin and took his bloodied hand in hers.

Yet it wasn't like she could assuage him or anything. Jonah had permitted Costin, a Soul Traveler, to basically borrow his body: Jonah sheltered him, lent him physical form so Costin, who existed as an immaterial being, could complete his mission to win back his soul for good. But Jonah had gradually learned how to take over their shared body.

Damn the guy, he'd learned *real* well, and it was tearing Costin into all kinds of pieces.

The good news was that Costin was in control of his host right this minute, but Dawn suspected that was only because Jonah was biding his time until the whim to take over seized him again.

The topaz gaze, which signaled Costin was in charge for now, burned feverishly, his dark hair slouching over his forehead, half shrouding his eyes while he watched Dawn inspecting his hand. She tried not to grimace at his bent, injured fingers.

"I want him out," Costin said, and to hear that kind of torture in The Voice—a deep, fingernails-over-bare-skin tone that had always held such great power over her—just about slayed Dawn.

As if to balm her anguish, guilt seeped through her, silencing her. Over a year ago, she'd been the one who'd locked Costin into

Jonah's vampire body. But she could even trump *that* fact because, after the Queenshill trip last night, when Jonah had hijacked his and Costin's body and taken it out of secure headquarters so he could prove to the team that he could also fight, she'd made a deal with him: the team would allow Jonah to aid in their missions, and in turn, he would let Costin out on occasion.

A trade-off so that they could effectively continue to track and then wipe out the Undergrounds.

A devil's bargain.

But she was used to making deals that involved a catch. Hell, she'd been the genius who'd *turned* Jonah and Costin into a vampire in the first place. It'd been the only option that would allow Costin to continue destroying the blood brothers.

It'd been the only way to save *him*.

While she wordlessly ran her fingers over his knuckles, she avoided Costin's intense gaze. God, but she could still feel it on her, so she watched while the bones under his skin subtly undulated, his injuries mending.

She only wished Costin's powers could also heal all those deep-down inner wounds he would always carry.

A stream of jasmine floated by, and she lifted her face to the scent, thankful for a distraction. Breisi, her favorite Friend spirit. One of many deceased vampire hunters who'd chosen to stay on and fight with Costin until the end.

"*Broken?*" Breisi asked while circling around Dawn and her boss.

Costin's answer strung the atmosphere together even tighter. "Not for too long."

"Bully for vampire healing." By now, Dawn's inner swell of anger and remorse had receded to a burn in her throat. Good thing, too, because tears were a waste. "It'll be interesting to see how long it takes for you to heal all the way."

"Yes, interesting." Costin eased his hand out of her palm, but it left streaks of blood behind. His breathing quickened, as if the aroma got to him. "It never grows old, being this ever-changing experiment."

Dawn tried not to take offense to that. No matter how much he tried to hide it, she knew Costin—a crusader who'd despised the monsters he hunted—couldn't reconcile himself to his vampiric state, much less her dominance over him. Ever since she'd exchanged blood with Costin in L.A. to keep him from expiring, she'd technically become his master. Of course, she'd had to kill her own maker to end his Underground, and that had turned *her* into a human again, but Costin didn't exactly have the option to do the same with his master.

Not unless he wanted to terminate Dawn in order to bring a semblance of humanity back to his own host's body.

Dawn started as Breisi flew to the back of the room, where her boyfriend, Frank, was sitting on a high stool. Pink marks slashed over his thick neck, the only healing evidence that he'd been badly wounded last night during the struggle with the schoolgirl vampires.

On their own stools, Kiko and Natalia sat to the left of Dawn's vampire father. They were both wearing those tired, half-victorious, hyperwary expressions that served as tonight's post-vamp-fighting costumes.

And then . . .

Then came Eva, Dawn's mom. She'd stayed here at headquarters because, after last night's escalation in activity, no one wanted her to go even a block away to the flat she rented above a pub here in Southwark, so she was their temporary guest. She looked as put together as ever with her blond hair and daisy beauty, which had gone quickly from an early-twenties vampire glow to a hint of her actual middle-aged wrinkles after she'd been changed back into a human in L.A.

She was still a head turner.

But when she sat a few subtle yet very obvious inches to Frank's right, her skin seemed paler than ever, just as Dawn's had become. Their pallidness was because of the blood they donated to Frank and Costin, respectively. That, plus the bags that Costin secretively procured from a contact in a blood bank, kept the vampires on the team fed. As for Dawn and Eva, they were on all kinds of vitamins and supplements so they could offer the taste of blood that satisfied Costin and Frank the most.

Near Eva, Frank had his head down, no doubt struggling with the sight of Costin's blood, but as Breisi drifted by, he lifted his gaze to her.

Eva looked away.

Kiko slid off of his stool, his short little-person legs cushioning the slight fall. He went for a low steel cabinet where some med kits were kept.

"Good thinking, Kik," Dawn said. "We'll need a wipe to get this blood off the boss before the vamps in this room start going nuts."

Now Frank was breathing as hard as Costin was, his nostrils flaring at the blood, even from across the bevy of experimental weapons and tabled experiments stored in the lab.

Dawn watched her dad with concern, but he waved her off. She rolled her eyes, her gaze ultimately landing on a freezer, which was stocked full of a mysterious, very dead commando who had, using night-vision goggles, tracked the team before falling to his demise about a week ago.

Yeah, a kid who'd been creeping around while the team had investigated the site of a vampire burial.

Just one more thing to worry about.

Kiko made it to Dawn in rocket time; Mr. Efficient had even already opened the med kit so she could yank out a packaged wipe.

She tore at the packet, extracted the wipe, then casually took Costin's hand again to clean it off.

"Next time," Dawn said to her patient, "maybe you should think about how much fight that wall has in it before you start whaling on it."

"I was at my wits' end," he said, his tone back to that low Wallachian accent that had always made her go a little liquid. "Jonah has grown too strong and . . ."

He didn't finish, and Dawn knew it was because a tough guy like him—a soldier who'd fought on fields of blood centuries ago—didn't allow themselves to break.

Fair enough. She wouldn't embarrass him by acknowledging any weakness he might be showing, so she just continued cleaning his knuckles.

But, at the same time, she felt the cold calm that kept her sane push even deeper into her bones.

Yet wasn't that what they needed right now?

Couldn't they all use a little alert frostiness?

The mangled cuts on Costin's knuckles were closing up, but Dawn felt as if she were the one still bleeding.

"I'm sorry," she said softly, disposing of the wipe by going to a drawer, retrieving a bag, and zipping up the refuse in it. She tossed it in a trash bin with a tightly sealed cover. "I wish there was something else I could do to help you with Jonah, Costin."

"But you made a promise to him." He held his gnarled hand near his stomach, and it was only now that her mind caught up and processed that he had changed out of the fight clothing Jonah had worn last night in favor of Costin's usual dark lounging threads.

Fine idea, really. Jonah had gotten blood on the fabric when he'd had the time of his life out there, feeding and running around.

Next to Dawn, Kiko spoke up. "Boss, she's only trying to work with Jonah."

"I know."

Costin closed his eyes, and Dawn didn't even have to enter his mind—to access their personal master-progeny Awareness—to know he was approaching the end of more than one rope.

How many times had she gotten him to this point since she'd come on the team?

He opened his eyes, then glanced at his hand, his face expressionless, and that scared Dawn more than any of the Underground vampires they needed to hunt in order to save Costin, or even to save . . .

Well, the world.

Uh-huh, she'd gone and thought it, and the idea wasn't any less of a hilarious nightmare. Her, the world saver.

Costin raised his chin, as if in defiance, and for a second, Dawn thought that maybe he'd shed something—his rage at Jonah, his fruitless attempts to change what couldn't be changed now with his host.

"I suppose then," he said, "that we shall require an adjustment in procedure from this point forward."

Kiko rubbed his hands together, clearly happy that the old boss seemed to have reappeared. Dawn only wished she could be just as sure.

"We've been pretty good about hitting curve balls out of the park so far," the psychic said. "What's one more?"

Dawn raised an eyebrow. "This is more like a cannonball, Kik."

"Things'll work out." He grinned, as if mentally adding, *How could they not when I'm clear, near, and on the case?*

In the background, Dawn could hear the other team members getting out of their chairs, and she turned to see Frank and Natalia coming forward to join them.

Eva just waited there, looking more out of place than ever.

Funny how she'd never come off that way back when she was a superstar-dusted Hollywood vampire.

"Maybe I should . . . ?" She motioned toward the open lab door.

As if on cue, the door creaked wider, and Dawn supposed that Breisi had pushed her essence against it in invitation for Eva to leave them alone. Clearly, the spirit wasn't stoked about how Frank's once-presumed-dead wife had come here to nurse her wounded former love last night. It was bad enough that gorgeous, perfect Eva carried a torch for Frank, and this was apparently beginning to wear on the normally accepting Breisi.

Eva smiled wryly at the air, catching the ghosty's message, too.

As she left—probably heading for the kitchen to make them all some tea—Dawn aimed an encouraging glance at her mother, and Eva's smile turned warmer.

They'd come a long way, Dawn thought as her mom departed. But as much as she wanted to make sure Eva was comfortable upstairs, the London vampire Underground was a priority.

Actually, it was everything.

Disturbed by this truth, Dawn focused on Costin as the team members formed a half circle around their boss.

She'd attempt anything for him—her Voice, her mentor, her lover. She'd even march through hell to clear all accounts. And she wouldn't be surprised if, someday, she found herself doing just that.

She owed him.

"So . . ." Natalia said, her Romanian accent tamed by a stint living in the States and an education at university. She also had a slight bump on her forehead from tangling with a spirit via a Ouija board, but she'd covered the injury with cosmetics. "What happens now?"

"Exactly," Kiko added. "We were talking about those Queenshill girls and whether or not they'll lead us Underground. They're vamps, all right, but are they the sort we're looking for?"

Even with his dark hair tousled by all the previous drama, Costin managed to look dignified in Jonah's body. "I know the lot of you were strategizing before I"—he stiffened and tilted his head as he used a euphemism—"had my altercation with the wall."

The team relaxed. Maybe their boss really was back.

"What did you come up with?" he continued.

Dawn stepped up before anyone else could get there first. "I'm going back to Queenshill because I'm the only qualified one who has a prayer of passing herself off as a student there. I can blend. See, Greta"—one of the Friends who was even now keeping watch on the schoolgirls' dorms and the rest of the campus—"reported a few hours ago that she saw a vampire student, Della, disappear into the housematron's room. Without the benefit of opposable thumbs and all that, Greta wasn't able to open the door. She couldn't even slip inside to follow, and the vents in Mrs. Jones's room are closed, too. But about an hour later, Della and the housematron reappeared. Then they went to each of the girls' rooms, where all four students stuffed their bags and then zoomed off. The Friends couldn't keep up with their vampire speed, of course, but at least we know that this housematron, Mrs. Jones, is one of them. *And* we have another starting point to find a possible Underground lair."

Kiko butted in. "We don't know where the Lollipop Guild went, but Friends are combing London, searching."

Giving Kiko an are-you-done-interrupting look, Dawn continued. "First order of business is to see what's in that housematron's room. I'll just—"

Frank crossed his arms over his wide chest. "You'll just what? And you'll do it at the risk of them identifying you and taking you down, Dawn?"

Uh-oh—he wasn't saying "Dawnie," that sweet little nickname he'd used since she was knee-high.

He kept inflicting his papa-bear tone on her. "Or don't you remember that, last night, when we snuck on campus for some reconnaissance, we found out these girls had the scenting power of wolves?"

Dawn thought about how the Queenshill students had even looked like wolves when they'd turned all vampy. Transmogrifying, it was called, and Dawn wasn't surprised by this talent of theirs at all, because worldwide folklore also cited vamps running around as things like wolves and bats. Actually, the Queenshill vampires were basically a cross between wolves and those weird hairless cats that rich women keep around their mansions—not that Dawn ever hung around with heiresses or anything.

"Dad," she said. "The vampires have obviously gotten scent and sight profiles of me and Kik. And if they were able to catch any sort of vampire aroma—however unlikely—they could ID you and Jonah, too. They might be able to make any of us if we stepped foot on campus again while they're around. I'm just volunteering to test that theory while they've stepped away from campus."

"We'll think of another way," her dad said.

Natalia—the only team member who'd stayed at headquarters last night—cleared her throat, but Dawn raised a talk-to-the-hand palm to the new girl. No freakin' way were they going to send someone so damned green in, even if Natalia had proven to be a top-rate psychic so far. In fact, the team had pinpointed Queenshill as a possible Underground location thanks to the newbie and Kiko's combined visions.

Still, even though Natalia had a kind of vamp-radar—and the ability to hear dead humans—she had no fighting skills to speak of yet. She wasn't ready to check out a possible lair.

"Here's the thing," Dawn said. "If the Friends are patrolling campus and telling us that none of those vamp girls are around right now, I don't see a reason why I can't recon the property again. Chances are that all the vamps evacuated and won't be around to sniff me or gauge my body rhythms—if they even have the ability to do that." Which they might, Dawn thought. They still knew precious little about how these schoolgirl vampires—and maybe even their Underground—worked. "All I have to do is put on a handy-dandy disguise and get a Friend escort or two to give me immediate backup. Dressed as one of the older students, I can tiptoe into the dorm, then wheedle my way into the housematron's room to check it out."

Frank started to talk, but Dawn wouldn't let him.

"If it doesn't work," she cut in, finally lowering her hand, "then we can try something else. But we don't know where those schoolgirls are right now, so our idea of having Frank ambush them to get a follow-up look inside their minds for information about an Underground just isn't realistic. *My* plan is." She addressed her dad in particular. "The rest of the team can be on alert just off campus, especially if I find something beyond that door."

Everyone was quiet, but it was Costin's silence that got to Dawn the most. He had to be thinking about what would happen if they *did* discover more, because back before all the shit had hit in L.A., he would've put the team, whose main purpose was to ferret out the Underground location, in lockdown. Then he would've gone with the Friends to question the leading blood-brother master, and then annihilated the Underground by emerging from Jonah's body to exercise his full, hypnotic, warlike powers.

But . . . not anymore.

Natalia, her curly brown hair barely held back in its barrette, joined Frank's team of doubt now.

"What if those girls sic more animals on you, as they did last night?" she asked. "Perhaps they can even do it from where they are off campus. Their mind powers seemed that strong."

"And *perhaps* they can't do anything to us right now." Dawn fingered the outline of the sharp crucifix just under her black turtleneck. "Don't forget that my head trips can be just as strong as anything they have to throw at us."

Nobody had the guts to say anything to that. They'd seen how Dawn's ever-growing psychokinesis had taken up puppet-master proportions—she'd even been able to restrain one of the schoolgirl vampires, Della, with her mind during the skirmish.

But Frank gave it one last Daddy try. "They're capable little girls, Dawn. Don't underestimate them."

"So why aren't they at our front door barking at us right now?"

Costin listened, as if weighing all of this. Kiko just laughed.

"Dude," he said, "I can tell you why they're not here. First, those girls are major naïve, unless they were just *acting!* And unfortunately for them, naïveté isn't so great a quality for a vamp to have. Second, they obviously didn't get along with each other. They were a social disaster waiting to happen. I mean, did you see them scrapping among themselves as they hoofed it away from us? And I don't even need to talk about the big-time tension between Della and her frenemy Violet. Who's to say they won't self-destruct before we even *get* to them?"

Frank shrugged.

"The way I figure it," the psychic added, "we'll just load Dawn up with a UV grenade or two. I don't know if a silver bullet or a dart or holy water will work on those hairless wolf-cats, but UV sure did."

"Pardon me," Natalia said. "But they move around during the daylight. How can UV affect them so much?"

Kiko scratched his blond head. "I imagine they can only stand so *much* sunlight. Our grenades have enough concentrated UV to knock them to the ground. It's like having one cocktail and getting a buzz as opposed to having, like, fifty drinks and getting alcohol poisoning. Dawn could take out a small hive of these vamps with only one grenade if she plays her cards right."

"She might need more than just a grenade," Frank added. "What if we're dealing with an Underground that has distinctly different levels of vamps, like the one in L.A.? We'd need for every Underground vampire to be a sucker for that kind of UV dose, too. If they aren't, then Dawn could be waltzing into a death trap."

In spite of Frank's argument, Kiko pointed at Dawn, shooting her with a wink and a smile. "Our girl can handle her vamps."

Thankful for his props, Dawn stoically winked back at him. But when she glanced at Costin to see if he'd been persuaded, her heart sank at the way his gaze had gone dark again.

Even though he'd never admit it, she knew that he hated needing their help to such an extent.

She touched the crucifix buried under her shirt again, the points sharp enough to let out pinpricks of bad blood if she pressed hard enough.

"Costin?" she asked, wanting him to give his blessing.

But if he didn't give it, would it make a difference?

Would he be able to stop her—his master—if it came right down to it?

The thought unsettled her, but it also made her feel . . .

Well, *powerful*.

And justified, too, because now he couldn't use her as bait, as he'd done in L.A.

Now he couldn't hurt her nearly as much.

But . . . God, it wasn't right to think that way. She wouldn't contribute to literally putting Costin's soul in hell, which is what would happen if his mission to exterminate the dragon and his blood progeny failed.

"So when morning comes," she said, putting an end to all this conversation, "I'll hop into some schoolgirl clothes and get myself to Queenshill."

Costin paused, and Dawn tensed. But when he nodded, his topaz gaze meeting hers, she knew that he felt just as helpless to control her as he did Jonah.

She wanted to fall into his mind, to tell him he was mistaken, that he was still The Voice. That he was still the boss.

But when a new blast of jasmine air blew into the room, she tore her gaze from his, something dying a little inside of her.

A Friend's voice—the French accent identifying her as Evangeline from one of Costin's eighteenth-century teams—whisked through the rest of the jasmine that was spilling into the room as other spirits joined her.

"Outside," Evangeline said, the words threading through the atmosphere. *"Get your weapons ready."*

Before she even finished, the team hopped to it, with Dawn grabbing a batch of velvet-wrapped throwing blades from her back pocket and heading for the lab door along with Kiko, who'd pulled his revolver from his shoulder holster. Frank joined them as they ran up the stairs.

About damned time those schoolgirls showed up to finish what they'd started last night, Dawn thought. In her craziest fantasies, she'd been wishing they'd just get on over here and put an end to the waiting.

"How many of them?" she asked.

"One vampire," Evangeline said as she trailed back to allow Breisi to take her place beside Dawn and Frank. *"And she is asking for 'the girl.' Asking for Dawn."*

Only one?

And she wanted Dawn in particular?

At the top of the steps, she exchanged red-alert glances with her teammates, then sprinted the rest of the way to the front door, where she looked out of the peephole.

And, indeed, out on the premorning street, right in front of the decorated gates of Cross Bones Graveyard, which was really just a slab of cement, stood a schoolgirl dressed in a long skirt, white shirt, and slender red tie.

Violet.

The leader of the Queenshill vampires.

FOUR

The Ugly Stepsister

"What does she want with *me*?" Dawn asked as she pulled back from the peephole.

"Who?" Kiko asked.

"That Violet girl. The queen bee of the group." Dawn went to the weapons panel in the wall near the door, opened it, then extracted a holy water bracelet that she strapped around her wrist, plus a mini flamethrower that she shoved into the waistline of her dark pants.

Kiko had come to her side, dragging a wooden stepstool so he could raid the weapons cache, too.

"Kik," Dawn said, "I'll take care of her on my own. She asked for me, and if all of us go outside to say a fond hi, she might bolt."

"Undergrounders don't usually ask for so many fights above, Dawn. It's a concern."

"Everything's a concern."

She donned a communication earpiece and grabbed a locator device for good measure, then stuffed a UV grenade in the pocket of the light jacket she was about to put on.

Frank's voice sounded from behind her. "How about I zip outside and get close enough for some eye contact? I can go inside her mind in a snap."

Dawn paused in her prep. "Let me run this by you all one more time—she asked for *me*. There's gotta be a reason, and I'm going to find out what it is."

"I can tell you what it is right now," Frank said. "It's easier to kill a team member if she's by herself. Ambush Basics—know what I mean?"

"Could be," Kiko interjected. "The rest of them just might be waiting out there, hoping we'll snag on their hook. Not that we couldn't snag them right back."

Dawn reached into the weapons hole again.

An exasperated sigh from her dad told her that he knew she was going to do what she damned well pleased. The fact that Costin hadn't stopped her yet probably even lent weight to her cause.

He wanted her to go outside, wanted to see just what Violet was here for.

And, gee—here she'd thought that her being used as bait for the Underground had stopped in L.A.

As she took a container of garlic essence out of the cache, she admitted that she didn't mind being sacrificed anymore, that it was actually what she lived for nowadays. Then she motioned for Frank to clear the area before she put some essence on her bod.

Even if these vamps ended up being immune to garlic, she was hoping the stench might confuse their senses a little, taking away their ability to keep track of her every movement if she ended up having to hightail it away for some reason; she'd spray the stuff as she went along, leaving a false trail.

Or maybe garlic wouldn't work at all if they could hear her body rhythms.

At any rate, Breisi had spent most of the last few hours brainstorming ways that might address both issues, and Dawn trusted that her Friend would come up with something. Hell, even before Breisi had been murdered, she'd been their official awesome mad scientist.

Since Frank didn't love being around garlic so much, he removed himself to the back of the room, melding with the dark wood, the ominous bas-reliefs featuring friars on the ceiling, the chubby angel faces, and the mirrors that gave such a twisted manor-house feel to this place. Meanwhile, Dawn slapped on the essence, barely even catching the much-more-appealing scent of the Friends as they swirled around her.

The spirits were probably outside, too, near Violet, and the notion gave Dawn that much more confidence.

After wrapping herself in the big, light jacket to cover the extent of her arsenal, she positioned a silver-laced throwing blade in her fingers, ready to rock.

"Hey," Kiko said, still standing on his stool. "Don't die."

"Don't worry." Dawn walked to the door. "You still owe me a game of football." The kind where you played with a triangle of paper.

"Dawn," Frank said from the back of the room, his own tone carrying an entire epic series of caution.

She stopped, hand on the knob. Damn the timing, but it struck her again how caring he'd become after being turned. Back when he was human, he'd been too drunk half the time to have a fully developed conscience, so Dawn was still getting used to this new, improved, vampire version of her father.

If "improved" was what you'd call it.

"Frank," she said, softening as much as was possible. Which still left a bunch of room for an awkward edge. "I'm not a kid anymore."

They locked gazes, but then he planted his hands on his hips and glared at the floor.

Kiko couldn't resist tossing one in there. "Admit it, Frank—your baby's all growed up."

Just as she was about to open the door, Costin's voice came out of one of the angel-face speakers, giving voice to the wooden cherub.

"It seems that Violet is not approaching, merely . . . waiting."

By now, Costin would've instructed Natalia to monitor the video screens in another room while he sequestered himself out of sheer habit. Last night, Jonah had proven that their body could survive outside, but Costin never risked what he didn't need to. The stakes were just too high, and Dawn couldn't really fault him for it.

Even though it might be a real game changer if he would just give his new vampire body a chance beyond headquarters . . .

But why worry when *she* could deal with Violet right now?

"What do you think the queen bee has in mind?" she asked Costin. "And I really hope you're not standing at our bedroom window just so you can get good reception." Although he hadn't been able to break out of his body with his full powers, he'd retained his ability to use his mind for hypnosis and such. "You'd be giving her a nice target."

"Thank you for noting it," he said, a hint of amusement somewhere in there.

Okay, Jonah had taken their body outside last night, but she was still worried about the safety of their ultimate weapon. She was a creature of habit, just like Costin was, and if they didn't keep him as secure as they could—even with his powers being as questionable as they were nowadays—it would all be over.

"At the moment," Costin added, "I'm as safe and sound as possible." Until Jonah decided to take over. Costin didn't say it, but it was implied. "Yet regarding Violet's motives? I cannot be certain of anything."

"Whatever the situation," Frank said, "we'll be ready."

Aw, Dad was backing her up now. His protective doggedness tried to break through Dawn's frostiness.

Tried, but she was too prepped for action to feel any of the warm fuzzies.

She addressed the angel face. "Costin, you're ready to control the UV lights outside and flood the area if Violet pulls anything funny?"

"Yes."

"Then I'm off."

She didn't want to wait around for any more gooey stuff. Everyone in the house knew . . .

Well, they knew that she wouldn't go off and die, so why linger and get all schmaltzy about it?

Deep breath and . . .

She opened the door, stepped through, then quickly closed it behind her as the near-sunrise air pawed at her cheeks. She took a deep breath of it as her pulse thudded in her temples, in the veins of her neck.

Across the wanly lit street, Violet leaped up to balance on the Cross Bones Graveyard gates, clearly not afraid of being caught on one of the many closed-circuit TV surveillance cameras that covered London. Nope, she just vamp-crouched on that gate as if she was expecting more hunters to come out.

Her eyes glowed a little in the dimness, outdoing the purple blush of the sky.

Dawn flashed a silvered throwing blade at the girl, warning her, showing her she was armed yet alone as she stayed on the stoop near the door. Simultaneously, she peered around for signs of other creatures . . . or maybe even one of those red-eyed shadow figures that had been tracking them at the vamp burial site.

In the end, they came to stare at each other—Violet, Dawn. Dawn, Violet.

She shielded her thoughts, just in case this girl tried to read her.

Otherwise, nothing happened except for a stir of the cards and letters tied to the gates. The mementos flapped in a sudden huff of breeze, probably the result of a patrolling Friend.

Violet sniffed the air, tilted her head, as if trying to understand what the jasmine meant. But then she smiled, as if she'd made a connection between the scent and the hunters. Then she canted her head to the other side, sniffed again, and the smile disappeared. She stiffened, holding to the top of the gates.

"I smell your and your little person's scent on someone else who's come outside," she said through gritted teeth.

"What're you talking about?"

The girl made one of those clucking, eye-rolling expressions that Dawn herself had perfected in middle school. "Someone else just stepped outside. Whoever it is, send them back. You're the one I want to see."

Aw, shit.

It had to be Frank, whose untreated change of clothing from last night had picked up scents from headquarters. He'd probably snuck through a belowground back exit, still intent on ambushing Violet.

"Stop it, you guys," Dawn said to her team in general. "Get back in the house."

A crackle from her earpiece, then her dad's resigned voice. "Had to give it a try."

Stubborn ass.

"All right," Frank said an instant later. "I'm in the cradle."

At the same time, Violet relaxed, then dropped from the gate to the ground to land in another crouch, her long brown hair raining to her back.

Dawn cocked her blade but didn't throw it.

Violet straightened to a stand, hardly seeming to give a crap that Dawn had her in a line of fire.

"Found you," she said instead, and the gamesmanship she'd exhibited last night in their skirmish was blatant in her tone now. When the girls had first engaged the hunting team, who'd been nosing around Queenshill for clues to an Underground, the curious vampires had been playful like this, as if the team were catnip and didn't pose much danger at all.

This told Dawn that the girls were either not Underground vampires or just way too cocky if they were.

But then the tables had turned, and the change in matters had caused the girls' flippancy to disappear.

"You bring your buddies?" Dawn asked.

"No." Violet's tone got ugly. "I'm alone. I had a slight . . . falling-out . . . with the others. I'm on my way out of London, really, but I thought I might see you before I scuttled off."

"Bullshit."

The other girl raised her voice and tremors skated over Dawn's skin.

"You can have faith that matters will change if our superior decides that things are steady enough to take the chance on leaving the temporary hiding spot where she's sheltering the others. I doubt she would risk another public face-off—we enjoy our freedom, but we're not daft—yet there's always a chance she could switch to offense and hunt you down just as effectively as I did. Fear can provide a lovely trail."

That amazing sense of smell, Dawn thought. Half-wolf, half-cat vamps.

"Calm about that, aren't you?" Violet added, looking like she wanted to put a little more scare into Dawn. "Don't be. You can rest assured that you're being searched for in other ways, even if most of us won't come out of hiding."

Dawn still tried not to seem rattled.

But Violet wasn't done.

"I'm quite fast, myself, and when I returned to Queenshill with the intention of tracking your aroma, it didn't take me long to be directed here. As long as I know what I'm hunting, I'm very, very good. We all can be."

She glanced around, as if keeping an eye out for the other girls, and it occurred to Dawn that Violet might be . . .

. . . nervous.

When Dawn narrowed her eyes, the schoolgirl added, "You can either listen to what I have to offer or not. Your choice, but we don't have long before I need to be on my way."

Dawn kept her throwing blade primed, secure in the notion that she was fast on the draw and so was Costin. Based on how the girls had reacted to the UV grenades, the lights outside headquarters had the power to give these vamps a screaming sunburn if necessary.

Best of all, it looked like Kiko might've been right when he'd said that the Queenshill vampires didn't like one another, that they might come apart at the seams after last night's brouhaha.

Or, again, this could just be a beautiful setup, and the rest of them would spring on her just when she let her guard down a notch more. . . .

"Forgive me if I'm suspicious," Dawn said, "but why would you be telling me all this?"

The schoolgirl smiled, and it sent ice gouging up Dawn's spine.

"Because," Violet said, "I want everything to be taken away from them, too."

She leaned back against the Cross Bones gates, and Dawn wondered if the girl had any idea of who was buried there in the unconsecrated ground—of how many other female bodies were in a mass grave under the concrete behind those gates because they'd been too wicked for a proper send-off.

An early-morning train rumbled by on the raised tracks to Dawn's left, emitting a clacking growl of warning, cautioning that Violet's comment was too good to be true.

After the train passed, it left everything else around them in the same sleepy post-witching-hour gloom.

As Dawn's earpiece crackled, assuring her that she wasn't alone in this, a Friend whizzed past.

Once more, Violet sniffed the air, casual as could be. "That perfume."

Dawn wasn't about to get into slumber-party mode and start revealing secrets, too. "My favorite essence—eau de impatient."

The vampire girl laughed, just like this was some kind of warped bonding moment.

"So you think you can talk me and my buddies into taking everything away from your friends," Dawn said, testing. "Just so you know, that isn't why we showed up at your place last night."

Violet crossed her arms over her white shirt and slim red tie. "I can't persuade you to aid in providing a parting gift to my classmates? A 'do unto others as they've done unto me'?"

Oh, too perfect, Dawn thought. She didn't dare believe it.

But . . . she sort of did. And maybe that's why Violet had chosen her to talk to. Because, with some kind of vampire power, she could sense Dawn might be a perfect target.

Whatever the reason, she'd be a fool not to at least listen for a second. "Okay, I've got to know what you're going on about, so keep on talking."

Violet scanned the sky, then shrugged. "For over a year now, I've been a part of a small, select vampire class at Queenshill. Seven girls, all of us told that we were 'special.' And what a bunch of bollocks that was."

"Because whoever recruited you betrayed you?"

There—an opening for Violet to talk about the Underground without Dawn having to say it out loud and give her own game away.

But the girl was still back on the "special" part. "I'm not the only one to have been disappointed. A few of us left, you know. One of us even ran away."

Briana Williamson? Dawn wondered. Through investigation, the team had come upon her history, and it had played its role in leading them to Queenshill in the first place.

"I'm running off, as well," Violet said. "There are other vampires for me to be with. Better ones."

Good God, was this girl insinuating that she wanted to join up with the Limpets, who counted Frank among their number?

Soooo not going there. But how could Dawn get Violet to tell her if she was a member of an Underground without actually saying "Underground"? If Violet had anything to do with one, the word could set off alarms for the vampires, especially if Violet was taking part in one of these types of vamps' favorite pastimes: Spying. Messing with people.

But the team used stealth, too. It was the best way to launch a final attack on an Underground, even though Dawn would cast a hearty vote for going into any lair and slaying every suspicious vampire imaginable. But her dad and Costin kind of put the kibosh on that; their mere existence proved that there were good ones out there, and wiping them out didn't sit well with what conscience she had left.

Since Frank had asked Della about Briana last night when he'd been trying to get into the girl's mind, Dawn decided to use this tactic to question Violet, too.

"Why did Briana run away?" she asked. "Did Queenshill disappoint *her*?"

The schoolgirl tilted her head at Dawn, her voice snapping. "Why does Briana matter?"

Careful. Use those mind blocks. "Just wondering if you're off to join her."

"Hardly." Violet traced a long finger over the gate. But then she caught herself, glanced around again, then talked fast, as if she wanted to get going. "Listen. Before I leave, I only wanted to warn you. You must watch out for one Queenshill girl above all others. Della."

Oooo, venom.

I want everything to be taken away from them, too, Violet had said. But Dawn would bet her life that this vamp had only meant Della.

"You don't like her much," Dawn said. "Do you?"

Violet chuffed, but then went back to tracing the gate. Her words had a tremor to them now—a little girl lost, and Dawn almost felt for her.

Almost.

"She took it all away," Violet said. "All of it."

"So everything's her fault," Dawn said, trying to return to the subject of the Underground, knowing her coworkers were taking in every detail over their earpieces. "*She's* the one who kicked you out."

A lowered glance from Violet. A vengeful one.

Dawn knew the girl was only going to tell her what she wanted to, and this might not help their cause at all.

Damn it, could Dawn distract her enough for Frank to get out here to surprise Violet and then read her mind, so they could get everything possible out of her?

But then how could Dawn get him out here without scaring her off?

"Do you really want to know?" Violet asked, shards of light in her eyes.

The malevolence of the question should've warned Dawn, but her adrenaline pulsed, and her need to save Costin moved her mouth, causing her answer to spill out.

"Yes," she said, and for that one instant, she stopped shielding.

In the next heartbeat, Violet sped close enough so that Dawn could discern some faint pinkish scars on her face. Then the girl's eyes went electric, her gaze seeming to blast against Dawn, shattering into her with a crash of color and image, just like the time when another vampire, Robby Pennybaker from Hollywood, had come into her head.

But Dawn had given permission this time, and she froze under the visual assault, the connection telling her why Violet had chosen to talk to her one-on-one instead of any of the others on the team.

She'd sensed a perfect target, all right—but it'd been because of the darkness that'd been growing in Dawn ever since the night she'd become a Hollywood vampire and then gone human again after killing her master.

It was because of the black hole in her, yawning open and sucking in all the hate Violet was feeling, too. . . .

The vamp schoolgirl shared punches of image and sensation: a small cavelike room with fairy lights strewn over the ceiling, a lava lamp, a poster of Orlando Bloom over a zebra-covered settee, girls—the vampires from last night—rolling over the ground and wrestling with one another like pups. . . .

One word laced through the image, long-drawn-out, sorrowful: *home*.

Dawn shrank under the yearning of it, Violet's pain in losing it.

Then there was a luxurious flat with leather furniture and swinging crystal chandeliers and, oh God, Kate Lansing, the young human the team had been investigating, and she was running up some stairs, trying to get away from the pack of laughing vampires. . . .

More words: *Recruit. Nightcrawl.*

Then a flood of girls dressed in historical and fanciful costumes, all of them flitting around a tavernesque room that rang with laughter and gaiety and blood as they chased males and sank their fangs into them. Girls, girls, girls, their mouths ringed with red.

Graduate. Reward.

And then, most keenly of all: a wild-haired man with golden eyes smiling down like a wolfish god.

Love.

Wolfie.

Warmth rushed through Dawn, but just as quickly, the ice of loss took its place, hardening to such hatred that Dawn pulled out of the mind-link and held up a hand, just to block and keep Violet from infusing more bitterness and bile into her.

That dark spot in Dawn swelled, as if thirsting for more, but she backed toward headquarters, away from the vamp girl, battling to get herself back.

Slowly, slowly, reality returned: the chalky street gaining color and form, the adrenaline ebbing to a sense of nausea that coated Dawn's stomach and shook her from fingertips to toes.

She turned to Violet, finding the girl's eyes alight while she took in breath after quick breath, like she was excited to have found a repository for her ill will.

Like that hatred was the only thing keeping her going.

As Dawn recovered, she realized something: girls running around, the tavern, the costumes . . .

Underground?

Had Violet just shown her a glimpse of it?

"What—" Dawn started to ask.

"It's all her fault," the other girl said, and as her hands flexed, Dawn saw that her nails had grown an inch, making her fingers into semiclaws. "Della's."

She raised her awful hands to her face, covering her expression, shaking with either overwhelming emotion or an effort not to change into her vamp form.

"Tell me more," Dawn urged. *Save Costin. . . .* "I can help you, Violet, maybe—"

"Help me?" The girl uncovered her face, and the sight of a growing snout and knifepoint teeth jarred Dawn.

But she didn't let the painful jerk of her veins or the shudder of her pulse stop her. "How do I destroy her? *Them?*"

The Friends were swirling around in a frenzy, but Dawn thought it was only because they were so close to finding everything out.

Yet Dawn should've listened to one of them saying, *"Hear that? Hear it!"*

The shudder of an approaching train hit the air, and Violet cocked her head again, her posture going rigid.

Something—a feeling—tickled the back of Dawn's neck in apprehension.

"Run!!!" Breisi screamed in Dawn's ear before pushing against her.

Dawn stumbled backward, toward headquarters, when it started.

Violet's eyes widened, her fanged mouth opening in what looked like one word—*DELLA?*—before she shielded her face with her hands.

Then . . .

The descent of a massive black shadow.

Breisi smashed against Dawn in earnest now, forcing her to lose balance and fall to the ground, dropping her throwing blade and then crawling backward up the stairs.

Partway up, she fumbled for her flamethrower, only now realizing what was happening.

Birds.

Ravens.

Was it possible that the other vampires were in hiding nearby now, summoning these animals to catch Violet?

Or to shut her up?

The birds crashed into the schoolgirl, their wings barely camouflaging the blood as they nipped at her, clawed at her, ate away at her skin and face and hair, pinning her to the ground with the force of their numbers.

The train continued on by, but Dawn could hear the cawing, could hear the trace of a girl's screech as Violet fought her way down, and feathers ripped into the air as she swiped at them with her claws in a counterattack.

Dawn crab-moved up the stairs, where Frank was already outside, reaching for her, intending to bring her to where Kiko waited in the doorway with his own mini flamethrower in hand.

The train trailed off, and the ravens finished up, several of them lifting away from the barely moving pile of rags and flesh that remained on the ground.

Violet was a mangled mess of gore and eyeless sockets and fingers that were still gnarled into barely flexing claws, and . . .

God.

It took Dawn a second to realize that the vampire's head was still barely attached, keeping her animated.

On the walkway, two ravens carried Violet's eyes in their beaks, waddling away from the action as three other birds dug into the girl's chest.

Dawn's trigger finger itched. So did the trigger of her mind, because she realized too late that she might've been able to stop the ravens with her psychokinesis.

Jesus, even if Violet was a vampire she had to be in pain.

But . . .

Bad vampire, said the dark place inside of her. *Kill or be killed.*

Frank was tugging at Dawn's jacket now, trying to get her all the way inside. He could've yanked her into headquarters if he wanted—he was the strong, fast one—but the quaking of his hands told her that the sight and smell of Violet's blood was overtaking him, even over the stench of the garlic.

Once she was in, Kiko started to close the door behind her just as a horrifying sound beat down from the sky: a cloud of ravens—the ones who'd gotten Violet—zooming toward the girl again.

The team threw their bodies against the door to shut it, and as Frank sank to the ground, Dawn sprang up to gape through the peephole.

"Come on!" Kiko said, wanting to see, too. They'd bricked up the lower floor's windows, so this was the only view available down here.

A nasty taste lingered in the back of Dawn's throat as she watched the ravens swoop down to tangle their claws in Violet's hair and brutally yank her head from her body.

Then, as simple as that, the schoolgirl withered away, just like she'd been covered by a quick-working acid that ate skin, bones, and clothing.

The ravens seemed to scour their wings over the walkway before taking off, leaving a new pink glow to devour the sky.

Dawn sank to the floor beside Frank just in time to see her mother coming from the back of the house through the gap of a dark hall, concern slowing her steps.

Dawn didn't have the words to explain to Eva about the

ravens—the animals that the other girls might've called to take care of Violet.

So what hell would they have in mind for the hunters?

Kiko spoke. "Once, the Friends told us that it didn't seem like these vampires can see through the eyes of the animals they call. They just use a command mind-link, like the animals are hearing orders. They probably tracked Violet, and the rest of the vamps might not know where we are. Not yet."

Dawn barely heard him over the "Holy shit"s stabbing her every thought. She caught her breath, the room a flurry of jasmine since Friends had whooshed in with her.

But she did have enough brainpower to realize that the Friends hadn't stopped the raven attack, either.

"Shit, shit, shit," Dawn finally said out loud, as if she'd never seen killing or maiming in her life. Or maybe it was just that she would never get used to it.

Yet when she felt the coldness spreading through her, like it'd come to protect her, she rethought the getting-used-to-it part.

She told them about what she'd seen, about how the ravens had finished off Violet.

"Well," Kiko said, plopping down next to her and watching Frank as he continued to recover. "At least we know for sure that decapitation works on them."

Dawn closed her eyes and allowed the cold, dark stain to spread even more until it calmed her.

Making her as frosty as she needed to be to go on from here.

FIVE

Once Upon an Implanted Tale

In the deepest part of the main Underground, where air hummed over the skin and darkness was lit by blue flutters from the banks of small telly screens, the new *custode* stood at attention, mask off.

"You called me back here just as I was getting started on tracking those attackers. Thirty minutes didn't give me any chance whatsoever."

"We've suddenly got larger issues at hand," Nigel, the head keeper, said. His sandy hair was slicked back, his athletic body encased in the black of their tight uniform as he lounged in the swivel chair in front of the monitors.

"Larger issues." A small laugh. "I see. You recalled me because you believe yourself to be more capable than I when it comes to outside duty. How just like a big brother."

Nigel's lime-hued eyes—a family trait—brooked no argument,

but the new *custode* wasn't about to present one. It was true that it would take time for a recently activated caretaker to master this job; Nigel would be far more effective in doing the highest priority fieldwork right now. A week wasn't a very long time to get used to what a newly attuned body and mind could do.

They weren't vampires, but they were the best sort of servants nonetheless.

"I called you back," Nigel said, "because expedience is necessary, and there's no time to dally with your less developed talents today."

"Yes, sir."

Nigel ignored the sarcasm.

Ah. So he was being quite the serious professional now that Charles was dead and gone. Pity Nigel hadn't been so vigilant before last week, when Charles had mysteriously disappeared at Billiter Street—and no doubt died there, too, based on the traditional vision/tales that had been fed to the new *custode* upon activation.

Tales containing the history of this particular vampire community, which the Meratoliage family had protected and served for generations.

But Nigel would never be able to make up for Charles's death. Not now, after failing so bloody miserably.

And that's the reason the new keeper had taken such secretive and risky measures to protect the Underground—to protect *while* serving. Frankly, Nigel didn't seem to be up to it.

Yet the new *custode*'s plan was a gamble well worth taking, based on what these monitors all around them had shown recently: The schoolgirl vampire Della staring at Claudia so suspiciously. Della keeping her distance from the elder vampire, as if she sensed more danger than the others did. Della taking the lead position among the girl vampires last night with such strength and barely contained ferocity.

Della: a perfect instrument, much like the tuner that had been used on her back at the hotel.

The new *custode* watched Nigel, wondering what he might do if he should discover this plan with Della—if he would agree it was necessary or wage punishment on a keeper who'd overstepped all bounds.

But why tell him?

Why take the chance that he would shut down a plan that was so beautifully conceived and bound to work in the end?

Even a new caretaker could see that security had fallen to shite Underground, and Nigel was partly at fault. Apparently, no previous *custode* had seemed to recognize just how weak Mihas was when he was with Claudia. His companion allowed him the freedom to be reckless but, without Claudia, he would have to think on his own, and think clearly at that.

Yes, Mihas had always been the more vicious, wilder soldier of the two—the most valuable. Yet coupled with Claudia, he had become a creature of his own appetites and didn't pay much mind to anything else.

The newest *custode* didn't stir as Nigel stood from his chair. Perhaps previous keepers had been too intimidated by the old ones to carry through with some sorely needed maintenance. Nonetheless, an hour or two ago, when Nigel had finally given the new caretaker an assignment that took place outside the confines of the Underground, where freedom of movement wasn't so simple, it had been the perfect time to act.

The new *custode* rested a gloved hand on a belted compartment where the tuner was kept, as if to protect the plan itself—the secret of it. The spindly object had been formulated a generation ago by an uncle, a maintainer who'd stepped down from service to the Underground when his body had grown old. It worked on the younger, more susceptible vampires, not the older ones, and *custode*s had found that it kept the main Underground's vampire girls in line if they required punishment . . . as they often did here in Mihas's hormonal, crazed community.

Not that they ever told Mihas that they used it on the girls.

Yet it came in quite handy when a younger vampire would wander too close to the *custode* area. Della herself had almost needed it the night before last when she had stumbled too near and the *custode*s had intercepted her, thinking she could use a lesson in never straying from the main part of the Underground.

But, tonight, the tuner had been used to imprint a new fear on Della's subconscious. Mind-to-mind via the implement, the new caretaker had vaguely shared only three of the tales that were given to each family member upon a *custode*'s calling. Della's own imagination would fill in the blanks of the purposely blurred faces, providing her own boogeymen.

Providing the fright that would make her the perfect conduit to whip Mihas and the Underground back into shape.

And Della should be afraid, really, with what Claudia was doing to the unaware girls in private. But, with success in this plan, the housematron's sins would be the very thing to bring about her downfall.

The *custode* would have seen to everything personally, but that would involve too much individual risk. Yet secretly implanting the tales in Della meant that the schoolgirl would never be able to reveal how she received her information, should she be asked. Although the keeper would have to be careful about manipulating her through the fear that would result as the tales turned her against Claudia.

Hopefully.

Certainly, though, there was a bit of rule bending involved with this strategy. But if this gamble resulted in removing Claudia from the Underground and shaking up Mihas, thus making him a stronger blood brother, the end would certainly justify the means.

The newest *custode* would bet the house on it.

Nigel was lending one last glance to the screens, most of which had been furtively tooled to pick up images from CCTV cameras in London's surveillance network, plus a few key lenses of the Underground's own. Although the *custode*s couldn't manipulate most of the cameras themselves—they could only see what the lenses were showing—the tellys revealed everything from views in the Queenshill dorm, where the vampire schoolgirls had lived, to feeds from places like Highgate, above the main Underground.

By combing through past footage, day by day, the *custode*s had been attempting to discover the whereabouts of the attackers, but they were having no luck, especially with the lack of anything such as facial recognition capabilities.

Yet it could only be a matter of time before they found something among the thousands of hours they'd captured.

While inspecting what they'd cultivated so far, they *had* come upon recordings that had been clouded for some reason, including the footage from cameras on the Queenshill campus last night. The fogged images, in fact, resembled the malfunctions from the night Charles had died while investigating the same clouded camera feeds at and around Billiter Street. Unfortunately, the *custode*s had been immersed in Relaquory—an every-night activity not to be deserted at any cost—during the goings-on at Queenshill, and it was only when they had returned to the monitor room to review the footage that they had noticed a pattern.

Quite the coincidence.

Quite the clue that, perhaps, these attackers were more than they seemed.

"Our present situation is this," Nigel said. "Shortly after you checked in on the schoolgirls—"

The *custode* didn't flinch at the assumption that the hotel visit had been all about checking in rather than implanting tales.

"—a camera showed one of them, Violet, appearing on the roof of the hotel and then running off in a burst of speed to who knows where. We'll have to slow down our recordings to isolate her image, camera by camera, and discover her destination." Nigel offered his associate the chair. "Claudia hasn't contacted me about this disappearance yet, and I'm not certain she even realizes the situation since she left the girls alone in the hotel so she could spend precious time with Mihas."

The new *custode* noted the slightly mocking way in which Nigel had mentioned Claudia and Mihas. Interesting.

"But," Nigel added, "we do need to act since Violet seems to have taken great pains to avoid detection for some reason."

Violet, the little bitch of the crowd. The sort of girl who made life pure hell, and it had been hard to watch how she treated everyone around her this past week. "You don't think she's merely off somewhere pouting after another fight with Della?"

"No matter her intention, she shouldn't have left in the first place. Our alert system"—a feature that highlighted particular screens and allowed the *custode*s to focus on where their vampires were when aboveground—"tried to keep up with her, but she moved faster than she usually does when the girls are outside on their own. It's possible that Violet even halted on the outskirts of the city, or in a place where there are no cameras. That would explain the reason the alert system hasn't isolated her by now."

With his fluid *custode* way of slipping across a room, he moved toward the exit. "And since there aren't cameras everywhere, I'll go afield to see if I might locate Violet. If nothing pans out, I'll check on Queenshill later. You stay Underground to access and slow down that footage from around the hotel, because you might be able to piece together a lead."

"But—" began the new keeper.

Big Brother held up a hand. "One of us must always stay Underground. You know that. No exceptions."

Yes. Right. There were only two of them.

Always two.

And, with that, he was gone, the black automatic door sliding shut behind him.

The *custode* stood there, feeling the chiseling buzz of the atmosphere, feeling a ripping sensation digging into every pore because of what resided down here with them.

But this was life now—the lot of the Meratoliage family—and the *custode* accepted that, sinking into the chair's leather comfort while the monitors flashed with activity.

One of the screens was rimmed with red, highlighted by their alert system, and the keeper saw that it came from the camera trained on the hotel where the schoolgirls were.

Nigel had obviously been keeping an eye on it while going through other footage to find Violet on the smaller console screens. But there was a different reason this particular telly caught the new *custode*'s attention.

Della was standing at the window, staring out at the waking sky.

The caretaker pushed a button that connected directly to this camera, and the lens zoomed in to magnify Della. The glass of the hotel's window provided an eerie sheen over the girl's frizzy hair, the intense expression on a face that was otherwise so sweet and innocent.

What was dear vampire Della doing?

The *custode* could only hope that the last implanted tale—the one given the most emphasis during the tuning—was emerging in Della, flickering in snippets that would make more sense to her with each passing hour.

A most bloody, beware-little-girl story that, mixed with the others, would awaken Della to what was really happening in her safe little Underground . . .

ONCE upon a few hundred years ago, on a path that stretched far into the woods, a lone figure ran and ran, slicing his way to where the moon couldn't peek through the branches and the scent of blood was like crushed berries staining the air.

The aroma grew thicker, and the figure halted, dust clouding around his boots as he froze, sniffing.

Searching.

He was a vampire, his facial features blurred by the night. A creature carrying a limp girl—an unconscious pile of long blond hair and bunched wool from her cloak—over his shoulder.

Again, the creature sniffed the night, shuddering as saliva dripped from the corner of his mouth to his chin.

Then, his eyes aglow, the vampire darted off the path and into the foliage, which held branches that clawed past his slight beard and razored straight to his skin, leaving gashes that screamed in pain.

Yet by the time he reached the cottage in the woods, his skin had already healed to pale smoothness, to a hue that could even be mistaken for human, with the correct amount of artifice.

The creature crashed through the door, the spill and splash of blood hitting his senses as he fought the instinct to become animal, as he battled the urge to feast on what the scent offered.

Instead, he controlled his overwhelming tremors while scanning the darkness with a bright gaze that cut right through the pitch of night.

He looked past the blood on the walls and floor, the ash-strewn hearth, the shattered wooden table, the mangled bodies of village men who had taken up axes and farm tools to enter the woods and hunt what they deemed a monster.

There. In a corner. Another blood-soaked body—one that had survived.

The one that had created all this carnage.

The trespasser lunged toward that body, dropping to his knees at the other vampire's feet. Around them lay the carcasses of wolves and other animals that the wounded creature on the floor had summoned for aid—an ability that both vampires wielded as personal talents.

Although the night would have obscured the other creature's face to anyone else, every feature was vivid to the first vampire. Besides, the other's hollow, sharp breathing was all too agonizingly familiar.

"Even from home, I heard your call for healing. . . ." The first one's words faded to a whisper. "What have they done to you this time?"

The wounded vampire attempted to smile, his fangs, which had not yet receded, bathed with evidence of blood play. His wild hair, grown long and free during his time away from Versailles, was matted with gore from the head injuries that were healing all too slowly. His clothing—the justaucorps, cravat, vest, breeches, silk stockings, and elegant buckled shoes he wore with such arrogant pride at court—was torn and ruined with red.

Worst of all, his face was caught between his pure hunting form and the more human one he used to masquerade among his prey.

He is too weak to shift back into regular shape, *the first vampire thought.*

Yet the injured vampire would never admit that he had almost been beaten by the angry humans this time. That sort of pessimism did not exist for him.

Rather, he held up a white ribbon soaked with her *blood. The latest young female conquest's.*

"You will be the death of us all," said the first vampire, allowing

his own poached village girl to tumble from her resting place on his shoulder and to the ground, where her hair spread like bright rays over her closed eyes. She had fainted when the creature had met her on the dusk-lined path that fringed the village, where she had been intending to meet with a boy, no doubt.

The wounded vampire began to laugh in flagrant disregard of the danger he had invited, but his mirth was cut short as he sucked in a deep breath of agony.

The first vampire felt his comrade's pain, sharing it, as the ribbon fluttered from his companion's fingers to land over the hair of the prone village girl.

"This is no laughing matter," the first creature said, reaching out to touch his blood brother's face.

The injured vampire avoided the contact, turning away. "From what we hear, the dragon himself takes risks far greater than the both of us, my friend. Do not be so alarmed."

Something seemed to sink within the first vampire as he hesitated, his hand still in the air. Then the creature schooled his expression to blankness while touching his comrade's head, whether his friend wished for the soothing contact or not.

Like this, the creature healed his friend's wounds, gash by gash, although every closing of an injury drained him of more energy.

Eventually, the wounds were in such shape that the injured vampire's own body could take over the healing. He leaned his head back in clear relief, his fingers glowing as he touch-healed the more minor cuts on his face, his chest.

The first vampire took the limp girl in his arms again and watched his friend.

"If you are not torn apart by wrathful villagers," he said, "then this questionable lack of discretion is bound to slay you nonetheless."

The second vampire raised an eyebrow.

"I refer in particular to your mistress at court," added the first creature, his voice tight. "She is sure to guess at your excesses one night."

"She waits for me to return from my time in the country as any other kitten would—unsuspecting and innocent." He grinned, a predator biding his time in the dark. "Isn't that so? They all *wait because they cannot resist us."*

The first vampire ignored the cutting jibe, thinking instead on the word "us."

Blood brothers. Powerful, enthralling, insatiable. Nothing seemed enough for any of them: never enough blood, enough gluttony, enough . . .

As the word "affection" dissipated in the creature's mind, he used a nail to cut the village girl's throat, then offered her to his blood brother to build up his strength yet again.

The other creature ravenously accepted, grabbing the girl and latching his mouth to her young, fresh neck, sucking, sucking until she was drained to a husk.

When he raised his face to the first vampire, his skin was high in color, his gaze flaring.

"What would I do without you?" he asked.

The first vampire did not answer.

He merely stood and left the cottage as he always did after healing his friend, knowing he would come every time the other vampire called. . . .

THE *custode* watched the monitor screen as Della gripped the hotel's windowsill, her eyes wide and bright, the veins in her throat standing out to such an extent that it seemed the vampire girl might explode altogether.

Were the implanted tales backfiring? the *custode* wondered.

Perhaps only a member of the Meratoliage family could withstand them. . . .

Or was something else happening with Della?

On another screen or two, the caretaker saw an oddity: ravens gathering.

Still, the caretaker monitored the hotel's screen while beginning to access earlier film from this same camera.

Violet's film. And the *custode* would find her, if only to facilitate some trouble for the bitch.

Meanwhile, Della backed away from the window on the telly, her hands covering her mouth as she sank to the floor out of camera range, so the keeper paid due attention to the job at hand, where other screens were showing larger gatherings of ravens heading south of the Thames.

Suddenly, the *custode* had the feeling that perhaps Della had not been undergoing the visions at all. That she was quite busy with another activity . . .

But the ravens were only the beginning.

Hours later, the cameras at the Queenshill dorms revealed something equally noteworthy.

The lenses, clouding over, just as they had on Billiter Street one week ago.

SIX

London Babylon, Still Temporary-Haven-Bound

Later

DELLA had not meant to go so far with the ravens.

Not so far at all, and even hours after it had happened, as a seething dusk enshrouded London, she sat between Polly and Noreen on the hotel's floor near the beds, wishing she could do something, *anything*, to redeem herself.

Their backs against the wall, they could hear Mrs. Jones talking to Wolfie on her secure mobile phone in the confines of the loo, reporting to the too-distant Wolfie what Della had confessed about Violet and the ravens. Their housematron had discovered it upon returning from Wolfie's. Bad welcome-back tidings.

Yet there had been no use in hiding it.

Actually, the sooner told the better, because Della was beyond fear now. She had lived so long in a constant state of waiting for reprisal that this last act had finally brought about a protective numbness, and she took a chance on using the mind-link that connected the class of Queenshill girls, even though Polly and Noreen had been staring straight ahead, avoiding her this entire time.

I didn't mean it, she apologized once again.

Polly turned her face away a little more, her hands splayed over bent knees that, in her human days, had been constantly scratched by the grass of field sports. Her fingers arched as if she were trying not to claw at Della.

Noreen merely slumped, the legs that she so loved to dance on stretching before her. She resembled a doll with red-thread hair left out willy-nilly after playtime.

You already apologized, Della, she thought back in response. Drained. Stunned. *Apologized a thousand times.*

In sharp contrast, Mrs. Jones's voice rose and fell from the muffle of the loo as she and Wolfie discussed what should be done about Della now. It didn't escape Della's attention that the housematron realized the girls could overhear every syllable, although Wolfie's sorrowful tones were slightly garbled by the mobile.

She didn't understand his sadness since Violet had recently fallen out of his highest favor. Still, Della supposed he had loved Violet because she was one of his darlings.

Della wished he were near enough to hear her apologetic thoughts, too.

She shifted on the ground as Mrs. Jones told Wolfie that he was not the only one to have lost quite a bit with the death of Violet.

Della wasn't exactly certain of what she meant, but the entire conversation was pressing a sense of dread against her chest, and she could hardly concentrate on anything else.

It was the worst form of punishment, this dread. It was torture that all but made her want to hurl herself out the window in an act of redemption. And wouldn't that be perfect? The slow wait of her broken bones mending, the inability to end her own life so that she would have to endure even more dread from Mrs. Jones's endless watching . . .

Della curled her arms round her bent legs, resting her forehead on her knees, but it did nothing to dash away the memory of what she had done with the ravens.

She had only meant to have them track Violet, to perhaps even scare her into returning by showing that there was no place Violet could ever hide from her pack.

But as the birds had searched the streets, Della's fear that Violet would do the girls harm had only expanded instead of abated. And by the time she had sensed the birds coming upon her fellow schoolmate—wherever she had been—Della's fear had stretched and birthed into something that resembled the viscous dark of justified hate.

Violet *had* to pay for running away from them, had to pay for every time she had made them all feel so small and bullied—

The ravens had responded to Della's temper in a black cloud of cawing, diving, tearing fervor, and she had not been able to stop them.

Stop . . . herself.

The loo door opened, and Mrs. Jones, with her sensible bun, shoes, and skirt, rounded the corner into the main room, snapping shut her mobile.

She crooked her finger at Della.

Come here, little girl.

But a tear of fright kept Della lanced to the ground.

Do you know what's in store for you, *little girl?*

Della squeezed shut her eyes at the niggle. She dug her fingernails into the carpet, more afraid than she had ever been, even as a human. As a vampire, she had been told she would be improved in many respects, but Della had brought so much emptiness and fear with her into this existence that she hadn't been able to let go of what had always been so much a part of her.

It was said that the masters were the same, though—they each had varying powers based on personal strengths brought over from humanity. Why shouldn't she have carried traits with her, too, even if they were more like weaknesses than abilities?

The housematron leveled an impatient glare at Della.

Get up, Della told herself. *Stand up, as you did last night. You can do it again.*

Unsteadily, she did rise, Violet's death screams coming back to her as a reminder of why she was in this spot.

But, oddly, those screams made Della . . . stronger.

Yes.

Much stronger.

On legs that didn't seem so ready to buckle anymore, she walked to Mrs. Jones, her gaze lowered, mostly because she was wary of the elder vampire entering her mind to see that, deep down, she didn't regret killing Violet at all.

A moment passed, two moments, as the housematron stared at Della. Then, finally, she said, "I am in a quandary as to how to address this, Miss Bennett."

"I'm so very sorry, Mrs. Jones." Sorry a bully such as Violet had not been taken care of sooner, and that was the truth of it.

Masquerading this regret as remorse for Violet's raven attack, Della opened her mind to her superior.

Just then, the housematron skimmed Della's thoughts, her head tilting as she narrowed her eyes, then withdrew. Did she believe it?

The older female looked her charge up and down. "My quandary is rather more complicated than your apologies, Della."

Yes. *Yes.* "I understand, Mrs. Jones."

She hefted out a sigh, gracefully resting her hands on her hips.

"Violet ran away when staying inside was extremely necessary. You and I know that she was up to no good, and I realize you only wished to stop her before she brought more trouble upon us."

Della quashed the urge to nod.

Mrs. Jones tapped her fingers against her hips, as if turning a decision over in her mind. Then her fingers stilled. "And this brings us to the bottom of it," she said. "You stepped over the line, yet you did it out of respect for us. In spite of what happened in the end, you started out by protecting the rest of your group, and I'm sorry Violet never wanted to do that, although we had such hope for her. Loyalty to the unit is valuable to us. Betrayal of the group is not."

Her statements were like a swirl of letters, separated until they coalesced into actual words for Della as she slowly raised her gaze to find Mrs. Jones frowning, as if torn.

But Della knew the reason for that. On the mobile, she had heard Wolfie defending her, even as he mourned Violet's passing. He had told Mrs. Jones that, perhaps, *she* would have summoned animals in such a case, too, if she had chosen to take advantage of the talent she—and even he—rarely utilized these days.

All in all, he had made a case for her to show mercy until he could talk with Della himself.

The housematron lowered her voice, her tone like the snap of a whip.

"Wolfie," she said, "insists that we finally return home. Our new home, where the rest of this will be settled."

The main Underground?

Joy trembled in Della's chest, even if she would receive a postponed punishment there. Even if Mrs. Jones was once again employing dread to stretch Della upon a mental rack.

"Thank you, Mrs. Jones," Della said.

"Your gratefulness is premature."

A catlike flicker lit her eyes, the pupils clicking to slits, then back again.

Something inexplicable flashed in Della's mind: two vampires with featureless faces in a cottage in the woods, one healing the other. Somehow she knew they were blood brothers, and they had a blond girl with them, on the floor, her eyes closed. . . .

She remembered all of it, the entire waking dream, and she blinked, raising a hand to her throat. But it was still there, whole.

Mrs. Jones left Della to stand in place, but Della's mind fuzzed with consequent flashes, mainly of a white ribbon soaked in blood.

Although she blocked her thoughts, both against Mrs. Jones and the assaulting images, the fear rose again to burn like slick black ice in the middle of her chest, causing rationality to slip and slide. But the ice did cool Della as the images faded, then thankfully disappeared altogether.

Behind her, the elder vampire was speaking to all the girls. "Both Wolfie and I feel it's time to get you to your true home after dusk tonight, mostly so he might have the opportunity to handle Della's latest issues. Besides, the attackers haven't shown themselves again, and I've started to believe they're not much more than last night's nuisance. So it's full speed ahead, young ladies."

Noreen asked, "We're not going to school yet, Mrs. Jones?"

"Not for the time being."

The idea of the main Underground held such powerful appeal that the two other girls twittered, excited about going back to the main Underground even before promotion, when they would have otherwise been transferred there.

As if she were the lone one who recalled Violet's death, Della stood rooted to her station. But it was only because she was hoping the images wouldn't return.

"Ready then?" Mrs. Jones asked Polly and Noreen.

Della could hear her classmates springing to their feet, already gathering their books and rushing to their bags.

They were so busy that they couldn't have possibly seen Mrs. Jones come back to Della, leaning close to whisper in her ear.

"Ready, my sweet?"

An inner alarm screamed within Della as the housematron backed away, smiling in feline menace.

Then, as Mrs. Jones moved toward the door to wait for her charges, Della's mind once again flickered on that white ribbon swirling down, down to the ground, where it withered over the hair of a girl who had probably been a lot like her.

SEVEN

The Bladed Tunnel

Earlier

BEFORE the sun even rose, Dawn had told the team all about what Violet had shown her via their mind connection. Then, a couple of hours before classes would even be in session at Queenshill, she'd taken a refresher nap for the big day ahead.

Generally, she didn't need many z's to operate, but a little slumber would give her that extra bit of energy she might have to rely on during this second trip to the exclusive girls' school.

Yup, she thought while standing under the pound and steam of a shower, *a second of quiet under some hot water and a nap should do it.*

Dawn slathered her skin with a neutral soap of Breisi's invention that would hopefully throw off any vampire's sense of smell. The soap hadn't seemed to do the trick last night—not altogether—but she suspected that maybe it didn't cover the scent of ultradread so well, and she and Kiko had been feeling just that while they'd waited in some woods to be discovered by those vamp girls.

But the dread wouldn't happen again. Dawn would make sure of it.

Scare me once, she thought, *bully for you. Scare me twice, and I'll already have my blades out.*

After Dawn got out of the shower and wrapped herself in a towel, Kiko came knocking. Steam wisped the air as she let him in and he held up a red sweater enclosed in a plastic bag.

"From the costume bin," he said. Back when they'd been preparing headquarters, they'd raided vintage stores for clothing, wigs, shoes, and all manner of disguise, which they could use for interviews and any necessary undercover work. "It still has a whiff of that former-owner smell, plus a different cleaning detergent than we use, so maybe it'll help with distracting the noses on these vamps."

She combed the tangles from her hair, which was the opposite of her mom's: brown, unspectacular, and more functional than glamorous.

"Nothing like a red sweater for undercover work," Dawn said.

"Don't be picky." Kiko tossed it on the bathroom counter and headed for the door. "You can thank me for saving your ass later."

"My ass is very appreciative now."

As he left, he gave her a smirk, and she grinned back while firing up a hair dryer that didn't have half the power of the ones in the States.

Still, not long afterward, she, Kiko, and Frank—who huddled under a protective blanket even with the darkened windows of their modified Kia Sedona—drove to Queenshill. Once there, in the relative privacy of the back, she stuffed her hair under a wig cap and went to work on her cover.

The wig she'd chosen was mousy—the ashy, wavy brown of a bookworm. She secured it over her head, then topped off the schoolgirl look by dressing in a calf-length checkered skirt, a white blouse that buttoned at the wrists, a pair of random, thick glasses she'd found among other handy costume wear, and, of course, the sweater.

After checking her weapons and stowing them, she headed from the sheltered cove where they'd parked toward the unguarded gates of Queenshill, thinking it was interesting that last night's ruckus hadn't resulted in more security. Bobbies had been called and everything, but Dawn supposed that they probably hadn't found much on campus besides the remnants of a wildlife fight from the animals the schoolgirls had summoned.

Even so, she kept her eyes peeled while traveling a gravel path that took her between a chapel and the gothic-tinged administration building. She clutched a pink folder to her stomach, her head down, her wig covering her features. A "book bag" was strapped crossways over her chest, and it was heavy with everything she'd need once she got past the housematron's door:

Two smaller stakes: One ash, one aspen. One tipped with silver, one plain.

Two UV grenades.

A mini flamethrower.

A mini machete.

Frank and Kiko were off campus with the bigger stuff, like her saw-bow.

Her earpiece came to life with Kiko's voice. "You there yet?"

"Not yet."

She barely moved her mouth. Not that anyone was really around right now to hear, but schoolgirls were supposed to be in class and she didn't want to draw undue attention. Then again, during a previous daytime trip to campus, Dawn had gotten the distinct impression that these students weren't exactly under lock and key. They were overachievers here at Queenshill and seemingly treated with the respect and freedom they'd earned, so a schoolgirl cruising to the dorm right now wouldn't be entirely out of place.

Yet as Dawn passed by the main buildings with their chimeras spreading their wings and gaping at her, she reconsidered the whole "watching thing." She definitely felt like there were curious eyes *somewhere*. . . .

Shaking it off, she headed past the classrooms, their leaded windows thick and fancy among the dark brick. Hell, ghosts of little, silk-clad kids would've seemed right at home peering out at this sky, with its gray clouds that looked like stuffing torn out of a clawed mattress.

"I'm just past the football field, so I'm close," Dawn added for Kiko's sake. He'd wanted to go into the housematron's room, too, just to see if he could get readings off of any clothing or objects. But they all knew that his psychometry didn't work on a vamp's items unless they were alive when they'd been wearing or handling them.

Besides, was she going to smuggle him in by using her book bag or something? Right.

Her wig fluttered as two Friends traveled by her side. Breisi and Greta, a spirit who'd been on campus this entire time.

Kiko was just now responding. "Can't wait until you get your camera on so we can see something."

A shushing sound followed, and Dawn guessed that Frank had already gotten tired of his teammate's commentary. Her dad had accompanied them here even though he was weaker during sunlight hours than at night. He'd inherited the ability to move around during the day from Eva, who'd turned him into a vamp in the first place, and Dawn had to admit that the Hollywood Underground's talents often came in handy for the team's purposes.

Ahead, the dorms loomed: all brick and modern gloom. But first, Dawn had to pass by the copse of trees where they'd encountered the demon dogs sent by the schoolgirls last night.

Good times.

Keeping her heartbeat steady, she blew out a breath, inhaled, then bypassed the trees by using a neat stone path. As she approached the dorm where the vamps lived, she noticed a dictionary propping open the card-key-accessible door.

Of course. Greta had already said that, to ensure Dawn's entrance, some of the Friends had pushed the book to the slit of the door after another student had exited.

So far, it was all running like clockwork.

"All right," Dawn whispered, "I'm almost inside. I'll get the camera on after I'm in the room, 'kay?"

"Cool," Kiko said.

Then he went silent, and Dawn imagined how Frank must've put his hand over the psychic's mouth to make the quiet possible. Good thing, too, because with Costin and Natalia also monitoring from headquarters, they needed room for any one of them to talk at a moment's notice.

With a sly look around, Dawn opened the door, kicked the dictionary to the side—hah, what symbolic pleasure she took from that—then slipped through.

Friends were patrolling the halls to make sure any cleaning personnel or supervisors wouldn't cross paths with Dawn. They knew that security was light at Queenshill, even after last night, and all there was to worry about, really, were some cameras in the dorms and an elderly security guard who normally wandered the campus after the sun went down.

Breisi's voice was wind-tunnel thin as she spoke, just ahead of Dawn.

"This way. Let's go."

"Hold your horses," Dawn whispered. "This idiotic skirt is confining."

"This, from a woman who's been known to wear a cocktail dress during a brawl?"

Dawn smiled sardonically at the jasmine air while they rounded a corner that led to the stairwell. If the time had been right for some chatter, she would've reminded Breisi that, hello, the brawl had been staged for a stunt during one of the movies she'd worked on during her "other life."

The one that seemed so irrelevant these days.

Dawn took the stairs two at a time, thinking that at least those choreographed fights and the physical training that went with them had allowed her to jump right into vamp fighting. When she thought of what it might've been like to try to find her dad, who'd been missing at the time, without all the skills she'd had . . .

She *didn't* think about it.

Near the top of the stairway, Breisi and Greta sped ahead to the door, and when Dawn got to it, too, she put on a pair of tight gloves, slowly applied pressure to it, then stuck her head past, glancing around the fluorescent hallway.

Nada. They were all alone.

But then Greta darted even farther ahead.

Leaving the stairwell behind, Dawn ran to where the Friend was guiding her, to a door marked "Housematron."

Heartbeat: calm. Breathing: take it down a level.

After putting her pink folder into the book bag, Dawn took out the tension wrench, rake, and short hook the Friends had told her she'd need. Then she went to work on picking the lock.

She only hoped that the vamps weren't the type to have used any sort of magic aboveground. If so, she'd know pretty soon whether or not there'd be trouble getting inside the room.

Within a minute, she had the lock taken care of and was opening the door, her lungs burning with a held breath.

No magic, she thought. *Please, no magic—*

But, without incident, she cracked the door open, allowing Breisi and Greta in before her so they could cloud any cameras.

As she stuffed her tools away, she noted that maybe these vamps weren't so keen on attracting suspicion aboveground after all, in spite of their more careless activities like burying victims' heads and other body parts at an abandoned construction site on Billiter Street. They'd also been real nonchalant about their master sending off Awareness signals, because that's how Costin had tracked them down in the first place.

When Breisi called to Dawn, she entered, then shut the door, locked it, and slipped off her bag while scanning the room.

The first thing she saw was a nondescript desk with folders neatly stacked in wire organizers and a computer glancing back with a blank screen. According to the Friends, the blasé setup described the vampire housematron in a lot of ways: Plain. Ordinary. Unsurprising except for what they now knew about her.

But there was something besides the desk that caught Dawn's eye—a queen-sized bed with an indentation on the duvet, as if Mrs. Jones had been slumbering on top of the covers the last time she'd been here. It was a personal detail that got to Dawn in a way that she didn't want to acknowledge, so she let it go.

Other than that, there was a bookshelf lined with plastic ferns and stacked with hardbound volumes of classics from the likes of Thackeray, Austen, and Dickens. And then there was the mahogany wardrobe against a wall.

In addition to some drawers for clothing, that was about it . . . except for the camera peeking out from behind the fern on top of the bookshelf.

Dawn knew that it would already be clouded, but she jerked her chin toward it anyway.

"*Greta's got it,*" Breisi said. "*Still, we don't have long.*"

"Gotcha," Dawn said. "Someone might notice the malfunction and decide to check it out."

She took out a hair band from the book bag and wrangled the wig into a ponytail, doffed the sweater and glasses and stuffed them in the bag, rolled up her sleeves, then slid a headlight over her head. "I wonder if clouded cameras were the thing that drew that commando boy"—the dead one in their lab freezer—"to us on Billiter Street."

"*A possibility,*" Breisi said. "*Now hurry.*"

Yeah, yeah. Dawn made it snappy, but she still went on wondering if the commando's group kept tabs on any of those cameras posted just about everywhere you looked around the city. They might have been monitoring the burial area, which would explain why the kid had been attracted to it.

Had the camera malfunctions made him—whoever he was and whatever his purpose—come running to snoop around?

Sometimes the influence of an Underground reached both high and low into society. How connected was *this* community here in London?

Good God—and was it only a matter of time before this Underground realized that "Limpet and Associates" had messed with the cameras near their own headquarters?

Gah. She shouldn't be dwelling on this right now.

Dawn attached a small camera to her headlight. Breisi and Frank had been developing the surveillance item over the past year, but it'd always shorted out or gone a little fritzy on field tests. Now it was time to give this improved version a go.

Flicking it on, she glanced around the room while Breisi darted about, getting her own good look at every nook and cranny.

Dawn's earpiece activated. Costin.

"Perfect reception," he said.

She hadn't been prepared to hear him, and her flesh seemed to roll with shivers that bled below her skin, too, burrowing down deep, low.

Nice timing.

"Kiko?" Dawn asked, mainly to bring herself out of it, but also genuinely wanting to know if he was getting a picture, too.

"Lovely in Technicolor," he responded.

Breisi's thready voice spun around Dawn.

"Here!"

At the urgency of her Friend's tone, Dawn followed the sound to the wardrobe while ducking under the strap of her book bag, putting it back on.

"Open the wardrobe," Breisi said.

"Wait a sec." Dawn extracted her machete from the bag. "Team members are the ones who're supposed to have the privilege of commanding you guys, not vice versa. Let's have some respect for decorum here."

"Cállate, *Dawn, I hear something. A breeze?"*

Holy creepies. "An opening."

Pulse chopping, Dawn jerked open the wardrobe door, only to find a space occupied by a few sweaters and skirts that hung in the air like specters.

But when she looked closer, she saw loose threads from two cardigans stirring.

A breeze, all right. Now, if she could just find an opening . . .

She'd read ghost stories before, so she pushed the clothes to the side in order to reach the back panel. She pressed on the wood, here, there, one corner, one side, the other—

It sprang and creaked open, the breeze huffing out of the resulting black rectangle. To Dawn, it sounded like something exhaling. Something hidden in the dark.

Costin, she thought, her purpose agonizingly clear, even if nothing directly in front of her was.

Save him.

Now her pulse was really going as she waited for Breisi to gush through the pitch-black rectangle first. Then she stepped all the way into the wardrobe herself, closing the door behind her as she entered the gape at the back of the structure.

Greta would stay behind to patrol and, more importantly, to uncloud the camera just as Dawn disappeared and before whoever might be watching it got worried about the reception.

As she stepped all the way through, one foot hitting what felt like wood planks on the other side, the darkness engulfed her, the cold so complete that Dawn couldn't even see an inch in front of her.

But the darkness?

It didn't feel so bad.

"Turn on your headlight," she heard Kiko say over the earpiece as Breisi went to scout ahead.

Dawn did, then sucked in a breath.

She was standing at the top of a steep staircase, over what looked to be an abyss, and a sway of vertigo made her balance tilt.

She let go of her machete and it tumbled away.

But Breisi was already there, pushing against her, steadying her, even before the machete hit the bottom after what seemed like a few minutes.

"Thanks," Dawn said as her Friend provided a crutch.

"Anytime. I didn't see cameras yet, but I'll keep you posted."

Together, they descended.

Slowly. Very, very slowly. Each step like a heartbeat dragged through thick liquid.

At the bottom, Dawn's shoes hit rock. Breisi went ahead again, then came back, reporting that she still didn't see any cameras.

Dawn swept her headlight over the enclosing rock and the darkness that burrowed through it. Then she scanned her lamp back over the stairs while taking a few breaths that cleared her head. Her blood was pumping, jamming.

"A tunnel," she said.

"A tunnel," Kiko repeated. "Now those are some real powers of perception you've got going, Dawn. No wonder you're 'key.' "

He was talking about the prophecy he'd made over a year ago—a precognitive vision that had persuaded Costin to bring her onto the team in the first place. Kiko had seen her standing victorious and covered in the blood of a vampire.

She didn't know how accurate it was, but it always seemed to give them hope when there wasn't so much of it going around.

Dawn reached into her bag to grab the mini flamethrower. "I wonder if this tunnel leads to the big show."

The Underground.

"Maybe," Breisi said, *"we should have brought Natalia here."*

The new girl's voice immediately came over the earpiece. "Yes, I would be able to feel if any vampires were near."

Kiko interrupted. "We shot that idea down earlier, Curls. Dawn gave us a description of what she saw in Violet's mind, so she knows what she's looking for. Plus, Breisi can scout ahead some more."

Was it Dawn's imagination or did Kik sound a little too protective?

"Dawn." It was Costin now. "Perhaps we should send Frank and Kiko in since there seem to be possibilities."

"Only if you want to take a chance on Greta clouding the housematron's camera yet again. If it happens another time before I get out and someone besides the school is monitoring it, it'll be a sure sign that something's up." She shrugged and added, "Besides, if I get caught down here, one hunter's death is more acceptable than three, and you know that's true."

No one said a word. But, weirdly, the thought of dying was probably scaring them more than it did her. Hell was relative, and as far as she was concerned, she'd already been through it. Physical death might feel pretty good if that death had a purpose to it. Besides, she was—

"—key." It was Natalia, and she'd been saying something that Dawn hadn't been paying attention to.

Then she repeated it, as if reassuring everyone. "You said it before—Dawn is 'key,' so how can she die?"

"Especially," Kiko added, "when she hasn't even fulfilled my vision?"

And it was a prophecy he'd made before his broken back, his drug habit, and his slow recovery. It'd been a solid vision, unlike some of the ones he'd had as an addict.

But . . . enough.

Dawn turned her headlight on higher power, the beam lighting over the walls, and—

Whoa-ho.

"Would you look at that?" Kiko said.

Dawn meandered closer, Breisi right next to her.

It seemed as if gnarled blades were coming out of the rock, but as Dawn closed the distance, she saw that they were only roots that had warped into thorny imposters.

She pointed the light down the tunnel, where the faux blades seemed to tighten into a thicket.

"Freakin' figures I'd be wearing a skirt for this," Dawn said, reaching into the bag to put the sweater back on.

Too bad she'd lost her machete, but destroying the property was a dumb idea anyway if she was just here to quietly scope things out.

"No flamethrowers," Breisi said, knowing how Dawn's mind would be working.

"No kidding." She wrapped herself as best as she could, then forged ahead.

But when her Friend seemed to hug her, as if providing a cloak, Dawn missed a step.

Warmer, she thought. Yet the feeling didn't necessarily have anything to do with the sweater she was wearing.

She swallowed, began to walk again.

Let Breisi be. It wasn't like a Friend could get sliced up, anyway, and maybe the layer of Breisi's essence would even work to cushion any cuts.

Probably not, but whatever.

The earpiece went silent as Dawn tried to make her body smaller, but even with Breisi's help, the roots snagged on Dawn's sweater, then her shirt, ripping, leaving her with stinging souvenirs on her arms and legs.

Had the schoolgirls used this passage often? Or had it been here for the housematron only?

Either way, the vamps probably healed so quickly that scratches wouldn't matter to them. Or maybe they were masochists who didn't even care.

As a particularly mean root clawed at Dawn, she grunted. But, strangely, the pain made her want to go even farther as a "screw you" to the vampires.

Maybe to everyone.

Next thing she knew, the roots were stubbornly grabbing at her wig, pulling it and the cap off her head. She didn't fuss, merely tore them off the sharp points and put them in her bag for now. Who cared, when she could see the end of the brambled passage just ahead?

When she got there, she took a hesitant step out, feeling

around with her foot and hoping there'd be something to hold her.

Yup. Big, wide, welcome ground, and as Dawn emerged from the tunnel, the air got even crisper, like a slap that just kept giving.

Breisi swept around the perimeter, and when Dawn heard what sounded like beads clanking together, she sought out where it was coming from.

"Breisi?"

"*Over here.*"

Dawn's headlight caught a swish of orange and red, a curtain of what really did look like beads.

She went to them, whisked them aside.

The oxygen left her for a second, but she got it back in the next heartbeat.

"It's one of the places I saw in Violet's mind," Dawn said. "The room with the fairy lights and seventies upholstery and Orlando Bloom."

It felt like her pulse was stabbing her now, leaving her perforated and a little weak.

Dawn wondered about the rest of Violet's images—the girls running, gnashing their fangs, and swinging from bone-studded chandeliers.

But this discovery was a start. Were they on their way to a real Underground?

"Remember," Dawn said, "Violet told me that the other place I saw, the more lively area, was a reward for the vamp girls. A place they went after they graduated?"

"Our own prize on this hunt," Costin said, startling her.

She heard the rush of dark joy in his tone, and something inside her clung to it.

He'd told the team that, over the passage of years, the blood brothers had seemed to embrace their own pleasures rather than the will of the dragon. So the more decadent, the better, Dawn thought, because that meant a master had forgotten his true mission of serving the biggest vampire of all.

And if Violet's images indicated an Underground, it looked like this master had totally forgotten his purpose in a nubile paradise.

Unless, she added while recalling how the Queenshill girls had fought, these vamps would be the best followers of them all.

As Breisi investigated on her own, Dawn began rooting around the room like a maniac—the zebra pillows, a beanbag, even the lava lamp—trying to find something.

But there was nothing. Not really. Just manga books, nail polish, an iPod.

The remnants of an area that didn't seem to Dawn like any part of an Underground at all—and she should know since she'd been in one before.

She was out of the room before Breisi could catch up.

"*Maybe there's more.*"

"We need to move on, remember?" Dawn reached the open space, closing her eyes and trying to listen for movement. For a sign. For hope that this wasn't another damned dead end.

When she felt Breisi nudging at her, she loosened up, allowing her Friend to guide her. And she did, to another tunnel, this one thornless.

"Wait."

Precautions. Dawn's locator was attached to her skirt so the others could find her, and Breisi would be able to navigate her way around any maze you put in front of her, but Dawn still reached into her bag to bring out a fluorescent tube, which she bent in the middle to activate before tossing it to the ground.

"Just in case I find myself on my own," she said to Breisi as they continued down the tunnel. She'd clean them up later.

"*You won't be alone,*" the Friend said.

"Better safe than sorry, yeah?"

As they continued, Dawn dropped a few more rods before Breisi stopped her.

"What is it, Breez?"

"Odd." She seemed to be moving up and down the rock, brushing against it with her essence. *"A crack."*

"You feel a crack? Like there's an opening or door?"

Costin immediately came on. "Dawn, let Breisi lead you while you move closer with the camera so I can see."

She went pliant, allowing Breisi to push her forward to where there really was a sliver of space. With nudging guidance from her Friend, Dawn was able to take off her gloves and follow the line with her fingertips, her heartbeat so sharp now that it felt like she was being flayed from the inside out.

"What should I do?"

Costin paused, then said, "I would put my very existence on the idea that this door is charmed, as if to hide what is behind it from the schoolgirl vampires who lingered in the Orlando Bloom room."

So there *was* some vampire mojo going on—they just hadn't done any of it aboveground, where it might be more easily detected by rival blood brothers or educated hunters.

For the first time, Frank got on the earpiece. "Unless we can perform some magic I'm not aware of, I'm coming down to blast through. Have the Friends find an open window to the dorm, then cloud any cameras as I run by."

"Dad, you're fast, but this is real chancy. . . ."

Yet about five minutes later, Frank was next to her, having used what he'd seen on her camera, the light rods, and his own senses to find them. He was bundled in protective, sun-shielding gear, not an inch of skin in sight. The clothes were so thick that the thorns hadn't even cut all the way through.

He nodded to Dawn, his masked face freaking her out a little until he removed the covering.

"With your mind and my body," he said, "we'll have an entrance soon enough."

Breisi swished by, and Frank cocked his head at the greeting.

In the meantime, Dawn was wondering if he really thought that she could punch that hard with her powers—enough to make up for what he was lacking during the day. She recalled back in L.A., when he and Kiko had tried to get through all the rock to help her and Costin in the other Underground. It'd taken a while.

But they might as well try, she thought, even if the charmed door put out some kind of signal that it was being breached.

She was used to the procedure now: all she had to do was access her darkest, deepest, ugliest thoughts, and that ball of fury shaped itself within her.

So she did it, thinking about how much she'd hated Eva while growing up. How much Frank had hurt her.

But even that didn't seem to be enough anymore, so she tapped into her frustration with Costin and Jonah.

Her guilt—

Just as she slammed out with her mind, Frank ran at the wall, shards of rock exploding outward with their combined effort.

"Again," Frank said.

She thought of how the Elite vampires had smacked her around and humiliated her just for fun during the final showdown in L.A.

And—*blast.*

Thought of that night when she'd needed to turn Costin into a creature that he'd always despised.

Blast!

Thought of how much she hated herself sometimes.

Blaaaaaast!

There was enough of a hole now that Frank made the most

of it, speedily hefting chunks of rock to widen the opening as he coughed for some reason.

"Faster," Breisi said. *"We've already used up a lot of time."*

Frank kicked enough in so that he fell through, landing on his hands and knees and springing right back to his feet.

But as Dawn and Breisi came through, he stood there, his expression a blank.

"Frank?" Dawn asked.

Alarmed by his stillness, she raised the flamethrower as she flashed her headlight over the room.

And when she saw the scalpels and knives and blades hanging from the ceiling like razored leaves, Dawn started coughing, too.

Or maybe "gagging" was a better word for it.

EIGHT
The Connections

AFTER dusk fell, Dawn sat in front of a gutted fireplace in a headquarters lounge, scribbling on a legal pad, trying to diagram her impressions of everything she'd found today.

Or at least she *had* been diagramming. Now she was just zoning out, hardly seeing the French sixteenth-century hunting tapestries on the walls staring back at her. Costin had said he'd chosen the artwork just because they pleased his aesthetic sensibilities, and that might've been the case for him, but for her, the men on horseback who were chasing creatures with long, dripping fangs had a real different significance.

Unimaginable beasts. Bloodthirsty monsters.

They were out there, all right, but what the hell kind of things had the team come upon *this* time at Queenshill?

And what did those blades in that underground room have to do with the images Violet had shared?

Dawn caught the sound of high-heeled footsteps on the wooden floor, and she tossed her legal pad facedown on the end table next to her.

Eva, who had taken it upon herself to become the hostess of headquarters while she was still around, arrived dressed in one of the outfits she'd quickly packed before being escorted here last night: some kind of designer glen plaid pencil skirt and sweater. That's what she'd told Kiko when he'd asked, anyway, and God knew why Kiko would even be interested.

She watched her mom set a tray on another stand near the leather wing chair Dawn was sitting in.

"You need to eat," Eva said, gesturing to the plate she'd prepared. "Egg and cress on soda bread. It's good for you."

Dawn was about to tell her mother that, thanks, she'd get around to eating in her own time, but like always, the sight of Eva tripped her tongue.

The surgically altered face, the melancholy lines of mortality that hadn't been there before Dawn had killed Eva's master and turned her mother human again . . .

Just another reminder of what Dawn had taken from someone else.

"Thanks, Mom," she said instead. To emphasize her gratefulness, she grabbed the sandwich, bit into it, then talked around the food. "Good timing, too—I'm waiting for the team to meet me back down here."

"Where are the rest of them?"

Eva's question was too casual, and Dawn knew her mom was more interested in Frank than anyone else. "Dad's taking a slumber, but the rest of us split up to do research on the Internet, Costin's database, and in his library, just to see if we could come up with some connections to what we found today. Links. Ideas."

"Sounds logical."

Eva tugged on Dawn's ripped blouse, which she hadn't stopped to change since they'd returned from Queenshill. The attention made Dawn more aware of the slightly pungent healing gel she'd dabbed over her injuries.

Her mom pointed to the puffiest, reddest scratch of them all on Dawn's arm. "Don't tell me—you barely got out alive. Again."

"It looks worse than it really is." After discovering that blade room, Frank and Dawn had explored the area while Breisi searched for any linked passages or trapdoors, charmed or not, that might lead to a bigger find.

A true Underground.

But they'd found nothing, so they'd called it a day. Yet Dawn was hoping they'd be able to return to Queenshill for a more comprehensive sweep.

If it'd do any good.

"Are you allowed to tell me what you found?" Eva asked.

Dawn had been about to take another bite of her sandwich, but she stopped to say, "There wasn't much there."

Denied.

But, jeez, even though it looked like Eva might be sticking around here for a while, just for safety's sake, that didn't mean she was a part of the team.

And when Kiko and Natalia walked into the room, side by side, he inadvertently backed Dawn up on that by clearing his throat when he saw Eva, obviously halting whatever he and Number Two Psychic had been chatting about.

Probably team stuff, and Eva seemed to know it.

Her smile was expertly forced, too understanding. Dawn could tell by now.

"There's more food in the kitchen if anyone's interested," her mother said.

Kiko took a seat on a low green velvet couch near the fireplace. "How about I take you up on that later?"

Natalia nodded to Eva in greeting while primly sitting next to Kiko, her ever-ready notebook in her lap. She was wearing a tweed skirt set and thick white stockings—practical, far less stylish than Eva's Rodeo Drive ensemble. Dawn liked that the psychic didn't seem to mind her lack of fashion sense, either.

One of the Friends swooped over to Eva, and the blonde held up a hand.

"I know, I know. It's time to go to a different room so I won't hear any of the team talk."

As the Friend escorted her out, Kiko turned in his seat, his gaze following her. "Hey, there're a bunch of *EastEnders* episodes on the DVR, if you want."

Before things had picked up with business, he and Eva had started watching the British soap together as just another way to fill her time. She'd been trying hard to get into the swing of life over here as a new person under a new name, "Mia Scott." She had no career and, truthfully, no family who required her attention, and it'd been hard for her.

Eva maintained that family had been her big reason for becoming a vampire back in L.A., but . . . Well, her plans hadn't really worked out. Not unless you counted her voluntary blood donations to Frank as making her a part of the family now.

Her mom acknowledged Kiko's TV suggestion then left the room.

No, you couldn't say Eva was much a part of anything nowadays.

Dawn could feel Kiko gazing at her and wondering what was going through her mind, but he didn't dare read her. He hadn't done that to her, or anyone else on the team, since Hollywood, when she'd broken him of the rude habit.

Needing something to do, she took another bite of her sandwich, then held it out to Kiko and Natalia. They both declined.

Frank ambled in soon afterward, his wiry brown hair sticking up in back from his resting time. Dawn wondered if he'd seen Eva in passing and, if so, how they'd reacted to each other.

Like exes, no doubt. Even though Dawn wished it could be different. She adored Breisi—hell, as much as Dawn could "adore" anyone—but . . .

She felt a rogue thrill tumbling down the back of her neck, indicating another presence.

Costin, she thought, putting down her sandwich.

She took a drink of tea to coat her suddenly dry mouth, catching their boss out of the corner of her eye as he moved toward the fireplace. He leaned against the mantel in his black lounging suit, which was all rustling, silken material.

Unlike Frank, Costin's every post-rest hair was in place, his midnight-hue locks curling slightly down his neck and bringing out the pale of his flesh, the topaz of his eyes, which were burning a little more than usual.

She could tell he hadn't fed from a blood bag yet, but he would have to do it soon, and the notion made her put down her tea before she spilled any of it. He'd drink a bit from her, too, since her blood gave him more strength and contentment than any other.

A feeding. A bite. Sadly, it'd somehow become the most constant and fulfilling component of her life.

"Our Friends," Costin said without preamble, "have relayed that Mrs. Jones has not yet returned to Queenshill or, more specifically, to her room. However, something else *did*."

Kiko said it first. "One of those pseudo-ninja figures? Like the kid we have downstairs in the freezer?"

"One of those," Costin answered, low and smooth. "It seemed to be investigating her room."

"So," Kiko said, "I guess we can now be pretty sure that those shadow figures are related to the schoolgirl vamps."

Breisi had entered the room, and as she swished in the door, her voice tunneled around them. *"The question is, do these vampires know about these shadow figures? Or are the figures* after *the vampires?"*

Great—more questions, but they were valid ones.

At any rate, Dawn felt justified in what she'd suspected earlier. "These shadow things must've finally noticed a pattern of camera clouding—on Billiter Street, last night at Queenshill, today in Mrs. Jones's room. . . . They're not just onto the vampires, if that's the case—they're onto us, too."

"But a few steps behind us," Kiko added.

Frank sat in a chair next to Dawn, leaning his bulky forearms on his thighs as Breisi settled around him. "So whatever these shadow figures are, they're using cameras to monitor. If we keep clouding the lenses, we'll tip them off to where we are because they know what to look for now."

"Then we don't cloud anymore," Kiko said. "We use disguises from this point on since I doubt the vamps—if they're even aware of the shadows and the cameras—get smell-o-vision over their screens. Maybe I'll have to go around dressed like a kid, and maybe it's time to pull out a lot of wigs and disguises for the rest of you."

"But," Dawn said, "if we're going to be creeping around vamp territory, we'll need *some* sort of distraction for those cameras. If the vamps are using the shadow things to monitor us, they'll catch on soon enough that we're a threat. According to what Violet said, it sounded like they still weren't sure about our status, and that's why they haven't risked hunting us down in public, where they could be identified by society at large. They're only being cautious with us because we're not exactly one of their 'nightcrawl' victims who disappear without much of a trace."

Natalia was at the edge of the couch. "I noticed a camera near our headquarters. One of the London surveillance network's?"

"Right," Kiko said. "The shadow things could be accessing the network somehow, so I guess we'd better hope that they take their time in recognizing us."

Costin's tone was terse. "Most unfortunately, the camera outside headquarters was clouded this morning when Violet appeared. A Friend was only following procedure in keeping our business private."

Right, Dawn thought, because the last thing they needed was for regular society to be all aflutter about vampires—especially since there were two of them on the Limpet team.

One of whom was particularly important to wiping out the dragon.

As they all let that knowledge soak in, Costin added, "It will be a time game with these monitors and possibly the schoolgirls: will they discover us before we find out who and what they are?"

Breisi's voice whirled around them. *"The Friends will be ready to defend headquarters if they show up, Costin."*

"Yeah," Dawn said. "We'll batten down the hatches even more than we already have. But to invade us, they'll have to be real good . . . and real ballsy to risk a public battle in the middle of a city. Queenshill was at least removed from traffic."

Kiko added, "We'll strike at them before they can identify who we are. Don't worry about that."

That seemed to assuage the boss for now, although he didn't look completely satisfied.

Natalia didn't, either, as she went back to taking notes.

"Anyway," Dawn finished, "this investigation really has gone a lot better than the last one and, if I'm not mistaken, most other Underground hunts. We're doing just fine on it."

"If these girls are even Underground," Breisi said.

"Yeah, yeah." Kiko was obviously beginning to get itchy to move on. He liked the research part of the job more than almost anything except the actual fighting. Oh, and bragging about his talents. "What's next?"

Costin took a sleek, black-cased object out of his shirt pocket, then handed it over to Frank, who barely glanced at it before passing it to Dawn.

"Explain?" she asked.

Breisi hovered over Dawn. *"It's a pulser I had Frank construct."*

Frank said, "She started developing one in L.A. 'cos of a vampire's sensitive hearing in general, and she figured one day we might need this to avoid being tracked."

"Bingo," Kiko said.

"But," Breisi added, *"I picked up the idea of a pulser again, knowing we'd need it more than ever."*

With a rush of adrenaline—of get-me-back-out-there-to-fight urgency—Dawn ran a finger over the slick casing, which was no bigger than a cigarette lighter, really. "So we can use this to confuse our body rhythms if they have the ability to track us like that."

"That's the hope," Frank said.

Kiko hopped out of his seat to take a gander, and Dawn yielded the pulser to him. But instead of keeping it for long, he brought it over to Natalia.

When he handed it to her she smiled at him.

Was it Dawn's imagination, or was he turning a shade of pink she'd never seen the likes of?

"Back to the task at hand," Costin said, prompting Natalia to give the pulser back to Kiko and pick up her notebook again. "Everyone here has had an opportunity to process what we saw at Queenshill today. What have you arrived at?"

Kiko reclaimed his seat. "I still think that, based on all those shiny tools hanging from the ceiling plus the sight of that fridge, we could guess we're dealing with a vampire who has developed a taste for a victim's organs. And whether this vamp—or even a human who's a monster just the same—is from an Underground or not, what we found was a torture station, complete with a bathtub for letting blood."

Natalia's brow furrowed with what Dawn thought might be the same repulsion that'd overcome *her* earlier.

But she was over it now.

Kiko had suggested the same slice-and-dice idea on the rushed ride back from Queenshill, but the presence of the bathtub had taken Dawn in a similar yet different direction.

"I told you guys that the bathtub"—which had been cleaned down to a sparkling shine, just like the fridge and the blades—"reminded me of Elizabeth, Countess Bathory. Even though her original story seems to have gone the way of legend, she's been called a vampire. So during research time, I looked into her."

Natalia furiously wrote as Costin straightened away from the mantel, his expression disturbingly serene.

"And what have you come to know about the countess?" he asked.

That look on his face . . . It wasn't just serene, but sinister, Dawn might call it, if she had guts enough.

With all the calm she could muster—all the coldness—she reached for her teacup and took a sip. Her mouth had gone cottony again, but this time, it wasn't because of what Costin did to her libido.

She put the cup back down. "She operated mainly from the late fifteen hundreds to the early sixteen hundreds in the region of the Slovak Republic. Some say it was Hungary, but either way, she lived with her war-hero hubby, who was absent a lot of the time. The legends say that she bathed in blood to preserve her beauty. I didn't have tons of time for research, so I didn't find any solid documentation to back that up yet, but there's a lot of speculation that the bathing story has been stretched to some mighty lengths of bullshit. Still, the countess did go to trial for torturing scads of young girls and women. The number of her victims varies—"

"Over six hundred and fifty," Costin said, his gaze clouded.

Everyone in the room glanced at him, and it was the type of glance where you'd rather not be looking, but you do it anyway. Hell, Breisi even stopped moving around.

He clearly recognized the need to explain. "I was involved with dismantling an Underground in Siam at the time the countess was at large. When I finished with my task, I heard the rumors about her, yet arrived only after her incarceration. Even so, I talked to many a villager who lived in fright of her and her accomplices. In addition to her reputation for . . . mistreating . . . servants, she had a predilection for enjoying the company of those who practiced the black arts. She was even supposed to have eloped with a man who was rumored to be a vampire, but she returned to her castle all alone, without him."

Dawn had been holding her breath while listening. Although she and Costin had a master-progeny Awareness, that didn't mean they had ever let each other all the way in, exposing and sharing everything. There were still personal shields in place.

It wasn't even too often that Costin spilled personal information outside of their Awareness, and when he did, she was never sure where it would lead.

If he had a purpose for doing it.

Nice to have trust in a relationship, she thought.

She exhaled, then said, "I read that stopping the countess was a lot of trouble. She was real well connected, even related to the prime minister of Hungary and a prince of Transylvania. Then there was an aunt at royal court, but she was supposed to be a witch, just like the other people the countess obviously hung with."

"A witch and a corrupter of young girls," Costin added.

A mental lightbulb went on for Dawn.

"Girls like the ones from Queenshill?" she asked.

Natalia lowered her notebook while Frank lowered his head.

"Well, slap me silly and call me Spanky," Kiko said. "I'm going to venture that corrupting young girls was a family tradition?"

They all looked at Costin for assurance, but he'd gone back to lurking against the mantel. That probably meant he agreed.

Dawn sat back in her chair, knowing when Costin was open to her using Awareness between them and when he wasn't. This would be a "wasn't" moment.

She continued. "The countess's accomplices would supposedly tempt girls to her domain with jobs, or if necessary, drug or beat them into submission. No one escaped alive."

Costin gave a subtle nod.

Hell—a contemporary of the countess at their disposal. As usual, Dawn *tried* not to let his age bother her, but the truth was, she wondered if that wasn't the least unnerving chasm between them.

Anyway . . . "The more sensational accounts say that the countess started the whole blood bath deal after she hit one of her maids and made her bleed. Elizabeth noticed that her skin was softer—"

"More supple." Kiko added in randomness.

Dawn didn't stop, even while shooting him a what-the-hell glance. "—than normal. So she bathed her face in blood. Some tales go on to say that she kept girls down in the dungeons beneath the castle, and she started using them for blood baths. After soaking herself, she'd make other girls, who were picked for their beauty and talent with the tongue, if you know what I mean, clean her off."

Natalia jerked, like she'd thrown up a little in her mouth. Dawn passed her the tea while continuing.

"Whether this is all true or not, the countess did go to trial, like I already said. Her accomplices turned on her, but, as we know, she had powerful connections in life, so even when her crowd was put to death, Elizabeth was just walled up in a room until she died."

Here, Costin spoke once more. "When she was put away, she was nearing her fiftieth birthday, yet even so, she appeared strangely . . . young."

Dawn canted forward now. "You saw her?"

His gaze was distant again. "The first time, I caught a glimpse when a meal was slipped through to her, for there were no windows or doors in her room. Since she wasn't a blood brother, and there was no indication of one recently around her, she wasn't a priority, in my estimation. I did attempt to question her, though, but she didn't yield significant information." He paused. "In the end, I determined she wasn't involved in an Underground and I was soon on my way, following a much stronger lead."

"And now?" Dawn asked. "Is this something worth pursuing?"

"Over the ages, I've learned to rule out no connection, regardless of how thin it might seem. The bathtub, the blades . . . Disturbing evidence to consider."

Frank ran a hand down his face, his features like those of a man frozen in never-ending battery, just like the bar bouncer he'd been in true life.

"What you're not saying out loud," he muttered, "is that maybe the countess is alive and well and we found her playroom today?"

"Oh, I wouldn't go that far." A bitter smile ghosted Costin's mouth. "But I would certainly wonder if she has served as inspiration."

"Good gravy," Kiko said. "What kind of vampires take a blood bath?"

Dawn knew. "Ones who subscribe to the countess's supposed method for staying young and beautiful. Sound familiar?"

Hollywood. Fame, fortune, youth, beauty . . . all worth selling your soul for.

And Dawn could testify to that, because she'd been beautiful once, during her own few moments as a vamp back in L.A. . . .

Kiko had already ushered in a related topic, keeping things moving. "Natalia was pursuing research about Thomas Gatenby, so there's even more to think about."

Focus on that, Dawn thought, because her dark spot was eating at her, reminding her it was there. Like she could ever forget.

But she did manage to force her attention on Gatenby, the man who'd donated the land for Queenshill in the first place. They'd speculated that the name "Thomas Gatenby" could be a pseudonym for a blood brother, so this could pay out.

"Besides the basics of what we already know about Gatenby," Natalia said, pushing back a brunette curl that had escaped her barrette, "I haven't much to report. I spent the afternoon attempting to find a historian who might be able to offer more."

"But you did find someone," Kiko said. "Over at King's College, with the University of London."

Natalia was pretty much aglow with the support from Kiko. It was a newbie, I-can-be-constructive-too thing.

Or maybe something else?

"I have an appointment to speak with Dr. Hopkins tomorrow," she said, "on campus at her office."

"I'll go with," Kiko said.

They exchanged smiles before Kiko cleared his throat and turned back to the group. He avoided Dawn's raised eyebrow.

"Anyhow," he added, "I, myself, brushed up on Bram Stoker stuff, just to see if anything jumped out at me." Kiko addressed Natalia. "You weren't with us before we settled here in London, before the boss isolated the vibes he was getting and pinpointed this city. But while we were tracking down vibrations from what he thought might be a master, we did a lot of research along the way—especially about Stoker."

As Kiko told Natalia about all the hotels they'd hidden in, all the times they'd sat around while Costin had tried to tune in to the night, Dawn recalled how she'd wondered why their boss hadn't been able to sense this possible London Underground before if these vampires were as careless as they seemed. But now she realized that, based on where Costin was at the time, he was more attuned to that specific area and nowhere else; he had to be in the proximity of a master to feel his effects.

This meant that, back in L.A., he'd probably sensed this most recent blood brother while the vamp was visiting the States. It was the only thing that made sense to them because, soon afterward, Costin had lost the master-level vibrations, only to find them again after picking up a trail that eventually led to London.

"We even spent time over in Ireland," Kiko was saying, "visiting in and around Dublin, where Stoker spent a lot of his life. Then we went on to his haunts, just to get any insight about what he really knew about vamps. About Dracula, in particular." He sighed. "Unfortunately—and I'll quote the guy's grandnephew, one of his biographers, here—Stoker's 'one of the least-known authors of one of the best-known books ever written.' "

"And that's made all the weirder," Dawn added, "when you consider his cause of death is sketchy."

Kiko said, "Some sources say he had syphilis. But it does make paranoids like us wonder, don't it? I mean, he hit a lot of nails on the head with *Dracula*, so a wild imagination might conjure up the theory that he was punished in some way for saying too much."

"He did extensive research for the story, so maybe he just tripped over some truths during his studies. Some say that there's no real basis for Stoker modeling Dracula on Vlad Tepes, but that could be a cover-up." Dawn shrugged, kind of surprised she knew enough to add to the conversation. "Even though our Underground vamps come from the same source—Vlad Tepes—Stoker could've changed or invented details about his vampire. For example, our Hollywood vamps could see themselves in mirrors, but Dracula didn't cast a reflection."

"Chances are," Kiko said, "Stoker was an innocent party in all this. But it was still worth checking out because we know that our individual masters develop different powers anyway. Then blood weakens their offspring from generation to generation—"

Frank interrupted, as if wanting to clear the room of the profound discomfort Tepes invoked.

"It was almost like Stoker was supposed to write a book about vampires in the scheme of things. He was a sickly kid, and his mom entertained him with scary stories. When he recovered, he played in places like cemeteries. Get a trend out of that?"

Dawn wondered what Stoker might've picked up among the graves, but she didn't ask.

"I thought," Natalia said, "he lived in London."

"He did." Frank again. "When he was an adult. He published stories for kids, continued a career in the theater and—"

"After that," Kiko added, "we got *Dracula*. And, by the way, the count had quite the connection with animals, just like our schoolgirls."

Dawn stood, antsy now. She could sense Breisi getting squirrelly, too, her essence heading for the door.

"And he got younger as he drank blood," Dawn added, "kind of like the countess. Guess what else? I read that her legend had a lot of influence on Stoker when he 'created' his most famous tale."

"'Created,'" Frank said, remaining seated. "The Underground vamps probably get a good laugh out of that one."

Exactly, Dawn thought. The dragon. The guy—whether he was mostly creation or myth—who'd really, truly created Costin and his former blood brothers, then commanded them to form Undergrounds so he might control them after going belowground himself to an undisclosed location until he gathered enough strength to take over the world.

She glanced at Costin, who seemed to be in another place again, at least mentally. The intensity of his thoughts sent a buzz through her. Even if he wasn't letting her in, she was still so achingly aware.

But it wasn't hard to guess what he might be thinking. Initially, the dragon had made him into a vampire, too, yet Costin had accepted a deal from a mysterious being to gain back his soul if he could wipe out the dragon and his progeny. That's when "The Whisper"—the name Costin had given to the force that had made him this offer—had shaped Costin into a Soul Traveler.

A creature with powers that had taken down many an Underground so far.

An idea prodded her.

"Costin?" Dawn said.

She felt him disconnect from his memories as he glanced at her.

"Yes, Dawn."

She steadied herself in the undertow of his voice. "What if we could get a stronger, more direct read on this new master, if there is one? If you visited the blade room and the schoolgirls' Orlando Bloom room, all under the ground, you might be able to sense the vibes of this master we've been looking for—if one lives near there and hasn't been shielding."

Back in L.A., he hadn't been able to sense Benedikte aboveground because the master vampire had been careful about disguising and blocking himself. But what about now?

"You wouldn't be blocked by the earth," she continued. "You'd be right *there* to clearly feel if an off-guard blood brother is at that location. And I'm not just talking about Jonah going there while he's in charge of your body. I'm talking about letting you be the dominant one—the one who gets everything firsthand. Then we'd know for sure that we're dealing with more than just schoolgirl vamps."

Caution, not fear—never fear, never from Costin, right?—skimmed his expression.

He didn't want to risk it, she thought. Not when they were still unsure about security for him. Yet how could they be sure unless they made a move?

Damn it, she didn't want to think he was being overly wary, but . . .

Well, wasn't it worth the risk, especially if Jonah had been right about being able to protect Costin if Jonah's consciousness pushed Costin's own essence deep down into their body?

Jonah could get him under the ground, then Costin could take over just long enough to use his senses. . . .

He must've seen how Dawn was still doubting his willingness to take a shot, because his jaw clenched, his gaze hardened.

Then he pointed upstairs, toward their bedroom, and she knew it was time to make this a private discussion.

Or maybe he just wanted to feed.

As the team started to disband, Costin told everyone to get sustenance and rest as they required, while he weighed the balance of the day's events and decided what course to take now.

The room cleared, and Dawn kept her gaze down as she ate her sandwich, sustaining herself for what was to come.

But as she finished up, she realized one person hadn't left the room yet.

Natalia.

The new girl was holding that notebook in front of her like she was a secretary in secondhand clothing.

Again, Dawn held out her sandwich, offering.

"No, thank you," Natalia said. "I believe I'll eat what Eva made in the kitchen."

"Have at it then."

Yet she didn't move.

That's when Dawn knew it was mentor time. Yay.

"What's up?" she said.

The great thing about Natalia was that she could be surprisingly straightforward. Dawn really did appreciate that, based on all the secretive crap that defined her life.

"Kiko," the other girl said. "He . . . he told me he was having trouble sleeping today."

"He's getting rest now, though, right?"

"Yes, he went upstairs. Through the hallway. With all the Friend portraits . . ."

It hit Dawn. Natalia was trying to tell her something more.

"Friends," Dawn said. "Is he using them to lull him to sleep?"

"I think so."

Dawn cursed under her breath, or maybe it was above it. From the way Natalia hugged her notebook even tighter, it had to have been above it.

"I cannot be certain," the girl continued, "but I thought you should know."

Great. Kiko had seemed to be doing well off the meds, but there were always addictions to take another one's place. Dawn could preach about that.

One hatred for another.

One mission for another.

"I appreciate you telling me," Dawn finally said.

And . . . still, Natalia didn't leave.

Dawn gave her a too-polite, go-ahead-and-say-it look.

"Kiko and I have had discussions lately, mainly about our skills," the new girl said. "Improving them. Consulting with spirit guides, perhaps, when we have more time."

"Let's cross our fingers that you'll be available for that real soon."

"I'm hoping . . ." Another pause, but Natalia came out of it sooner than Dawn expected. "When we're done, I intend to use my abilities to continue solving what the team leaves behind."

Dawn looked away. At the beginning, when she'd started hunting, it'd seemed so wrong to leave all those victims—bread crumbs on their path to an Underground—behind in favor of pursuing the vampires.

Not so much now.

"Kate Lansing was murdered by the schoolgirls," Dawn finally said. "Thanks to Della last night and Violet this morning, we know that for sure. Case closed."

"But the other voices I hear . . . Not Kate Lansing's, because I haven't been back to her burial site—"

"We can't go back to Billiter Street." That's where Natalia had first heard the victim, the team's initial lead.

It's where the hunt had started going down, here in London.

"But I can hear so many others." Natalia sighed. "They keep coming."

Dawn tried not to imagine what it must be like, having to control some of what you received as a psychic.

Natalia traced the spiral wire of her notebook. "I want to attempt contact with Briana."

Oh, God, Dawn thought. Briana Williamson, one of the schoolgirl vamps. She'd gone missing even before the team had come on the scene, and they didn't know if she'd been terminated or had run away, as the status quo maintained.

When they'd contacted Briana via a Ouija, they hadn't known if her soul, which the Underground vamps lost during the blood exchange, was in hell or if maybe they were talking to the real vampire girl herself.

Or maybe even something worse.

"Natalia," Dawn said, her voice sounding deceptively cool. "Tell me you're not crazy enough to really do this."

The new girl was shaking her head. "No, not crazy. Not . . . yet."

Dawn fisted her hands, hating that she understood why Natalia needed to do this.

A mission, she thought. A purpose that was taking her over. Dawn could tell right now, just looking at the determination on her teammate's face.

Dawn leaned forward, hoping her point got across and they wouldn't have to discuss this again. "Keep any and all Ouija boards away from here, Natalia. You don't know what you might bring in."

"I—"

"*No.*"

Before Natalia could plead her case and break Dawn altogether, Dawn turned away and left the room, heading upstairs to Costin.

Where she would continue her own damned mission.

NINE

The Good of the Many

THE second Dawn got into the bedroom, she began to unbutton her shirt so she could pull the collar away from her neck.

She was in a hurry to get fe—

No, to feed *Costin*. To supply him with blood.

The light in the restroom was on, so she headed across the floor to it. She couldn't shake Natalia's worries about the victims, and maybe working it out right now with Costin might help. She didn't want to be dwelling on this during the . . .

Yes, she'd admit it. During the high that a feeding gave her.

"Costin, I was thinking," she said. "Your contact in the City police force"—Detective Inspector Norton—"is still working on Kate Lansing's case. With the Friends keeping their eye on him, we know he's running into walls with the investigation."

The good inspector had too much sense to talk to his colleagues about the possibility of something paranormal being the culprit in

Kate's murder, and real-life explanations kept setting him at a dead end in the case.

She added, "Do you think Norton'd be willing to come on board with us? In an unofficial capacity, I mean? He might be a good addition."

No answer. Just . . .

. . . breathing?

"Costin?"

She came to the bathroom door, finding him braced over the basin, a hand on each side of it as he panted.

She dropped her hands to her sides, her shirt gaping halfway open.

Jonah. He was probably ready to come out, and Costin was wrestling with him. Shit, it always seemed to happen at feeding time, too, where all the biting and rough intimacies that went with it lured Jonah most of all.

An ache clawed through Dawn's chest, maybe because Costin's black hair, unfurling over his high cheekbones and full lips as he leaned over the sink, made the vampire into something more like a vulnerable man.

So *un*like the arrogant, powerful enigma she'd first met.

She worried about the color of his flesh—he needed to feed soon. Still, it was easy to ignore that when the rest of him was so diverting. Even though his skin tone was pale, its texture was beguilingly smooth, like the pearled marble they'd used to refurbish this bathroom from something old and crumbled into a place with golden handles and etched glass over the shower stall.

He'd been refurbished, too, Dawn thought. Before going vampire, there'd been self-inflicted, crisscrossed scars over his face, thanks to Jonah. But when she'd exchanged blood with them, Jonah's soul had departed, leaving only his personality.

Then a preternatural healing had taken over, building their

body into a room—a shelter—for Costin that came awfully near to perfection. But perfection or not, his body, his room, was a prison—not just for him but for Jonah, too.

Thing was, though, that Jonah loved this vampire body. He wanted to claim it while Costin only wanted out.

Over the sink, he steadied his breathing.

"You okay?" Dawn asked after a moment.

He glanced up, facing his image in the mirror. The Hollywood line of vampires could cast reflections, and sometimes Dawn didn't know if it was a blessing or curse that he could look at a form that wasn't really his own.

There was that feral burn in his topaz eyes. Hunger.

It was feeding time, a need that Costin only gave in to because he had to; otherwise, it repelled him and, boy, didn't *that* make Dawn feel great, even though she knew it wasn't really about her. Actually, he thrived on her blood, and that's why he nipped it time after time while supplementing his diet with the bags.

That's what she told herself, anyway—that his disdain for feeding had absolutely nothing to do with her technically being his master and his having to submit.

"I'd ask what I can do to help," she said, "but we've been over this before."

Costin's voice came out as an abrasion. "He's the one in charge recently. Jonah. I'm only still speaking with you because he hasn't taken over just yet. But he's there, waiting."

And, last night, she'd been the one who'd made a deal with Jonah: work with him as a teammate and he'd stop causing Costin—and the team—such trouble.

Jonah was only keeping his part of the bargain by giving fair warning that he was en route, and if she wanted to help destroy all the Underground masters efficiently, she'd have to maintain her end, too.

Even Costin knew it was the only way, although he raged against being put in an even more submissive position.

Pushing down a twinge of betrayal, Dawn undid the rest of her shirt buttons. "Let's feed before your hunger gets out of control and it's a big bloody mess we're dealing with."

He was still a relatively new vampire, requiring nightly blood, and if he went without or got too excited about something, she had to restrain him. Add Jonah to the equation, and it'd only be worse.

But a shiver of yearning in the pit of her belly told her that, deep down, she enjoyed the challenge of taming them both. That it did something for her that regular sex never had.

Costin straightened from the sink, jamming a hand through his hair, grabbing at it. Yet then he let go, as if Jonah had backed off for now.

"Talk to me." The Voice, a rasp. A dignified plea. "Keep me here, Dawn."

She should say his name—it would help him to stay, she knew—but she'd made a promise to Jonah, and it was a vow that would help the team. Help their mission.

The good of the many outweighs the good of the few. That's what Costin had told her so often in justification for using her, dangling her as a lure for the Master back in L.A.

But she couldn't turn her back on Costin so easily.

"Queenshill," she said. "We were going to talk about Queenshill."

There. She wasn't outright defying Jonah by calling Costin's name to keep him here.

Costin nodded, knowing the thin line she was walking. Seeming to accept it a little more with every passing second.

"You think if I were to go to below the ground there," he said, his tone defying a tremor beneath it, "it would truly benefit us?"

She grasped one of his hands, his skin so pale and cool. His breath caught, but she thought that might have to do with the scent of her healing gel, which he had a slight aversion to.

The aroma of her need probably got to him more.

"My gut," she said, "tells me you should go down there. If there's a master around, you wouldn't be able to easily detect him aboveground because the soil separates you from where he lives . . . or lived."

He ran a thumb over hers, skin whispering against skin.

"Last night," he said, "Jonah was able to use this body to fight well."

He was on the edge of ushering his host to dominance. She could tell.

Costin added, "He fought bravely. Thoroughly. Perhaps I would be able to do the same, even if I cannot unleash my full powers outside of this body as I used to."

"I know you would do well out there, Costin. And the team would be there to back you up. Plus the Friends . . . None of us would ever let you fail."

It was pure truth. She herself would do anything. Just look at what she'd done back in L.A., making him into this creature only so she could save him. . . .

In a bid to forget, she rubbed her free hand against her neck, priming herself for the bite, even though her skin there and over her arms was still tender from the healing cuts.

He watched her, a shattered longing in his gaze, and she could see that his moments with her were ticking down, beat by beat.

Get him fed, she thought. *Before Jonah comes* . . .

"I only wonder," he said, "what would happen if I should come to stand before a fellow brother and—"

She stopped her priming, taking his face in her hands.

"We don't know how you're going to match up to a blood

brother. You can't do what you used to do, Costin, but we have to find out what's in store at some point."

As her hands fell away from him, he caught one, raised it to his chest, where she felt his heart beating.

When Jonah had lost his soul in the exchange, it had left this body still functioning but with heightened senses and powers. These vampires couldn't procreate except via a blood exchange, so that made them seem even less human sometimes.

But Dawn had started to believe that being an Underground-related vampire was more about mutating into a form beyond humanity—they were spiritually dead rather than physically. Breisi even had the idea that the presence of the dragon's blood, carried generation through generation, was an altering agent when it was introduced into a human body that had lost its own blood and soul after a draining bite. The death of a maker only opened that body to the soul again, allowing the spirit to consume the body, changing it back to its pure state.

But . . . theories.

Who could say for sure, except for the devil or even something like The Whisper himself?

Dawn spread her fingers over the tattoo of Costin's heart, and she could've sworn that it jumped, either out of barely checked fear about whether Costin would ever reclaim his soul, or at her touch.

Probably the fear, she thought. Or maybe just lust.

That was all.

"Every one of us has something at stake, don't we?" she said. "You more than the team. But . . ." She'd wanted to ask him about this for some time, and she knew Jonah would hold back on appearing because he'd enjoy the confrontation between her and Costin.

"But what?" Costin's voice soothed her, gave her a sense that he was inside as well as out, softly abrading her, making her bleed both ways.

"But," she added, "you've never really told me why you haven't used the same team twice. You always said it was because of secrecy."

A tight smile whisked over his lips. He knew where she was headed.

"Natalia said something the other day," Dawn continued, emboldened, "about former teams going insane because of what they have to face on this job, and maybe you retire them before insanity happens. Except you didn't have that option with us because you don't know what to expect from yourself now. You need seasoned backup." She'd tightened her fingers over his chest, almost like she was subconsciously trying to dig out of him more than he ever gave. "Is that true?"

"Yes." Zero hesitation. Zero baiting or secrets.

But just as she was getting happy about that, he added, "And no."

She told herself not to be frustrated, to just work through this. "I don't understand."

He twined his fingers through hers, providing a barrier between her and his heart. "Yes, I have retired teams before they slipped into a state that I would never want them to be in. And I have been watching to see how you and Kiko have been holding up under this extended tour. He is not doing as well as you, Dawn."

Something within her—the dark spot—stirred, and she knew it was probably the only reason she hadn't gone over the mental edge by now.

Because she was too much a part of what lurked around a corner at midnight.

With a descending curtain of realization, she thought, *I'm never going back to the way I was before. This is home. This is it.*

She should've been stunned, but she wasn't. There was only . . .

Acceptance.

And now that it was fully revealed, her load lightened a bit. This was what she was. This was where she was going from now on.

Costin tightened his fingers in hers. "Understand that I would do most anything to have different hunters in place. I have told you before that there is danger for a team in knowing too much about what dwells under the ground. With experience, members begin to believe that they know better than I how to handle matters."

"If you're referring to me, I'm 'key,'" she said. "I *should* know a thing or two."

"I have also told you that you are like no other, and this is what drew me to you. So yes. You would be correct. As 'key' you would have to know more."

He bent forward to rest his forehead against hers, his flesh cool where hers was hot.

"Yet, tell me," he said. "If I had not required such help from you . . . If I had not turned into this creature . . . this *vampire* . . . and you did not feel so responsible for it, would you have wanted to leave the team by now?"

If she'd allowed him inside her head lately, he would've already known. But these issues had reared up too recently, the truths defining themselves maybe because she'd had the time to think on her own while being so blocked off from him.

And the thing was . . . she didn't know if she had an answer.

If they'd defeated the Hollywood Underground unscathed, would she have wanted to leave Costin to pursue life as she'd known it before? Would it have even been possible with her being "key"?

Or would she have stayed with him out of love or . . .

God, she wasn't sure what was between them besides a force field of guilt.

As if to disprove that—because *couldn't* she love?—Dawn nestled against him, her face to his neck.

His cool, hardly human neck.

Like a trail of sultry, mixed-color smoke, he curled his way into her consciousness, and she allowed him in, relieved that he was finally there.

What will come of you once I am saved? he asked.

She held to him tighter. *Don't know, so don't ask.*

He tried again, coming deeper into her, saturating her until she needed to grasp his shirt to stay standing.

He thought, *Back in L.A., you were open to Matt Lonigan.*

She blocked him, hating that putting up a shield was such an automatic response. But she did answer.

That's before I found out who he really was—Benedikte, a guy only pretending to appreciate me for myself. But he really wanted Eva. He was trying to make me into my mother.

Hurt spilled from Dawn into Costin, and he held her closer. It was the first time she'd allowed herself to even think about what Matt had done to her, much less to tell Costin about it.

She went on. *I was ready to let down my guard with him for the first time ever, with any man. And I started to . . . but look what happened.*

We happened, Costin thought, and his words felt like glimmers of hope cutting through her.

But then there was something else—a gathering wave of gray pushing at her and grabbing her at the same time.

Jonah.

She pulled out of Costin, feeling as if she'd been stripped, exposed, even though Jonah knew everything Costin did.

"Dawn—" Costin sounded like a man who'd lost even more than his soul, but she knew his anguish was only temporary. His soul meant a hell of a lot more than she ever would.

She offered her neck to him, feverish, urgent.

"Feed, Costin," she said. "Before he gets here."

Was it jealousy that spurred him? It looked like it as his gaze took on a possessive air and he cupped the side of her neck with a palm.

She shrugged her shirt off both shoulders, ignoring her healing cuts, the material slumping at her elbows and revealing the tight, black sports bra she'd worn for her errand at Queenshill.

He slipped a finger under a strap, and his touch brought primitive heat to her skin, melting her above and below it as the tips of her breasts went hard.

Impatience thudded at her, and she leaned her head back even more while angling closer to him.

"Now," she said in a strangled whisper.

His eyes went vampy, silver and wild, his fangs emerging as he grabbed her waist and roughly sat her on the sink counter, knocking over a vase.

It crashed to the floor, also breaking apart the lily it'd held.

As Costin yanked up her skirt, bunching it around her waist, Dawn felt the marble, cool and sleek, on the back of her thighs, and she wrapped her legs around him, her shoes digging against his rear.

He lowered his mouth to her breast, nuzzling against it with his lips and a snag of fang. She flinched as it scraped her, her hips arching forward against the rise of his erection.

"Hurry, Costin."

Just at the feel of his cock between her legs, where she ached and pulsed, she was crazed. Wanting the pierce of his fangs in a vein, needing to feel the pleasure and pain of her blood being sucked out until she crashed down from the high it would bring.

He used his tongue to circle her nipple, tracing her, bringing her to a silent scream. Even through the cotton of her bra, she felt the wetness of his mouth, but she wanted more.

Something rougher, meaner.

Something that would fill.

She shucked the straps of her bra down her arms, going only far enough to bare her breasts. She was pinned by her straps, but the slick feel of his tongue on her peaked nipple made up for any sense of entrapment.

Then he tongued her nipple all the way into his mouth, a fang on each side of her as he flicked the nub.

She slipped her hand between her legs, just to ease the sharp agony of her clit. Rubbing, pressing, massaging, she tried to make it go away, but it didn't do any good.

"Costin," she said.

And he understood, skimming his hands under her ass and lifting her as he bent and brought his mouth to the heat between her legs.

There, *there* . . .

He tore at her panties with his fangs and, oddly, she laughed, the sound ragged and just as off balance as everything else in this messed-up world.

But she forgot to think about that when he licked his way up her slit, careful not to nick her, although the thought of his fangs so close, so dangerous, did a lot more carnal damage than he probably meant to.

She was really wet now, pulling at his hair as he used the tip of his tongue to paint her to a building bliss. Her legs fell open even wider, unable to get enough, wishing he'd . . .

She went ahead and said it, almost screaming it at the level of a whisper.

"Do it, Costin."

He stopped, his breath coming in pants against her. She felt his thoughts prodding at her skull to get in, but she was so immersed in a world of black ecstasy—the inside of a bubble that was straining to burst—that she mentally pushed away, even while she physically urged him closer.

"Costin—"

She shifted her hips toward his mouth.

"No," he said, his voice all but recognizable in its escalating starvation, although she was sure it was still Costin, not Jonah.

Or was it . . . ?

No, it was Costin.

"Do it for me," she said.

She could feel the weight of him giving in to her, mostly because he was probably craving the taste of the most tender flesh, too.

As if testing, he grazed over the swollen inside of one of her lips, and she hissed in a breath.

Hurt.

Good.

Deserved.

She panted for more, maneuvering so she could look him in the face, plead with him if she had to, in order to get what she wanted.

But Costin was staring up at her with those silver eyes, and they seemed to be swirling with as much speed as her mind.

Her mixed-up, fucked-up mind.

When he slowly rose, his eyes a solid silver hue now, Dawn could sense the change in his posture.

The more casual assurance of Jonah.

He tugged her skirt down over her hips, then took her by the lapels of her blouse, pulling her forward until she was flush against him, her open legs bringing her against his cock.

Then, in one of those moves that Dawn could never understand, Jonah eased away, and her body cried out.

She fought to silence it, because she wasn't going to give anything to him. Not to Jonah, goddamn it.

But she was in sheer agony, splitting from the middle outward.

She didn't know what was going on with her own body, how

she couldn't just shut it down with Jonah here. Then again, before joining the team, she'd screwed her way through a lot of nights, taking what she could and trying to feel good about it. Sex had been a competition with her beautiful, wonderful, superstar mom, who'd been presumed dead until Dawn found out otherwise.

But now, what the hell was she doing?

Jonah spoke in his amused American accent—except he didn't seem all that amused right now.

Just famished.

"I'll guess that you're done flirting with sure trouble," he said.

Want, she thought, the need for fulfillment cracking through her, making her hate him and what his body did to her, whether it was Jonah at the helm or Costin.

Yet she knew what the inevitable outcome would be. They both did.

"Just get it over with," she ground out, turning her face away from him.

Even as she said it, she craved it—the bite.

And Jonah obliged her, lowering his mouth to her neck, where the pop of his fangs into her skin made her press her legs against his sides.

Made her mind into a red blank as he sucked and sated himself, finally soothing her to a numb purgatory.

TEN
Drink Time with Eva, I

Eva lingered in a hallway, near a stretch of walls that boasted a line of Friends portraits.

Although one of the spirits had been watching her during the team's meeting, the Friend had left now that there wasn't much for Eva to eavesdrop on and, as she watched, her invisible bodyguard became visible in a nearby portrait, which featured an idyllic prairie.

Her wheaten curls came into focus, her blue eyes, her face, her chemise flapping in a still wind that couldn't be felt outside the painting.

Ultimately, the Friend closed her eyes, at rest. Within the paint's textures, she would prepare herself for when she was needed, just like all these other spirits who lined the hallway.

Eva started walking, trailing her fingertips below the portraits, just under the frames.

She knew Dawn was on the next floor with Costin, alone with

him, feeding him, and Eva fended off the maternal instincts that shouted for her to go up there, knock on the door, and tell her daughter to keep it open while her boyfriend was over.

But Eva had forfeited the years when that would've been acceptable. She'd abandoned Dawn and Frank.

On the way past a portrait of an Egyptian Friend, she touched its wooden frame. At least, since Hollywood, Eva and her daughter's relationship had gotten better, but she knew she'd never really be Dawn's mom, just a "mother." One who'd, for all intents and purposes, been absent and then suddenly, shockingly reappeared.

Hi, I'm here. Love me.

Yet she didn't expect any more than an attempt at reconciliation from Dawn now, and she was lucky to get even that. Eva owned what she had done—selling her soul to the Hollywood Underground and faking her own murder so that she would rise again as a plastic-surgery-enhanced "other" superstar.

She deserved all those unsure glances she caught Dawn sneaking at her. Actually, she even deserved Frank choosing Breisi's affections over hers, although Eva would sell the soul Dawn had won back for her by the Master's death if Frank would just give her one more try.

Near the end of the hallway, she stopped, her pulse jiggering at the sight of a half-open door.

Ironic, she thought. All she'd ever wanted was her family. She'd become a vampire because she'd believed her Hollywood handlers when they'd told her that going Underground would be the best thing for her loved ones' futures, her stratospheric legacy ensuring they'd never lack for money. At least, she'd thought that's why she'd wanted to go Underground—not because of the never-ending adulation of the fans and society.

Eva contained a shiver of self-awareness, then reset herself.

No, no. She really *had* gone Underground for Dawn and Frank.

That's right. But while she'd been staging a return to life Above, Frank and even Dawn had started to create their own versions of families.

Dawn, Frank, Breisi, Kiko . . . They'd developed into a tight-knit unit, and all Eva could do was watch from the fringes.

She'd tried to become a part of them by volunteering to donate blood for the bags that Frank drank from, parceling them out so they'd last. She owed him at least that much for making him a vampire in the first place, but most of the time she only felt like more of a burden, someone to be watched over.

And she'd earned the spot she was in.

From inside the room down the hall, she heard his voice saying good night to someone—Breisi—and Eva knew that the spirit had gone to bed in her own portrait, now that the team was getting its bearings.

Eva hesitated, telling herself to leave, to go back to the guest room Limpet and Associates had given her, just until it was safe to return to her own nearby flat.

But then she heard Frank moving around, turning some late fifties music on at low volume, and her throat tightened.

Oldies but goodies. Their kind of tunes back when they'd both been human.

She found herself closing the distance to his door, knocking softly, then listening for his voice so it would wash over her, just like it used to, alone on the couch, snuggled together, them against the world.

He paused, then said, "Come in, Eva."

He'd vampire-sensed her, she thought, laying her hand on the door.

But just before she pushed it open, "I Only Have Eyes for You" began to play, and a twisting sorrow made her dig her nails hard into the palm of her hand by her side.

Blood, whether she'd meant to draw it or not, barely started to creep out of the sting.

She wondered if she should leave, because the scent would get to Frank. It might scramble his mind and make him break the promise he'd made to Breisi to only drink Eva's blood secondhand, not from *her*. It might . . .

Eva hung her head, waited, almost rushed away.

Then, unable to help it, she pushed the door open.

As he looked up from one of the gizmos he was working on—all Eva could see were wires and metal—his green eyes lit with something so familiar that she smiled at him, hopeful.

Never losing the faith that he did still love her deep inside.

Then his gaze flicked to the side, to Breisi's portrait, where the Latina with Louise Brooks–bobbed hair rested against the painted backdrop of the lab she'd kept in the L.A. house.

A weight, like a sharp rock with a death note attached, sank through Eva, dividing her.

But then a cajoling voice from the back of her mind—instincts that'd always looked out for her, instincts that had advised her to go Underground—whispered that she had what Breisi could never give Frank.

Blood.

So use it.

A second passed. Another.

Then Eva opened her palm.

It felt damp from the blood she'd drawn from her long, manicured nails.

She could see when the hint of her blood consumed Frank, because he pushed the bundle of wires and metal he was working on onto the table, where it moaned across the surface as he kept pushing, his head down.

"Frank?" she asked, afraid. Excited. Because she recalled what it was like to want blood, too. How irresistible the temptation could be.

His voice was like a thousand raw welts. "I already fed, Eva. From one of the bags in the fridge downstairs. Go away."

But the sustenance hadn't done much for him, she knew. It kept him functioning, those bags, yet it couldn't be the same as drinking from Eva, whose blood stimulated him more than anyone else's.

Use it.

Even as she raised her palm to him, offering so much more than just her blood, she told herself not to do it.

He reared back his head, and self-loathing was nicked all over his face.

His expression ripped through her, even when he lunged toward her hand, grabbed it, buried his face against her palm, her skin . . .

She dropped to her knees as he cradled her arm, opening the small punctures on her palm with his fangs then sucking, hurting her with the force of his need.

But it felt good.

Bad.

No. So, *so* good—

A scream of echoing, otherworldly rage shook her just before she was knocked to the ground from behind.

She didn't have to smell the jasmine to know it was Breisi.

The spirit kept barreling against her, pounding her toward the exit, and Eva rolled with every punch, not fighting back.

Taking it.

Deserving it.

When it was done, Eva sprawled on the hall floor, her pumps

off her feet, her skin tender with oncoming bruises, as Breisi circled back into the room, not even bothering to curse at Eva or acknowledge her any more than she had to.

Then, just before the spirit hefted her essence behind the door to slam it, Eva saw Frank's repulsed expression.

She ran from the horror, the shame of it, yanking a small towel out of a washroom on the way and wrapping her bloodied hand.

Down the stairs, through the foyer, fumbling with the locks on the door, then tripping barefoot outside, where a flood of UV lights revealed her for who she really was.

Then Eva ran and ran, never stopping until the shame finally caught up with her again.

ELEVEN

Once Upon a Blood Bath

In the main Underground, in a training room lined by wall bags, hitting boards, and dummies propped on stands, the atmosphere pulsed, murky and oppressive, as the two *custode*s paused an instructional DVD and proceeded to apply what they'd learned.

Since contact outside the Underground was shunned, the virtual training was necessary. But, all the same, it worked quite nicely as the new *custode* ducked under Nigel's restraining arm then mimicked the flash-quick breaking of his bones from leg to head.

The entire attack—a flurry of hands, arms, and elbows—was over in the time it would take for any normal human to even register what was happening.

Energized, the new caretaker sprang away from Nigel, hands up, giddy from the action.

"Not bad," Nigel said. "Not bad a'tall. If you hadn't merely been sparring, I'd be a pile of mush."

The *custode* only smiled at the sport of this Keysi Fighting Method. In KFM, everything around you and *of* you could be a lethal weapon.

Proper fun.

Before being activated, the new *custode* had been drawn to other martial arts classes, such as karate and Krav Maga. But those had only been instinctive interests that hadn't gone beyond amusement—not until the call to duty had arrived, revealing who the Meratoliage family had always been and always would be.

Sweat plastered Nigel's hair to his head, his dark clothing damp. "Perhaps I need to put you outside on patrol again if you're this keen."

The *custode* tried not to seem too pleased. "Tonight?"

Nigel nodded. "Tonight."

The pair retreated to the side of the rock-faced domain, where iced water and towels awaited them. After replenishing themselves, then cleaning up, they would engage in Relaquory—a ritual that could never, ever be missed. Afterward, they'd eat a protein-rich meal in the monitor room while they reviewed any outside activity that the alert system had picked up during their training.

Then, finally, it would be patrol time.

However, unlike earlier, there was no present urgency since Claudia had informed the keepers of Violet the vampire's death.

Yet, the new *custode* thought while gulping the water, there were many other pressing matters to see to. Many, many opportunities to clean up the Underground.

This morning, when the *custode* had watched Della on the hotel camera, it had seemed prudent to simultaneously follow the odd progress of those ravens on the other screens while accessing the camera footage from around the hotel in order to track Violet. Then the malfunction of Mrs. Jones's cameras at Queenshill had interrupted this process, but after the keeper had reported the fogged lenses to Nigel and he had directed his efforts to the housematron's room earlier than expected, the new *custode* had gone back to what had by then become previously recorded footage of those ravens.

And it had only been a matter of following the cloud of them until the birds descended on the borough of Southwark, below the Thames River.

Although the *custode* hadn't seen precisely where the ravens had gone or even witnessed Violet's death on camera, there had been a brilliant discovery all the same.

A fogged lens near the Cross Bones Graveyard.

Filing the location away for a time after Nigel would return, the new *custode* had decided that Southwark would be the first place to visit on the next patrol. The location wasn't near the main Underground, so the fogged lens didn't equate to an alarming security threat, yet a malfunction such as this had to be just as significant as the ones on Billiter and Queenshill.

By the time the *custode* had decided this, Claudia, who had rarely ever contacted the keepers before recent events, had called off the search for Violet, informing the caretakers of the young vampire's fate and Della's part in it.

Well then, the new *custode* had thought. Rest in peace to that little twat Violet, but the schoolgirl's passing had thankfully allowed the caretakers to concentrate on that fogged camera in Mrs. Jones's room all the more.

By using a handheld unit that had been programmed to sort out scents, much like the vampires themselves could, Nigel had registered confusing smells in the area, including a lingering whiff of jasmine. Certainly, the aromas could have been the result of random human schoolgirl visitors to Mrs. Jones's room before Claudia had locked it tight last night.

Yet Nigel had also plucked a long, wavy hair from the floor.

Subsequent processing had identified it as synthetic, a hair from a wig, and the *custode*s had wondered why it might be in the room.

Was it a remnant from Halloween in the girls' quarters?

A stray, floating piece of hair from a doll collection that one of the girls displayed in her room?

Nigel hadn't the opportunity to find out.

After he'd checked Claudia's personal wardrobe entrance to the sub-Underground—no obvious signs of forced entry there—the vampire herself had summoned him to escort her and her girls to the main Underground.

He'd never made it past the entrance, to the tunnel or the sub-Underground.

Since it wasn't often that the vampires interacted with the *custode*s or even made requests, an escort had become first priority. Hence, in an effort to see that the creatures safely arrived at an earthbound entrance on the heath, Nigel had rushed there to guard it; concurrently, from the monitor room, the new *custode* had provided a type of escort, as well, by slowing the feeds to belatedly track the vampires' progress as far as the cameras would allow.

After watching to see that the creatures were inside, Nigel had gone Underground also, but he'd taken a different tunnel, heading toward the *custode* section to program the alert system, which would track any more fogged camera malfunctions so they would be aware the exact moment another one happened.

Ideally, he'd explained to his partner, the clouded lenses would lead them to the troublemaking group who had appeared on campus last night.

The new *custode* had only smiled, saving the news of Southwark in the hopes of a personal patrol tonight.

In general, the keepers rarely handled agitators outside of the Underground—their main focus was set on the possibility of the appearance of any fabled blood brothers who had begun to attack others' communities over the last century. Supposedly, these brothers worked to forcibly take over or, perhaps, even peacefully join forces with the existing Undergrounds.

But this Underground wasn't open to any joinings.

Never.

That was the main reason the *custode*s had then gone into their database to pull up the last-known profiles of all the blood brothers before the vampire masters had gone underground. The intention had been to match them to the attackers from last night.

However, since the brothers had isolated themselves and lost touch with one another after the dragon had commanded them all to form secret communities, their profiles were hardly updated, and the project had yielded nothing.

But the new *custode* was thinking that it might not be such a terrible scenario if the attackers *had* been in the housematron's room. Should they be interested in Claudia, it might bode ill for the vampire. Besides, there was little danger of the attackers stumbling upon Highgate from Queenshill.

And the scenario could work for the *custode*'s plan to oust old Claudia, too. . . .

The caretakers finished in the training room and exited, the door whishing shut behind them as Nigel swiped a towel over his face, which bore all the aristocratic angles and identifying quirks of the Meratoliage family: the wide lime green eyes with a burst of thick lashes, the slim nose upturned at the end in such a way as to portray a modicum of dignity, the lush lower lip balancing a slight overbite, the pointed chin.

"It seems you've come in to the family destiny just as matters have become far more exciting," Nigel said.

Had he construed the new *custode*'s verve in training to be "excitement"?

"Charles dying is not 'exciting.'"

"Oh, sod off with the judgment, would you?" His tone had a defensive bite now. "Our family was built for this job over a century ago, and upon activation, every one of us becomes aware of the danger. Charles accepted it, too."

It was true that, long ago, the dragon, along with his allied practitioners of the black arts, had crossbred the Meratoliage ancestors, using the best soldiers and the most wily women available. They had experimented on them until they were all but mutants, and the family had bred accordingly thereafter.

At times, their efforts were blocked by what seemed to be weak hearts in many offspring, and this presented its challenges in populating their kind. But, otherwise, they were perfect for the calling: agile, servile, useful, and loyal minions to this Underground.

Yet the new *custode* wondered if anyone had questioned whether the family was more than that—if they could be just as valuable as a master himself.

Lethal thinking. Yet it was a query worth some thought.

Jaw tight, Nigel accessed the door to their quarters. "Why do I get the feeling," he said, "that your arrogance is going to be a troubling sideshow?"

Arrogance? The new *custode* thought of the implanted vision/tales in Della, the plan to expunge Claudia.

"Arrogance" might not be quite the word. Perhaps "foresight" would be more appropriate.

They went through the door, closing it behind them, and Nigel headed for the washroom. But he seemed to have a bit more to impart, as he halted in his tracks, lifted a finger to the new *custode*, and pointed it.

"When Charles died," he said, "I took his passing on my shoulders. I could have done more, I thought. I could have prevented it, perhaps, though I cannot really say how. Yet I do know this."

He took a step toward his sibling, and the new *custode* didn't give him the satisfaction of reacting.

"Charles was meant to last a long time in this calling. Long enough so that more acceptable family members would be of age to replace him when required. Yet he died much too young, and your presence here is nothing but an aberration. You were activated only because there was no one else in our generation to draw upon." He lowered his finger. "So any arrogance you're carrying is unfounded. Recall *that* in your more self-satisfied moments."

On the whipping tail of his pronouncement, Nigel turned back around and shut himself in the washroom while the newest *custode* tried not to take this evidence of Nigel's resentment personally.

He's going to see, the caretaker thought, wondering perhaps if this private plan to stamp out Claudia was about more than strengthening the Underground.

If it was more about proof of self-worth.

They're all going to see.

Chin up, the *custode* went to the icebox on the other side of the cavelike room with its soldier-simple beds and wiry furniture.

No matter *what* this personal plan was about, it was going to uphold the vow the Meratoliages had made ages ago.

The caretaker only hoped that Della, who was pivotal to making a change Underground, would soon recall all of the implanted tales, that the cleanup could soon begin. . . .

ONCE, over four hundred years ago, long before the vampire found himself bloodied and beaten in that cottage in the woods, he took a mistress whom he brought with him to a land not so distant from Wallachia.

A land where a castle lounged on a hill under a veil of night.

In this castle was a countess, and she had invited the vampire and his mistress, who had already disguised themselves as humans, to be her guests. The countess had a shrewd sense of darkness and collected as company those who shared her adoration of the black arts.

Incredibly, the vampires were the tamest of these guests—sorcerers and witches, lovers of pain and torture—yet for a while they found a home among them.

On this night, the vampire's mistress had decided to indulge in a bath. A special type of bath particular to this vampiress, a bath that was infrequently—but most definitely—required to restore the beauty one inevitably lost after the first blush of youth.

A bath that would do more than merely feed the body, as more regular blood meals did.

Falling against the high back of the tub, the mistress reveled under the stream of blood pouring from the human girl whose throat the vampiress had just torn asunder. The prey dangled upside down from a beam, eyes sightless, and the creature drank of her.

But not only via the mouth.

Skin—such aging skin—also opened its pores to gulp and savor and replenish.

The mistress was so enthralled with the blood that the sound of a door opening barely registered. Even so, all pores sucked closed, and the vampiress sat straight in the tub.

Around a sheer curtain, the countess herself, with her breathtaking dark hair and pale skin, appeared. She held up a hand as she smiled, her eyes as wide as a child who had discovered an unexpected gift.

"One of my maids saw you bring the girl to your rooms," she said. "I only wished to watch whatever you had in mind for her, as I have done with our amusements on other nights."

"And I welcome you to it," the mistress answered, knowing of the countess's unfathomable curiosity and hunger for new entertainments. She would not think this bath odd.

Not *unless she had seen the skin mouths.*

The countess's gaze lingered on her guest's breasts, where, under the glow of blood, skin was already softening, smoothing.

"What manner of art is this?" the countess asked, reaching out to touch a breast, to cup it and explore the rounded, slick texture.

The mistress shivered at the contact.

Meanwhile, blood continued to trickle from the girl above them.

The countess turned her palm upward, catching the red spill, her smile widening as she glanced at the vampiress, then at the blood again.

The mistress wished to tell the countess that, perhaps, blood would not provide answers. Certainly, lovers could be stunned into adoring your youthful visage again after a blood bath, yet the glow would always fade. It would not keep those lovers from cavorting with girls whose freshness was real—as the mistress's lover was doing even now in the dungeons. It would not stop the wrongfulness of loving him.

The glow would last only until the next blood bath and, even then, the change was only skin deep.

The countess licked the blood in her hand, and the mistress only hoped that it would be enough to fulfill her; the other woman's own pores would not open to drink and bring youth to her flesh, and the vampiress refused to initiate an exchange to accommodate it.

It would be such a responsibility to create a child, the mistress thought. For *it would be necessary to leave the countess behind when she departed this castle soon, as planned, while following a great love, winning it time and again, bath after bath. . . .*

Yet the countess did seem satisfied, leaning back her head in ecstasy, red dripping from her mouth to her neck. "Oh, how it begins to work." She opened her eyes, gazing at the mistress. "In return, I have many spells to share with you. Enchantments to bind and create love where it has waned."

"Spells . . . ?"

The countess's smile faded. "I have seen how his gaze wanders. I have seen how it tears at you."

The mistress said nothing.

Yet . . . Spells. Would *they aid in a lost cause?*

With one more glimpse at the countess's eager expression, the mistress caught a stream of blood from above in her own palm then lifted it to the dark-haired woman's cheek.

She rubbed the crimson against the countess's skin, slowly, circling with ever-increasing pressure.

"Yes," the woman said. "Yes. My flesh drinks it in."

She leaned forward to scoop blood into her own palms, then splashed it over the rest of her face, her throat. Then, laughing, announcing her intention of finding her own source of blood for a full bath, she finally left the room.

As the last drips from the girl above the tub flicked over the vampiress, the creature leaned back again, pores reopening and slurping until they finally closed in their own contentment.

Then the mistress stepped out of the tub, body shifting back to original form before coming to a mirror. There, the creature touched a soft, refreshed face that was hardly even recognizable, even to the vampire's own eyes now. . . .

TWELVE

London Babylon, Main Underground Below Highgate

After Della and her classmates had zoomed away from the hotel and through darkened London, toward Highgate, then to the very edges of the heath where an Underground entrance lay in wait, a fresh batch of images had started creeping in on her.

A tub of blood . . . The drip of red from above . . .

Now, on her newly assigned bed in the girls' Underground quarters, the pieces of the scene suddenly crashed into one another in Della's mind, exploding into a full vision.

Bathing in that blood . . .

The mouthlike pores on an unidentified vampire's body . . .

Della pressed her hands over her eyes. She and her classmates could do that, too—drink blood in such a manner. If they wished, they could open their skin and slurp it into their flesh and bodies and—

She shook the thought out. Was her subconscious twining real life and nightmares, holding her accountable for all the terrible things she had done recently?

Across the room, which seemed to Della like a fuzzed, frilly blur of lace and pink paint, the group of girls who had been welcoming Polly, Noreen, and her to their new home stopped gibbering in order to survey Della instead. Little by little, she could see them go from barely defined shapes to sharp, clear entities: girls with long hair, short hair, flounced skirts, smart dresses, wrinkled trousers.

The first time Della had encountered the more seasoned girls who resided in this main Underground, they had been in costume, partaking in a masque. Now they weren't so much different than she.

Except none of them seemed on the edge of a scream.

After a moment of curiosity, they went back to fussing over Polly and Noreen, who had taken to the rest of the crowd quite easily. Della had been too occupied with the scattered, guilt-induced images attacking her mind.

Yet it was time to mingle, she thought, lest she be marked immediately as an outsider and have to pay for it eons afterward.

She stood as if all was well, then arranged the fluffy furred pillows that had been waiting on her bed. She, Polly, and Noreen had been given a room of their own, as had the other students who had managed to graduate from Queenshill in previous years. Queenshill girls were the more precious type of vampire, fewer in number among the runaways and disenfranchised youth whom the high-class students had recruited from the lower echelons of society.

Yet they all combined here in the Underground, female soldiers-in-training for the dragon's future armies.

"Della?"

Someone across the room had called to her, so Della gave one last pat to a pillow then turned toward the others.

It was Noreen, who seemed to be a great favorite with the Underground group. One fellow vampire even kept touching Noreen's red hair as if she had never seen the like.

But Noreen's tone struck Della as being rather removed, as if she were only seeking Della's attention because it was wise to do so. She had closed herself off, so Della could not get much of a read on Noreen in general.

"Our new friend Raine," her classmate said, gesturing to the girl who had been winding her fingers through Noreen's hair, "has some naughty paparazzi photos of Zac Efron. She copied them from an Internet café aboveground last night while staking out a backpacking tourist."

"Then I brought the photos with me for inspiration," Raine said, her pug nose wrinkling as she giggled. "And tonight, we can use them as an appetizer to a meal we'll get in the common area afterward. They show quite a lot of skin. And what lovely skin, too."

The group giggled, as well, and Della wondered just how old Raine was—one of the eldest or youngest, just out of her teens?

Della knew only one thing: every single one of them craved the feeling of being as loved and cherished as little girls normally were, before they lost what Wolfie often referred to as their "dewiness."

He took care of them, coddled them, and several lifetimes would never chip away at the everlasting happiness he would give them.

When Della didn't respond straightway to Noreen's invitation, Polly took it upon herself to head toward the door. "Della should probably stay put. She's awaiting a serious talking-to."

Violet's death, Della thought. Polly wasn't about to let Della forget.

Blast—didn't Polly recall how Violet had bullied her, the so-called best friend, too?

Unwilling to allow her classmate any leeway, Della joined the group as they followed Polly toward the door. Then, as one, they walked down the rock hallway of the quarters section, which stood apart from the common play areas where the girls laughed, chased dispensable young male prey lured from aboveground, and pounced on their victims when the chasing became utterly boring.

Della caught up to Polly and extended a mind-linked thought. Polly was caught off guard, her consciousness open.

It might be prudent for you to stop chatting to these girls about my talking-to.

Polly lost a step, then answered quickly. *I'll be quiet about it.*

Then she fell behind Della in order, her mouth quite shut now.

A tickle of success feathered along Della's skin at how easy it had been to put Polly back in line, but the aftermath of it felt heavy, too, as if it had left a mark that didn't belong on her.

Raine guided them into the common room she shared with at least eleven other vampires. The crowded feel of an activity holiday camp told Della that Raine was one of the recruits, not a former Queenshill student. No, Queenshill girls wouldn't have these bunk beds, complete with down mattresses of a lower quality.

On those beds, females loitered, all of them of the European stock that Wolfie preferred, their gangly legs hanging, feet encased in Mary Janes and Skechers. Some of the vampirelets sucked on lollipops laced with blood, a treat they had whipped up in the experimental kitchens where some young male prey were kept in confinement. On a higher bunk, Della even saw three girls toying with pretty butterfly knives, playing Truth or Dare with cuts that they cooed over and healed with ecstatic, glowing touches to the flesh.

Della's own skin tingled with the thought of joining in, playing such games. . . .

But then she saw a curly-haired blonde in a corner, dripping blood from a dainty perfume jar onto her skin and dizzily watching as her pores opened like tiny mouths to sip the sustenance.

A flash of a bathtub, a spill of blood made Della squeeze shut her eyes to flush the image away.

Yet it stayed, hovering just over every giggle, every exclamation in the room.

Raine reached under her lower bunk pillow to retrieve those promised naughty pictures, but they ended up being so innocuous that Della wandered toward the blonde in the corner, with her drip, drip, drip of blood on skin.

She felt something brush against her boots and glanced down to see a gray cat sliding past her.

The room went quiet as the other girls saw the cat, too. When it fixed its ominous gaze on Della, then padded out to the hall, she followed, knowing she had been summoned.

A buzz of conversation swelled in the room behind her as Della tried to keep her feet moving in slow, deliberate progress.

No running away, she thought. She was ready for this talking-to from Wolfie and Mrs. Jones.

Perhaps she even wanted it—the warped attention. The reckoning.

But why would a person *want* a punishment?

The thought rooted, but didn't develop. It didn't have time to since Della was already trailing the cat back into her own quarters.

Once inside, the creature stretched, undulated, and grew into the figure of a grown woman.

Mrs. Jones.

Without modesty, the housematron remained naked, leaning back against a wall while she looked Della up and down.

Della herself didn't know where to lay her gaze. Mrs. Jones had always worn clothing in front of the girls, but Della could see the reason she might not wish to. The elder vampire's body was flushed with gorgeous, smooth skin, her breasts round and beautiful with pink-tipped nipples.

Just as Della was beginning to wonder what turn her newest punishment had taken, Wolfie stepped out from a shadowed corner.

Della held her hand over her chest. She had been too preoccupied to pick up his hair-in-sunshine, leather-clothed scent before, but the sight of his thick, wild brown locks, golden eyes, and wolfish grin slammed into her now.

And not in the usual blood-fluttering way.

A cottage in the woods . . .

Her veins twisted as they never had before. Caution.

But why? She loved Wolfie.

Why so frightened?

Mrs. Jones's voice raked over the room. "Any words for Della, *Mihas*?"

She had dissected his name with her tone, yanking his attention from Della to her. And when Wolfie's gaze absorbed Mrs. Jones's bare skin, he looked just as lost as he had been last night, when Della had stumbled upon their rendezvous.

While she stood there, not knowing what to do with herself, Della remembered the night she and her classmates had been turned into vampires. Seven of them, some of whom had left school under odd circumstances. Both Wolfie and Mrs. Jones had bitten them that night, exchanged blood with them, and as a result the girls resembled both superiors when they changed into their vampire forms.

And, even on that night, Della had got the feeling that, perhaps, Mrs. Jones took joy from the girls' wolf/cat ugliness.

Now, under the glare of her superior's beauty, Della felt even uglier.

Preening under Wolfie's lustful scrutiny, Mrs. Jones ultimately seemed content. "You'll take care of this situation? I must research longer-term arrangements to explain to the school where Violet, Della, Polly, and Noreen have gone."

"Hurry back then," Wolfie said, completely under her spell.

Slowly, as Della watched out of the corner of her gaze, Mrs. Jones turned back into her cat form—the one she often used to skulk around and keep tabs on the girls.

Then the housematron departed, her tail high as she slipped through the crack of the door.

The instant she left, Wolfie smiled even wider. But as a haze seemed to lift from him, his eyes focused on Della.

He opened his arms to her, and she found herself running to him and burying her face in his loose white shirt.

"How I've missed you!" he said.

She held on, knowing this moment would bend to a worse one at any time.

"Me, too, Wolfie," she said, smelling the leather of his rock-star-like jacket, trousers, and boots.

When his grip on her loosened, she knew it was over, and sadness closed her throat.

He held her at arm's length, his gaze just as sorrowful. "What have you done, my darling?"

The question was rhetorical and, out of sheer desperation, she fell against him again, embracing him so tightly that she started to believe that maybe she would not ever have to let go.

He rocked her, petted her hair, the frizzed bunch of it crackling under his touch. "My little love," he said, all but cooing. "My wayward Della."

During his rocking, he had moved her in full view of the door, and when she saw the cat's eyes glowing from the crack, she raised her head from his chest, the constant visions twisting into thoughts as her mind spun:

Blood is youth . . .

Last night, when Mrs. Jones had suddenly seemed so much younger . . .

The girl dripping from above the bathtub . . .

But before Della could completely reconcile everything, the cat's eyes were gone.

The urge to run consumed Della because, all of a sudden, Wolfie's arms didn't feel so secure.

Without letting him know this, she backed away, her head down.

But why? She was home. She would always be safe with Wolfie here.

He clearly misconstrued her response as fear of punishment, not anything darker or deeper.

"It was on the news," Wolfie said, referencing Violet's termination. "The terrible conspiracy of ravens witnessed as they flew early this morning into Southwark. You're fortunate nothing else has come to light. Very fortunate."

"I know."

"Why did you do it?" he asked.

"Because Violet wanted to avenge herself on us." The truth. Her best hope of ending this quickly. "You know I bested her last night, Wolfie. I humiliated her and brought her down, and she wasn't about to tolerate being at the bottom. So she told us we would be sorry, then she sneaked out of the hotel."

He was shaking his head, his shoulders slumped. "Violet."

A flicker of hope warmed Della. He believed her.

Sighing, he sat on Polly's bed, among a cheetah stuffed animal and an embroidered pillow featuring a football.

"She was the most difficult of any of you," Wolfie said. "I held out hope for Violet, yet Mrs. Jones always . . ." He trailed off, then recovered. "She always lobbied for her to . . . leave."

Della froze. Leave?

"You mean," she whispered, "just as Briana and Sharon and Blanche left?"

All members of their small Queenshill vampire class.

All mysteriously run away from the group or taken by estranged parents who hadn't seemed to care for their child before reclaiming her and never allowing their girl to return to the school.

Here today, gone tomorrow.

Della's brain flickered.

Young girl dangling over a tub, the vampire with the blurred features beneath, her pores drinking and drinking . . .

Slowly, she chanced a look at Wolfie, who had not said anything since Della had mentioned the three other girls.

Wary, she thought. He seemed to be looking at her in a different light now.

If Della had any stones, she would enter his thoughts, as she had done once, yet she knew it would be an unforgivable act this time. Even Wolfie, with his love and tolerance, had his limits.

"Violet," he said, "has nothing to do with your classmates who have left us, my dear."

It seemed as if he were about to pat the bed next to him, inviting her to nuzzle up against his chest, but he stopped himself.

He exhaled, planted his hands on his thighs as he engaged her with a serious stare. "You've put me in quite a position, you know, with your raven games."

"Mrs. Jones also said that. Even if Violet required action, I went too far. I did more than track her."

"I can understand how you might have gone overboard. Mrs. Jones and I were out of range, out of touch, and you had to make decisions on your own. We've trained you to realize that a good soldier does that, Della, even while following orders. And I have always attempted to instill the will to fight in you—the urge to win at all costs."

Perhaps he was *not* going to terminate her, Della realized. Yet she knew he was hurting from the loss of Violet.

"I'm ready for what's due," she said, straightening her posture, exhausted in this waiting and dreading.

A strange smile darkened his eyes. "Just like a good soldier."

This time, she knew he was not going to be lenient, not as he had been before whenever she had misstepped.

He rose from the mattress, his muscles rolling under his clothing with every footfall as he walked toward the door. "Follow me."

She obeyed, steadying herself, staying on the lookout for the cat as they took the hallway where the scent of blood traced the air on the way to the common area.

As they passed the recruits' rooms, Della noticed the silence, the lack of presence from any other girls, and she supposed it was feeding time for one and all.

Except her.

In the near distance, the thin sound of wailing graced the atmosphere—males. Victims.

White ribbons . . .

She shuddered at the image, but it had also become colder, dimmer as they rounded a corner and went deeper into the Underground, where the wails defined themselves as weak cries for help. The lovely scent of male flesh, bitten only recently, filled the tunnel.

Yet the blood—and the boys' faint murmurings—filled her with courage, too, just as the screams had done earlier at the hotel when Della had recalled Violet's death shrieks in front of Mrs. Jones.

"Wolfie?" she asked softly.

"Yes, my dear."

She stopped walking, halting him, too.

"Have there been others for you?" she asked, thinking of the tub images, the skin-mouths. "Companions such as Mrs. Jones? Or has she been with you for centuries?"

The question took him aback—she could sense it.

"Well, now. That's quite the private query."

She already could guess that he would not answer, at least not at this moment.

But she thought it might be important to know, for some reason she had not fully come to terms with yet.

He pushed against a door, and it moaned open, fully introducing Della to the blood here in the kitchens.

Her sight adjusted to a thicker darkness that barely hid the counters with their pots and pans for mixing flavors. Along the walls, cages dwelled, embracing teenaged boys gone bad, boys who had been tempted down here by all the lovely girls.

Wolfie went to an empty cage, then opened the door.

Without question, Della stepped in, and he shut the bars. Then he went to the enclosure to the right of her, motioning the prey forward with one hypnotic, "Come, boy."

The prey obeyed, stretching out his arm for Wolfie, who scratched it lightly with his nails—not enough to maim or drain, just enough so Della would suffer the scent in her hungry state.

He did the same with the male in the cage to the left.

She thumped to the padded floor, trying not to sense the immediate blood, to crave it.

But it was already too late.

Shudders began to wrack her body; she had not eaten for over a day.

Wolfie came to stand in front of her cell. "Anyone who visits the kitchens will see you and wonder why you've been treated so. You won't tell them, Della, but Polly and Noreen will know. And although I understand why you did what you did with Violet, you took her from us. From *me*. That cannot happen again."

"Yes, Wolfie."

It seemed as if he wished to say something more, but he instead left the room, the cries of the captives growing in volume once Wolfie had shut the door.

"Mercy," one teenager said from across the way.

And, in the cage to the right of Della, a young man stuck out a thin bloody arm to her, although she could not even dream of reaching him.

"Mercy," he said also, and she realized it was because he wanted to be put out of the misery of his own punishment.

His yearning to be sucked.

Della held her hands over her ears, but it did no good, because she could still hear them. Smell them.

And she could still see the formation of yet another vision rotating in the dark of her mind, where all sorts of scattered, formerly unthinkable pieces were beginning to fall into place.

THIRTEEN

The Dearly Departed

At headquarters, a miasma of colors expanded behind Dawn's eyelids as Jonah continued to draw from her vein, pressing against her, sucking and sucking. . . .

She gripped his shirt, the strength ebbing from her, but it was replaced by the high of weakness and—

Her bubble of ecstasy broke open, shattering into a dark so blinding that it swallowed her in the cold comfort of knowing that she had given just as much as she'd taken from Costin and even Jonah.

That she'd done her time for the night.

As Dawn struggled for breath, Jonah recovered, too, his open mouth against her throat. She squirmed away from him, using the remainder of her strength to lift her leg, plant her foot against his torso, then shove him away.

He veered back, crashing against the wall. Strung out on blood, which reddened his fangs and lips, he planted his hands against the marble, using it to slide to the ground, where he closed his eyes.

Dawn leaned back against the mirror. God, she wouldn't have pushed him if Costin had been dominant in that body. But this creature on the floor wasn't her lover. It was Jonah, who was obviously enjoying the taste of her way too much.

A spiral of sensation—maybe it was appreciation for *being* so appreciated—drilled through her, and she slumped off the counter, one palm to her neck as she used her other hand to pull her bra over her breasts. Even with the healing gel, her skin stung.

"Hold on," Jonah said, holding a hand out for her and opening his eyes.

"Fuck off."

"Would you stop being so stubborn?"

The silver of his gaze was deepening to the normal blue of his humanlike facade, but his fangs were still evident as he reached out farther to latch his fingers around her arm and pull her to him.

Too weak to react normally, Dawn slid across the marble floor in his grip, coming to bang against his leg. She made the token effort of bringing up an elbow to jar it down into his thigh, but he had his fingers on her neck before she'd even raised her arm all the way.

"Just sit still for a minute," he said softly, impatiently, pressing against her bite punctures. "Then you can beat me up all you want."

Healing waves streamed through her, but she didn't move, didn't let him see that it felt good with the heat flowing down her neck, through her chest, into her gut, where it unfurled and tickled her in spots that shouldn't have felt anything when it came to Jonah.

She tried to think about anything else—the need to get some supplement juice and food into her, the necessity of scrambling as far away from him as possible—but her pitiful libido was boss now.

A sharp stiffness needled her between the legs, and her skin prickled until he took his fingers away and let her go.

"I can heal all those cuts on you," he said as she rolled from him, then crawled for the door.

"You wish."

"Dawn," he said before she made it out.

In spite of herself, she glanced back.

His fangs had receded, his eyes a full blue now, his skin a healthier shade of pale, his lips still red with the mark of her blood.

The sight of that speared her, and she squeezed her thighs together, hoping this would get rid of the sensual twang.

It didn't.

"You happy now?" she asked. "Glad to be back?"

"Very."

And she could tell it was true by the way his gaze was taking in every detail around him, as if he'd just been born again. Whoever was dominant in that body was the one who experienced everything firsthand: the texture of marble against fingertips, the stream of air from a heater over skin, the taste of blood.

Back when Costin had recruited him, Jonah had accepted the deal based on an opportunity to escape a sheltered life. He'd possessed all the money a man could want but had lacked so much more. Passion. Purpose.

And Costin the Soul Traveler had given those to him. That's why Jonah loved being a vampire—because it provided everything he'd never had, a million times over.

Jonah smiled as he finished his survey of the room, and he sprawled, long legs like a cowboy leaning against a fence at the OK Corral. "So the plan is for me to go under the ground at Queenshill?"

"That's the plan for Costin." Dawn's neck still tingled, as if Jonah were still touching her. She brushed at the area, like you did when you tried to clean off a fly you'd just killed. "As cool as you think you are, you wouldn't be able to detect any master if one was around."

"Then I'll just get Costin belowground safely and he can come out to do the detecting. Afterward, I'll bundle him up and protect him again when we go back above."

"Protect." Dawn just about spit the word.

She wiped her hands on her shirt, lending skids of blood to the material. Then she crawled the rest of the way out of the room, toward the walk-in closet with its minifridge and her supplement juice.

"Maybe you misunderstand me," Jonah said from the bathroom.

As she pawed open the fridge and took out the plastic juice bottle, stripping off the cap and shakily lifting it to her mouth, she heard Jonah rustling around, coming out to stand at the entrance to the closet. Juice trickled down her chin because she could barely control herself.

He stood there in Costin's lounging suit, strong and flushed from the feeding, but the tousled hair, the nonchalant stance told her he was all Jonah.

"Do you still think," he asked, "that I would ever let Costin get hurt? Everything I do is for our own good in the end."

She kept drinking while eyeing him, trying to avoid how sincere Jonah sounded. She hated to admit it, but she knew that he was just as devoted to their cause as the rest of them. He just wanted a chance to prove it, after being relegated to the shadows in the pit of his own body for so long.

He began perusing a line of black clothing that hung from the rack, no doubt getting ready to change into his own kind of hunting wardrobe. His assassin ensemble from last night had been perfect for all the blood-spraying trouble he'd caused by showing up at Queenshill to scare the schoolgirls off.

"Like you," he added, "I would do anything to make sure Costin gets these Underground guys."

She finished drinking, swiping her sleeve over her mouth. "I guess we'd be shit out of luck if the romance and adventure of all this didn't appeal to you."

Picking out a black pea coat, he shrugged. "But it does. And you never know—maybe one day you'll even realize that I've got a little nobility lurking somewhere in me."

She didn't want to argue, because every time they did, she always ended up understanding too well that no one—not even Jonah—should have to live like he did: pressed down into his own body for as long as the Underground hunts or this vampiric state lasted.

And that could be for centuries.

Dawn grabbed a cookie from her stash, filling herself with it as Jonah continued to choose his clothes.

Meanwhile, a stream of jasmine slithered into the atmosphere via the heating vent.

Goody. Whenever Jonah took over, Kalin, Dawn's least favorite Friend, appeared.

"Back from searching for the schoolgirls?" Dawn said to the Friend, a.k.a. Fire Woman, a nickname earned because of her portrait of flames.

Jonah greeted Kalin, too, but this time he didn't seem as exasperated as usual. The Friend had a crush on him, and he wasn't that into it.

At least normally. Maybe he was just tolerating her tonight.

"You didn't find any of them, Kalin?" he asked.

"*No schoolgirls out at play,*" the spirit said, her voice a reedy swirl of words that reflected a lower-class British accent from years and years ago. *"Not in the places I was searchin' along the Thames."*

"Thanks for the progress report," Dawn said. "Now leave us alone."

Kalin laughed, a tumble of mirth.

Jonah didn't react, and Dawn realized that he genuinely didn't mind Kalin's presence right now.

Dawn took a stab at what was going on. "Is she going to be your protector, Jonah? Your best Friend?"

"We all need our allies," he said mildly, checking out a pair of badass boots he'd pulled out from below the hanging clothes.

Great. Kalin and her hurt feelings had switched loyalty to Jonah because she'd always felt that Costin didn't pay her enough attention. Bitter twit.

But Dawn wasn't about to let them off the hook so easily.

"Kalin, bind Jonah."

He raised his eyebrows at Dawn while the jasmine air went still.

Dawn got to her knees, waiting for the Friend to obey the command. They were supposed to take orders from team members.

The spirit began to laugh again, and she even nudged Jonah . . . who wasn't laughing.

"Dawn," he said, a trace of disappointment in his tone, "you know a Friend can't obey an order that harms Costin."

She got to her feet, her legs still rubbery, even though growing anger gave them some steel. "You're not Costin."

"Yes, I am." He cocked his head in vampire consideration as he watched her. "I'm very much a part of Costin, and he's a part of me."

Dawn took the empty juice bottle and flung it at him, knowing he'd have the instincts to avoid it.

And, yup, he did avoid it—gracefully. Easily.

As she pushed past him out of the closet, Kalin's jasmine flared around her, and Dawn swatted the Friend's essence away.

But her hand only caught air.

"You know that Costin's gonna banish your ass when he gets back," Dawn said to the Friend.

"Oh, Daaa-aawn," Kalin called. *"Almost forgot. You're needed downstairs. . . . Urgently, I'd say."*

Her first instinct was to tell Kalin to go to hell, but she was a Friend, first and foremost, so Dawn chose to believe that there was something going on that she needed to check out.

While buttoning her shirt, she busted past the bedroom door, and when she got to the lower floor, she ran into Natalia.

After recovering from a wave of dizziness—it was too soon to be up and walking around, even with the supplement in her—she realized that the new girl's eyes were wide, her fingers plucking at her skirt.

"Your mom . . ." Natalia said.

Maybe it was the half-panicked tone her coworker was using, but it set Dawn off. "What? What about Eva?"

"I saw her run out the door a few minutes ago—"

She hadn't even finished before an adrenalized Dawn had taken off for the front door, where she found the locks in place.

"I shut it and locked up," the psychic said as Dawn's legs went weak again, "because Eva left it partway open—"

"Where did she go?" Dawn flung open the weapons cache and began to raid it.

Then she realized something.

"A Friend's going to be with my mom," she said, relief washing over her.

Idiot Kalin. She'd freaked Dawn out for nothing. Eva had probably decided to go back to her flat for some reason and a spirit would be escorting her. Nothing to go Armageddon about.

Then again, Eva had left the door half-open. . . .

"I don't know what happened," Natalia said. "And I don't know where she went. But Dawn? She's alone."

Dawn stopped, an illegal revolver halfway to the hip holster she'd just donned. "You mean 'alone' as in she's got a Friend with her. Right? That kind of 'alone'?"

A bolt of jasmine rushed down the stairs, and Dawn glanced in its direction.

"*No,*" Breisi said, her voice angry even in its melodic flow. "*No Friend would go with her* anywhere."

Dawn shoved an earpiece in, grabbed a few more weapons plus her jacket and phone, then bolted to the door.

"Try calling Eva on her cell," she said to Natalia before she changed her mind about going out the front and headed for the back.

And no one stopped her.

FOURTEEN

The Meet and Greet

Dawn had no idea where to start looking for Eva except for her mom's nearby flat, which sat over a pub called the Bull and Cock.

So she sprinted straight over after having the presence of mind to take the belowground back way out of headquarters, where she thought she could avoid the front door camera that'd been clouded earlier. But, even with all the talk about getting IDed by cameras, Dawn didn't put on any wigs or change the raggedy schoolgirl shirt and skirt she'd been wearing since this morning's Queenshill visit.

No time for anything else, she kept thinking, as much as she even *had* the capacity to think, what with her still feeling woozy after Jonah's feeding.

As she booked it to the Bull and Cock, the air stamped her face with a cold burn, but she wasn't outside for very long before she barged into the warm pub.

Everyone, from the guys throwing down ale at the bar to the couple getting cozy by the fireplace, glanced over to see what kind of freak had come through the door to let in the chill. But Dawn just flashed a "hi" sign at them, pulled her jacket around her, and headed for the stairwell that led to her mom's rented room.

Halfway up the steps, leaving behind the rock music playing in the common room, the adrenaline failed Dawn and she rested her hand against a wall, leaning forward so she wouldn't fall backward.

All she had to do was get up the stairs, and if Eva was in her room, bring her mom back to headquarters to sort through whatever had happened.

That's all.

Her earpiece crackled. "Dawn?"

It was Frank, and he sounded as sheepish as a kicked Doberman.

But his voice got her going up the rest of the way to Eva's room.

"You gonna tell me what the deal is?" she asked.

"Yeah, but first you should know that your mom's not answering her cell. We could hear it ringing in her guest room. She left it here."

"I guess she was so busy running from something or another that she forgot it, huh, Frank?"

At the door, Dawn realized that she didn't have Eva's key with her—she didn't even have her lock picking tools—and she let out a word that probably even made her dad cringe.

She decided that the music in the pub might be loud enough to distract from the noise she was about to make, so she said, "Dad, give me a sec before you start explaining. I need to get into Mom's place."

"Tell me if she's there," he said.

"I will."

Then Dawn stepped back from the door and closed her eyes, focusing.

Damn Eva for doing this, she thought, allowing her anger to gather. *Damn vampires for making me scared that she's not safe out here. Damn—*

She blasted out with her mind, but the door only suffered something like a lame kick.

Good God.

So she pictured Jonah, and the door blew open with a splintered crack.

While rushing in, Dawn trained her silver-bullet-loaded revolver around the room, where the heavy curtains huddled like bulky shapes in the moonlight and the dark wood seemed to mask something ready to spring at her.

Knowing her mind was on overdrive, she targeted the rest of the room, with all the modern paintings on the walls, then the huge bed in the corner, just in case something was under it.

But that was stupid, she thought, finally hitting the lights. Eva had run away. It wasn't like something had swooped in and forced her out of headquarters just to bring her to her own apartment.

All the same, Dawn inspected every corner, every possible hiding place before returning to the door. It didn't really close right, even though it shut most of the way, so she lugged over a heavy oak chair and jammed it under the knob to take the place of the lock she'd blown out.

"She's not here, Frank," she said, accessing the earpiece and holstering her weapon.

He sighed.

Then everything hit Dawn at the same time—the dizziness from Jonah's nip, the aftermath of an adrenaline rush that'd sapped her even more.

Legs quivering, she made it to the small kitchen, leaned against a counter, then yanked open the fridge door and grabbed the first food she could find.

Baked chicken.

As Frank spoke, Dawn ripped the plastic covering off and bit into a leg like an animal, sinking to the floor as she thought about where to go for Eva next.

Normally, she would've consulted Costin. But with his absence, she'd been left in charge once again, and she didn't know what to do.

How about think?

Frank didn't help by interrupting. "Dawn? When you find Eva, tell her not to worry. We'll talk it out when she gets back. We just want her behind safe walls again."

If she found Eva.

But Dawn wasn't giving up so easily. They'd find her.

There was a disturbance on Frank's end, and it sounded like Breisi's ethereal protests.

Then he came back on. "Okay, *I* want her behind safe walls again." When he continued, it was obvious that he was talking to Breisi. "Is that better?"

Another ghostylike sound in the background—one that resembled a yes.

Dawn finished swallowing the chicken. "You gonna tell me about what happened or do I have to guess why no Friends were available to escort Eva or find her right now?"

As she rummaged in the fridge for a bottle of water, she could almost see Frank running his hand over his face.

"I don't rightly know what happened," he said. "One second, she was at my bedroom door, and I thought she was just popping in to say hi. The next, I smelled her blood, and I . . ."

Oh, God.

The water bottle only made it halfway to Dawn's mouth. "Tell me she didn't. Tell me *you* didn't."

"I started to." If his tone had been remorseful before, it was worse now. "I couldn't think. I just smelled . . . saw . . . *needed* her blood. It was right there. The next thing I knew, I was going at her palm, where she was bleeding, and Breisi woke up and kicked Eva out of the room."

"And that's why Breisi put the big no on any Friends going after Mom. And the spirits will side with her out of loyalty."

Jesus, Frank. But more importantly, what had Eva been thinking?

It had obviously been the last straw for Breisi. And why not? Her and Frank's relationship—a spirit and a vampire—was tough enough in the first place; add a former wife who still had the hots for Frank and you got a brew that'd been set to blow from the start.

Dawn wanted to sit both her parents down and give them a good . . .

What?

Gah, she didn't know what. But her mom was out there somewhere, and so were the vampires, who might or might not have identified the fogged camera and figured out where the Limpets were housed. They might've even seen Eva come out of headquarters on that camera.

"Frank," she said, "talk to Breisi. I know she's mad, but if Eva gets hurt and a Friend isn't there to help . . ."

"I know it."

There was another muddled Breisi-like exclamation, and to Dawn, it sounded like the spirit said, "You reap what you sow."

Shit. Like any other hunter Costin had ever recruited, Breisi had a firm sense of justice—that's what The Voice had always depended on to operate—and Eva had thrown all Breisi's goodwill back in her face tonight.

"So where do you think she went?" Dawn asked, closing this conversation up so she could get moving. "This is a big city and without Friends to canvass it for Eva—"

"Hampstead Village?" he asked. "She talks about how much she likes that part of London."

Oh, super, a location on the opposite side of town.

"Or," Frank added, "she could be anywhere."

"Thanks, that'll narrow it down." Dawn controlled her temper. Frank had only been obeying his natural instincts when Eva had marched into his room, bleeding, but Dawn was pissed that he hadn't controlled himself. Pissed at Eva for making him that way.

But . . . Calm, cool, collected.

Deep breath. Another one.

Okay.

"Maybe," Dawn said, "a Friend who's already on patrol will see her somewhere around the city. I'm assuming Breisi hasn't been outside to get ahold of any of them yet, so they wouldn't know that they should be giving Eva the cold shoulder."

"Wrong." Now Frank's tone was tense, as if he were staring in Breisi's general direction. "Seems as if my girlfriend decided to be as efficient as always and send a Friend out to spread the word from one to the other."

Enough was enough.

"Breisi?" Dawn said. "Listen to me. I know you can hear me."

Silence on the other end.

"Breisi, Eva's my *mom*. Sure, it sounds like she made a stupid choice, and she should account for it. But not like this." She rested her head against a cabinet, suddenly feeling like she was always trooping through thick, heavy muck. "Not like this."

An instant passed where Dawn actually had enough energy to imagine her Friend relenting, but then Frank intruded.

"Breisi left the room, and I doubt it's because she's gonna tell the others to find Eva."

Dawn banged her head against that cabinet. Like they didn't have enough to deal with. Now this.

Breathe.

"Just keep me in the loop," she said. "I should probably grab a hat and different clothes from Eva's closet for some kind of pathetic disguise so I can move around in front of those cameras. After that, I'll aim toward Hampstead since I have no other idea what to do. But while I'm floundering, work on your woman, would you?"

"This is as much my bad as Eva's," he said. "I'll work on Breisi all night if I have to."

Frank signed off, and Dawn wrapped up the rest of the chicken, shoving it back into the fridge after one last drink of water.

Then she rested, just until the thought of standing up didn't seem like such a big deal.

Meanwhile, she reviewed the plan: hop the tube to Hampstead, because she sure as hell wasn't going to sit in headquarters twiddling her thumbs and waiting to hear something on a local newscast about a middle-aged blonde going missing or . . .

Dawn didn't want to think it, but she did.

. . . or going dead.

She shut out the possibility. Drank more water. Wiped the grease off her hands on a fleur-de-lis dish towel.

Then, just as Dawn felt strong enough to get up, her cell vibrated.

She answered before it went off a second time. "Hello?"

"Hi, Dawn." Eva's exhausted voice.

Thank God, thank God . . . "I know the story, Eva, so you don't have to explain. Just tell me where you are."

"Don't worry—I'm in a public place. A nice wine bar in the area of the London Bridge tube station." It sounded like she was holding the phone away from her and confirming with someone else that this really was the right location. Then she came back on. "After running out, I just ended up in here. It looked like a safe place."

"But you left your phone—"

"I've borrowed the barman's because I thought you might be . . ."

"Jumping around like the devil's been poking hot arrowheads in my ass? Yeah, I was."

Relief was inching through Dawn, and she actually pressed a hand over her thudding heart like some maudlin soap queen. But this was her mom. She'd lost her once, almost twenty-five years ago when she'd just been a baby, and she'd had to grow up without her. The thought of losing Eva again hurt more than Dawn would admit if anyone else were in the room.

Her mom hadn't responded yet, so Dawn tried to smooth out the dead air.

"Dad says that you should come back so you can talk it out."

"I don't think that would make Breisi very happy."

Damn it. "And having you traipse around the dark streets of London as vamp bait is a much better option."

Dawn quelled her temper again. It was just that this episode was so minor in the scheme of things. Why couldn't it just be over?

Vaguely, though, she realized that maybe Eva was fighting to find her own way, just like Costin was.

It's just that Costin's way needed to come first. Always.

"I'm really sorry this happened," Eva said.

Her shame was obvious, just like the loneliness Dawn also heard in her tone.

"Mom." She hoped the word said everything: how scared she'd been, how her mother dying for real this time would beat Dawn back down to the confused, aimless girl she'd been before getting Eva back.

But her mother seemed to get it.

Or at least she sounded happy that Dawn cared enough to be angry.

"Do you want me to stay here, with all these people around, just until . . . ?" Eva asked.

"Until I come to get you? Yeah." Dawn reached up and used the counter to get to her feet. "What's the name of this place?"

"Just a minute."

She heard Eva asking someone, then she came back on line with the name and directions.

But, even though Dawn heard all of it, something else had captured her attention.

A soft thud on the ceiling.

She took out her revolver and meandered in the direction of the window, thinking that, of course, if there was something on the roof, it'd be a great time to be wearing this pain-in-the-ass skirt.

She hiked it up, trying to get it out of the way, but it only slipped back down.

Whatever.

Whispering, Dawn said, "I'll be there as soon as I can, Eva. No matter how long it takes, just stay there."

Not waiting for an answer, she folded the phone with one hand and stowed it in a jacket pocket. Then she doused the lights and glanced out the window.

Nothing outside except a wanderer or two—businesspeople on their way home.

She waited until they passed. Then, not hearing anything else, she accessed her earpiece.

"Were you listening to Eva, too?" Dawn quietly said to whoever was on the other end: Frank, Natalia, or, God help her, even Jonah.

But it turned out to be Natalia, probably because Frank was talking to Breisi. Jonah was probably trying on bitchin' clothes or something, and Kiko was likely sleeping, lulled by a Friend.

"I heard everything and noted it," the new girl said.

Good, dependable Natalia. "Where's Jonah?"

"He was getting ready to run out after you."

Aw, how devoted. Yeesh. "Tell him not to even think about taking unnecessary chances."

"He discovered that on his own after hearing you with Eva. So he turned his attention to Frank and Breisi. He's mediating, you could say."

Dawn didn't know how to react to that. It was actually a pretty constructive thing for Jonah to be doing.

She decided to get going, but first it'd be smart to report the thump on the roof. Sometimes it was the little details that counted the most in hindsight.

"Natalia, just FYI, I heard something on—"

Dawn started backward as a *thing* with red eyes and a black-masked face appeared in the window, hanging upside down.

With a spurt of adrenaline, she took aim with her revolver, hardly caring if a blast from the illegal firearm would draw the attention of the entire neighborhood.

But the thing—the shadow, the twin of the dead boy the team was keeping in the lab freezer—disappeared from view.

Dawn's limbs were frozen as her mind took a second to race with possibilities: what she should do, what she shouldn't do, what needed to be done.

Vampires.

Save Costin. . . .

But before she geared into motion, the glass shattered, and the dark thing crashed through the window, kicking the revolver out of Dawn's hand, then grasping her wrist to flip her to the floor.

The oxygen slammed out of Dawn, and the communication device flew out of her ear. As the shadow thing got into an intimidating hunch, its boot crunched down on the earpiece.

Even out of breath, Dawn had just enough clarity to grab a silver-bladed knife from her jacket, and she back-stabbed toward the shadow thing.

It arched backward, out of the way, and Dawn used that split second to bound to a crouch.

As they faced off, reality set in: the red night-vision eyes right here in front of her, the figure suited in black from head to toe. It was about Dawn's height, just like that dead boy in the freezer, but Dawn could already tell the shadow thing was quick and strong.

One heartbeat passed . . . another . . .

Neither of them moved as the shadow thing just stared, like it was getting some kind of read.

Dawn's pulse kicked, hammering away at rational thought.

"What the hell are you?" she found herself asking on an escaped breath.

The shadow thing looked sidelong at her, as if amused by the question, and that bought Dawn just enough time to come to her senses and reach for her pocket-bound mini flamethrower.

Yet as she brought it out, she raised her finger off the trigger when she saw that the shadow thing had a flash grenade in its own hand.

Prickles gnawed their way up Dawn's skin at the sight of the box. The shadow boy from Billiter Street had been carrying one, too, and the team had analyzed it after his death.

But could the device do more than temporarily blind an opponent? Had Breisi and Frank found out everything they could about it?

The stare down continued as Dawn wondered if she could fire at the shadow thing—or even chuck the knife in her other hand at it—before the intruder activated the blinding box then darted out of the flames' way to come behind Dawn and inflict some major hurt.

Maybe some defense-lowering bullshit wouldn't be amiss right now . . . ?

"Listen," Dawn said. "I'm not out to piss your kind off. Whatever you are. I'm just looking for someone I know here in this flat."

The shadow thing hunched a little lower.

Then it talked, its voice electronically mangled, and in all the temple-pounding confusion, Dawn could only think of the sound of snakes slithering out of Medusa's head.

"Attacker," it said.

"No, not at all." Dawn clutched her flamethrower. "I didn't attack you. You came here."

"Last night. Queenshill."

Dawn tried not to change expression, because the moonlight was going to show any cracks in her poker face.

Even so? *Fuck.*

Had all the clouded cameras from Billiter to Queenshill to Southwark finally led this thing here, near headquarters, and it'd been watching the area before picking up the sight of Dawn running around in the streets?

She'd have to divert this intruder from headquarters, have to make it think that she didn't want anything to do with hurting vampires at all and that it should just go on its merry way.

The shadow thing started to circle her, but Dawn didn't allow that. She stalked it, too, still face-to-face.

And with every step, she prepared a different weapon—accessing her inner darkness, feeding it with thoughts of Jonah,

Costin . . . everything that was wrong with this world that she couldn't set right.

The anger rolled, gathered.

"I have a few questions for you," the shadow said in that eerie voice as it stopped circling.

British accent, Dawn thought while the thing's finger moved, as if to activate the box in its hand.

With a desperate push, she blasted out with everything she had, her power licking around the thing's wrist and yanking it.

The untripped flash grenade flew into the air, and the shadow figure jumped backward, trying to get away from whatever Dawn was wielding.

But she wasn't done throwing down just yet.

Dawn gave as good as she'd gotten earlier, pushing with her mind, connecting, then flipping the shadow thing over and slamming it to the floor.

Yet what it did next broke her concentration, broke her mental hold altogether.

It . . . laughed.

Laughed.

By the time Dawn processed that, the shadow thing had levered itself off of the floor and sprung to its feet, ready to grapple.

Fight? Dawn thought. *You want a* fight?

The dark spot in Dawn expanded, folding outward into a different shape that boxed her and squeezed her temples, warping her judgment and causing her to raise the flamethrower.

She didn't care what kind of damage the weapon would do to Eva's place or even to this thing that might be a decent prize to capture alive for questioning.

Dead, was the only thought she had. *Gone.*

Kill them all.

Just as she was about to pull the trigger, the figure kicked out at her, a dark streak, and the weapon spun out of Dawn's hand, leaving her fingers numbed. Then, in the next heartbeat, the shadow thing swept Dawn's legs out from under her and she crashed to the ground with a chest-punching grunt.

Her knife jarred out of her other hand and rattled to the floor, and her brain scrambled as the shadow thing braced itself on top of Dawn, pinning her to the ground.

Dawn prepared for the worst, but when the shadow didn't make another violent move, she realized that it wasn't going to kill her. Not yet.

Like it'd said before, it had a few questions, and Dawn wondered what kind of persuasion it might have in store if she didn't feel like answering any of them.

Rage—at being used, just like she'd been so often—balled up.

As the shadow thing laughed again, Dawn ripped out with her mind to tear at its face, and the force caught its goggles and mask.

The items flew through the air, clattering to a landing, but the thing kept laughing, this time in surprise.

"Feisty," it said in that same altered voice.

Dawn just stared, because the thing wasn't an "it." It wasn't even a boy like the shadow figure from Billiter.

It was a young woman with light brown hair that came to her neck. A girl whose light green eyes were wide and thrilled with this playtime Dawn was providing.

Channeling her shock, Dawn punched out again, this time launching the shadow figure high enough so that she stopped laughing just before thumping back down to Dawn's stomach.

As Dawn heaved out a pained breath, the female jammed an elbow down.

Dawn ducked it, but the shadow was so fast that within a blink, she was already plastering Dawn to the floor again, her hands on Dawn's arms, shins pressing down on Dawn's legs.

Both of them were panting now as Dawn tensed under the woman's hold.

Strong, she thought.

Almost vampire strong.

But the boy in the freezer hadn't been a vamp. He'd had physical irregularities, like a heart on the wrong side of his chest. . . .

The female hovered over Dawn. "Now. Time for those questions."

No, she thought, on the edge of panic. She'd let every bone in her body be broken before she gave in to any kind of torture and gave up Costin's secrets.

Her anger was like a creature raising its own head to show a face so ugly that it was unbearable to look at.

The female lowered herself closer, and Dawn noticed that she didn't have a scent.

With a lethal whisper, the shadow said, "Mind powers. You do have them, don't you?"

The young woman bent even nearer, her lips against Dawn's own.

A shock lit through Dawn and, instinctively, she tried to turn away.

But the female kept her lips against the corner of Dawn's mouth.

"Just what sort of servant are you?" the shadow asked.

Dawn's heartbeat pistoned, punching against the dark spot, pounding. . . .

Then her mind shattered into a thousand pieces, forcing out more energy than she'd ever experienced—enough to push the woman off of her in a spinning arc.

But the shadow managed to land on all fours, smiling, as if she'd been looking forward to a test like this and nobody had ever given it to her.

Just as she looked ready to spring again, she froze, then righted herself and glanced toward the window.

Then she went for her mask and goggles, scooping them up as she lunged toward the exit, easily tossing aside the chair with one hand before yanking open the door.

Once she'd slipped through it, she slammed it hard enough so that it actually closed all the way.

Dawn got to her hands and knees. What the hell had just happened? Had the female gotten some kind of call or—?

Not taking the time to figure it out, she dove for her flamethrower at the same time she heard something that resembled a scream of air.

Jasmine, she thought, just as a flood of it entered through the broken window.

"There!" Dawn pointed her flamethrower toward the door. "One of those shadows!"

She heard the Friend bash against the wood, but there were no open spaces to get through.

"Bleeping . . ." Dawn heard the Friend say, and she knew it was Breisi from the thwarted attempt to cuss.

She'd come, Dawn thought. It'd been too late, but she'd come, probably after Natalia had finally figured out that Dawn's earpiece had been debilitated.

Dawn ran toward the exit and braced her foot on the wall as she pulled at the door. It protested, then opened, and the moment there was a larger crack, Breisi darted through in hot pursuit.

Dawn joined in, but before she'd even climbed down the stairs, through the pub—with its patrons standing up and wondering what the hell was happening—and gotten thirty meters into the cold streets, Breisi had already circled back.

"Gone," the spirit said, disbelief winding through her voice. *"I never even picked it up to track the thing."*

But Dawn had the feeling that they hadn't lost the shadow girl at all.

That, in fact, she was somewhere on a rooftop, watching them even now, still laughing.

FIFTEEN

Drink Time with Eva, II

Eva folded shut the mobile she'd used to call Dawn and handed it back to the barman who was wiping glasses behind the mahogany counter.

"Thank you," she said.

As he accepted the phone, he smiled, teeth white and a little crooked, but still, a charming gesture. "How're you getting on then?"

"I told my daughter to pick me up when she could."

"So she's on her way?"

Eva nodded, settling into the corner of the bar among a pile of daily newspapers and tabloids, where people couldn't easily see that she was barefoot, having lost her pumps back at the Limpet team's headquarters. She wouldn't have been able to run in them, anyway, but the dirt and a few small cuts on her feet didn't sell that point very well. She also didn't care to show off her wounded hand, which was covered with the bandages the barman had given her after he'd seen the blood on her palm.

He worked a cork out of a bottle of Sauvignon Blanc and splashed some of the wine into a glass he'd been shining. Then he slid it over to her.

"Don't you worry yourself about anything, not even this," he said.

She could see it on his face: he knew she'd had a wildly rough night and was only being kind to her.

Maybe his first clue had been when she'd opened the wine bar's door, trying to look as dignified as possible, even in bare feet and hiding her hand behind her, as she'd entered. She'd only come inside because she'd realized that there wasn't a Friend with her, and her survival instincts had told her to be around people, where danger was less likely.

The barman had greeted her, probably judging her well-tailored clothing against the rest of her. And after she'd bandaged up, then asked to use his phone for an urgent call—she'd lost her cell, she'd explained—he'd handed his very own mobile right over.

He'd probably thought she'd been attacked, and he wanted to play the good guy. When he'd seen that she didn't require a call to any officials, Eva could also tell that he thought she was attractive, even with all the signs of age on her skin.

Thanks to the reconstructive surgery she'd had after being turned back into a human, the barman wouldn't be able to see that she was *the* Eva Claremont, or even Jacqueline Ashley—the name Eva had used during her cosmetically and vampirically altered comeback.

Yet that didn't seem to matter, because he had still smiled at her, seemed . . . interested . . . in her.

But Eva had pushed all of that aside in favor of calling Dawn, and she'd felt bad for making her daughter run around outside of headquarters and for even causing a second of worry.

Though at least someone had missed her, Eva had thought. Someone had cared enough to look for her.

Now she picked up the wine and wryly toasted the barman, who winked back.

To Dawn, she thought.

Then she paused and added, *To what I did to Frank.*

At the upsetting memory, she drank deeply, and the fruit-laden liquid slid down her throat, warming her. She drank more, until there was nothing left.

The barman had gone to serve someone else—a man and a woman in thick sweaters and carefree attitudes, maybe tourists—and he returned to find Eva's glass empty.

He glanced around, as if to see if anyone noticed, then refilled it.

Yes, he liked her, and as the wine spread through Eva, the knowledge lent her an anesthetic awareness of his every move, his every glance.

She tucked a strand of hair behind her ear. "Are you sure? I lost my wallet, too."

"I'll pour just as long as you're safe and sound here. You're in my care now."

As he left to serve an elderly gentleman who was interested in some cognac, the warmth in Eva turned sharp.

How long had it been since she'd been wanted?

Not since she was Underground, back when men would've died for one night with her.

Heavy-limbed, she toyed with the stem of her glass, in the mellow hold of the alcohol and attention now. Every time the barman checked on her, with his ginger hair and freckled hands busy on the glasses and counter, it became easier to forget the look on Frank's face, the rage in Breisi's reaction. Eva wondered if forgetfulness was what Dawn had found, too, years ago, when she would have sex with all those men Eva had heard about.

She and Dawn never talked about that, though. There were some things they'd never be able to discuss.

But here, now, Eva flirted with the idea that Dawn could've inherited all those needy sexual impulses from her mother, and Eva had only guided her own urges in a different way: she'd preferred to be admired by the masses instead of only a relative few.

An untouchable goddess who got off on being adored.

It might have been lonely if Eva hadn't been kept company by the hope that Frank would be hers again one day, after she persuaded him to come Underground, too. . . .

She went for another sip of wine, then slowed herself down.

How was she ever going to face Frank again after tonight?

Someone sat a seat away from her, but she didn't look up at whoever it was.

Not until the person placed a linen handkerchief next to her cocktail napkin.

Eva stared at the cloth for a moment, at the embroidered initials—"KN"—stitched in a corner.

Then she realized that she'd been crying.

Too embarrassed to acknowledge it, she ignored the handkerchief, using the paper napkin instead.

When she finished dabbing near her eyes, she pushed the handkerchief back to its owner, then looked up to thank him, anyway.

The warmth in her turned to heat as she found a man in a dark business suit, his chin-length black hair slicked away from a face with light brown eyes that angled in exotic appeal, his cheekbones high and defined.

"I only thought to offer," he said, his voice brushed by a British accent as well as another foreign quality.

Asian, she thought. Chinese and British?

Hong Kong?

She thought that maybe finding out would make her feel better as she turned her body toward him and did her best to smile as Eva Claremont would have done, once upon a better time.

SIXTEEN

Once Upon a Big Bad

"DID you program the alert system to isolate all Southwark cameras?" the new *custode* asked, mask off, voice modulator deactivated, hair stuck to her neck as the door to the monitor room whooshed shut behind her.

Nigel turned the swivel chair toward his sibling, gesturing to a cluster of bigger screens that boasted footage from the borough where she'd been earlier. "Done."

The keeper surveyed the screens, which revealed no odd activity as she'd seen earlier when she'd been investigating Southwark, where the mind-power woman had been running through the streets as if her life, or someone else's, depended on it.

That's how Lilly, who'd been let out for patrol, had first seen her—the female attacker who matched the schoolgirls' descriptions from last night. Dark hair flying out behind her as she ran toward the Bull and Cock Pub, athletic in her speed and style . . .

She'd immediately caught Lilly's notice from the roof where the *custode* had been scouting, hoping to find a reason for the fogged camera she'd discovered earlier.

The keeper had then moved in, using her night-vision goggles to watch this young woman through the window of the flat above the pub. And when Lilly had seen her aiming an illegal gun—naughty, naughty—as the female scoped the empty room, her interest had been snagged indeed.

Could this be one of the Queenshill attackers?

Lilly had set out to discover an answer, only wishing to stun the woman with a flash grenade, disabling her until Lilly could get her restrained for a round of questioning. And, if the interrogation had not panned out, Lilly would have released the subject.

Subtly, she touched her mouth, where she'd brushed her lips over the other woman's.

Maybe she would have released her.

The woman was by no means striking. She wasn't even pretty. But she was certainly intriguing. Lilly had underestimated her, and she liked that there were still some people in this world who could bring that about.

Unfortunately, she had not done as well as she'd hoped in fighting off the mind blasts that the woman used. Although Lilly's body had been adjusting nicely throughout activation and training, she'd found that engaging a true opponent was nothing like sparring. In real life, the blood boiled and the mind and body had to work in tandem, and that wasn't what had happened tonight.

But Lilly would improve.

"I must say," Nigel noted as she continued smiling to herself, "that you hit it on the head, the right place at the right time."

"I was peering at those screens all day long, remember? I just happened to notice a fogged lens near Cross Bones, and I thought it might prove worth my while to investigate."

"Even though I sent you to Queenshill for a follow-up."

"I was making my way over there. Eventually. I'll get to the sub-Underground and Mrs. Jones's tunnel later."

Her brother was wearing quite the expression—as if he wanted to chide her yet couldn't justify it in the face of her small success tonight.

Arrogance, his tight mouth nonetheless hollered.

"Nigel," she said. "Stop looking like such a prune. You do realize that I found one of the Queenshill attackers tonight, yeah? It *has* to be the female with the mind powers that Claudia described based on Della's description. She matched the details in appearance and behavior, and she was in the area of a camera malfunction. That's enough coincidence for me to go on. May we assume that she and her group reside somewhere in Southwark?"

"We could," Nigel said, turning back to the monitors. It chafed that he was doing everything within his power to avoid giving credit to the new *custode*.

Yet it'd been much like this while growing up, too. Charles had been the sweet younger brother while Nigel was the elder who seemed to think a little sister was no more than a thorn in his side. One night, Nigel had left to "strike out in the world," never to return. Then, years later, Charles, her favorite, had left school and departed home, as well.

She should have noticed how odd it was when her parents didn't grieve for Charles's absence or his lack of a full education, which they'd always insisted on for their children. She had only attributed their stoicism to their usual stiff upper lips, and their uncaring attitude toward her to a repressed longing to see their sons again. After all, Lilly knew that, long ago, they'd lost four other sons due to the Meratoliage curse—the heart defects. So her parents had learned to cope accordingly.

Then, all too soon, before any of her nephews had come of age, Lilly had been activated, the vision/tales put upon her.

That's when she had understood where Charles and Nigel had gone off to. She'd also realized the reason for her father's remoteness and occasional bitterness—he was a never-called *custode* who had been passed over for other keepers during his own prime.

She leaned against the console. "What do you mean by 'We could' assume that our attackers are based in Southwark? Your answer sounds rather passive."

Nigel shook his head, as if having to deal with a developmentally challenged charge. "Do you have proof that these attackers have the Underground itself in their sights? Or is it possible, just in the slightest, that they told our schoolgirls the truth—that they were genuinely seeking the company of other vampires and they stumbled upon a few of ours? Naturally, with Violet's and Della's immaturity, matters escalated and then fell to pieces, but can you blame the 'attackers' for defending themselves from the dogs and animals the girls set upon them at Queenshill?" He went back to the screens. "Why poke at them if they're only incidental?"

Lilly crossed her arms over her chest. "So you'd rather just keep monitoring them."

"Lilly. The Underground has survived all these years because the *custode*s refrained from overreacting. You've seen the visions. You know."

"But *custode*s have never come upon a nuisance like this before." She leaned toward him. "These attackers have help, Nigel. The jasmine you smelled in Mrs. Jones's room—it's somehow connected with an invisible entity who was out to chase me."

"You're certain that this 'invisible entity' wasn't part of that woman's mind powers?"

Lilly pushed away from the console. For all the good this was doing, she may as well have been talking to one of those grainy telly screens. If Nigel had been with her on patrol, he would have heard it—smelled it—screaming past her as she dodged into a building's crevice while the entity passed.

"Mark me," Nigel said, his gaze boring into hers. "There's a difference between what Underground vampires do and what we do. When they kill aboveground, it's done with runaways and no-goods who have already dropped out of their families and society. But these attackers could be different, and even Claudia, as questionable as she is, knew this and refrained from going after them. Mihas even used a bit of discretion."

Lilly's interest was piqued at his strong opinion about Claudia.

How would he take the news of her plan to dash her out of the community?

Then again, hadn't Nigel been a victim of the same male-devised hands-off philosophy that had got the Underground into such a vulnerable position in the first place?

She kept her mouth closed as he continued.

"These attackers," he said, "might be missed from society, and unless you're ready to take a chance on covering up their deaths, we keep monitoring until we must act."

"And if we ever find them tip-toeing around Highgate?"

He finally turned to her. "Then we rethink our position. We need more proof of their identities and intentions." He gestured to the Southwark screens. "To do otherwise might reveal us, and that's the last thing we need."

She knew that, while her instinct was all *she* needed, Nigel would respond only to steel-clad proof.

And there it was. Lilly was definitely on her own.

So be it.

"Then regarding Queenshill," she said. "I can go back there tonight, through the woodland sub-Underground entrance rather than the school's. We need to see if anyone made it past Mrs. Jones's room and into her private tunnel, since you were interrupted before you were able to cover that area earlier."

"If you don't mind, I'd prefer to take that on after my rest. Queenshill will still be there, deserted and sad without its little vampires in it." With the energy they absorbed during the Relaquory ritual, they could avoid slumber except for an hour or two per night cycle, even though this rest was still imperative for maximum performance. "Are you ready to take over the monitoring?"

"Ready." And she had an idea in mind to pass the time, too.

As Nigel retreated to their quarters, Lilly sat in the chair and, while keeping tabs on the main screens, began to access more of the previous footage, determined to catch sight of the attackers on camera.

Yet, this time, she brought up recent images from in and around Highgate.

A daunting job, to be certain, with all the hours she would have to cover. But if she could find any proof that the attackers had been anywhere nearby, perhaps Nigel would believe that the *custode*s were facing more than he knew.

While she did this, she also monitored a well-hidden camera that was located in the main Underground, its glass eye on the kitchens where Della waited in a cage among the male prey.

Anytime now, Lilly thought, wishing she could speed up the visions that had to be blooming in the vampire girl's mind.

Anytime . . .

ONCE, long, long ago, just before the vampire found himself in need of healing in the woodland cottage and much after the vampiress shared the ecstasy of bathing with the countess, there was a big bed in a hushed, candelabra-lit room in a country estate.

In that bed was the vampire, a seemingly human male who had been masquerading as a foreign noble at court so he might gain entrance to such high company, which he felt was his due.

He held a young auburn-tressed mortal girl in his lap, reaching between her legs, strumming her until she buried her smooth face against his neck in a fit of anxious, innocent response.

Delighted, he howled softly into her ear, and the girl giggled all the more, so nervous, so new to a nighttime rendezvous with a mysterious man about whom she knew so little.

Then the sound of a door easing open and shut caught the vampire's hearing, and he raised his face from the girl's fragrant hair.

When he saw his comrade in a corner, standing with his arms crossed, the vampire on the bed sighed.

"Is it too much to ask," he said, "for my valet to remain in his own quarters during certain times of the night?"

"Valet." The other blood brother had done away with his beard, and his brown hair, pulled into a queue, was dull in the dim light, his gaze just as flat.

"Yes, my valet." *The vampire ran a finger through the moistened folds of the girl on his lap, the curious virgin who was set to marry an old wealthy man by month's end.*

She winced into his neck, hiding her face from the intruder.

"Oh, now, now." The vampire kissed her forehead. "You have embarrassed Cerise. She did not anticipate an audience."

The interloper's eyes began to burn with ire. "I am ready to leave this place," he said, then added with a blood-brother mind connection, And I am *not* your valet.

The vampire sent his companion a warning glance, thinking that they should act like humans among humans—at least until it was too late for the pitiful prey. It was all part of the hunting.

"You know my invitation from Madame Bontecou to play here extends for more than a day or two," he said while nuzzling the girl.

"And I have not yet enjoyed all the natural delights to be found in the country."

She had started to tremble against him, and the vampire knew he had to finish this seduction soon before it soured.

But didn't everything? Even at court, where a certain clever wit was twisting folktales into new parlor distractions—stories meant to teach lessons to "attractive, well-bred young ladies"—the vampire had been chased away for fear that the tales would churn up the truth: that the rash of nearby woodland killings—new and *old—had served as too much inspiration for the storytelling.*

That these amusements would expose him.

Thus, a trip to the country, a change in location, was precisely what a vampire such as this one had required.

His blood brother used their Awareness to communicate again. So you plan on being careless here, as well? Just as careless as you were at court before you called me to cover all evidence of your follies?

Careless? *the vampire in bed volleyed.* I am not the one who has visited the old woman in *these* nearby woods for love spells, my friend. Just who is the careless party?

His comrade's gaze seemed wounded, and the vampire knew he had gone too far.

I am sorry, *he said.*

As if out of quiet desperation, his friend began to shift shape into one that had always pleased, that had always stoked the ever-burning fires in the gut of a vampire who never could satiate himself.

The vampire covered the girl's eyes, lest she see. Yet her face was still pressed against his neck, as if to erase herself from the situation altogether.

Not now, *the vampire in bed thought to his comrade after it had shifted fully.* Please. Later?

After a moment of stunned hesitation, his friend whipped back into another shape—one that could glide away almost undetected through the halls. Through existence, really.

His comrade then slunk out of the room, melancholy, leaving the vampire with such hunger, such thirst, that he looked down at the girl—the untainted font of blood to be had.

When she slowly looked up at him, she must have seen it in his face, because before his fangs emerged with terrible thrust and speed, before he twisted into the grotesque that he was, she heaved in a breath.

Yet when he tore into her throat, she ceased to breathe any longer, becoming merely one more body to dispose of after the vampire had finished. . . .

SEVENTEEN

London Babylon, Main Underground Kitchens

It was only the dependable onslaught of images—Della's lone constant in these past hours—that had kept her from grasping the bars of her cage and yelling for someone to release her.

To get her out and away from the tempting blood and scent of the boys in the cells around her.

Yet instead of going over that edge, Della had found that the visions were like morphine, something steady to sedate her while she lay on her side with her knees cradled against her chest.

As the most recent vision furrowed through her, she truly welcomed the sight of the blurred vampire with a young girl on his lap as he softly howled into her ear before going on to tear her apart. . . .

Upon finishing, the visual pieces gently settled into Della, as ingrained as all the others had become. But there was one jag of imagery that remained floating on top, as if reluctant to mix.

Howling.

It reminded her of Wolfie.

Just like Wolfie.

Della drew her knees closer to her chest, hugging, clinging.

She didn't want to believe that those visions featured her master. Yet was he the wounded vampire from the first one about the cottage, and now the creature with the girl on the bed?

Yes.

No.

Oh, she couldn't stop thinking that it very well might be him, just as surely as she believed the vampiress in the bathtub was Mrs. Jones, centuries ago, perhaps after she had first met Wolfie and he had claimed her as his mistress.

After all, hadn't a mistress been mentioned in the first vision with the woodland cottage? Hadn't that rescuing vampire—the vague blood brother—said that the wounded creature—Wolfie?—had a mistress back at court?

A question rustled around Della's mind.

Who was this other blood brother and where had *he* gone?

It was as if that one question had given birth to a slew of them: Could this blood brother somehow be connected to last night's attackers? *Had* the blood brother sent a troublemaking group to take over Wolfie's Underground for some inexplicable reason Della wasn't grasping?

Jealousy?

Revenge?

She rolled onto her back and stared at the ceiling of the cell, repeating to herself that her mind was playing tricks on her, conjuring warnings out of her misery and fear, giving her something to muse over besides the stirring scent of these boys around her.

But it did no good. Perhaps she would never be able to explain where the visions originated, yet her brain was in a frenzy to solve what they meant. To identify a clear face among the blurred features . . .

She felt something poke into her shoulder, and at first, she ignored the sensation, thinking it was only a part of another oncoming vision.

Then Della felt it again, and she jerked to all fours.

They have come to get me, she thought. *Wolfie and Mrs. Jones.*

Then she focused enough to spy Noreen on the other side of the bars, where her classmate was holding a long stick—a snooker cue that was sharpened at the blood-stained end for playtime with the boys in the Underground common areas.

Della arched her back, hissed at her, warning her off.

Noreen, clearly flushed with a recent intake of blood, took a crouched step backward, a strand of her red hair falling over one eye.

They stared at each other, the caged males around them suspending their cries.

Finally, Della relented, wishing she could find that morphine-like state once again as she crept to the corner of her cell.

Noreen was most likely here because she had been excited by the play in the common rooms and had found that easy blood wasn't enough. It never was for their kind: they were made of sugar, spice, and anything they could gnaw their way through. Unlike most girls, the wonders of entering a sexual world did not drive them. Violence did, and the letting of blood marked a very special rite of passage into a never-ending girlhood for Wolfie's darlings.

Noreen cocked her head at Della, then slowly stood, clutching the cue stick. "I only thought I might get here before Polly did, because when she does come, it'll be with a bigger toy."

"Then let her come."

"Della."

She glanced at Noreen. It was the first time Della had ever heard her classmate's voice harden beyond a light note.

But Noreen didn't give anything away with an expression; her face was half-hidden by her red hair as she bent to undo the top of a Thermos flask that Della had just now noticed by the foot of the cage.

Noreen had brought blood. Della could smell it.

She leapt to the door of the cell, landing in a crouch, while the boys on both sides began to beg Noreen to notice them. To suck their cravings away.

"Belt up," Noreen told them. Then to Della, "Hold out your arm, you."

But Della had already rolled up a sleeve and presented herself, the juices in her mouth hot, her fangs pushing at her gums in anticipation. The other girl dripped the blood onto Della's skin.

At the first splash, her pores opened like desperate baby mouths, gulping in as much blood as they could, and Della groaned with the intake—the sucking, intoxicating absorption that made her tingle in her belly and between her legs.

Her hunger grumbled, awakened from its stupor.

Yet all too soon, there was no more to imbibe, and Della grabbed at Noreen's wrist just as the other girl pulled away from the cage with her emptied container.

With an impatient huff, Noreen twisted her way out of Della's grip. "It was dicey enough getting this bit of a meal to you. I'm not about to stay and risk even more."

"Why did you even dare it? There are cameras round, you know."

Noreen cradled the Thermos flask. "Pity, I suppose."

Della had spent over a year with this girl: They were classmates of a special breed. They had been good friends.

And, truthfully, they had been more family than either one had ever known.

"Noreen," Della said, sensing how closed the other girl was to her—all shields up and blocking any classmate thought-links.

Nonetheless, she reached out with her mind, rubbing up against Noreen's mental walls, wanting so badly to come in.

The other girl's gaze softened, connecting to Della's need, yet she still didn't drop her defenses all the way.

Della whimpered low in her throat.

Noreen sighed, as if extending this one token. "Perhaps I understood what you did to Violet and seeing you punished for it doesn't sit well. Perhaps . . ." She glanced down, then back up. "Perhaps I even wish it had happened sooner."

Encouraged, Della kept pressing her thoughts against Noreen's closed ones, and when her classmate finally gave in, it was like breaking down a door to a clean, uncluttered room that bore a resemblance to Della's own mind before it had become so foreign and possessed.

In their link, Della felt everything Noreen had been suppressing: The glee when Della had impaled Violet with the tree branch last night. The justice when Della had sent the ravens.

Then the other girl's gaze hardened, just as her voice had earlier.

Violet was irredeemable, Noreen thought, *and if you ask me to say that out loud or think it in front of Polly or Mrs. Jones or Wolfie, I won't. I've learned how to stay out of trouble the best I can. I've learned to fade when I need to. You used to be good at that, too.*

Then Noreen nudged Della out of her mind, closing herself off once again.

But Della knew the reason. Her classmate would continue to fade as long as she thought it was the easiest method of survival.

Yet it wasn't, Della thought. It was the toughest way of all.

Noreen brushed a hand over her long skirt, clearly attempting to set matters back to normal. To fade away again.

"I'll be leaving now," she said, "while everyone's still distracted by playtime with Wolfie. He's in the middle of it all in the tavern room, with the girls scratching at him as he laughs and urges them on. And who knows when the cat will be back."

Mrs. Jones.

A flash of that vampiress in the tub with the hanging, dripping girl roared through Della.

As Noreen walked toward a steel kitchen basin, where she no doubt intended to clean the Thermos flask of its blood, Della stopped her progress by knocking at her friend's mind.

Reluctantly, the other girl opened up again.

Mrs. Jones, Della thought, because saying it out loud would be unwise. *Be careful of her, all right? Be very, very careful.*

I always do my best. Noreen turned toward the basin.

Della halted her friend again by thinking, *Briana, Sharon, Blanche . . . ?*

At the list of their departed classmates, Noreen glanced over her shoulder, the anguish of losing their companions mapped all over her expression.

Della grasped the cell bars as the boys next to her watched both vampires, back and forth, while cowering in their own cages.

You've always played the dancing jester, Noreen, Della thought. *But you've also wondered about what became of our classmates. Haven't you? You just never thought about it too much, because you didn't wish to know the answer.*

I only wondered why they left.

You never saw a pattern? You never had questions?

Noreen stared at the Thermos flask in her hands. She was fading.

Yet Noreen was still open to a mind-link, and Della took the advantage and shared a few of the vision images she had been experiencing, every picture like a slap that caused her to cringe while giving it.

But when she had finished, it felt like a burden shared.

The Thermos flask fell from Noreen's hands and clattered to the rock floor.

You think Mrs. Jones . . . she began, and there were mental tears soaking her thoughts.

Della nodded, even while keeping what had to be the worst part of the visions to herself.

Wolfie.

Did he know about Mrs. Jones's baths, if she were indeed the one taking them? Did he know what precisely caused the youthful glow Della had noticed on their housematron's flesh recently?

Or had Mrs. Jones managed to keep the secret for centuries?

Yes, that had to be it, she thought, seizing upon the excuse. Wolfie would never be an accomplice to the sacrifice of his darlings, his little loves.

It had to be all Mrs. Jones.

Noreen had wandered closer, a hand over her mouth, as if to keep herself from screaming, just as Della had been trying to do for hours now.

And Della had been so hoping Noreen might only tell her that the images were rubbish.

Perhaps if Della explained a bit more.

Every six months, she thought to her friend, *one of our class disappeared. There were always justifications: Running away. Disinterested parents suddenly becoming interested enough to claim their child from Queenshill.*

Tears were seeping from Noreen's eyes now, and Della felt the oncoming ache of them, too.

Their beloved classmates. Their friends.

Their trust in the elder who had been tasked with protecting them when they had been told over and over that, in the Underground, they would be cared for by Wolfie, always.

This was no rubbish.

It was somehow all too true, wasn't it?

Della forced herself to continue. *That was the reason Mrs. Jones would never reveal who was in her select Queenshill vampire classes before us. She was hoping we wouldn't discover a pattern of disappearances.*

Noreen's hands had only tightened over her mouth. More horror. More tears.

Della looked away, trying hard not to picture each of her friends hanging above a bathtub, their blood slipping from a gash in their throats. Unlike humans, vampires like Blanche, Briana, and Sharon would not have fully perished with only a cut to the throat, for if they were dead, their bodies would have fully disappeared, just as Mrs. Jones had always warned.

They would have still been as alive as a vampire could be.

Torture, Della thought. They would have needed to be tortured and somehow restrained mentally as well as physically for Mrs. Jones to procure the blood that was still young and fairly pure from the class of new vampires.

Her very own handpicked harvest.

What should we do? Noreen asked.

Shaken, Della looked into her schoolmate's saucered gaze. *Act as if you don't know anything, and don't ever go anywhere alone with Mrs. Jones.*

But should we tell Wolfie?

The question rocked Della, even if somewhere in the black of her mind, she had been wondering the same.

No, she answered. *Let's not.*

Was it because she feared breaking his heart if he knew what Mrs. Jones had been doing?

Or was it because she was scared witless that he did know?

Della could tell Noreen was stashing the Wolfie questions away, too, as her classmate reached up to grasp a cell bar just above one of Della's fists.

Then what happens now? Noreen asked.

Della already knew. In a way, she had known ever since Wolfie had put her in this cage with no assurances of ever getting out.

She hadn't realized until now that he had refrained from promising anything to her, even though Wolfie always tried to make things better for his charges.

Do you know what's in store for you, *little girl?*

The reminder mauled her, and she found herself giving impromptu instructions to Noreen, unable to hold back.

Perhaps a short, anonymous note for the others to find, Della mind-thought. *Disguise your writing. Mention something very cryptic about the patterns of Queenshill students' disappearances. Leave it in a Queenshill girls' room and be there when they find it, then destroy the note before anyone else can see. It will be as if it never existed, yet if the previous Queenshill girls feel as strongly as we do—if they haven't forgotten their pain in all the excess down here, as Mrs. Jones probably hoped they would—they'll talk and spread the subject, hoping for answers they might have never found about their friends. Perhaps they will even discover courage to find those answers now. And no one will know who left the note unless you let down your shields, Noreen.*

The other girl seemed confused, but then understanding gradually dawned.

Della moved her hand up the bar, covering her friend's.

There's power in numbers and in the hurt of losing friends. If any of the surviving members of previous Queenshill classes had suspicions, we'll know soon enough. If it doesn't work, we'll both keep up shields as to what we know. By then, we'll realize there's no hope for discovering anything.

Noreen shook her head. *What are you saying?*

Della backed away from the bars and absently ran her fingers over the slim red tie that all the girls in her class had chosen to wear because it reflected their oneness.

I'm saying we need to get to the truth before it gets to us, Della answered as she thought of the vampiress in the tub again.

But then, just under the pulse of that image, she saw the vampire in the bed, tearing and gnawing at the girl he had once held on his lap.

EIGHTEEN

The Drunk Patrol

Dawn had basically guilt-tripped Breisi, who'd already been put through the remorse wringer by Frank, into escorting her to the wine bar where Eva was hanging out. They needed to get her mom back while avoiding any more encounters with that shadow girl. Breisi had already said that the only reason she'd blazed over from headquarters was because Natalia had reported that Dawn's earpiece had gone out, and that news hadn't sat well with the Friend.

What a pal, huh? But Dawn knew her Friend would defend her and probably even Eva, like a ghosty wildcat if it came right down to it. Breisi was too upright to ever really turn her back on someone.

That was the hope, anyway.

They were moving at a rapid clip along Borough High Street on their way to Tooley Street, where the bar was supposed to be located. At the same time, Dawn kept up a conversation with Breisi.

It didn't matter that people were staring—for all they knew, she had a Bluetooth device on.

"Believe me," she said while keeping one hand in her jacket pocket, her fingers touching the reassuring heft of the mini flamethrower. "I do know where you're coming from, Breez. I'd have been a jealous wreck in the same situation, too. I don't fault you for that."

"Listen to you—the voice of experience," Breisi said next to her.

Dawn thought about Matt Lonigan, who'd almost had her convinced back in L.A. that she might be able to do the boyfriend thing for once.

Breisi seemed to realize her verbal blunder. *"That didn't come out the way—"*

"Sure it did." Dawn cupped a near-frozen hand over her nose as they maintained their tempo. It felt like half of her face was about to fall off from the chill. Jolly old England didn't have anything on the jollier Southern California weather.

Breisi took advantage of the awkward pause to fly up to scan the rooftops, then dip back down by Dawn's side again, and when she continued the discussion, Dawn sighed, occupying herself by scanning for any sign of Shadow Girl.

"Really, Dawn, I've tried to have patience."

"Yup, you sure have."

This girlfriend talk was harder than it sounded, but Dawn hung in there, mostly because Breisi seemed in need of some hard-core counseling.

"I knew Frank had a history with Eva and that it wouldn't disappear anytime soon. But I was ready to weather that."

"And you did for a long time. I know—I got it. You just hit a wall tonight." Dawn thought of Eva walking into Frank's room, her palm bleeding. "A big, fat, bloody wall."

"I'm glad you understand, Dawn. It's only that . . ." She faded off.

It didn't take a PhD to realize that Breisi's shut-out of Eva tonight was bothering her, so Dawn spared her Friend the agony of continuing. Or maybe she was sparing *herself* from hearing it.

"Breez, no matter who you are—a spirit, a person, whatever—there's a time when everybody has to draw a line. There's only so much you can handle, and sometimes, when you get to that point, a person who's generally a little nicer than others regrets taking the stand they need to take because it isn't 'nice' at all."

Dawn paused as she played chicken with a drunk guy in a green and red scarf who wouldn't move to his side of the pavement. She won as he swerved to her right, where he should've been in the first place. Hell, even though she was a foreigner, she knew how traffic worked in London.

"Sometimes," she finished, "you can't be nice. I just wish it hadn't come down to you finding that line with Eva."

They turned onto a crowded Duke Street, and on impulse, Dawn slowed her speed walking, lifting her hand to feel Breisi skim the tips of her fingers. The airy contact was just as reassuring as the slickness of her flamethrower.

Then she began walking full throttle again, and Breisi's essence lingered behind, like she'd been taken aback by Dawn's almost-affectionate gesture.

That made Dawn speed up even more, hunching into her jacket, mostly in embarrassed reaction to what she'd just done. To forget it, she combed her gaze over her surroundings for any red eyes in the night. Any shadows bounding over the rooftops to track and maybe even attack for another round of attempted questioning.

A buzz traveled her skin, maybe at the idea of being watched and hunted. But she was up to the challenge of smacking Shadow Girl around if they came face-to-face.

The phrase lingered like the light fog clouding the streetlights.

Face-to-face.

She ran the back of a hand over her mouth, wiping, remembering how the girl had brushed her lips there.

Discomfort got to her, so she called Breisi's name, just for the company.

A couple of people gave Dawn and the space around her disconcerted glances, but she just stared them down as she muttered to her Friend, putting closure to the conversation they'd been having.

"Let's just make sure that nobody associated with us—and I mean *nobody*—is ever left in the lurch like Eva was tonight, no matter what dumb thing they do. Then we'll never have to get all touchy-feely, Oprah-couch-conversation again. Okay?"

A whisk of jasmine traveled over Dawn's head. *"In the future, I'll find another way to remind Eva where she stands with Frank. And when this hunt is over, we'll find a better blood source for him, no matter how much hers does for his taste buds."*

A skip of panic interrupted Dawn's pulse. Was Breisi talking about cutting Eva loose?

Dawn tried to figure out why that bothered her. Maybe having her mom supply Frank with sustenance meant a lot to Dawn, too, in some surreal way. Maybe the blood tie between her parents was another way of keeping her family knotted together and she didn't want to undo it.

Resting her hand against the pocketed mini flamethrower, she led Breisi past pub goers in their cheery scarves and coats, past The London Dungeon, a tourist attraction marked by a hovering sign that stated, "Enter at your peril."

Kiko had taken Eva here once. He'd loved the whole torture-as-grand-entertainment vibe, with its Jack the Ripper and Sweeney Todd flamboyance, yet Eva had avoided all Dawn's questions about her visit there. Dawn had just assumed that maybe her mom hadn't loved it quite as much.

But had her lack of response meant something else?

Had Eva gotten flashbacks of her own time in a blood-steeped world?

Had she . . . liked it?

In light of what had happened with Frank tonight, Dawn had cause to wonder, so she walked even faster until they came to the wine bar—a bright, full-windowed establishment with a burst of foliage out front. A black cab was just pulling up to the curb, and Dawn ran to it, confirming that he was here to pick them up since she'd called for a ride earlier.

After the elderly gent, who was decked out in a newsboy cap, responded that he'd be at her service, she asked him to wait while she fetched Eva. Then she subtly addressed Breisi as she walked toward the bar.

"Wait here?"

"I'd prefer to stay as far away as possible," the Friend said.

Boy, Dawn thought while she pulled open the glass door and entered. Nothing like a good catfight between dysfunctional creatures to liven things up.

She came to a fancy bar framed by bottles, the scent of wine, cheese, and fresh bread seeming utterly out of place in her world right now. Going to a corner of the counter, she waited for the bartender to notice her.

He had reddish hair that stuck up a bit near the back, accompanied by freckles, all of which made him seem nerdy and sporty, like he rowed in one of those boats she sometimes saw on the Thames. The type of decent guy who usually took one glance at Dawn and quietly tried to avoid looking at her ever again.

But he did look, probably because Dawn was a car wreck in her tomboy jacket that covered her ripped and bloodied shirt, her skirt, and postfight hair.

"Hey," she said as he braced his hands on the bar, towel in hand. "I'm looking for a blond woman, fortyish—"

"With bare feet and a duchess's bearing?" He gestured toward the back of the bar, where faux candlelight burned from sconces near a line of high wooden booths. "She ventured back that way."

Dawn caught a nick of something like tightness in the guy's tone. "You the one who loaned her his mobile phone?"

"I'd be the one, yes."

"Then thank you. I appreciate you looking out for her."

"Was glad to be of aid. She . . ."

Dawn waited for him to finish, but he only began wiping down the bar.

"Go ahead," she said.

He stopped, then laughed. But it wasn't a ha-ha laugh. Like his words, it had some tension to it.

"She makes the rounds, your mum," he said. "Doesn't she?"

As Dawn tried to figure out what he meant by that, he stepped over to some customers who wanted to order.

And she kept watching him, even as she went to the rear of the bar, where there were murmurs from the patrons nursing their reds and whites over plates with food that wouldn't keep a sparrow happy.

Dawn looked around. Looked again.

But she didn't find Eva.

All right. Maybe Dawn had misunderstood the bartender and her mom was in another spot. There was a stairway leading downstairs. Maybe Eva had gone there?

Or had she left altogether?

Dawn's fingers curled into her palms in a flash of worry.

Or had something taken Eva . . . ?

Turning around, she darted toward the front, powered by the chill running through her veins.

Yet when she saw what had to be Eva's long, slim, barefoot leg sliding into a booth, as if she had just returned from someplace else and was sitting down again, Dawn halted.

Then she gingerly stepped toward the booth.

With each thud of Dawn's pulse, Eva became more visible.

Her mom's hair was loose and finger-tangled, draped on her shoulders and clouded near her face like she was partially hiding behind the flow of it. And she had this look in her brown eyes . . . a dreaminess. Same as the languid smile she was wearing.

Drunk, Dawn thought.

So much for Eva taking what she'd done with Frank seriously.

As Dawn started getting angry again, her mom leaned back in the booth, then slowly raised her gaze to Dawn as if she felt her watching.

After blinking, like she'd caught sight of reality in the form of her daughter, Eva gradually straightened in her seat, caught.

But caught doing what?

"Mom?" Dawn asked. Like, duh, maybe it wasn't Eva and she had to make sure.

Her mother made a show of glancing at her slim golden watch while straightening her décolletage or whatever the more fashionable people called it. Her hand was bandaged—evidence of what she'd done to Frank.

Dawn spoke before her mother could. "I know—I took longer than I thought I would. There were some . . . complications. Are you . . . ?"

"I'm fine," Eva said, slurring a bit. Smiling like the cat who'd eaten the canary . . . and the parakeet . . . and even the dog. "Time to go?"

"Yeah, time to go. You mind telling me how much you had?"

Eva waved her hand in airy dismissal. "Not much. I didn't have my wallet so the barman spotted me a glass or two."

Here, she made a dizzy-drunk gesture with her fingers, parceling out just how little her intake might've been. After she inspected the measurement, her fingers indicated more. Then, with a small laugh, even more.

"This is so uncool," Dawn said, extending her hand to help Eva stand.

"I think the barman liked me. But then . . ."

Eva's comment was taken over by a secretive smile.

"God, what?" Dawn asked.

Her mom hesitated. Then she got that goofball smile again.

"I came back to this section to wait for you," she said, almost coyly.

She headed for the exit, leaving a trail of interested gazes from the customers along the way, their necks craned at the barefoot lady lording it past them.

Always the queen, Dawn thought, the old envy creeping back on her. Always the superstar, even when nobody knew who the hell she was these days.

As they passed the bartender, he watched Eva, a frown on his face.

From behind the fluff of her hair, she sweetly thanked him, and Dawn pulled her by the sleeve toward the door. She wasn't about to play porno nanny.

"Drunk moms aren't cute," Dawn said as she guided Eva outside and toward the cab.

"I'm hardly drunk. Just . . . tipsy."

She said it like she was a teenager who'd been experimenting with booze for the first time, and Dawn wanted to wring her neck, especially after everything she'd put the team through tonight. As it was, she, Breisi, and the rest of the Friends guarding headquarters would have to hope that nothing would end up watching Eva and Dawn slip in through one of the back entrances.

If there was any karma in this world, Dawn thought, Eva would get a killer hangover.

She put her mom in the cab. "We've got a long talk ahead of us."

"Mmmm," Eva said as she curled into a corner of the backseat.

Breisi whooshed by just as Dawn was climbing in, too, and Dawn gave the spirit a don't-you-say-anything glance.

To Breisi's credit, she stayed mum.

After settling in, Dawn turned to Eva to say something else, but she only found her mom with her eyes closed, a sedate smile brushing her lips as if she were finally having nice dreams.

Anger easing—but not by much—Dawn left her alone for the time being, thinking that maybe they all could use a sweet dream or two.

NINETEEN

The Test

The next day, in an oak-laden alcove that hid their modified Sedona just outside Queenshill School, Dawn glanced away from her window's view of green fields and toward her thick, black wrist-watch.

A little after four o'clock, and the sun was already setting here across the Atlantic pond.

"Unless your watch has a time travel feature," Jonah said from the backseat, "I don't see how bothering with it's going to get Kiko and Natalia here any sooner."

Dawn shot him an exasperated look in the rearview mirror. Like her, he was dressed in a disguise, but instead of coming off like a student, he was more of a maintenance man with his rugged brown coat, cords, and a flannel shirt. He'd also tied his hair back into a poet's tail, like Lord Byron on a lumberjack kind of day, then topped that off with a plain baseball cap.

Sitting comfortably, he reclined against the passenger-side door, his long legs stretched from the left to the right, his hands clamped behind his head.

"When someone puts you in the backseat," Dawn said, "that's a strong hint that they don't want to hear even a peep from you."

"Even with all the modifications on this hunk of junk, I don't think your banishing me to the backseat will make me disappear." He compounded that with a grin.

Okay, he had her. She couldn't wish him away because Jonah might be the only means of getting Costin to those rooms below the surface, where they'd be heading just as soon as Kiko and Natalia arrived from their Friend-escorted appointment with the historian at the university. Hopefully, the two had gleaned some intel about Thomas Gatenby, the long-deceased man who'd funded Queenshill and could have a connection to their vampires.

But more importantly, today was the day they'd all see if Costin could sense any master vibes up close and personal in those vamp rooms, where he'd be unblocked by the earth.

It was the big test, and Dawn couldn't stop fidgeting in the front seat. It wasn't even that she was jittery about sneaking back into that dorm, because the Friends had discovered that there was a school event—a meeting where the prefects would address the students then host a concert on the main campus that would take away a lot of traffic from the housing area. No, she was just nervous about the possibility of Costin not being able to sense anything at all in those rooms.

Then again, Dawn thought, catching herself tapping an impatient foot, maybe she wasn't too stoked about having Natalia with them on this trip, either—a decision they'd come to this morning when Dawn was forced to admit that they really should bring a psychic who seemed to have a sixth sense about the presence of vamps. Since Dawn had done the preliminary scoping of Mrs. Jones's room yesterday, it was time to use their bloodhounds to uncover more details.

In the backseat, Jonah said, "So what's around here to eat?"

Dawn had the feeling he was asking for a bite. "Not me. You can make do with part of a bag in the cooler in back."

"Not even a nip?"

"You took more than the small amount I can handle last night."

"You know that your blood is the best for Costin. It powers us more than any other."

That was no lie, but she had the feeling any blood would do for Jonah himself.

"Cooler," she said with finality.

She heard him rustling around in back for the blood, then drinking his fill. Afterward, he kicked back again.

Then he began to whistle softly.

"Why don't you just rest," she said. "And by that, I mean your mouth."

"I don't need any," he said, gesturing toward a dark-tinted window. "Besides my regular rest today, I had a good catnap on the way up here under all the blankets that were piled on me. I'm set."

"That's more than I can say about Eva," Dawn muttered.

"What?" Jonah asked, even though she knew damned well he'd caught it with his uberhearing.

"Forget it."

When they'd left, her mom had still been lolling in bed with the covers over her head. It looked like that karmic hangover had come around after all.

But maybe a nice, long nap for Eva was a good thing, because without Natalia or Costin there, Frank had needed to stay back at headquarters to organize communications. Breisi had, not so mysteriously, decided to remain behind, too, so the longer Eva stayed in the guest room, the better, and maybe she knew it.

Dawn stilled her restless foot again. No need to get jumpy. Everything would go okay, from the drama at home to Costin's test to the safeguarding of headquarters, where a number of Friends were posted in case the team needed to stand against any vamps—or shadow girls—dumb enough to bring the fight above-ground.

Yet that hadn't kept the team behind brick walls. Hell, no. Fear of attack would get them nowhere. The only way they would advance was to keep on investigating, whether or not it meant that they had to disguise themselves in public and use one of the back headquarter entrances like sneaky sneakers.

Jonah leaned forward, and Dawn shifted in her seat when she felt an electric awareness of him—of the body she'd been so intimate with hundreds of times when Costin was dominant.

"Just so we have this straight," she said, "you follow my lead out there. Are you clear on that?"

"You've already drilled it into my head."

"Your head's pretty thick."

He came closer, enough for his words to stir a few stray hairs on the back of her neck from the short blond wig she was wearing.

"*Whose* head is thick?" he asked.

"Don't you start bitching at me again about last night, Jonah. I went after Eva because there was no other choice."

"You could've waited until Breisi simmered down. Or I might've been able to talk Kalin into helping instead."

Outside the windshield, branches bobbed against the graying sky. Probably Kalin, who'd insisted on accompanying Jonah here.

As Dawn kept track of the tree's motion, she wondered if the Friend would really have gone against Breisi's wishes or if Kalin owed more allegiance to her group than to Jonah.

She filed the question away, just as she had so many others that might be useful in the future.

"In any case," Jonah added, "you almost got captured by that shadow girl when you went hightailing it out of headquarters, and you put the team at risk."

"I didn't expect rescue or backup. I told all of you to stay put."

"Well, aren't you the anti–princess in a tower."

Dawn huffed out a breath, hoping he'd sit back against the door again. As far as she was concerned, the encounter with the shadow girl had only given them more information to use.

So what if she hadn't told the team about the strangest part—the girl's mouth brushing over hers? Dawn thought that she'd just leak that info to Kiko later, when she could laugh about it instead of feeling a little . . .

God, what was the word? Not violated. Just . . .

Surprised?

Refusing to rehash the scene—she'd been doing that off and on all night while trying to rest—Dawn watched as a lone raindrop hit the windshield.

Jonah sat back, thank goodness.

But he still reminded her he was there by saying, "Do you feel it?"

Her hand went to her book bag, where her weapons were waiting. "Feel what? Vibes? Some kind of Awareness you're developing?"

"Calm it down, hotshot. I'm only wondering if *you're* feeling watched. The shadow girl might be around, you know, here, there . . . everywhere."

At the false alarm, Dawn relaxed—sort of. And it wasn't because she welcomed another round with Shadow Girl. Hearing casual speech in Jonah's own mild tone—not Costin's brooding, mysterious cadence—always kept her edgy.

That's when Natalia and Kiko pulled up in a second black Sedona that had been subtly tricked out with protective outfitting and weapons.

Natalia got out of the driver's side, wearing a dark blond wig, creased pinstriped pants, a creamy sweater, plus an overcoat with a scarf and gloves in her own version of schoolgirl garb. Kiko came around from the other side of the vehicle, decked out in black cargos and boots. He was going to stay behind, off campus, to play backup, just in case something happened.

That was highly unlikely, though, Dawn thought, especially with itching-for-action Jonah around.

The duo got into Dawn's vehicle, Kiko staking out his usual spot up front, Natalia in back by Jonah. Dawn pressed a button near the steering wheel to prepare the outside UV lights if they were suddenly needed.

Kiko scanned Dawn's own schoolgirl getup, which consisted of newish jeans and a turtleneck with a dark, fashionable, thick raincoat this time. No damned skirts for her.

"You look like the preppy activist on campus," he said.

"And you look like you're in a pretty good mood. You get some decent juice during your interview?"

Kiko nodded. "I figured me and my Padawan could hash through what we learned, then give you the scoop when we got here."

At his comment, the apprentice Natalia's full cheeks turned pink, but Dawn thought that might be more out of excitement for getting to go belowground with the team than anything.

Natalia had also taken out a colored sheet, which looked like it'd been spit out of a computer. It featured a proud poof of a guy with sharp features and a Victorian wardrobe straight out of *The Prestige*.

Damn, Dawn loved that movie.

"Thomas Gatenby," she said.

"Right." Kiko pointed a small finger at the man's peacock stance. "Would you ever guess he was a ladies' dude?"

Jonah offered his own take. "Appearances can deceive. We know that better than anyone."

Dawn bristled at the "we." But he was here, a part of the team, whether she liked it or not.

From a speaker in the dashboard, Frank's voice interjected. "Breisi's telling me to ask if Natalia or Kik had any visions connected with this interview about Gatenby?"

Kiko shook his head. "I didn't get to touch anything that belonged to the man, so I didn't get any psychometric readings."

"And there's no precognitive help from me," Natalia said.

The two psychics exchanged a glance that probably only they could understand. Dawn thought it might be about some kind of bonding moment between two so-called experts who hadn't come through as much as they would've liked.

As Dawn looked away, it felt like Kiko had gone across a big, unreachable space toward Natalia, getting all buddylike with the new girl just as he had with Dawn when she'd first joined the team.

But that was silly, she thought. Kiko didn't belong to Dawn.

No one really did.

Another raindrop splatted against the windshield, and she reached for her umbrella—or "brolly" as it was called around here—to have it ready for when she finally got to go outside.

"So what *did* you guys get?" she asked, and it sounded abrupt, even if she didn't mean it to be.

Jonah raised an eyebrow at her, but she put him out of mind.

Kiko, who usually jumped all over any opportunity to showcase his smarts, gestured to Natalia, encouraging her to talk.

She grinned at him, then started up. "Per Dr. Hopkins, who has made a career out of studying colorful local characters, Gatenby was once the toast of society. At the same time, he was considered to be eccentric enough to have some mystery about him. He often took secretive trips out of town, leaving very little information behind. There is a distinct lack of journals or letters, for instance. Dr. Hopkins said that oral tradition—nothing written—maintains that Gatenby took up with a group who had a terrible effect on him, and these friends even caused his familial relationships to grow distant. The family worked hard to cover up these acquaintances—the Gatenby clan was social-climbing and would brook no scandal—yet there was always unsubstantiated talk about their very own black sheep."

So he had pals, Dawn thought. Friends who had led Gatenby astray.

"Great," she said. "Could be that those buddies of his are linked to the vamps we tangled with the other night . . . and maybe they involve even more than that."

Like a blood brother?

Had one of those friends even insinuated himself far enough into Gatenby's life to overtake it for the purposes of an Underground?

Kiko couldn't help himself—he'd stayed quiet long enough. "We didn't ask Dr. Hopkins about vampires—the conversation wasn't opening itself to it—but it sounds like they could've been involved, don't it?"

"Especially," Natalia added, "since Gatenby's inheritance upon his parents' untimely deaths began to be spent in ways that didn't resemble him. Before, he wasn't a notable supporter of charities, and when he donated land for what came to be Queenshill, it was quite a surprise. He also spent his fortune like . . . how would you say it? . . . like water, as well."

Jonah spoke. "What happened to the money when he died?"

Natalia held up her hands, an empty gesture. "Gone. All of it. No trace."

"And how did he die?" Dawn asked.

Kiko answered. "Tuberculosis. There're medical records that say so, but Dr. Hopkins has been looking into whether or not they were forged."

Right. Undergrounds always tried to tie up their loose ends.

"Before his death," Natalia added, "he was a recluse. Dr. Hopkins couldn't even identify a stable home for him. No one seemed to know where he'd gone."

"Reclusive?" Jonah asked.

As Natalia nodded, Dawn checked him, curious about what expression he might be wearing. He'd been a rich recluse himself when Costin had found and recruited him.

Easy pickings, those discontented guys with lots of dough.

But Jonah only looked thoughtful. Dawn wasn't so used to that.

He said, "And Dr. Hopkins doesn't know the identity of these friends?"

Both Natalia and Kiko shook their heads before she said, "*No one* seems to know who they were, although there are local rumors—legends, really—about sightings of Gatenby in Highgate before his parents died."

"Highgate," Dawn said.

They all looked at one another while her pulse picked up momentum. Not long ago, part of the team had gone to Highgate Cemetery, where Natalia had clocked in some pretty heavy discomfort from what they thought might be a nearby bloodsucker presence. But they'd attributed it to the legend of the Highgate Vampire, who was said to haunt the graveyard.

But now . . . ?

"Looks like we might have ourselves a good lead," Dawn said.

As she congratulated the two on their work, Natalia beamed and Kiko shrugged, as if taking his due as he checked over his projectile weapons and blades. Jonah just peered out the darkened window, a faint smile lighting his mouth—a cool customer who didn't seem that affected by what they had to do now.

Go under the ground to those vampire rooms.

Dawn had to give it to him. He was brave. Maddening but brave.

While Kiko stayed in the vehicle—where Dawn noticed one last look exchanged between the psychics—she checked that their new pulsers were working, then trooped with Natalia to the stone fence that separated Queenshill's land from the road. They were taking a different way onto the campus than usual, pretending like she and Natalia had left the assembly early and were strolling the property with their umbrellas overhead. After they arrived at the dorm and gave the all clear, Jonah would speed over to meet them, then they'd see to the abandoned underground rooms.

Dawn helped Natalia over the fence, and they began walking, keeping radio silence for now.

Luckily, the Friends who were already on campus had come up with an idea to take the place of camera clouding. They'd discovered that, with at least two of them, they could exert enough pressure against the stubborn cameras to adjust their positions, and they were hoping to push the devices off-kilter so the resulting pictures wouldn't show Dawn and Natalia at all.

Problem was, this technique took away Friend power: two or more had to do the job of one.

Soon enough, Dawn and Natalia came to a path, and they took it toward the dorms, which waited under a sky that was shedding sprinkles. Kalin was somewhere behind them, hardly as buddy-buddy as Breisi usually was, but things got less awkward when Greta the Friend greeted them.

With every step, Dawn's excitement grew, the pulser thudding at her chest like a counterheartbeat.

Once, a few months after the team had brought down the Hollywood Underground, Costin had told her that there was more than one way to destroy a vampire community.

Chaos.

Introduce a hint of suspicion and trouble to an Underground, and there was normally a domino effect, he'd said. With chaos, any vampire who had problems with a master would have an opening to confront him at a sign of weakness. Take away another constant—like the illusion of safety—and change could take out a community hour by hour.

Dawn had seen the theory in motion in L.A., where the vampires had begun collapsing under the weight of their own machinations and paranoia. Chaos had definitely helped the team at first . . . until Dawn had introduced her own brand of it into the equation.

Or maybe it'd all gone wrong when Costin had stayed too long out of body during the ultimate attack and had to pay for it when Dawn had to save him.

But what could she have done differently? she wondered. They'd been successful in wiping out the community, yet how could she have avoided the sacrifices she'd forced?

Natalia laid a hand on Dawn's arm, her fingers wrapping around it as they neared the dorms.

Dawn looked down to find the new girl pale, her breathing fast.

As a newbie, Dawn had been this freaked out, so without really thinking much, she rested a hand on Natalia's shoulder.

"No sweat," Dawn said. "You've been in the field before. You did fine then and you'll do great now."

Natalia's nod was brusque, and Dawn guided her team member along until they came to the door, which was propped open with a dictionary like last time.

Actually, everything seemed kind of rote as Dawn brought

Natalia up the same stairway and down the same hall while the Friends manipulated cameras and distracted any girls who weren't over at the theater on the main campus.

As she'd done before, Dawn put on her gloves, picked the lock, then urged Greta and Kalin ahead of her and Natalia. She opened the door enough for her to enter and pull the psychic inside, too.

Since they didn't dare disable any sound from the cameras this time, they worked quietly and efficiently. Within a minute, Dawn had on her headlight and mobile camera, and had a small machete in her hand as she opened the wardrobe leading to the hidden spring door.

She opened that, too, switching her headlight on full power. She'd already told Natalia about the darkness and the height issue on the stairway, so she hoped the new girl was prepared.

But Natalia was surprisingly unafraid of heights as they descended those steps into the pit of blackness, where the coldness wormed its way into every exposed pore.

Since no cameras had been found in these tunnels, Dawn felt all right about talking.

"You doin' okay?" she asked Natalia.

"I don't feel anything yet," she said, referring to her vamp radar. She ran her gloved hand over the tunnel walls, her own headlight making squiggly patterns over the rock.

Dawn accessed the earpiece—a new one since the old had been crushed last night. "Jonah, you can come on down now."

The air around her got heavy with jasmine, which seemed to quiver.

Kalin, getting excited about Jonah's big appearance.

"Hey," Dawn said to the spirit. "Focus, would you?"

The Friend swept by Dawn, knocking her a bit.

Could anyone be more useless? Dawn thought. Sure, Breisi had told Kalin everything she needed to know as far as directions belowground went, but Dawn didn't have half as much faith in Fire Woman as she did in her old faithful. Maybe, if Kalin had retained the fire-throwing powers she'd possessed as a human hunter, things would've been different, but as far as Dawn was concerned, the older Friend was a menace waiting to happen.

Soon, Jonah came below, halting in his speedy run to appear in a blink before Dawn and Natalia.

"Now I feel something," the new girl said.

She was zeroing in on Jonah, but if other vamps were near, chances were Natalia's tuning fork perception would increase in volume—or however she felt the creatures' presence—depending on how many were around.

That's how the team thought she worked, anyway. They were learning on the job.

Jonah was glancing around, and instead of a grin, he was frowning.

"What?" Dawn asked.

It looked like he was about to give her the patron saint of dismissive answers: *nothing*. But he seemed to decide against it.

"It's the boss," he said, avoiding Costin's name. They'd learned enough to know that saying it in the open wasn't smart because you never knew who might recognize the moniker. "He's doubting the wisdom of being here."

Dawn wished Jonah hadn't said anything. She didn't want to be afraid for Costin in any way.

"If something goes wrong," she said, "you'll get him right back inside of that body. But this is going to go like clockwork. He'll see."

Jonah seemed pleased that she'd just extended a vote of confidence in him.

Deciding not to explain that it'd been for Costin's benefit, not Jonah's, she followed Kalin's quivery lead until they got to the thorn tunnel.

Her pulser beat at her chest, jousting with her own rhythms.

"Here's where the good times start," Dawn said, buttoning her thick jacket. Even though her cuts had healed significantly, thanks to the gel, she'd still made sure she and Natalia had worn a stretchy, wetsuit-type neoprene layer under their regular clothes to protect their skin.

But as Dawn's headlight shone on the roots, she noticed that the points were strangely . . .

Clean.

She reached out to touch one, then drew her hand back. "Huh. It's like . . ."

Descriptions escaped her.

Natalia peered inside, too, multiplying the force of light. "Like what?"

"Like they're really spotless. Wiped down, even more than I tried to do when I left the first time."

Jonah crouched down to get a look. "Maybe these are movie monster roots. They eat whatever gets on them."

Dawn held back a retort. If Kiko had said it, it would've been funny.

Damn if Jonah's theory wasn't a bad one, though. Not with the crap she'd seen in life recently.

She took off her wig because she knew she'd lose it anyway, stored it in her bag, then entered. Natalia followed suit before she ventured into the thicket, and Jonah rounded them off.

At the end of the short journey, their outerwear was worse off—jagged and torn—but they'd avoided cuts.

That brought them to the Orlando Bloom room, and as they stood outside the orange and red beads that were swaying with the push of Kalin's entrance, Dawn turned to Natalia.

"Anything?"

The new girl shook her head, her headlight whipping back and forth as she denied any blips on her vamp-dar.

Dawn looked to Jonah and said, "We'll wait for Kalin to make a sweep then . . ."

Then they'd let Costin loose.

Her heartbeat seemed to hammer at the pulser. What if something did happen to their ultimate weapon?

What if Costin . . . ?

Don't even consider it, she told herself.

Jonah didn't make her finish what she'd been saying about their plans, but Kalin burst past the beads before Dawn might've gotten another word out, anyway.

"*Clear,*" the Friend said.

Now Dawn's pulse was knocking around like something in a straitjacket running into padded walls.

"Ready to let out the boss?" she asked Jonah.

His tilted grin returned. "Don't miss me too much, Dawn."

"Oh, don't you fret about that."

Kalin had gone eerily still, and it wasn't beyond Dawn's notice.

He didn't waste any time—he was that confident of the switch and the ability to reassume his place after this was over.

Dawn's headlight caught the change from blue eyes to topaz, from a casual posture and grin to a straight back and stoic pride.

Her skin heated, her chest caving in on itself.

Costin.

As his gaze adjusted to her, she took his hand because it was okay to touch him now that Jonah was gone. His cool flesh balanced the sear of hers.

A moment stretched—an instant where she had no idea what to say or how to define what she felt at having him back.

Natalia strangled it. "Hurry?" she said softly, as if chancing to remind them that this wasn't the time or place.

And she was right.

"Any vibes?" Dawn asked Costin, still holding his hand.

He gripped it, as if getting used to her again.

But then he let go.

She tried not to make it a big deal. He needed to concentrate.

As he surveyed the area, Dawn noticed that Kalin had backed off, as if waiting for Jonah to return before she got excited again. It was odd because, once, she and Costin had been close.

Very close.

He sauntered toward the beads but didn't go beyond them.

"Something," he said. "Something barely here. A remnant of energy that is disappearing even now. But that happens shortly after they leave. One has been here recently—not more than two days past, though, or else I would not feel it."

A master.

Dawn almost collapsed in relief. This place *did* have something to do with an Underground. Costin's vibes had just validated it.

Even Kalin was whizzing around in celebration, and Natalia was smiling above at the Friend.

"Let's get to that blade room then," Dawn said. "Maybe the vibes will be stronger if it's any closer to the big show or if a master has been there any more recently."

So they rushed forward, following Kalin, until they arrived at the entrance, where they'd previously done their best to clean up any trace evidence of their presence from the rubble, though they couldn't hide how they'd smashed through the wall.

Costin stayed outside the room again. Actually, he didn't even come within ten yards of it as Natalia and Kalin entered to look around.

"Don't you want to see it?" Dawn asked.

"No." His voice sounded raw.

"Why . . . ?"

"Because I can feel it from here. Whatever was down here is gone now."

"But—"

He touched her cheek, and she shivered at the contact, at the sorrowful cast to his gaze.

Then, before she even knew what was happening, he reared his head back.

When he righted it, his eyes were blue.

"Jonah!" Dawn shoved him. "Bring him back!"

He didn't even stumble under her push.

"Bring him *back*!" she repeated.

He didn't seem smug now. He didn't even seem cocky.

"Dawn," he said, as if working up to bad news. She knew the tone.

She bunched her hand into a fist.

"I wasn't the one who pushed him under," he said, stepping forward to cup his palm over her hand.

Her arm trembled as she tried to raise it, but he wasn't relenting.

What did he mean, he wasn't the one who'd pushed Costin back under . . . ?

But she understood, even as he lowered his voice so no one else would hear.

"He voluntarily went back in, Dawn."

As Jonah let her go and walked toward the blade room to inspect it, she didn't go after him.

Not this time.

TWENTY

The Highgate Chronicles

THE sky had folded from dusk into full night, the rain letting up, by the time the team finished at Queenshill, where they were as careful as possible to clean up any further traces of themselves in the tunnels and rooms under the ground. Anyone who saw the ravaged blade room entrance would know it'd been breached, but there wasn't much they could do about that.

Afterward, thanks to the Dr. Hopkins interview, they turned their attention to Highgate—the village where Thomas Gatenby had once been sighted with those bad-news friends of his.

Since the team had previously visited the cemetery there, they knew a little about this fresh-aired spot high on a hill overlooking the city. Highgate was bursting at its seams with tourists, shops, and pubs. Everyone, from Dick Turpin, the famous highwayman, to wealthy professionals raising families, to rock stars, was associated with the place.

Parking their Sedonas near the tube station down the hill from the graveyard, the team took the opportunity to change their disguises so that anyone who might be tracking them on a camera would have a harder time establishing a pattern from Queenshill to here. There was no way they could wander around the village as themselves, because almost a week ago, Dawn, Natalia, and Kiko had gone into the eastern portion of the cemetery to check out psychic leads.

Now, after banishing the males to the other vehicle and going to the back of the Sedona to change, Dawn put on another wig, a brunette bob, then donned some subtle makeup to age her face. She'd learned some tricks on movie sets, and it was as useful as hell now.

When she checked herself in a handheld mirror, she almost laughed, and it wasn't in hilarity. It's just that she looked how she felt—way older than just twenty-five years.

But she wasn't going to dwell on what had happened with Costin at Queenshill today: How he'd *allowed* Jonah to take over. How he'd retreated when, until recently, he'd always pressed forward.

Where was the line between careful and cowardly? she thought. And why couldn't she stop wondering if Costin had crossed it?

But she squashed it all to the back of her mind. To even think that Costin lacked bravery . . . it was appalling, something she didn't want to question.

Something she really had no *right* to question, she added as she put on a different pair of jeans than before, these weathered instead of new. She added a long-sleeved cotton shirt, a striped scarf, then a long brown coat that lent her the casual blending factor of an American middle-class tourist.

From now on, she definitely wasn't going to question Costin, even though a constant heaviness was still dogging her.

In the backseat with its blackened glass, Natalia was putting the finishing touches on her backpacker garb, complete with a braided red wig plus khakis and a flannel scarf over a down jacket and gloves. But she also wore a frown—a result of her frustration from their Queenshill visit. The psychic hadn't heard any voices from the dead in any of the rooms, and Dawn suspected that Natalia often felt useless when she couldn't get in contact with those victims she wanted to help so badly.

The new girl kept looking toward the windshield. "There's something going on out there, Dawn. I feel what I felt the last time we were here. It's like walking into an empty room that's really not so empty."

When Natalia had met Frank for the first time, she'd said something real similar, so Dawn could only think that the psychic was talking about vampiric presences nearby.

A lot more than just a few, too, because Natalia usually had to be close to a source in order to feel it, and no one was in the vicinity of their vehicle right now.

If there were a lot of them, they'd be having a bigger effect on Natalia.

But could her stronger reaction have something to do with the Highgate Vampire and its minions wandering around the cemetery? Dawn wondered. The creature was legend, and a valid candidate for an Underground connection. Maybe Natalia was tuning in to him and his group because they were above the ground, just up the hill. . . .

Dawn gave the other girl a stalwart pat on the shoulder as Jonah and Kiko knocked on the back passenger-side door, then climbed into the car, locking up behind them. The entire time, Dawn kept scanning out the windshield for any shadow figures tracking them, but she knew that the Friends were patrolling the area, too.

It reassured her a teeny-weeny bit.

Kiko, who was dressed in a generic baseball cap, a heavy gold jacket with a Manchester United Football Club patch on the sleeve, and a scarf that would cover half his face, looked young enough not to be buying any booze in a pub. But as he sent a far more mature glance to Natalia—a questioning glimpse—he seemed older.

"You're feeling it again, huh?" he asked her.

Natalia shrugged, then pulled her jacket closed.

Dawn interpreted her response. "We're near *some* kind of gold mine, but for all we know, she's reading the Highgate Vampire and his cronies in the cemetery. We just have to figure out if they're all connected to what we found below Queenshill."

Jonah pressed a key ring alarm button and aimed it at the other Sedona, causing it to *whoop*. If Dawn didn't know any better, she would've spent a lingering glance on him, with his purple-tinted wire-rimmed glasses and sporty baseball cap that matched Kiko's. Even in jeans, Doc Martens, and an L.L. Bean jacket, he managed to stand out, which was the last freakin' thing they were supposed to be doing.

"Jonah," Dawn said, "the idea is to have people *not* look at you."

Kiko scanned Jonah's appearance, too, then gave her a what're-you-talkin'-about? glance.

"He looks normal," Kiko said. "For a vamp."

Dawn stopped herself from arguing that anyone with eyes was going to notice Jonah—especially chicks. But she didn't want Jonah to know that she'd noticed the draw he had on females.

Yet he evidently did, because he got that cocky grin. "I think I come off like an everyday hubby just hanging out with the family on vacation."

He grasped both Kiko's and Dawn's upper arms in solidarity, suggesting that she could be the mama and Kiko the kid. At least, that's how she took it.

She was a second away from smacking his hand away when

Kiko took it upon himself to make the situation even more intolerable.

"If you and Dawn had a kid, he'd probably be all dark-haired and not a blonde like me. Details, Jonah."

"Perhaps," Natalia added, probably trying to be helpful, "you were adopted, Kiko."

Gah.

Dawn shrugged off Jonah's hand and tugged her own baseball cap onto her head, over her wig. "If anyone is nosy enough to ask, we tell them that we're all cousins who met up here in London for a vacay and are in the mood for some good pub grub for the adults and kid. But, except for Kiko partnering up with Natalia, we should casually separate ourselves unless we need a powwow. It might be harder to ID us if we look like individuals instead of a group."

"Sounds fine to me." Kiko slipped on his weapon-filled backpack. "On the same note, we should be careful while we're talking to people around here. This Underground could have servants aboveground, and they might go back to their community to report anything out of the ordinary. As far as everyone's concerned, we're gung ho tourists who love to hear scary stories about the area. What visitor doesn't?"

With that, they activated their pulsers via tiny handheld remotes, then got out of the vehicle separately, with Jonah going first, then Kiko and Natalia, then Dawn.

All the while, her pulser pounded against her chest.

After everyone else had started up the hill, she got out and hit the alarm button on her car keys, glancing around more out of paranoia than need; the Friends were patrolling *and* manipulating the cameras with their essences, so everything should go smoothly.

Problem was, the camera manipulation required more than one

Friend, and the team needed the spirits to be as spread out over the area as possible.

But they'd make do while sticking to the plan they'd formulated before leaving Queenshill: sidle into what would hopefully be a locals' pub, then strike up conversations with any casual historians to see if there were juicy rumors about Thomas Gatenby.

There was also the possibility that Kiko or Natalia might be able to channel visions based on touch or their precognitive abilities, and Jonah might be able to make eye contact and carefully reach into the mind of anyone who appeared to be holding back information.

But that was a last-straw option—*if* he could even do it without losing control of his vampire self, just like he had when he'd come to the team's rescue with the Queenshill schoolgirls. Besides, using his vamp powers might open him up to a reading by creatures that the team wanted to get the jump on themselves.

After walking up the hill, Dawn came to a village square where a cozy pub named the Figurehead awaited with its white walls and brown trimming. Tudor style, it was called.

She saw Kiko and Natalia going in together, and she guessed that they were tailing Jonah.

Dawn slyly made sure her earpiece was tuned to Frank back at headquarters so she wouldn't get feedback from the other team members, then she entered the pub while extracting the crucifix on her necklace so it would be in plain sight. She hadn't done it before out of a grudging awareness for Jonah's comfort.

She was welcomed by planked walls and a small collection of ship figureheads that mainly featured wooden women with bared breasts. The decorations mixed with long trestle tables and a bar populated by people who looked British and local enough.

Kiko and Natalia, who were already ordering meals from their server, had taken a seat at a rustic table near a duo of salty-looking older men. Jonah had gone to the far side of the bar, near a gray-haired old woman who was knitting and nipping at a glass of whiskey.

Avoiding them all, Dawn cruised the room, playing the tourist as she surveyed the mermaids and assorted ladies with abundant boobs. But she was really listening for who might provide the best conversation.

As her pulser thumped, she focused on a man who looked to be in his sixties, sitting at the bar opposite Jonah and easily talking to the bartender while cradling an unlit pipe in one hand and holding his place in a magazine with the other.

Target fixed and locked.

Dawn claimed the stool next to him, then ordered some tea and the curry special. Afterward, she smiled at her possible fountain of information, making sure he saw her crucifix.

He didn't react.

"Is that pipe for show?" she asked lightly.

He peered at it, his eyes crinkling while he smiled. He reminded her of what Rupert Everett might've looked like if he had lots of gray hair and hadn't gone into movies: a less polished version of suave.

"We're following in the footsteps of the States with our smoking bans," he said, his tone dry. "I'm still weaning myself from the habit."

She knew all about bans, and the last time she'd met a smoker ignoring one in a pub, she'd gone off on him with her mental powers. Accidentally.

Or maybe not. She still wasn't sure what the hell had happened when her temper broke and she'd turned into a puppet-mastering fiend.

"And here," she said as the bartender brought her tea and all its trimmings, "I thought you just wanted to seem like an intellectual."

He smiled wider, showcasing tobacco-stained teeth. But somehow that didn't make him any less professor-like attractive.

Not that Dawn was "on the pull" or trying to get laid here.

Not these days.

She dug into the bag she'd plopped onto the stool next to her. As she took out her guidebook and a notepad, she hoped that her neighbor would take the bait and comment on what she was doing.

And . . . yup.

"A guest in our country," he said. "If you need a recommendation or two, I'd be more than happy to provide."

"Thanks. To tell the truth, I really could use some advice. This isn't just a fun trip to England for me. I'm here to study."

"Really."

"Yeah. I know I'm not exactly a coed"—she motioned at her face, laughing, hoping she'd done a good enough job with her aging makeup—"but I went back to college, and I'm taking a semester off to do some research for a project I'll need to finish for graduation."

"Oh?" He tucked his pipe into a pocket.

She shoots—and she scores.

"And what subject moved you to come over here from the colonies?" he asked.

The colonies. How droll. She ignored the jibe because getting into a discussion about the Revolutionary War wouldn't just be a distraction; it'd be embarrassing because she didn't really know about that shit.

She just laughed a bit, and he looked as if he regretted that he wouldn't be able to engage in a debate about Loyalists and Patriots or "America's imperialist bent" or . . .

Whatever.

"I'm into the formation of legends. Sociology," she said, like she knew exactly what area she'd be studying for that subject. Like he'd know, either. "And London seemed to be the place to go for good stories."

"Highgate has its share, so you did find a cozy little niche."

In Dawn's peripheral vision, she saw Jonah charming the old woman across the way. Hopefully he wouldn't get an itch to bite her or anything.

"In my studies so far," she said to her own target, "Highgate stood out."

"Let me guess. The vampire of the cemetery." He took a quaff of his ale. "And the supposed ghosts of the Gatehouse pub up the way."

"Wow." Dawn pushed the friendly act even further, stoked that she was actually successful at it. See what happened when you tried? "I'm really lucky that I ran into you."

She positioned herself to visually touch base with Natalia and Kiko. The new girl was listening to the old gentlemen at her table, and one more had even joined the group while Kiko kept his head down and did his best to hide that he was an adult dressed like a kid. His main purpose was to be there in case Natalia needed him.

Dawn grabbed her pen, like she'd taken Natalia's place as the best note taker ever. "I dug around for a topic that my adviser might not have seen before, and I came across the name of a guy who no one seems to know much about. Are you local?"

"Yes."

Sweet. Her blood beat in time to the pulser, and she felt like she was at the edge of a forest, ready to run and chase.

Then he added, "I even happen to be Sting's neighbor."

As she gave him an "ah, good for you?" glance, he laughed.

"All right, I hardly live next door to him. But I can never resist the opportunity to impress others with the fact that the stars live among us here in Highgate."

Dawn smiled politely again, but not enough to encourage any kind of pickup. She didn't want to be impressed.

Her unknowing informant went back on track. "What's the name of the chap you're keen on researching?"

"Thomas Gatenby."

"Ah, the infamous dandy who was led straight into near obscurity, though no one knows exactly by whom . . . or how. Quite the challenge you'll have tracking down his precise story."

"Any ideas about what happened to him?"

"I've had many a conversation about it in these parts. We do love our speculation."

"And . . . ?"

"It's said that Gatenby favored the pub at the top of the hill, on the old main road. The Lion and the Lamb. Byron and Keats once enjoyed it, as well."

Dawn wrote down the name of the team's next stop.

She said, "I've heard talk about some pals who might've guided Gatenby in the wrong direction, like you mentioned. I think there's something to that story. Was he ever seen there with any of them?"

"There are rumors about such sightings, yet most involve Gatenby drinking to excess and then stumbling into the night in the company of one man who was as wild-eyed as they come."

Wild-eyed. Could that describe a vampire who had Gatenby under his influence?

Or was it the other way around?

"This is great," Dawn said, egging him on. "I'll have to check out this pub."

"Oh, do. There're said to be hauntings, too, and if you plan to dig into the history of the place, there were tunnels discovered under the building, as well as secret rooms. They believe highwaymen used them for smuggling, since the road was a well-traveled thoroughfare. The Lion and the Lamb would be a brilliant place for you."

"Think they'd let me look at those tunnels?" She meant to sound like she was kidding.

But in reality?

Not even.

"They don't open that portion to the public, as far as I know. It's a danger, they say, and as business-minded people, they don't need that risk."

"I'll chat up the employees there anyway. Can't hurt."

She heard a mellow ruckus behind her, from where Natalia had been talking with the old men, and when Dawn turned around, she found both Kiko and Natalia walking out of the pub.

When she turned back around, her meal had arrived, and she made eye contact with Jonah, who shook his head then quickly snapped his gaze away when he saw that her crucifix was in plain sight. All the same, he didn't want to leave the pub yet.

Just to ease out of the topic, Dawn asked the man beside her—Damian, she eventually found out—to give her a few restaurant and theater recommendations. And by the time she'd finished eating her food, Jonah had gotten off his stool and was kissing the hand of the old lady, who laughed like a young girl and bade him a fond good-bye.

While she rubbed her skin, as if noting how cool his own had been, he left without even a glance at Dawn.

She settled the bill while thanking Damian, who seemed slightly disappointed that she hadn't asked him out or something. The guy must've been desperate for company, she thought. But she did quietly make arrangements to pay for his bar tab in gratitude.

The second she stepped out the door, she furtively tucked her crucifix back in her shirt, then reactivated her earpiece to group mode, which caused it to come back to life.

"We're in the bookshop to your left," said Kiko's voice while

Dawn walked away from the pub. "The Friends have taken care of any cameras for us, and they don't see anyone following."

Fetching a stick of spearmint gum from her bag—curry was yummy but strong—Dawn spotted the quaint bookstore and headed toward it. Out of new habit, she kept her gaze on the rooftops for any signs of Shadow Girl.

Nothing.

Inside the shop, activity was muted except for the shuffle of shoes and the serenity of quiet classical music. It didn't take Dawn long to find the rest of the team huddled around a New Age book section, Jonah on one side of the shelves, Kiko and Natalia on the other.

Dawn took a spot next to Jonah, but she could see through the spaces between the books that Natalia seemed upset.

Kiko stuck his head around the shelves, then whispered, "Limey bastards. We left because they started talking smack about Romania and Gypsies when they heard her accent."

From the other side, Natalia whispered, "It's okay, Kiko. I paid no mind."

"Bullshit."

Dawn had never seen him look so affronted.

"Really, Kiko—" Natalia began.

He continued talking to Dawn. "The last thing we needed was a scene, so we split before I got out a dart gun."

Dawn stopped chewing her gum and glanced at Natalia, who had her gaze lowered as she paged through a paperback about crystals. There were splotches of color on her cheeks, revealing her embarrassment.

Natalia, who'd recently immigrated from Bucharest, was trying hard to be a productive member of this new society, but she had a hot button about being called a "Gypsy," a derogatory term that people tended to use for criminals who'd immigrated from her homeland.

"Natalia?" Dawn whispered.

The new girl didn't glance up, but Dawn could tell she was listening.

"They don't know you. They don't know jack about what you're made of. It's their problem, not yours."

Natalia nodded stiffly, like she couldn't talk because that might open the floodgates.

Dawn sighed, not knowing what else she should do. And when she felt Jonah watching her, as if he approved of her trying to make things better, she pretended to be totally into the book titles.

She didn't need the blessing of a psycho. She hadn't forgotten how Jonah had slashed his face to keep Costin in line back before the two of them had been turned into a vampire. She hadn't forgotten how voracious he'd been that night at Queenshill.

"I got some great info back in the pub," she said to all of them, talking softly and getting back to business, the most comfortable place she knew. "How about you guys?"

"Nothing worthwhile, as you can imagine," Kiko said.

Jonah ran a finger over a volume about self-healing. "I never even got around to asking about Gatenby. My lovely lady friend told me how much I resembled her long-gone husband and then reminisced about how they'd met as children in a bomb shelter during World War II."

"That's okay." Dawn motioned all of them closer, then shared what Damian had told her about the Lion and the Lamb and the tunnels below it. "I vote we make our way up there to see what we can see."

"I'm your Huckleberry," Kiko said.

Jonah and Natalia agreed, too, and as they left the bookstore piecemeal, Dawn stayed behind for a second, grabbing the book that Natalia had been so interested in and buying it.

What the hell. It was just an impulse.

They were all walking toward North Road, which had been visible from the square, and it wasn't long before they spotted the Lion and the Lamb, with its red bricks and faded shingle sign.

They were about twenty feet from the entrance when Dawn passed Natalia, slipping the paperback to her.

"Looked kind of cool," she said, moving ahead and not waiting for a thank-you.

"Dawn," Natalia said.

There was something in her voice that begged for a good look, and Dawn turned around.

The new girl had come to lean against a wall, almost sitting down, one hand pressed against her temple. Dawn went back to her, letting Kiko and Jonah go farther ahead.

Without even asking, she had the feeling this was about Natalia's vamp radar.

"It's stronger than ever," the psychic said. "I—"

She doubled over, both hands vising her head now, and Dawn rushed over to her while talking into her earpiece.

"Kiko, get back here and take Natalia to one of the vehicles. I think she's done her job for the night."

It seemed like there were a thousand pulses thrashing around in her now.

Vampires. Near. There had to be.

"What's going on?" Kiko asked.

Up ahead, Dawn could see her coworker turning around, then start jogging back to them when he saw Natalia. Meanwhile, Jonah waited under a streetlight—a lone figure, lean, mean, and ready to go.

Kiko was patting Natalia's back as she squeezed her eyes shut and kept pressing her palms against her head.

"You're going into the pub while I get her out of here?" he asked Dawn.

"Yeah." She kept watching Jonah, her pulser too loud in her ears and against her chest because, somewhere inside that body, Costin was waiting for them to find that Underground location so he could come out and kick some—

Doubt cut off the thought. *Would* he come out again?

Dawn just wasn't sure anymore.

Leaving Kiko and Natalia behind, she walked in Jonah's direction, even though she started to wonder if she might be entering a vampire hive for Costin . . .

. . . or maybe just for herself now.

TWENTY-ONE

London Babylon, Main Underground Kitchens

THE rumors about what might have truly happened to all the missing Queenshill girls had gone round much sooner than Della had expected.

She looked out of her cage at the gathered students who had been promoted from Queenshill throughout the years—girls who were staring at Della as if they were about to blast into her mind to see if she was lying.

Actually, she thought, trying to stay calm, the speed with which the news had circulated was stunning.

Yet, honestly, she was most shocked that each and every one of these so-called caring classmates had been so wrapped up in the excesses of the Underground that they had left their pasts at Queenshill behind with nary a thought to their own missing friends from years gone by.

But perhaps that had been the very idea. Perhaps that was the reason for this eternal play park where the girls lacked for no diversions. Wolfie had enchanted them all, and Della wondered how long it might have taken for her, too, to forget about her beloved mates.

As the Queenshill girls cocked their heads at her, she spied Polly in the rear, her expression sullen. Noreen was at the forefront, closest to the cage. And round all of them the caged boys begged, reaching beyond their bars, only to be ignored.

Della used her classmate mind-link to Noreen, cutting the rest of the group out. *Somehow, I suspect that you did more than leave an anonymous note for the others to find.*

Noreen didn't shy away. *So I risked volunteering answers when I realized that the girls were more than receptive to the anonymous note, Della. The news awakened something within them. Everyone here has wondered about their own missing friends at some time before they came Underground.*

The remainder of the girls—lovely upper-class, well-raised girls—were still watching Della as if she were an . . . oracle?

Was she?

No. She had only been desperate enough to speak aloud because she suspected she had nothing more to lose. If she had been out of this cage, would she have ever found a voice?

I suppose, she thought to Noreen, willing to accept whatever consequences were in store now, *it doesn't matter if everyone's privy to what I believe about Mrs. Jones. For all I know, I might not ever be released from this cage, anyway.*

A girl wearing her platinum hair in a chignon, her slim body draped in a white dressing gown, moved next to Noreen, emanating maturity. Della had no doubt this was an older vampire, even though she appeared to be sixteen.

How did you come upon this information about Mrs. Jones?

she asked, looking into Della's eyes to reach a mind-link, since they weren't born in the same Queenshill class.

Like Della and Noreen, the older vampire clearly knew to keep silent about this, refusing to broadcast their doubts in case any cameras should pick them up. They needed to stay quiet on all counts, even though Noreen had already told Della that a good deal of the recruits were either still playing in the common areas or flitting round aboveground in the Lion and the Lamb, where Wolfie had a deal with an owner who never asked just what the girls who brought such good business were. And Mrs. Jones was nowhere to be found at the present time, either—she was probably still finishing business at the school.

Wolfie himself had gone above to run about the heath at such an eye-blurring pace that no human would ever be able to mark it.

So their thoughts were safe . . . unless the Queenshill girls decided to tell on Della.

She braced her arms over her stomach. Hungry. She couldn't think of how to protect herself when she was so hungry.

Yet her answer was safe enough. *I can't explain how I came to know about Mrs. Jones*, she told the older vampire, who seemed to be in charge of all these gathered ex-students.

Noreen made eye contact with the lead Queenshill girl, and Della could hear what she was saying because of her and Noreen's opened classmate mind-link.

I told you, Stacy—dreams. Della had vivid dreams that make all too much sense in the context of what we've experienced.

All the girls looked at one another, all the different schoolmates who'd survived Mrs. Jones, making eye contact and silently spreading the word. Their communication created a flurry of sound because of the class mind-links.

Dreams, they said.

Visions . . .

Amidst the buzz, Noreen kept glancing at the older vampire named Stacy while also thinking to Della, *After I spoke up about the note, we started talking, the lot of us, new students and old. Comparing. And it seems that, each year, one classmate would leave school about every six months from* every *class.*

Stacy added to that, her tone bitter. *Their absences never seemed terribly connected and, once Underground, the pain faded for the older ones. Wolfie was here, and that was all we wanted. We didn't think about Mrs. Jones anymore. She never came round much, so it was easy to forget how she would look at me as if . . .*

As if she wanted to devour you? Della finished.

Nodding, Stacy glanced at her own classmates for their reactions. They, in turn, peered about the room and shared with the other girl vampires who hadn't been in their exclusive class. Soon, they all seemed just as haunted as Della, and she was more certain than ever that she had done well in having pursued her suspicions, because even if some of the girls had forgotten during the passage of years, there was a part of them that still hurt for their missing friends—girls who they believed had abandoned the class.

Yet then Stacy lanced Della with a look. *You've got us interested, and we're all too willing to believe this about Mrs. Jones. But, then, what of Wolfie?*

Della was quick to come to his defense, perhaps because it covered her own misgivings. *No! He couldn't have known about what Mrs. Jones was doing.*

Even if he'd been with his mistress for centuries.

Soon, the other girls were shaking their heads, as if, in a chain reaction, they were all refusing to believe Wolfie was just as guilty.

Mrs. Jones was the only one responsible, Della told herself. Just the cat. Wolfie loved them too much, whereas Mrs. Jones had always seemed to resent them, even while pretending to care.

However, that trickle of uncertainty remained. That thin line of trembling "what if?"

Della could only take strength in the obvious need of the Queenshill alumnae to believe in him. The willingness to place the blame far away from the benevolent master who had always treated them with such affection.

All the girls had come closer, as if creating a hive that would enclose them in this new knowledge and keep them safe until they knew how to emerge.

She could hear the droning of connected thoughts from all the girls as she looked into Stacy's light eyes.

There was always a sense of jealousy from Mrs. Jones, they were thinking. *When she and Wolfie first began turning us into vampires—even long before she became a housematron—she took part in the exchange with the very old girls almost reluctantly. . . . She was always slinking around in her cat shape whenever Wolfie came near us in the sub-Underground. . . . It was as if she wished to disappear, yet she couldn't bring herself to leave him alone with us. . . .*

At this last thought, Della recalled how she herself had seen the cat's eyes glowing through the darkness of doorways and in hiding spaces when Wolfie was close. How Mrs. Jones had watched while he frolicked with her and her classmates, three of whom had disappeared.

Wolfie, one of the girls thought. *If he only knew, he'd—*

Stacy raised a hand to silence the notion. *We leave Wolfie out of this.*

They all glanced round as one of the boys in his cage laughed madly to himself, breaking the quiet.

Della disconnected from Stacy's eyes and, with no small amount of paranoia, opened her senses full force while trying to feel Mrs. Jones's returned presence anywhere in the Underground. But she could not.

She connected back to Stacy, to the network, just as another schoolgirl thought, *Why would she do it?*

It sounded like Polly, even though she still loitered in the background, hunched over, her straight hair hiding her face.

Stacy tilted her head as she waited for Della to respond. They thought she had an answer.

Youth? Della finally thought, remembering the dream of the vampiress in the tub. *Blood baths make Mrs. Jones seem younger, even if she's a vampire born centuries ago. Drinking through the skin—*

Gives her a glow. Stacy ran her fingers over her own arm.

A fraction of the other girls shifted, touching their own skin, frowning.

Since Stacy was so close, Della took in the other vampire's face. There *was* something different about this older Queenshill girl, as well as a few of the others. Nothing obvious, but perhaps less of a flush to the cheeks, less of a sparkle in their gazes . . .

Yes, the start of something that wasn't the same as what Della saw in *her* eyes in the mirror, no matter how young the other vampires seemed everywhere else.

Had they—the older ones—begun to long for youth treatments? The other girls who had been Underground even before Mrs. Jones became a housematron had even more of a maturity, now that Della truly thought about it.

Would they all be just like Mrs. Jones, their cocreator, as the years passed?

What are we? Della asked. *What did they make us?*

No one knew, because neither Wolfie nor Mrs. Jones had ever explained the particulars. They had given them long lives of affection and adoration—promises as bright and sweet as truffles—and as with all overwhelming gifts, none of them had ever thought to ask what the price would be as long as they were happy.

Yet that had not stopped Della from wondering, upon occasion, where her soul had gone and what might happen to it should she ever want it again.

Noreen had huddled near the entrance of the cage, and she aimed her next mind-question at Della.

So what do we do now?

Della looked into Stacy's eyes, seeing that the older vampire had come to peer right back.

Why? Della was only one of them, no more special, no more . . .

In her mind's eye, a flock of white ribbons fluttered, and she realized she had somehow become more.

Della Bennett of the frizzy hair and classroom daydreams . . .

She rose to her knees, grasping the bars of her cage. *I want to know,* she mind-said.

Stacy's own missing classmates were at the front of her thoughts—Della could feel the bruising presence of them.

Want to know what? the other vampire thought.

I want to know what happened to them. Definitively. I want to see, and if what we suspect about Mrs. Jones is genuine, I want to show Blanche and Briana and Sharon that I haven't forgotten them. That I never will.

Your injuries from their absences are too fresh, Stacy mind-said, acting as if she had grown out of the same phase. Yet Della could tell—they all could tell—from the pang in the older vampire's tone that those injures had come back with the introduction of Della's dreams.

Every youthful hurt, every twist of betrayal.

None of that ever really died, Della suspected, no matter how many years flew by.

I want, Della added, staring at Stacy, *to see all of it and know that it's true before I pay Mrs. Jones for what she did.*

The schoolgirls stirred as Stacy thought, *You want to look inside Mrs. Jones. Is that what you're saying, Della?*

Together we could, Della said, putting it all on the line, because she knew she would never have another chance. *Strength in numbers. We've been raised as a future army, haven't we? On the nightcrawls that Wolfie used to stoke our hunger and train us, we were schooled in how to work together. We've just never tried it outside of hunting humans.*

It's true, whispered one girl in the network of their minds. It was Noreen, whose anguish matched Della's.

The older vampire narrowed her eyes, and in the other girl's gaze, Della could see the ghosts of Stacy's own missing friends resurrected by the possibility of a reckoning.

If we acted, Stacy thought, *it would change everything, you know. If we were to be caught by Mrs. Jones while forcing ourselves into her mind, there's no punishment she wouldn't exercise.*

Della leaned against the bars. *Then again, Wolfie deserves better than Mrs. Jones, and we can make certain that he gets it.* Do *you recall his sadness after the disappearance of each student, and can you imagine how he might feel if he knew what Mrs. Jones was doing?*

They remembered.

And she could also feel that their anger about their friends had shaped itself into a rage for Wolfie's sake.

How dare Mrs. Jones do this behind his back? they thought. *How* dare *she?*

And, in that moment, she thought that there was absolutely no possible way Wolfie *could* know. He would never sacrifice them for Mrs. Jones's vanity.

She kept repeating it, clinging to it as gazes disconnected, leaving each girl to her own musings. Then, little by little, they drifted into small groups most likely composed of the survivors from each class.

Except that Noreen was the only one of Della's classmates to come near her. Polly stayed on the other side of the kitchens, near the basins.

A lock of red hair fell over Noreen's eyes. *What will you do if they don't have enough courage to go through with this and they all turn on you?*

Della pressed a hand to her chest, where it felt as if her heart were cracking, coming close to its own suicide—something the girls weren't supposed to be able to accomplish, even though there were times when she had thought about doing it.

After what seemed like hours, Stacy glanced over at her.

The older vampire didn't say a word out loud or in their minds, but in her expression—a savage, cold stare—Della knew that the other girl was remembering the confusion, the agony of thinking that a friend—an ally—had left them nearly alone to contend with all the unfairness life had to bring.

Then, as Stacy walked from group to group, as if monitoring them and hearing everyone's decision, Della sensed a chill in the room—a hatred that was growing.

A mob mentality that made her grip the bars.

As the steel pressed into her palms, she thought of what might happen if she should attempt to pull the bars apart. She hadn't tried for fear of reprisal, but if she were to pry them, she could get out—

Then a pall shrouded the room, causing shoulders to stiffen, backs to hunch, hair to rise on flesh.

Before Della even saw the gray cat slithering into the midst of them, she knew Mrs. Jones was here.

Had she heard what was going on in their minds?

Wouldn't they have sensed her intruding on them, though?

Stacy's gaze snagged Della's again, and there was no doubt that the older vampire was wondering the same.

Did Mrs. Jones know?

Stacy smiled, and Della's hackles rose.

For my friends, the older girl vampire mind-said before springing across the kitchens with a growl-hiss and landing just in front of Della's cage. Then, just before she grabbed hold of the bars, she added, *But especially for Wolfie.*

She tore the bars away, and it was only in that moment that Della realized just how badly Stacy—and no doubt the others—needed to protect what they had in the Underground: how they needed to believe Wolfie had been betrayed by Mrs. Jones just as their friends had been victimized.

Free, Della burst out of the cage, leaping over all the girl vampires in her injured anger and crashing in front of the cat, who flashed sharp teeth and hissed in furious surprise.

In wavelike reaction, the girls mutated into their vampire forms, hair receding to leave wrinkled, hideous skin, their eyes slanting, their faces growing snouts, their fangs protruding as they growl-hissed at the intruding creature and mobbed her.

The cat gave a wrathful cry and jumped up and away from them, warping into the naked, womanly form of Mrs. Jones for only a second before she, too, turned into her true vampire: a large, fanged cat creature with claws and fur and burning eyes.

She grasped on to a light fixture swinging above the kitchens, her back arched as she continuing hissing while clinging to it. Below, the girls prepared to go after her as the boys yelled, laughed, clapped in the cages.

"Kitty!" one screamed. "Here, kitty!"

Della's stomach rumbled, so hungry, but not only for food.

It was for all that anyone had ever dared to take from her.

Stacy, in a cat-wolf form similar to the rest of theirs, stalked in a circle underneath Mrs. Jones and the light fixture as she kept eye contact with Della for communication.

We know all about you, Mrs. Jones, she mind-said. *We know what you've been doing to us.*

The cat vampire's hiss choked off. Then she smiled, those needle teeth gleaming while her voice calmed, as if this was only a mistake that they would regret. "Oh, girls."

All of them, Della included, laughed, sending the air to vibrating.

The hair spiked on Mrs. Jones's body, and her voice grew in screechy volume. "If I find it within myself to excuse your temporary lack of judgment—"

Always watching, Stacy interrupted, still stalking and looking at Della, as if she were a touchstone. *Always trying to see who Wolfie loves more, then planning who might provide your next blood bath.*

Their housematron's features froze, as if a light had been shone upon her and she didn't know where to hide.

Della's dreams *had* been spot-on.

The names of her friends ran through her head, her heart: Blanche. Briana. Sharon.

A roll call of dangling, bleeding girls above a bathtub.

Mrs. Jones could apparently see the same thoughts on every face below her, and she flashed her thin, sharp teeth. "Wolfie will not abide this. And I certainly will not. Stop being bad girls this instant."

This time, Della wasn't afraid to mind-speak back to Mrs. Jones. *But you made us bad girls.*

They all crept closer together, anticipating the moment they could see the truth in their housematron's eyes.

Power in numbers.

A good little army who, by virtue of the nightcrawls, had been taught not to drink in dainty bites, but to devour.

It didn't even occur to Della that they might be mismatched with Mrs. Jones's age and experience trumping theirs.

They were many. And they'd been wronged.

Della's mouth flooded with juices, her veins purring with appetite.

"Do you know what happens if I perish?" Mrs. Jones said, her voice hardly as imperious now. She could obviously smell blood in the air, and it was her own. "You girls are partly mine, so your abilities—even if you don't have all of my own—would be halved. The dragon wouldn't be so happy with such a change. Think of your ultimate master and what sort of punishment *he* would impose."

I believe, Stacy mind-said, *you ought to be considering what he might do to you first, Mrs. Jones.*

Della came to Stacy's side, where they rubbed against each other in unity, and the others joined in, the sound of panting even louder than the voices of the boys who were urging them on from their cages.

"Girls—" Mrs. Jones began.

But they had already flexed their muscles in preparation, and now they jumped toward her, en masse, clawing at the light fixture.

It crashed to the ground, and they all pounced on Mrs. Jones, weighing her down with multiple girls, including Noreen and Polly, on each limb as Della, Stacy, and a few others used their nails to spread the cat vampire's eyes open.

Mrs. Jones attempted to use her voice, her strength, her charms to subdue them, but the girls had been bred from the blood of two vampires, and they were only one generation removed from both of them.

And they'd been wronged. . . .

Sharon. Della's mind-voice rose with each name she called. *Briana! Blanche!!!*

They peered into the cat vampire's eyes as Mrs. Jones screamed in protest, but the sound faded in Della's perception at what she saw in a wild, slanted thrust of images that cut into one another. . . .

Each of her friends, charmed asleep in a room where blades hung from the ceiling, casting wretched shadows like the most crooked of nightmare branches—

The girls awakened, then given charmed blood to drink so that they would be lulled to a sleep that would still keep them alive—

Strapped above a tub and bled out while Mrs. Jones showered under them, her skin-mouths gaping, drinking—

Then, the blades . . .

The blades slicing into Blanche/Briana/Sharon's flesh to extract hearts and livers, and Della knew that the girls had been kept alive so the cat might enjoy those treats—

And, finally, *finally*, when Mrs. Jones finished with each girl, she decapitated them, erasing all evidence that they had ever been in the blade room at all.

Della tried to pull out, even as she saw Mrs. Jones strolling out of that bladed room and down the hall, into the sub-Underground lounge where the girls would normally chase and pounce with Wolfie.

The big question clogged in Della's throat, but she mind-said it, anyway, even if it was just a tortured mental whisper.

Wolfie?

Had he tried to do anything to stop this?

But at his name, Mrs. Jones's mind became a black wall, and it felt as if Della were falling into it until she forcibly yanked her consciousness away from Mrs. Jones's.

She rolled off the housematron while the other girls continued to hold down the cat vampire. Mrs. Jones had put a block around anything that had to do with Wolfie, and even under attack, she was refusing to let them see the one answer Della really wanted.

She struggled for breath, numb, as the urge to scream and cry welled up in her.

Do you know what could have been *in store for* you, *little girl?*

At the blackout, the other girls who had gone into Mrs. Jones's mind had also drawn back from the old creature, and that gave the cat vampire an opening.

With a steel-on-blackboard yell, she swatted out with her claws, catching Noreen and another girl on the sides of their faces, sending them hurling across the room.

Stacy and the others bounded away from Mrs. Jones before she could get them, too, but Della was too caught by shock to join them quickly enough.

Wolfie . . . ?

The thought held her in its grasp as Mrs. Jones clamped her fingers around Della's neck, taking her and aiming toward the door as Della choked and tried to free herself.

The old vampire sped off through the tunnels, holding Della to her, but Della didn't really feel the incredible speed or hear the Queenshill girls giving chase.

That's because she had already decided that she wasn't going to be another Blanche or Sharon or Briana, and she went limp in Mrs. Jones's grasp, sliding down until she tangled with the housematron's legs, slowing the cat vampire to a skidding, dust-blaring screech that chewed at Della's limbs.

But she didn't care, because before Mrs. Jones could recover, Della used her claws and teeth to tear chunks out of the cat vampire's legs.

The old creature screamed and swatted her attacker away, but Della crashed into a wall, scrambling to her feet just in time to see the cat vampire already trying to self-heal her ripped limbs.

Della glanced at her fingers, gore-heavy claws, not having realized that she could inflict such damage on her superior.

That she would ever dare.

In the back of her mind, as she heard the other schoolgirls grinding to a halt in the tunnel, Della remembered how good it'd felt to sic the ravens on Violet, and she mind-said one last thing to Mrs. Jones.

For our friends. Her mental voice was just as mangled as Mrs. Jones's legs. *But especially for Wolfie.*

As the schoolgirls jumped at Mrs. Jones, the cat vampire's expression went . . . soft. It was as if his name had shredded her far more than any claws or teeth ever could.

But like the long-living thing she was, Mrs. Jones glared at the oncoming girls, then darted toward the ceiling, and Della realized that they were just below a trapdoor that the housematron must have been targeting.

Blood so delicious in her mouth, Della sprang, too, wrapping both paws around Mrs. Jones's neck in an attempt to pull her back down.

She thought she heard—and felt—the housematron's throat rip as the cat vampire's velocity punched them both aboveground, through the earth and wood and into the night, where the moon bathed a heath sprinkled with light rain.

But on the way back down, she lost her grip on Mrs. Jones.

Actually, it was as if the vampire had disappeared as Della felt a pair of hands grabbing at her ankles and yanking her into the hole until she smacked the ground.

Everything spun—the tunnel, the darkness—as Stacy loomed above Della.

"Are you mad?" she asked Della as some other vampires prepared to jump up through the door after Mrs. Jones, as well.

"Stop!" Stacy yelled.

And they did.

As Della clambered back to a stand, splinters of wood sticking out of her bare, wrinkled cat-wolf skin, Noreen said, "But she'll get away!"

"I think I might have got her." Della panted, going beneath the door, looking up into the night as she tugged the splinters out of her skin. "I might've taken her head off at the neck."

The other vampires began panting, excited.

Stacy stared at Della for a moment, then leaped up to the exit, bracing herself on the sides of the hole as she glanced around then gracefully fell back to the floor, staying in a crouch.

"She's nowhere in sight, and I imagine she would've been, with all her injuries slowing her."

The panting increased in rhythm and volume from every girl.

"Maybe," Noreen said, "Della killed her and her body disappeared already."

Several schoolgirls began gleefully applauding, but Stacy merely stared at the opening above them. It would need to be covered quickly, Della thought in a discombobulated cloud.

The older vampire shook her head. "Let's take care of this door, and then we'll have to decide what comes next. We don't dare go out there for any sort of ambush from that smart old cat, if she's still whole."

But one of the other girls was already humming, "Ding dong the witch is dead," as they scrambled to find materials for a new covering.

Yet, as Della helped, she realized that none of the schoolgirls had stopped to consider that if Mrs. Jones had aided in creating them, her termination would have affected their composition.

They would have lost half their powers, unless Mrs. Jones had been lying.

And, even worse, none of them except Stacy seemed to be thinking of what they were going to tell Wolfie when he returned Underground.

TWENTY-TWO

Once Upon an Omission

IF the main Underground were a body, then the room where the *custode*s kneeled before a long wooden box would be the heartbeat.

The atmosphere felt like a field of electricity round Lilly, vibrating and pressurizing her flesh, muscle, blood, and bone, weakening and strengthening her at the same time. A *custode* never missed the Relaquory ritual, because it was here that they gained energy while giving it at the same time, joining only to separate, absorbing purpose and will.

Heads bowed, both keepers extended their bared arms over the tightly packed dirt in the box—the earth that covered everything except for a nose and mouth barely peeking out. Then the *custode*s sliced their arms with the curved ritual knives that had been in the Meratoliage family for over a century, when their servitude had started.

They allowed two drops of blood from each of their bodies to soak into the soil—a small token of sacrifice and worship, a symbol of their devotion.

As they remained on their knees, holding hands, they withstood the vibrations that fed them, like all *custode*s had in the past, their lungs heavy with the oppression, their bodies gaining power until they needed no more.

Then, rising to their feet, they left, locking the door behind them in layers of steel-clad security. Even so, the air outside the room stayed weighted and quivering as they returned to their quarters, where they tended to their knife wounds, which flared next to the other arm cuts culled from night after night of Relaquory.

Afterward, they checked the monitor room for any pressing activity, but there was only a gathering of vampire girls in the kitchens to note. So they nourished themselves with normal food, then walked to the monitor room again, where they planned to watch the Southwark cameras for any more signs of those attackers, as well as review the footage they had missed during the ritual that fueled them beyond the ordinary.

Before Relaquory, they had made plans for the night: while Nigel went on patrol, Lilly would continue to investigate older footage of Highgate. Thus far, she hadn't found anything to indicate that the attackers who'd invaded Queenshill had been in the area lately, but she had a lot more recordings to cover.

"So you're going to check the Queenshill rooms belowground first thing on patrol?" she asked her brother.

He nodded as they rounded a corner of the rock hall. This morning, while it was still dark, he had finally got his bum up to the school, using the wooded entrance in lieu of the one in Mrs. Jones's room. There, he had found a curiosity or two, the most interesting being the blood on some tunnel "thorns" that had grown quite naturally in one part of Claudia's sub-Underground.

The thicket wasn't an intentional trap—Claudia had thought herself strong enough to decline any major security precautions in her belowground domain. But in Lilly's view, the refusal was only another sign that these vampires wrongly depended upon the *custodes* for protection when they should have been providing more for themselves. The keepers had other important matters to attend to, yet sometime during the past century, these vampires had got more dependent than ever.

According to rumor, though, they hadn't been the only ones to become complacent. It seemed that time had dulled the fire of purpose in many of the blood brothers who had been so voracious and loyal on the battlefield centuries ago.

Or perhaps those stories about the other Undergrounds weren't true at all, Lilly thought. Perhaps the tales were created by wandering masters who were bored of waiting for the ages to pass and for the dragon's armies to rise against the world.

All the same, Nigel had cleaned off those bloodied thorns in the sub-Underground, taking samples that the vampires might be able to use to identify a trespasser once the *custodes* handed over the blood to them. Her brother had also found a hair matching the other one that he had discovered in Mrs. Jones's room during his initial inspection of it.

But that hadn't been the most disturbing find. Part of the wall that used to cover Claudia's private room, where she'd killed her girls, had been demolished. Nigel had no explanation for it, but Lilly knew.

The attackers. They had to have been there.

Lilly had asked him if he had noticed a jasmine scent at any time in the sub-Underground, but he had said no. Nonetheless, she wondered if Mihas had received her communication to beware of jasmine altogether.

"I wish," she said, as the monitor room's big black door came into sight, "there were cameras in Claudia's part of the Underground. We would know for certain what happened down there."

"She wanted to do all the watching herself, without surrendering her privacy to the modern eye, as she calls it," Nigel said. "And no wonder, with what we know she's been doing to her classes of girls down there. Mihas was only accepting of the cameras in his section because of what we protect here. That's the only difference."

He didn't add that previous *custode*s had insisted upon surveillance in Mihas's section of the Underground, whereas it hadn't mattered so much with Claudia's portion.

They arrived at the door's access panel, and Lilly hopped in front of Nigel to open it.

"You'd bite my arm off to get in there first," he said.

"There's a lot to do."

Like finding that dark-haired woman with the mind powers, Lilly thought, hitting the button to release the door. Discovering the woman's whereabouts seemed even more important than most everything else for some reason, and Lilly hadn't been able to stop thinking about cornering her again, beating her this time in any game of cat and mouse they might take up.

As the door slid to a gape and Lilly burst into the room, she and Nigel were stopped short by the red-rimmed screens that the alarm system had highlighted during their short absence.

"What now?" Nigel murmured. "They've been putting us through the paces lately."

Fascinated, Lilly merely watched what was happening on the Underground cameras trained on the kitchens: the knock-down, drag-out fighting between the pack of girl vampires and . . .

Was that Claudia, in full cat-vampire form, in the midst of them?

A thrill speared her. Had Della finally recalled every tale that

Lilly had implanted? Had she put all the pieces together, and that's why the girls had gathered?

She leaped toward the console, but Nigel was already reaching for the mask hanging on his belt.

"What're you doing?" Lilly asked. Surely he wasn't about to interfere.

"What do you think?"

Quick as a flash of panic, she was on her brother, her hand grasping his hair to wrench his neck back, her curved Relaquory blade to his throat.

He was too stunned to move—she could feel it in the way he raised his arms, pausing in retaliation.

But she wouldn't give him the opportunity.

"Listen to me," she said evenly, though she felt his body now tensing in readiness to disarm her. She brought the blade closer to his jugular, showing him she was serious.

And when he loosened his muscles—for the moment, at least—he seemed to cooperate, perhaps believing that she really would cut him.

Or perhaps her cold tone had persuaded him, so she continued to use it.

"We're *custode*s, only connected to the Underground, not a true part of them."

"Lilly . . ."

"No—there'll be none of this 'you're only a new keeper' talk out of you."

Rage sizzled just under her skin, because she knew what he was—a scared caretaker who'd become just as misguided as the leaders of this particular Underground. Instead of fixing his attention on the future, he'd focused on the vampires, forgetting his true purpose in being here. Lilly saw this error as having led indirectly—but just as certainly—to the needless death of Charles, since her other brother had been on patrol round the vampires' careless burial ground.

If Mihas and Claudia had been minding the bigger picture instead of chasing their common appetites, she thought, she wouldn't be holding a knife to her brother's throat. She would die for the future of the community, but she wouldn't do it for these ridiculous creatures that housed them right now.

"You truly believe," she said, "that interference is the best policy?"

Still loose-limbed, Nigel didn't move, and Lilly knew she needed to state her case quickly, to stay on guard against the defensive move she anticipated from him.

"Together," she said, "Claudia and Mihas are weak and predictable. We know this because of all the vision/tales."

Tales numbering far more than what Lilly had implanted in Della. Old tales of this particular community's history that dated before the dragon's command to create Undergrounds.

She added, "Based on their past, I can tell you precisely what will happen with these two if Claudia survives those little girls. Whatever she did to upset Mihas's darlings, she'll just think of something new to lure him back into her good graces. Then she'll give him what he wants—in this case, the guarantee that he can keep his Underground while she continues to hold him in thrall after her blood baths. Her routine never changes. His doesn't, either. Mihas will, of course, take her back, but he'll concentrate on his own desires, keeping Claudia on a hook, just as always."

She whispered in Nigel's ear, harsh and brooking no argument.

"We must keep the cycle from going round, don't you see? Claudia should've gone her own way centuries ago, before she started clinging to Mihas, and it seems the girls are going to finally send her off."

When Nigel spoke, Lilly could feel his throat working under the knife. He sounded like a negotiator trying to reason with her.

"We can't allow the citizens to destroy each other."

"Can't we? This is a tiff that concerns only them. Where is it said that we have to interfere in their messes—unless we're specifically asked or unless the Underground itself is threatened to a destructive degree? Where is that directive, Nigel?"

Out of the corner of her gaze, she saw Claudia now fending off the girls in a hallway. Fortunately, Lilly knew Mihas wouldn't come to the cat vampire's rescue anytime soon. He was galloping over the heath, having a brilliant, silly old time on his own.

But Lilly would get around to returning him to full blood brother form soon enough.

"As *custodes*," she said, "we're meant to ensure that this sanctuary thrives, and that's what's going to happen without Claudia here. You know that as well as I."

"They're eating themselves up from the inside out, Lilly."

"Yes, because we all destroy what makes us weak," she said, softer now. "I recall your telling me that once, when you and Charles were playing army on the lawns, and I wished to join in. Charles was all for it, but not you. Never you."

Unthinkingly, she pressed the knife against him until he sucked in a breath. A hint of blood wet her hand.

"You told me," she said, as she felt him tense again, "that I would be a weak link. I would cause your deaths because I was merely a girl—one who was useless in so many ways." She had been deemed sterile, but in those years, she hadn't known what that had meant. "Naturally, I argued, so you took me in the house and stuffed me in the wardrobe. Do you remember that, Nigel?"

He barely made a sound, but the silence seemed to hold a hint of remorse.

"I was locked in there a long, long time," Lilly said. "Enough time to realize that you had learned this attitude from Mum and Dad. No one but Charles, who ended up getting me out of that wardrobe, believed I would amount to much. The girl of the family. The—what did you call it? Ah, yes." Her voice hardened. "The *aberration* who was not meant to go Underground like the most important of Meratoliages."

As his muscles went even tauter—he was about to attack—she released his hair and flattened her fingers to chop him with the side of her hand at the middle of his arm, on the hollow triceps muscle. He began to sink to his knees, and she struck the other side, too, immobilizing both of his arms.

"Thank you for the lessons on pressure points," she said as he tried to recover. "They've allowed me to relieve you of your command."

To emphasize that, she bent, holding the knife with one hand and levering back her other arm to strike the lower edge of the bottom of his jaw with the heel of her palm, toward the hole in the bone, up and in toward the center of his skull.

Knocked out, he fell backward, and Lilly watched him hit the ground.

As she calmed her heartbeat, her breathing, clarity came upon her.

She hadn't killed Nigel, because who would be called to take his place until her cousins came of age? But if her brother should discover that she had any role in orchestrating Claudia's ouster, he would be justified in terminating *her*.

It was time for the backup plan.

She unhooked the tuner from her belt, then moved toward him. She would have to make certain no one ever knew what she had been doing, and if that included using the tuner to adjust Nigel's mind and to tame Della and the other girls into subservience—if they managed to do away with Claudia—Lilly would take up the necessity of it.

It was for the good of the future, she thought. The ends justify the means.

But what if those girls, even while tamed, began to question if Mihas was aware of Claudia's blood baths?

Lilly didn't even flinch as she connected one end of the tuner to Nigel. She would see to that, as well, because Mihas needed to command these soldiers at all costs.

Yet she was quite sure that, should the girls think too much and turn on Mihas as they were doing with Claudia, he would have them in hand with his great charms. Their psychological makeup assured that they were the types who needed a protector, and since Mihas required them just as much—he could not cope with adult relationships, as far as Lilly saw—she was counting on their symbiotic neediness to win the night.

Everything would work out, she thought, for Mihas had always been the hungriest of soldiers. She only had to find a way to remind him of the time when he was the terror of the battlefield.

She finished with Nigel, binding him with restraints, reviving him, then tuning him, his eyes closed afterward as he adjusted to the absence of these last fifteen minutes. Then she watched the monitor screens, where the gnawing, famished girls had wounded Claudia, slowing down the old vampire as she made her way to an Underground exit. A quirk of regret actually dug into Lilly as she saw how desperately Claudia fought back.

Really, the old vampire had been fighting throughout her entire existence.

Pity the creature, Lilly thought, as, while keeping up with the action, she also began to access a new batch of recent Highgate recordings—these focused on the cemetery.

It wasn't even that Lilly disliked Claudia. It was nothing personal at all. There was actually more to the vampire than Della or any of the girls would ever know, and in many ways, Lilly admired the old beast for her perseverance and loyalty.

Truthfully, if Lilly had just included one key vision for Della's viewing pleasure—one more tale, this one unblurred and unadulterated—Della might have found a spot of sympathy for the housematron, even as the girl warped into the fearful instrument that would hopefully bring about the moment when Mihas would have to make a choice between his darlings and Claudia. . . .

ONCE, centuries ago, before any of the other tales, there was a tent of rough silk, its walls billowing in the night as, in the distance, the primal laughter of newly made vampires rode the air.

Out in the woods, they were on the hunt, yet inside the tent, one of the young blood brothers was testing his new powers.

As he dripped blood from a gutted rabbit onto his flesh, he found that his pores opened to drink. But the sustenance did not seem to feed him, survivalwise, as much as it fulfilled another appetite that the vampire could not yet name.

He heard the sound of paws hitting the ground outside as another creature galloped out of the woods, and he used his senses to identify the other.

His blood stirred in his veins.

Then, the second newly made creature arrived at the tent, whipping open the entrance, revealing a face with golden eyes and a wide, pointedly charming smile.

The first vampire's pulse tripped, reveling in secret joy to see the other.

And it was always secret, he thought. It was never revealed, for the cost would be heavy if the other blood brothers—or especially the morally upright dragon who had exchanged with them and given them this new life—were ever to discover it. They might think it a sin, just as the first vampire feared it truly was.

As the other creature entered, the first one raised his arm, showing how his pores drank of the blood.

"Wonders never cease," the other said, drawing closer to inspect the miracle. "Each of us is different in some ways, yet the same when it comes to blood appetites and allegiances to our sovereign."

Along the edges of the tent, the first vampire's white cat—a remnant left by his deceased wife—slunk from corner to corner. He had given great care to the animal, had often understood how the feline seemed to keep secrets behind its mysterious gaze.

"I gather," he said, "that we have taken on the aspects for which we feel an affinity. You have always been the wolf of the battlefield, hence your abilities. . . ."

Indeed, the wolfish vampire glanced hungrily at the white feline slinking round the tent, then grinned at his comrade, letting him know that he would graciously spare the pet.

"And you, the cat," the blood brother said. "Clever, cryptic, always quietly planning new strategies."

The night outside was hushed, and as the first vampire put aside the rabbit he was holding, the second one came even nearer.

The first creature's blood thumped so loudly he knew it consumed the air. "Mihas . . ."

As Mihas reached out, resting his fingertips on the first vampire's flesh, the skin drinker wondered if they would ever be able to speak aloud of what was between them. Mihas's wife, all his mistresses and secret male lovers . . . There were times when the first vampire wondered just how much his companion truly felt the love he often professed behind locked doors.

Even now, he could see a waning interest in Mihas's gaze. He had already moved ahead to the next conquest, the possibilities brought by this new existence.

But the first vampire would not be left behind—not when they were surely meant to be together. Why, both of them even had so many emerging talents in common, such as the instinct to assume animal forms as well as to summon creatures when required.

They were two of a kind, and the first vampire believed he had found a way to ensure their unity.

"There are methods," he said, "we might use to be together more freely."

"Are there?" Mihas asked in a whisper as his fingers drifted to his comrade's throat. He was intrigued.

The first vampire's hope expanded. "You change from what seems like a man to another form when you hunt, do you not?"

"I do."

"And I am comfortable as the hunting cat creature . . . and as something else, as well, I have found." Other blood brothers had shown a talent for shifting into diverse humanlike forms thus far, and this vampire had found it had a more limited inclination, as well.

"Yes?" Mihas asked, insistent.

"I am able," he said, excitement churning in his chest, "to alter more than my hunting form."

Mihas had become absolutely enthralled, and the first vampire contained his joy.

"Is this true?" Mihas asked. "How so?"

"You said yourself that each of us is different in some ways. We all have personal strengths that have been carried over into these altered bodies."

Slowly, he concentrated on changing, as he had been learning to, bit by bit, these past few nights.

And when he was finished, Mihas's gaze was burning.

The first vampire's flesh seemed to waver under his companion's perusal—the intensity. The longing.

He did not even mind that what Mihas was now seeing was not his true self, for Mihas was all his, and this was what mattered most.

Now Mihas would not be thinking of those other lovers and more stimulating adventures to be had. He was seeing what the first vampire would, in the future, genuinely believe to be an "it" stage of being—a compromise to be reached until Mihas realized that all he needed was standing in front of him.

Then there would be no more need for "it."

"Is this possible?" Mihas whispered as he looked at the new body: The more delicate face, still strong yet also feminine. The breasts under the rough shirt. The slender waist.

"For as long as we need it to be," the first vampire said, thinking to adjust its voice to fit its outward manner. "There will be no more hiding for us once we have left our old lives behind. Until then, we make do."

"Tell me," Mihas added, "can you alter yourself further?"

The first creature did not understand.

Then, as it noticed how its companion's teeth had grown even longer, saliva wetting his fangs, comprehension dawned.

Younger. Mihas wished it could be even younger. He loved women, but his dalliances with maids far and wide testified to his affinity for the young.

The first vampire tried to alter itself further, yet from the look on Mihas's face, he was not entirely pleased.

It rushed to the bed, where it had placed a mirror. It saw a girl in the reflection—its hair in lush curls, its features even smaller and more immature. Yet there was a lack of freshness, a wisdom in its eyes that told of too much experience.

"No matter," Mihas said, coming up behind the first vampire. "The initial form is fine. Your talent is very *fine, Claudius."*

And as Claudius took him at his word and changed back into the older female form, where its mature gaze would not seem so unnatural, Mihas embraced him.

Perhaps his comrade genuinely was *enamored with its new, though necessarily adult, appearance.*

However, years down the roads they traveled, with Claudius passing himself off as "Claudia," Mihas's mistress, or even going back to his own male form as a helpful valet, Mihas grew tired of the charade. Even after they settled down to make their own community of dragon-mandated vampires, he turned to other, truly younger pursuits, as he never did grow older in mind or temperament.

He wished for the new as he became old, and Claudius, who in later years had become Claudia so fully that it would not have recognized its true self even if it changed back into its other half full-time, knew that this womanly form was not enough. Even the blood baths, which seemed to temporarily return it to the twenty-eight-year-old glow it had started with all those years ago when it had first been turned, did not work for as long as they used to.

There was no way to make Mihas believe that it was younger.

Still, the first vampire would never stop believing that there would come a day when Mihas would love Claudius as Claudius loved him. And he never stopped hoping, even as Mihas's Underground grew with lovely young girls who would take centuries to become as old as it was now.

Even as Claudius heard society call people like him an "it." And he believed them, losing all sense of who he truly was, solely for the benefit of someone else. . . .

LILLY was still watching the screens and keeping tabs on a resting Nigel when one of the girls—she couldn't see which of them—nearly ripped off Claudia's head just before the old vampire used her shredded legs and the last of her strength to propel herself out the exit.

Then she watched the girls tussle among themselves about going after their housematron to see if she was indeed terminated. But the *custode* had an advantage that they didn't—she could access a camera hidden in the ground near the Underground door, and she could see the old vampire speeding away as fast as she could manage with those unhealed legs, and hiding among a copse of trees before one cat-wolf vampire popped her head out to see if Claudia was still round.

My, my, Lilly thought. The girls had certainly been brassed off, hadn't they? Imagine, nearly decapitating Claudia. They were strong, fast, lethal bitches, and the Underground would be better off because of them as soon as Mihas got his girls under some real control.

Meanwhile, Lilly diligently went to work on reviewing Highgate Cemetery footage from nearly a week ago, waiting to see if Claudia would contact the *custode*s for aid and refusing to move from her seat until the call came.

If it ever would.

TWENTY-THREE

The Lion and the Lamb

THE Lion and the Lamb Pub had a couple of its upper-level windows bricked up, showing that the structure had been here for a while because there used to be a tax on the amount of windows for each residence and the dwellers had gotten around having to pay more by blocking up windows.

It was a sign of ingenuity if Dawn had ever seen one. Still, the sight was unsettling, mainly because it reminded her of that Edgar Allan Poe story where a guy was bricked up behind a wall, screaming to get out.

And that must've been pretty close to what Natalia had gone through just a few minutes ago, Dawn thought as she and Jonah prepared to enter the pub, sticking together this time for security since they might be that much closer to an Underground. For the new girl, there had been a wall of sound pushing at her temples, and now that Dawn thought about it, Costin had something pressing at him, too, with such force that it bricked him up inside that body of his.

She walked toward the pub's door, reminding herself that she needed to remember that Costin hadn't necessarily *wanted* to even retreat back inside his body earlier. She needed to do everything she could to empathize with him instead of falling into some trap of resentment about how he was too content to wait in the shadows, as he always did.

As she and Jonah entered the building, she realized that he was also walled into that body and was only doing everything he could to keep from being buried, too.

Maybe they all were buried in some way.

She scanned the place. Unlike the outside, things seemed pretty homey with a flag floor and country pub atmosphere. Hell, there was even a puppy resting its sleepy head on its oversized paws near the door.

Then, as they got farther in, the rest of it hit her: the sight of over thirty young girls hanging around a large back room, mingling with people who resembled Dawn and Jonah in their tourist disguises.

She noted that none of the patrons were from the vampire schoolgirl group who'd attacked them the other night at Queenshill. And, praise it all, there weren't any shadow things flitting about, either.

Even so, were these girls the reason for Natalia's radar going off?

For a second, Dawn toyed with the idea of opening her mind to Jonah so they could communicate silently, but if they were close to an Underground, she didn't want to risk giving off strange vibes that any vampires might pick up.

But she did shut off her pulser, using the remote device in her pocket. And the instant she was away from Jonah, she was going to display her crucifix necklace, just to see if she got any reaction from the girls.

She leaned over to her damnable temporary partner, talking over the driving beat of a Rihanna song coming from a jukebox in the corner.

"Estrogen galore," she said.

He leaned over to answer. "I noticed."

His words brushed against her ear, making her cross her arms over her chest. But there was no other safe way to communicate, so she rolled with it, giving the back room an even more detailed sweep now that they were nearer: Girls at a pool table, playing snooker. Girls laughing with some guys who seemed like American frat boys as they tossed darts at a board.

Interesting that none of the gals—whom Dawn assumed were either old enough to drink or were carrying fake IDs—had any beverages near them. That was odd for a pub. Plus, their skin was more than the average shade of pale.

After doing the math, the evidence really did seem to equal a reason for Natalia to go on radar overload. Before tonight, the most she'd encountered at one time was the four Queenshill vamps during a stealth visit. But now, the psychic had obviously sensed way more than a small group.

Dawn kept watching the girls without looking like she was doing it, yet at the same time, she thought of how they'd have to train Natalia to withstand her radar in the future.

If there was much of a future ahead of them.

She jerked her chin toward the bar, and she and Jonah went over there, standing instead of sitting on the stools.

A barmaid—her curly brown hair sprinkled with gray, crow's-feet liberally camping out around her dark blue eyes—came right over.

After ordering two pints of cider, just so they would fit in with the human crowd, Dawn made chitchat as the woman drew their drinks from a tap.

"Young clientele here."

Dawn noticed that the barmaid kept glancing at Jonah about every two seconds, even though his back was to her. He was standing out, all right, such a cool customer in those purple-tinted glasses.

"These your regulars?" Dawn added.

The barmaid set their drinks on two coasters decorated with ugly, big-nosed creatures carrying axes and advertising Hobgoblin British Ale, and Dawn paid up while the woman answered.

"We seem to attract the young girls. Even though they're old enough, they're not much for drinking. But the owner doesn't mind them here all the time—they bring the boys like you wouldn't believe, and *they* put away pint after pint."

Now Dawn realized why Natalia had gotten vibes even when they'd visited the Highgate Cemetery over a week ago—it'd probably been all these girls swarming the nearby pub.

Either the barmaid knew exactly who they were but was lying about it, or she was telling the truth and the possible vampires were keeping their activities under wraps.

Should Jonah look into her mind to see if she was fibbing? Or would that be a red-flag alert?

Dawn decided to just go on questioning, keeping that all-powerful element of surprise for when they needed it the most—during a final attack.

She wrapped her fingers around the sweating glass of cider but didn't drink. Meanwhile, the barmaid kept checking out Jonah's back, as if hoping he'd turn around.

"Nice place," Dawn said. "We heard a lot of recommendations, so we had to stop in. We're history nuts."

The "we" seemed to bring the barmaid's interest to another

level, because it included Jonah. "The pub's got quite a bit of business from word of mouth lately." She took the pounds Dawn had laid out on the bar. "The owner refurbished last year, and everything conforms to the conservation society's standards. If you walk around, you'll see historical details like writings on the wall in the second back room"—she pointed to an area that the girls weren't occupying—"as well as original furniture kept upstairs for private parties."

Dawn was hoping she'd mention tunnels. No luck.

But Jonah finally turned around to smile at the barmaid, and that seemed to pave the way for better answers.

"Is it true about the highwaymen around here?" he asked. "We heard they smuggled loot from the main road using tunnels."

Smooth, Dawn thought. Jonah was an okay detective as long as he wasn't being an asshole.

The barmaid gave him a flirty look. "Now who's telling you those tales?"

Jonah flirted right back with his grin.

Ugh. Dawn guessed that Costin's influence had given Jonah this confidence. He might've been a shy recluse back in the day, but now he was living it up.

"We took a walking tour around Highgate with a guide," he said, leaning his arms on the bar. "But they told us that those tunnels aren't usually open for a look."

"It's *not* actually part of what we offer here." The woman leaned on the bar, too, flashing some cleavage at Jonah.

Dawn almost barfed. She felt sort of territorial, not about Jonah, but about Costin, even though he wasn't the one flirting.

"Too bad," she said, getting closer to her partner, but only because she wanted to stick her elbow against his arm in a reminder that this was gross.

In the first back room, a burst of giggles spiked the air, and

Dawn saw a girl standing on the pool table, using it like a catwalk while she teased an audience of guys wearing things like *Superbad* sweatshirts.

The barmaid sighed and went over there with her hands planted on her wide hips, just as if she'd dealt with this behavior a thousand times before, while Dawn wondered how these vamps operated.

Did they take blood from their frat-boy victims and mind-wipe them?

Was erasing memories allowed in their community?

Dawn thought about Kate Lansing and what the team had found on Billiter Street, at the body dump. Bones. Kate's head.

No, she thought. When the vamps that the team was targeting decided to eat, they ate well, so they probably chose prey more carefully. They wouldn't want their victims to be easily missed.

She canted toward Jonah, taking care to talk softly enough to make it hard for any possible vamp to hear clearly. "We've got to get to those tunnels."

"Our server invited us to look around this place, didn't she?"

This time, when Jonah grinned, Dawn grinned back. If he was thinking what she was, maybe they could get under the ground. Then Jonah could let Costin out, just to see if he sensed a master down there.

But what would happen after that? If there was any indication of a master around, should they retreat or summon Kiko and the Friends to go for it right away?

Dawn didn't know. In L.A., after they'd uncovered the location of the Underground, the team had gone into lockdown and Costin had taken his time in getting there. He'd had a methodical plan.

Unlike this time, it seemed.

Jonah was already walking toward the second back room, where the barmaid had said there were historical writings posted on the wall. Dawn left her cider behind to back him up.

But when she saw two different entrances on each side of the white-planked space, Dawn got Jonah's attention and indicated that she was going to take one of them instead of scoping out the obvious.

He glanced around to see if they were being watched, but everyone seemed to be focusing on the pool table activity in the other room.

They slipped into a hallway lined with surplus straight-back chairs and closed doorways.

Jonah pulled down the sleeve of his coat, masking fingerprints while covering his hand in order to try the tarnished knob on one of the doors. It didn't open.

"Locked," he said.

They both laughed quietly. Locked wasn't a problem for either of them.

Still, now wasn't the time for a show of vampire strength or psychokinetic boogaloo.

While Jonah covered her, Dawn took out her lock picking tools and went to work, thinking that the loud pulses from the jukebox might be enough interference to mask these vampires' hearing.

"So what do you think Gatenby has to do with all this?" she asked.

"No ideas yet. But he frequented a place where there're tunnels and rooms underground, and Natalia felt something going on in here. I'd say it doesn't look good for our boy."

She took care of the lock, but when she opened the door, a bunch of old table linens fell out, and she and Jonah had to push the flood of them back in. He followed up with the door itself.

"Looks like we're gonna have to play treasure hunt," she said. "Or do you think there's some trapdoor hidden in the floor?"

"I think—"

He whipped his head around, sensing something a fraction of a second before jasmine bolted into the hallway.

Kalin's voice whirred around them. "*Update!*"

A cold thrust invaded Dawn with images of Natalia and Kiko. Were they in trouble, even though Kiko had driven the new girl back to headquarters to get her out of the way?

She backed off from the door and followed Kalin and Jonah down the hallway, toward the pub itself. But the Friend stopped them before they emerged into the open.

"*We found one of 'em on the heath nearby,*" the spirit said, her tone high and excited, chopping up her speech. "*We're trackin' 'er out of Highgate now—a cat woman lookin' older than 'em schoolgirls. She's fast, but she seems to be wounded, so she's not as fast as most.*"

"She's no schoolgirl?" Dawn asked. "Because we might have a few of those kind in here, Kalin."

"Not *a schoolgirl.*" Although the Friend was invisible, she got in Dawn's face. The jasmine was overwhelming. "*Older than one of 'em!*"

At first Dawn hoped this new, older vamp might be a master—*the* master they were looking for—but Kalin had said the creature was a female.

She turned to Jonah. "A wounded and vulnerable vampire. Sounds like a prospect for questioning to me."

"Much easier pickings than what we've got here."

As she and Jonah rounded out of the hallway and into the back room, that point was only emphasized by a blockade of girls, their heads tilted as if they'd heard something and had come to investigate.

Dawn's heartbeat seemed to crackle to pieces, all with their own rhythms, even without the pulser. She debated taking out the crucifix pendant from underneath her shirt, but then one of the girls sniffed the air, sensing Kalin.

Then they all sniffed.

Right. If these weren't vampires, Dawn was going to eat her flamethrower.

Then, with a barely perceptible laugh, Kalin—damn her—nudged against a few of the girls, just to be the bitch that she was.

God, Dawn was going to get her when this was over.

But it was enough to draw the girls' confused attention, and Dawn took the opportunity to calmly walk away from them, Jonah right behind her. Acknowledging that something was out of the ordinary would only give them away.

Then the girls started to giggle.

Dawn turned around in enough time to see Jonah making a subtle gesture that hinted at a reason they might've been back in that hallway.

A mile-high-club gesture.

In any other case, she would've gotten after him, but she had to admit that he'd thought fast, finding an excuse that had the girls breaking apart and going back to the other areas of the pub as Dawn and he opened the door into the night, where Kalin sped ahead of them.

"Just so you know," Dawn said as they began walking fast to where their Sedona was parked, "I saw that."

Kalin reared up behind Dawn and pushed her ahead, jealous as hell.

"Go," she said. *"Just get yourselves ready for word on when you're needed."*

"Okay, okay." Dawn picked up their pace, her breathing quickening, too, as they passed through the square near the Figurehead, the first pub they'd visited tonight.

Kalin sucked, but she was right.

This could end up being the big one.

TWENTY-FOUR
The Waiting Game

WHY did history seem to repeat itself? Dawn wondered as she and Jonah sat in their vehicle, still parked down the hill from the Highgate Cemetery.

He was in the backseat and she was in the front, just like hours before. Except this time, they were waiting for word from a Friend as to where they could find this running vampire and wrangle it for questioning, or if the Friends would need help when they had the chance to circle back and inspect the heath where they'd first spotted the vampire. The spirits guarding headquarters in Southwark couldn't be spared, so the team was the only backup available.

Meanwhile, Kiko had already used his driving modification equipment to take Natalia back to headquarters, where he would be leaving her, picking up Frank, and going to any new locations with him if needed. It was best to leave Natalia out of this, even though, as soon as she had gotten away from the Lion and the Lamb Pub, her profound discomfort had abated.

Still, they didn't want to take the chance of having her lose it during this crucial time.

"The Friends said this vampire was a 'she,'" Dawn said to Jonah as the time display on the dashboard stamped out each second. She absently played with the crucifix that was outlined under her shirt. "They said that the vamp's also older in appearance than one of those schoolgirls. Do you think she's something in between a top-level vampire and a lower one?"

"If it's a 'she,' it can't be a master," Jonah answered, taking off those hip glasses from his disguise and stowing them in a coat pocket, "and it also can't be a schoolgirl at its age. That's all I know."

He leaned back and watched a group of people laughing as they passed the Sedona on their way up the hill to the village.

Dawn watched them, too, her gaze stuck on a man and woman at the back of the small crowd. They were grinning at each other, and she could tell that they were in some sort of courtship stage.

Weird. She couldn't even connect to the innocence of their shared smiles or the way they stayed just far enough apart so that, when their coats brushed, it was a big deal.

She took her hand away from the crucifix and glanced the other way. Adrenaline was scratching through her, into her, as if coring her out.

But it was only anticipation, Dawn thought. Anxiety for her to get her hands on that running vampire and coax some answers out of the enemy.

Yeah, that was it.

She felt Jonah skimming the edges of her consciousness, like he was curious about what she was turning over in her mind and he wanted in. Thinking that she could and would withstand anything now, she didn't shove him away.

So he entered her, tentatively, then threw her a curveball by slipping out soon afterward.

But even more surprising was the extra-tingling haze he left—just like he'd infused her with a double shot of cool energy.

"So many things weighing on you," Jonah said, his voice low and even mildly comforting.

She didn't want comfort, though. She needed ice. Frostiness. A zone to prepare her for what was coming.

She wanted more of what she'd just felt from him, but there was no way she'd ask him for it.

Dawn fixed her gaze on a second-story window across the street, where the panes were covered with sheer red draping. "It's nothing I can't handle, Jonah."

"I know that. But you still can't stop wishing you could understand what the boss is doing—why he retreated earlier."

He'd nailed it. She wasn't anxious about encountering any vamps tonight. Her limbs and chest were heavy with running nerves because of Costin. She just hadn't admitted it until now.

Dawn found herself saying things she never would've said before, maybe because it was so damned quiet in this car. Maybe because she couldn't stand to keep it to herself anymore.

"I hate this," she said, anchoring a hand on the bottom of the steering wheel. "I hate that I think he's backing away from going banzai and fighting when there's a way for him to get out and take care of business now."

"What do they say?" She could hear Jonah moving forward in the backseat. "There's a slight difference between stupidity and bravery. The boss is only being smart. Safe."

"I know. It's just . . ."

How could she put it into words?

Jonah's voice went even lower—not Costin low, but there was a definite change.

"You can't possibly understand what he's doing, Dawn. Not when you're the opposite of him."

She turned slightly, seeing Jonah's profile, the false tranquillity of streetlights through the windshield providing only a little illumination. For a second, she could've sworn that he and Costin had joined more than they ever had—that Jonah had even become an intermediary.

Would it be easier to tell Costin how she felt by using a go-between? Even easier than going mind-to-mind with him when he was dominant?

God, something was wrong when Jonah had to be the middleman.

"The opposite of him," Dawn repeated. "What exactly does that mean?"

When Jonah looked at her, his eyes heated a low blue in the dimness. "You're impulsive, rash—everything he can't afford to be. But you're also strong, and he needs you to stay that way while logic forces him to hold back for the time being."

She paused, thinking she should stop dwelling on this now, but knowing she couldn't. Costin—a former minion of the dragon. A once loyal follower who had exchanged with his ultimate master and come to despise himself for it. The vampire who'd almost wasted away in a dungeon cell until The Whisper—the one who'd given Costin the powers of a Soul Traveler—had offered a bargain for him to win back his soul.

Dawn couldn't help but think that Costin had chosen to stay in just another cell right now, and she wondered if it'd always go back to that with him.

She was disappointed. That was the bottom line, because even though he'd screwed her over in Hollywood for the greater good, he'd seemed like so much more than she could ever be: Someone smarter than anyone she'd known. Someone she'd actually looked up to in a world where she hadn't looked up to many others at all.

"Was he like this as a soldier?" she asked Jonah.

"Are you asking if he retreated back then?"

She nodded stiffly, fortifying herself for an honest answer.

"When strategy demanded it, yes." Jonah sounded even closer to her now. "He always had an eye for the right move. Unlike some of his comrades, he never took a risk unless it was calculated. That's why he killed so many men on the fields of battle—even before he became a vampire."

"And that's how he's operating now." She said it more to convince herself than to continue the conversation. "He's the chess master."

"The best. And you're queen of the board." He waited a beat for that to sink in. "You really do mean everything to him, Dawn, and *you're* the one who's out here now instead of him. He needs you."

Her chest went tight at what Jonah was saying, mostly because Costin had never put it so simply. Where he was cryptic and as reserved as a soldier needed to be when everything was on the line, Jonah just put it all out there.

But she couldn't believe that she meant more to Costin than just a piece on a board, because first and foremost, that's what she was, and she'd never fooled herself into thinking beyond it. *Feeling* beyond it.

"Yeah, you're right," she said. "I'm 'key.' "

"Dawn."

She looked away from him, because seeing that face only reminded her of Costin.

But that didn't faze Jonah. "Someday you're going to know your value."

And what was that? she thought. Was she worth Costin's soul? Her own?

Even though Jonah wasn't in her mind, her thoughts must've been written all over her posture, because he inched even closer.

In spite of herself, she glanced at him.

Mistake, because his gaze held hers. Jonah's eyes.

But it was Costin's face she saw, only because she wanted to.

Yet his gaze . . . blue.

So blue.

She wasn't sure she could separate them in her mind right now, and when he touched her neck, she knew he wanted a bite, not because he needed blood, but because he desired it. From her.

Just her.

As his fingertips traced her jugular, her skin came alive, tingling every nerve ending, and she tilted back her head, her eyelids going heavy.

A bite.

God, it sounded like such a good idea.

And her body, from bottom to top—each thud of her pulse pushing toward the center of her and threatening to meet in a dark explosion—agreed.

She could see his eyes lightening to silver—a color that meant either personality might be dominant—and the evidence of his appetite for her made her bang even more, melting her, weakening her.

As he stroked her neck, persuading her to lean her head back even more, her eyes began to close.

Costin, she told herself. Because, to her, it *was* Costin moving in for the bite, his breath on her flesh. It was Costin brushing his lips against her neck, priming her until she went damp and crazy with an inner heat that consumed everything—

Then, with a growled sound of frustration, he backed off.

Dawn's eyes flew open, her heart jarring as if it'd been jolted into rhythm again.

It didn't help when she heard the slam of two nearby car doors, then soon after, a quick knock at the front passenger side of their vehicle.

She already had her mini flamethrower out and aimed by the time she realized that it was only Natalia. Jonah had obviously heard her way before she'd gotten here.

Mortification enveloped her with clammy heat as she tried not to look at him while unlocking the doors and summoning Natalia inside.

While the new girl jumped into the seat, Kiko got into the back beside Jonah, his jumbled words urgent.

"We decided to come back, and don't yell at me for not calling, because you'd only have told us to stay away."

Dawn was all business now, brusque in the face of what she'd almost allowed Jonah to do. She noticed that the new girl was holding a small silver-tipped stake, the weapon's point gleaming in the faint light.

"Frank taught me how to use this and more," Natalia said. "Kiko agreed that it's time to test me. Especially after what we . . . came upon."

"What you came upon?"

Kiko was already following up. "There's . . . Well, something happened to bring us back here, Dawn. And even though I wish Natalia would get her butt to headquarters"—he'd changed his tone, telling Dawn that he and Natalia had debated this and she'd somehow talked him into it—"I don't think that's what the team needs. I thought we should get back to you as soon as possible. Her radar can only help, and Frank can always rush to us if we need him."

"Plus, I'll be able to fight," Natalia said.

Kiko "uh-uh"ed. "Not before you hide, first thing, then engage only if you need to."

Dawn broke up the party. "Just why did you two come back here?"

"Tell her," Kiko said, but the new girl only shook her head.

Dawn realized that Natalia looked like a second grader who'd taken mama's favorite jewelry out to play with and accidentally dropped an earring down the sink drain.

"All right then." Kiko turned to Dawn. "Don't kill us because we were just doing something we thought might speed up the investigation. And I didn't even know what Natalia was up to in the backseat when I was driving her to headquarters. She was *supposed* to be lying down and resting."

Natalia spoke up. "But when you found out, you stopped driving and joined in quickly enough."

"Okay." Kiko's swallow was obvious, even from the backseat. "Natalia was carrying a small Ouija board, so we went ahead and contacted Briana Williamson."

"What?"

Dawn turned to the female psychic, remembering their conversation from a couple of nights ago: How Natalia wanted to get back on the Ouija to try to get in touch with the dead girl from Queenshill they'd contacted before. How she would do anything to help those voices that called to her.

"You know that we can't afford to open ourselves any more than we already did when we talked to Briana the first time," Dawn said. "What the hell were you guys thinking?"

She could hear Jonah stir at the curse, but she was beyond caring.

"I realize it sounds like a terrible idea." Natalia was hanging her head. "But nothing bad happened, and we were far away from headquarters at the time. Friends were escorting us, and it seemed the perfect opportunity based on what I felt in Highgate tonight." She peeked up through the bangs of her red wig, the braids dangling over her shoulders. "Briana—and I have a strong feeling it was her—came back to us."

"And," Kiko interrupted, "there was something a little different to what she said, so that's why we hightailed it back here."

Natalia had taken out her notebook and flipped to a page. "Perhaps it means nothing at all, but we thought you should see."

"Remember," Kiko said as Natalia showed Dawn what she had written, "how Briana had spelled out 'wicked master' on the Ouija during our first session with her, but then she was cut off?"

Dawn nodded, recalling how Natalia had passed out from the stress of the contact. They'd thought that "wicked master" was a warning or a game that Briana might be playing on behalf of a possible Underground.

"Well," Kiko added, "it looks like Briana didn't finish what she had to say, and tonight she had a chance to complete her thought."

Dawn glanced at the note page to find WICKED MASTER written on it, but with one little—yet freakin' huge—difference.

WICKED MASTERS.

An *S*.

Plural.

It was enough to make Dawn forget that she was avoiding Jonah, and she showed him the paper, too, knowing that Costin would get the information through his dominant host.

As Jonah stared at it, that gluttonous black spot in Dawn gaped, teased by the message. Taunted.

Stoked by the possibility that there was something much bigger than she'd first suspected on the horizon.

"More than one master," Dawn said. "A joint Underground."

Kiko nodded. "Either we're in for a fucking roller-coaster ride or we're just fucked altogether."

Twenty minutes later, when Kalin sped over to their vehicle to report that they'd tracked the running female vampire to the east in Dalston, Dawn started the engine and revved it to a roar that only halfway filled that dark spot inside of herself.

TWENTY-FIVE

London Babylon, Main Underground

THEY'D made a pact, the lot of them.

Never tell about what had really happened with Mrs. Jones—not unless Wolfie came into their minds to discover the truth for himself.

But even then, the schoolgirls had vowed to block the details as best as they could, to fight for what they possessed here in the Underground, because what *did* they have except for Wolfie?

What would be the use in continuing if he found out?

Of course, Della was certain that Mrs. Jones was still alive out there, somewhere; the old vampire had told them that they would lose half their powers if she were to perish, and it only made sense since she was their cocreator.

And all the girls still felt whole.

Yet they were willing to pit their own word against the cat's, if the ancient thing were ever to return. They were willing to have their master choose between her and them.

Because the girls had no other choice.

So, as one—a pack with a secret so terrible that it bound them—they sealed and camouflaged the broken Underground exit. Then they crept through the halls, sniffing in the hope that they would catch the scent of Wolfie's hair and leather clothing while avoiding the recruited vampires who had returned from aboveground.

After almost an hour, they simultaneously identified him, then traded glances and headed for the common area as that one unit.

His Queenshill darlings.

The girls he indulged, hated to punish, hated to lose.

They found him in a tented room, with its gold and silver and blue silks flowing from roof to ground over satin beds. It was one of Wolfie's favorite areas, and Della thought it might be because of his days as a soldier, camping out under a night sky.

But Wolfie's desire for fine things decorated the area, too: golden pitchers traced with blood that he had already sipped, diamond and crystal chandeliers, gem-studded posts, all derived from the swindled fortune of Thomas Gatenby.

Their master was presently stretched over a bed, alone, his eyes closed, his hands clasped on his chest, his hair spread over a pillow after his frenzied gallop over the heath.

Seeing him lying there, Della believed that he *was* good, innocent in everything, and the power of that belief sighed through her, even if, in the back of her mind, a niggle remained—a tweak of knowing that reality was what one made of it.

But it was her choice to have faith in what she wished.

Their choice.

As they padded closer to him, his chest rose and fell, but then he sprang up, giving a hearty growl that caused the group to jump back.

He laughed, but not a one of them giggled as they normally would have.

A pause clicked by.

Clearly realizing that Wolfie would think something amiss, Stacy forced herself to be jolly. She squeezed Della's hand next to her, so Della imitated the gaiety, squeezing Noreen's hand on her other side, sending the message down the linked chain of the gathered girls.

Soon, they were all laughing, just as Wolfie would expect.

Yet he still cocked his head. "What troubles my dears?"

Della's skin prickled.

The schoolgirls had silently mind-discussed at length what they would tell him. They had concocted a story that could be supported by what had been recorded on any cameras, if he should ever look.

Stacy stopped smiling, her tone dropping to a quivering whisper that would have made any actress proud. "We're so afraid, Wolfie."

It had its intended effect: he stiffened into a protective hunch for his girls.

Della remained silent, even though it didn't seem as if Wolfie minded that she was out of her cage. Perhaps he believed that Mrs. Jones had taken her from it; he hadn't been round to know any better.

Besides, Wolfie was Wolfie, and water slid off his back so very easily.

Would that be the case now?

"You see," Stacy added, "Mrs. Jones came into one of our minds and made a threat beyond imagination. She saw Noreen jesting, pretending to dance with you for our entertainment. Although Mrs.

Jones didn't outwardly react at the time, she became . . . jealous. Frighteningly so. She linked to Noreen's mind and told her to beware in a most awful manner."

They had chosen Noreen to be the victim because she did enjoy her dancing—any camera would validate that. Also, Wolfie had been paying a great deal of attention to her back in the sub-Underground.

Noreen, for her part, trembled quite convincingly next to Della, and the still-healing gashes on her face from that deep swipe Mrs. Jones had given her during their fight made her seem all the more vulnerable.

Wolfie knit his thick brows.

"Noreen told us what Mrs. Jones said," Stacy continued, "and while we were reeling under the shock of what she threatened, our housematron entered the room just as we were at the height of our fear. We overreacted, not thinking clearly."

"Overreacted?" he asked, as if not understanding the word.

Stacy went to Wolfie as planned, getting to her knees and lowering her head so she didn't meet his gaze straight on.

It was time for the clincher, Della thought, holding tight to Noreen's hand.

Time to see how Wolfie reacted.

"We weren't certain how to handle what she told Noreen," Stacy said. "She'd never before informed any of us that she would string us up by the ankles and bleed us dry."

Wolfie flinched, and Della wondered if it was because he was shocked by the very notion of such violence against his girls or if there was no way they should have known the details of Mrs. Jones's activities.

"She . . . said this, Anastasia?" Wolfie asked Stacy, his voice thin.

All the schoolgirls nodded, their eyes wide.

Stacy pawed at his thigh, and Wolfie glanced at her hand, his gaze going a deeper shade of gold. Even Della realized what that look meant; all of them did because they had seen it during playtime while leaning against him.

However, although the most recent class hadn't been graced by his bite yet, the older girls had known every one of his desires once they'd been brought to the main Underground.

"We didn't think of the consequences we would receive for protecting Noreen and, by extension, ourselves," Stacy said, her voice choked. "And as we defended against what we thought to be an imminent attack against one of us, Mrs. Jones ran away. We only thought we should be honest with you, Wolfie."

For a moment, he seemed as if he didn't believe that his companion had retreated. He closed his eyes, clearly attempting to contact her, but Della had no doubt Mrs. Jones was far, far away from the Underground and still above the surface that blocked mind communication.

When he opened his eyes again, Della didn't know if he was about to enter their minds to see the truth of this for himself, or if he was angry enough to skip that and slay them all right here and now.

What if he didn't believe them? What if they had driven out a mistress whom he would love more than all of them?

But when Stacy—experienced, knowing Stacy—moved her hand between his legs and stroked him, his eyes went hazier with gold heat.

And when the rest of them moved in to cuddle against Wolfie, to force him to make the choice between going after Mrs. Jones or staying here with them in this Underground he'd populated with a veritable feast of his greatest passions, he seemed lost. Especially when Della, Noreen, and Polly joined in.

He had never tasted their blood before, had never fully consummated his passion for them, and Della wondered if it had anything to do with Mrs. Jones's possessiveness of her harvests.

Della thought to her classmates, *Let him drink from the others*, and they seemed to understand that, perhaps, the three of them should withhold what Wolfie had been missing in case they required the leverage later.

As the other girls lowered him back to the cushions, their lips and hands all over him, he sighed, as if temporarily defeated.

"I suppose," he said, "Mrs. Jones will return if she chooses, and we can settle matters then."

It was all they wanted to hear for now, and while Stacy slipped off Wolfie's shirt, Della clung to his thigh in utter gratitude, trying not to pay mind to all the lies pinning her to the one individual she'd always believed would love her forever.

TWENTY-SIX

Happily Never After

In a rundown Dalston building with a Flats to Let sign in a glass-webbed front window, Claudia sat across from the bathtub that held its captive, a twentysomething woman who had tarted herself up for a night on the town. She wore a black dress that showed her curvy, nubile body to every advantage as she cowered. A flop of brown hair fell over one wide, terrified eye, brushing a sealed mouth that Claudia had charmed shut so the victim wouldn't scream so loudly anymore.

The vampiress had plucked its victim from the dark streets outside, famished after hiding in the woods near Highgate and taking an exorbitant amount of energy to self-heal its legs and neck to the point where its head wasn't lolling to its shoulder. There were still shreds of skin and a peek of tendons, but Claudia had at least been able to travel on afterward, moving at a visible blur—much more slowly than it would have preferred had it been perfectly healthy.

Although the victim's blood had given Claudia strength, the creature still yearned for more as it visually devoured the young woman's skin, its own flesh tingling while the small mouths chewed open.

The victim's eyes bulged at the sight—all she could do instead of screeching.

"It's moments such as these that define a life," Claudia said in its husky voice. It had long ago altered its speech to reflect that of a woman's, and the charade had fooled so many . . . even itself. "Choices we make, directions we follow. But I did the right thing tonight. I don't regret a bit of it."

The captive, with mascara running from her eyes to create ghoulish tears, nodded slowly. Claudia thought how its victim's eyes would carry wrinkles within a decade, but now, the skin was flawless.

Just as Mihas liked it.

Mihas . . . By now he would be Underground again with those traitorous schoolgirls. Somehow, they had discovered Claudia's beauty regimen. How? It didn't know, but it was going to find out after returning. And it wished to come back in grand form, looking its enthralling best so Mihas would agree to terminate those little monsters. Claudia and her companion would be able to cultivate many more in the future, so these defective rebels would hardly be missed.

The creature reached toward the woman in the scum-lined tub who cringed away from Claudia's touch. But the vampiress slid her fingertips over the woman's cheek nonetheless.

"They wanted to know if he"—Mihas—"was privy to the blood harvests," it said, thinking of how silky human skin was. Naturally warm. "But I didn't tell those girls. And because of that, he will know that I love him truly, forever. He'll realize that I did everything to protect him, and I always will."

It had been protecting him from the beginning: from the time when they had exchanged with the dragon through all their travels, even as Mihas had secretly loved other males, other females—anything that had tempted him.

But, mostly, he had loved his girls.

They had got him into such trouble, too, from the village mobs that had hunted him to the courtiers who had heard tales of a wolf on the prowl in the woods and forced Mihas to flee from polite society. Yet Claudia, in either womanly guise or that of a subservient male, had always been there to heal, to catch him each time he fell from grace.

And he had fallen so many times, especially when he had decided to take up with Thomas Gatenby, who had provided them with their present fortunes before he had taken ill—a condition that Claudia had advised her companion to hurry along. The man had been smitten with Mihas and his charms, and Mihas had seduced him into giving over every last bit of his riches, even at the risk of attracting attention from gossip-prone London.

Even at the risk of alienating Claudia.

Shortly thereafter, the dragon had commanded the blood brothers to create Underground communities to breed and train soldiers, and although settling had taken a while, Claudia had managed to persuade Mihas into some restraint years afterward. It had even stayed under the ground, the two of them joining to create what was sure to be the most formidable army of them all; it had seen to the formation of their society while Mihas had gone on more of his erotic journeys above. And when he returned from his wanderings, Claudia would always make certain to be beautiful for him.

This time when they reunited, though, would that be enough?

As the vampiress's fingers sprouted claws that scratched against the victim's cheek, Claudia wondered how long it could continue like this . . . how many new tricks it would have to invent to keep Mihas.

The woman in the tub was shaking, closing her eyes, sweating such fear that Claudia took its hand away, but not before skimming the healed bite marks on her neck where it had taken blood from her earlier.

"I wonder," it said, trying to make its voice soothing before it fully charmed the woman's mind to a deep, sleepy peace before a bath, "what those girls have told him. They're far more clever than anyone suspects, aren't they?"

The victim's eyes darted back and forth, searching for an answer in Claudia's gaze.

The vampiress tilted her head at that, for the victim presently reminded it of Della—that sweet, earnest student who had at first seemed quite harmless but was actually as vicious as they came.

Yet Della was its child, after all, only taking after the vampire parents that had borne her. And Claudia had chosen to create progeny because of the dragon's mandate. Go forth and give him a well-trained army.

There had been another reason, as well, because Claudia had believed that sharing children with Mihas would create a bond that might never be broken. It thought this connection might hold him beyond beauty and the passion it always temporarily created.

When Claudia had seen their first batch of children, it had been gratified, because when the girls turned into their vampire form, they were so very ugly: cat-wolves that looked older with wrinkled and hairless skin.

This was Claudia's petty revenge, and when it realized that Mihas didn't always like to see the girls in this form, or even when a few years had passed and they lost the immediate freshness of their true youth, Claudia had experienced something like relief.

No more the "blossoms" flowering into womanhood, entering a time that Claudia had left far behind in its own mortal life. There was an empowering element to that. And when it became a housematron at Queenshill to make the harvesting of beauty treatments all the easier, it had taken satisfaction in banning Mihas from taking the blood of Claudia's girls, too.

Everything had been going so well, it thought. Until tonight.

The creature stroked its victim's cheek again, and the woman choked on a silent cry.

Claudia sighed, then turned away to dig through the female's purse, where she found a mobile.

"He must be wondering where I am," the vampiress said, the echo of its voice against the dirty tile sounding hollow as it rang Mihas.

But he didn't answer.

Of course he wouldn't, Claudia thought while redialing to connect with his answering service instead. If he were Underground, his mobile would lack reception. Same with their Awareness, which was also useless now because of the distance between them.

It tried not to think of the alternative: Mihas cavorting with his girls. Mihas listening to their lies about what had happened with Claudia tonight. Mihas under their eager mouths.

Keeping its voice steady, Claudia spoke on the mobile, telling his answering service all about the attack. But with every word, it kept seeing him kissing the girls, his teeth scratching their lips for a taste of blood. . . .

What if it came down to a choice between them and Claudia? it wondered.

Like so many times before, it despaired of ever truly being loved by him.

So why keep trying to call? Why dial his mobile number again, just to see if he might pick up this time? Why not contact a *custode* to facilitate Claudia's entrance back into the Underground instead?

A gush of jasmine halted Claudia from dialing anymore, and

the vampiress stood, waving away the scent. The smell had been round since the escape from Highgate.

"What are you?" it growled.

Suddenly, the scent was gone, yet Claudia didn't relax. Instead, it turned to the victim, and this time in the woman's young face, it saw Della, Stacy, and the accompanying schoolgirls who had attacked.

Yet then it saw the *others* from the past, as well: the classmates Claudia had used for blood over the years.

The mouths on its skin were really working now, yowling without sound, and the vampiress flicked its claws to a longer sharpness as it assessed the woman in the tub.

Beautiful. Claudia had to be as beautiful as possible for its return Underground.

"There is so much I've tolerated from him," it said to the victim. "It's been the only way to hold on. Not even spells or potions or anything else I've tried over the centuries worked."

The question of when toleration became masochism poked at Claudia's mind, but it had asked itself this so many times before that the meaning had become vague, like the wind or the night.

Yet now?

Now it genuinely wondered how much more it could take from Mihas, especially as it kept picturing him with the girls.

But how could it care so much when it had allowed the behavior for centuries? Claudia had enabled him, even if it had thought it had found a form that controlled Mihas to a certain extent, that had enriched itself in a shape that had supposedly been so much weaker than any male.

It caught a glimpse of its own reflection in a grimy mirror to the side, and it cocked its head, realizing that it didn't even know who it was outside of Mihas.

All these years of being with him, and here Claudia was, in

a fetid bathroom, naked and cast out while wondering if he would even care.

Claudia's body rolled and twisted, and before it even knew what was happening, it had changed back into the true shape that had been pulling at it for so long.

Claudius.

Whole now, he looked closer in the mirror.

How long had it been? Years? Nearly a century, ever since going Underground?

The woman in the tub was kicking now, as if to get as far away from the vampire as possible.

A hurt laugh escaped Claudius. "At least Mihas was never *horrified* by this body."

He ran a claw over its stronger features: the aquiline nose, the broader cheekbones. Then his throat burned around his next words.

"The wandering masters used to tell him that we vampires either lose emotion or gain it to a level that would drive any human mad. I've loved him for so long that I don't know any other way to exist but this, yet . . ." Claudius got to his knees again. "He's never going to feel about me as I feel about him, is he?"

The woman began to weep, making no sound.

"It's taken me this long, but he's never going to accept what I am," Claudius added, leaning over to her. "He's never going to see that I'm not an 'it.' "

The victim stared at him, and although his first instinct was to revert back to "it," he stayed in his real form, feeling stronger for some reason.

What would Mihas do if Claudius returned to him *this* way? They lived in a far more open-minded culture now. Couldn't Mihas adjust to that as he had adjusted to every other societal convention in order to, one day, bring change to the world?

Claudius didn't know, because his mistake had always been in changing for Mihas.

He hesitated in pulling the woman out of the tub so he might hang her and become gorgeous once again for the one he so loved.

What if he refused to be "it," anymore?

He was so occupied in the asking that he never heard the footsteps coming up the stairwell. He didn't even hear the door to the apartment creaking open, nor the one to the bathroom.

Yet he did feel the biting line of a long blade as it nestled against the back of his neck.

TWENTY-SEVEN
The Trouble with Brothers

Dawn had both hands on the hilt of her machete as she fit its blade to the back of the naked vampire's neck, which was rough with bloodied wounds and the stringiness of tendons from the side to the front. Even his legs were scribbled with crusting gore.

There'd been a fight with this one, she thought, and the team was going to find out why.

Jonah was backing her up; so was an armed Kiko, even though his first priority was to guard Natalia at the door. All of them had no doubt this was a bloodsucker because the new girl had indisputably IDed this vampire after the Friends had manipulated the cameras around the area and guided them up here, into this empty apartment building. Natalia might not be able to differentiate between various vampire levels, so the team was on major guard if this vamp was more powerful than one of the schoolgirls from Queenshill.

Dawn didn't look away from her target as she talked to Kalin, who hovered back by Jonah. "Thought you said this one was female."

They'd even seen her outside, when she'd turned back into a full woman before attacking her victim, and the Friends had identified her.

Mrs. Jones, Dawn thought. Right in front of them.

"It shifts," Kalin said simply.

A regiment of Friends crowded just outside the room, too, waiting, and Breisi was even on her way here from Southwark, leaving an even bigger contingent of spirits there to guard headquarters along with Frank. She wasn't about to miss something that could lead to their endgame.

Jones stirred under the machete, probably because of Kalin's ethereal voice. Dawn took a moment to scan him: shining brown hair, his nudity showcasing a long, sinewy, smoothly pale body.

"So we've got us a shifter," Dawn said. "I've encountered a vamp before who was real good at that, and things didn't turn out too well for him."

Benedikte.

Dawn's pulse began to echo in the darkness at the center of her, and adrenaline made each breath tight and laced with an excitement that had, somewhere over this past year, mutated from a healthy fright into this.

There was a kicking sound from the bathtub.

The victim. Dawn had been watching Jones, so she'd almost forgotten, but not quite.

Without being told, Jonah went to the woman, gently scooping her into his arms before rushing her out of the bathroom. Dawn wondered if he was going to soothe her, then have a Friend lull her to sleep just until a spirit could see her safely home after they took care of matters here. Maybe he'd even mind-wipe her, even though the Hollywood line of vampires only did that under dire circumstances.

But this would count, Dawn thought.

The vampire moved under her machete again.

"Not if you want your head to stay attached," she told him, her tone sharp and icy. "We've got other blades ready to go, too, so don't think you've got room to maneuver on us."

Dawn could hear Kiko readjusting his grip on a saw-bow—a mix between a crossbow and cutting machine that was generally too big for him. But he'd insisted on bringing it up here from the car because it offered coverage at a distance. He had good enough aim to swipe off any vamp's head if Dawn were to get out of the way in time, so she hadn't argued.

As for Natalia, she'd chosen a machete just like Dawn's, even though the new girl had been directed to stay out of things unless the team got desperate.

"Who are you?" the creature asked from his lower position. His accent carried only the barest indication of the East in there, much, much less than Costin's. Dawn might not have been able to pick it out if she hadn't been so used to the hint of it.

She still hadn't seen the vamp's face because his brown hair was covering most of it.

"I'm afraid that you misunderstand how this all works, Jones," she said. "You're going to be telling *us* who you really are, and what you have to do with those schoolgirls."

The vampire started laughing while raising his hands in a mild surrender. His shoulders shook, so Dawn pressed the machete blade harder against his neck. She wouldn't kill him because there were too many questions that needed answering.

Well, she wouldn't kill him *yet*.

A line of blood appeared as Jones kept laughing, sawing his own flesh under the blade as if he didn't care about wounds at all.

Masochist, Dawn thought, even though the slice was already starting to heal.

But just as she was thinking it, the vampire whipped around with such speed that she barely had the machete raised before he smacked her across the room.

No—

She zoomed through the air, slammed against a wall, her head thunking against the tile. Her wig was only a slight cushion, sending her brain to reeling as she slid down to the floor while hearing the grinding *swick* of Kiko's saw-bow, which he'd aimed only to disable the vampire.

She tried to get a grip on herself as the metallic blade winged across the room, moving lazily in her dizzy perception.

Costin's soul, she thought, and it sounded like a tape that'd been left in the sun for too long.

Helpless anger gathered, mostly at herself for being taken out so easily and so early.

She couldn't have failed him again. . . .

Then a flood overcame her—the blackness, filling her with strength and drive, slowly pushing her to her feet with such looming rage that all she saw was the color red bathing everything: the once-white room, the saw-bow blade as it took its time in sparking and spinning toward Jones, who was already calmly stepping out of its path.

While anger loaded itself into Dawn, as if she were a weapon herself, the saw-blade flew past the vamp and ricocheted off the wall, flailing into a corner where it bit into the floorboard.

Jones leveled a long, fiery look at Kiko, who had dropped the unloaded saw-bow and was standing in front of Natalia, guarding her, drawing a gun loaded with silver darts—the better to stun and poison the creature for questioning.

The anger was still bringing Dawn to the point where she'd be able to do some damage, clarifying her sight and thoughts. But before it all came together for her, she blinked, bringing everything into better focus while Kiko fired.

The dart *thwack*ed into the vampire's pulped neck.

Jones only flinched with the contact, then curiously plucked out the silver with two delicate fingers.

Silver . . . It'd poisoned the Hollywood crowd, but it was no good on this one.

Laughing again, the vampire began talking—his voice a limb-melting lull.

"Come here, little one. Come, all of you."

The darkness tugged Dawn toward itself—herself—but she found her body disobeying her mind, and she took a leaden step forward, just like Kiko was doing, too.

Couldn't she fight it?

And, God . . . where was Jonah? What was keeping him out of the room—a struggle with Costin for dominance?

Was Costin refusing to come out?

"You're the attackers from Queenshill," the vampire continued with its charm-laden tone. "I can put two and two together because there aren't many little men interested in my kind in this area—"

As Kiko and Dawn took another step—damn it, why couldn't she stop herself?—Natalia leaned forward into Jones's words, too.

But then she lifted an arm, aimed her wrist, and sent a stream of holy water at the vampire from one of the team's Spidey bracelets.

Was she . . . immune?

How?

On contact, the water singed the surprised vamp, and he lost his power over Dawn as puffs of smoke curled from his bare skin. He cried out and attempted to shift into another form, his eyes slanting, his body growing dark gray hair, his teeth needling, leaving him looking only half-human now.

Holy items were obviously the ticket, so Dawn mentally pushed the darkness through her, clearing herself. Then she targeted the thing with her own bracelet, and when the bolt of water sizzled into the vampire's flesh, she felt the resurgence of dark joy giving her power. Control.

As Jones's yells of pain grew louder, she increased the water's pressure, wanting the agony to go on and on. . . .

"Stop, Dawn."

It was a voice she'd never thought to hear again, and the sound of it jerked her out of the murky stupor.

Costin. And he'd said her name like *she* was the bad guy here.

She glanced at him, and with the way Jonah—no, Costin, *Costin*—was looking at her, Dawn knew he'd only stopped her from utterly losing control and tiptoeing into a place she shouldn't be going.

But she also saw a personal accusation in his gaze, too, and she knew why.

The almost-bite, back in the car with Jonah.

Yet this wasn't a therapy moment; Costin had already turned toward the creature, and Dawn realized that the boss would have dared to go closer to the vampire for only one reason.

If he had sensed a master from the other room.

But this couldn't be a master, she thought, her core still swirling with the craving to hurt. This vampire didn't seem even half as powerful as Benedikte had been.

The cat thing was staring at Costin, his arms shielding his face as he stayed caught in a stage somewhere between human appearance and full vampire.

"That voice," he said.

"You recognize me, Claudius?"

Claudius. During the past year, Costin had shared the names and traits of his former blood brothers with Dawn. He'd told her that Claudius had been the brightest of them all—the planner who used his brain rather than brawn. Costin had even predicted that Claudius, whose thirst for violence was relatively lacking on the battlefield, would never have survived on his own all these centuries.

But he was a master vampire now, and the smart creature had been masquerading as Mrs. Jones.

As the master vamp shook his head—he didn't recognize Jonah's body—Dawn churned inside, raging to get at him, to get to the question about the dragon's location so they could tear this thing apart and be that much closer to winning. Killing Claudius would hopefully turn his own progeny human again, his termination restoring his children's souls, and that would disable the Underground until the team could go to it and clean it up.

But was that how a joint Underground would work, too? Costin had never told her. . . .

Dawn fisted her hands, her short nails digging into her palms.

In the meantime, Claudius's flesh was already healing from the holy burns Dawn and Natalia had inflicted.

"I only recognize that you're the vampire who tore at the dogs and went after the girls that night at Queenshill," he said to Costin. "You match what I saw in Della's report. Am I supposed to recognize more about you?"

Costin smiled, almost sadly at having to take responsibility for Jonah's bloodlust.

"Not yet, Claudius," he said. "But you *will* recognize me."

Dawn moved forward to help him, but he violently held up a hand to her. The ferocity of his gesture halted her more than anything.

But she couldn't stop what had obviously repulsed him in the first place—the brutal longing inside of her.

With a swish of jasmine, Breisi arrived to stand by Dawn, as if she'd sensed her turmoil, yet it only got worse as Costin fully focused on Claudius, who seemed so quiet—too quiet—in his corner.

The enemy was about to throw all he had at them, Dawn thought. And what if Costin, who didn't have access to his greatest powers while locked in Jonah's body, couldn't defend against it?

She kept her inner fires burning, allowing the ire to consume her.

She'd protect him, even if he was momentarily pissed at her.

"You're open to holy weapons," he said to Claudius, tilting his head, a fellow, curious vampire. "There are other masters who aren't. Perhaps you carry some guilt about a sin or two, and memories of your upbringing—the beliefs that you once held dear—consume you?"

Claudius tightened his lips, and that's when Dawn knew the creature wasn't going to spill any information whatsoever.

She mentally sidled up to Costin's consciousness, throwing caution about using their connected powers to the wind. There could be no holding back now because they were so close to getting somewhere.

At first, he barred her, but she pressed harder, and he finally allowed her in.

Yet she could tell he was guarding everything from her.

Let me make him talk, she thought. *You can't go out of that body to best him anymore.*

I still have a few tricks up my sleeve, he answered. *I need you to restrain him, Dawn, and that's all. Do you understand?*

She felt leashed, and the darkness ate at the restraints.

Trust me, she thought. *That's all* you *have to do, Costin.*

But he blocked her out of his head, leaving her in a cold place.

Alone.

Yet then the darkness reared up to swallow her, letting her know that *it* wanted her.

That it would never let her down.

By the door, Kiko had abandoned his dart gun in favor of his mini flamethrower, covering Natalia, who was holding her machete like it was a crucifix.

Costin stepped closer to his old blood brother.

"Talk to me, Claudius," he said, a deeply hypnotic sway to his tone. "Tell me everything, including where the dragon is."

Since the persuasion was targeted at Claudius, it didn't affect the team, and the other vampire, still in half-cat form, closed his eyes, resisting. His claws grew, his sharp, thin teeth pushing over his bottom lip.

Still not talking, Dawn thought.

Well, they'd see about that.

A black rush ripped through her, then out of her, pushing out toward Claudius. It wrapped around his neck, digging into the exposed tendons and meat with nailed force while sliding him partway up the wall.

She heard Kiko and Natalia gasp, then smelled jasmine surrounding her as Breisi whispered, *"Careful, Dawn!"*

Careful of what?

Hurting a master?

Going soft on a thing that wanted to wipe out humanity and keep Costin's soul from him?

The darkness rebelled against all arguments, shooting Claudius farther up the tiles until he banged into the ceiling, dangling there like a wilted leaf.

Costin had told her to restrain him, and that's all she was doing.

Either he was too far into his hypnosis to come out of it and correct her or he thought she hadn't gone overboard this time, so she didn't stop, even as Claudius gripped his neck, gagging.

"Tell me *all*, Claudius," Costin said, and she could feel his mind opening so he could attack with his Awareness.

But, baring his teeth, the other vampire blazed a look at Costin first.

He stepped back with the force of it, and Dawn knew that Claudius was using his Awareness to rip at the opened link between the blood brothers.

Without weighing the consequences, she busted into Costin's gaping mind, finding herself in the midst of their communicated images.

The night they had been turned by the dragon . . .

The blood-smeared battles against the enemies of the cross . . .

The love Claudius had for another brother . . . Mihas? . . . and the years of pining for his comrade . . . Claudius's shame and fear of how others would judge his love a sin . . .

Claudius, changing himself into another, more acceptable shape, a woman . . .

Then, in another time, another place, this woman grandly entering a set of doors that led to a bed where this Mihas was writhing under love bites from vampires who looked similar to the Queenshill schoolgirls . . .

Dawn's thoughts wove into the images. *An Underground of joint masters.* Wicked *masters.*

She found her voice, even while she was entangled in their Awareness.

"The dragon," she yelled at Claudius, asking the question that had to be asked before Costin destroyed each master. "Where's the dragon?"

It was like a black wall crashed down, blocking the rest of the images, but Dawn rammed against it, one time, two—

Costin pushed her out of the Awareness, and with the snapping of her concentration, she lost her grip on Claudius and he fell to the floor.

As Dawn recovered, mentally pinning the master vamp so he

couldn't move, she noticed that Costin had sunk to the ground, too, weary from losing the energy he'd expended, even while doing something that would've been so easy for him before he'd been trapped in Jonah's body.

But she didn't lag on that, because the faint smile on Claudius's face told her that he knew about the dragon, and he damned well wasn't going to tell.

Or that's how *she* saw it as her gaze flushed red again.

Was the dragon in this joint Underground of his?

Then she heard something—a sound in the near distance—and Claudius's needled smile got even bigger.

Barking dogs, and they were approaching.

Kiko heard it, too. "He's summoning animals, just like those Queenshill girls did."

"If he's their master," Dawn muttered, "he gave them that power."

She moved her mind quickly, releasing Claudius only for the second it would take to shut the apartment door, slam abandoned furniture against it, then come back to hold him down again.

Yet, it didn't work that way.

Just as she'd shored the door with the final chair, the enemy sprang to his feet, changing again, but this time, he seemed to be altering himself into the womanly form Dawn had seen in the Awareness.

Mrs. Jones.

For an instant, she seemed confused to be in this kind of state.

Yet then she raised her chin and became male again before mutating into a full cat-vampire form, seething, wielding fangs and claws while aiming his body at Dawn.

She armed herself for his attack, darkness sweeping around inside her, rising. But then Costin . . .

Costin stood and flashed his own fangs at Claudius, warning him off.

Costin, who hated what he'd become and was finally using it.

The two creatures jumped at each other, colliding as they ripped and clawed on the way down.

While the Friends scrambled around, Kiko targeted with his flamethrower.

"No!" Dawn said. He'd get Costin while trying for Claudius.

"Then separate their asses!"

Before Dawn could blast out with her mind, the Friends charged the fighting vampires, jamming against Claudius, trying to force him away, their voices raised as they tried their own lulling powers on the enemy.

But they were ineffective against this master.

Dawn was scared to death that Jonah's body—which couldn't possibly stand up to even a weak master—would get destroyed and Costin would expire along with it, so she fired away with her mind power, hoping that the surge would help the Friends part the two vampires.

Instead, the push of it banged Costin and Claudius against the wall near the tub, and they smashed down into the basin. Even though Dawn couldn't see Costin anymore, it was obvious from Claudius's position on top, where he slashed down with his claws, that he was tearing through Costin's clothes to his skin.

Oh, God, oh, God, this was it. She'd failed, and there was nothing she could do. . . .

Wait, she thought, coldness settling inside of her.

There was something.

She concentrated. Concentrated. Whipped herself to the height of a frenzy.

Higher.

Higher—

It punched out of her, connecting to Claudius and jerking him by the cat hair out of the tub, arcing him up, then down to the ground.

The crack of bones punctuated the vampire's screech, but Dawn wasn't done.

She pounded him to the floor again and again until the vampire went limp. Then, before it could start healing, she wrapped around his ankles and hung him upside down from the ceiling.

Meanwhile, Costin stayed in the tub, no doubt healing what damage had just been done to him.

"You know where the dragon is," she said to Claudius. "Tell us!"

The vampire stayed silent, swinging back and forth from the ceiling, his mouth pressed shut.

Dawn sliced out with her mind, and a rip formed in the vampire's stomach.

Her heart seemed to suspend its beating. Had she just . . . ?

Everyone else in the room froze as Claudius cried out and pressed his hands to the wound. Even so, his blood poured out, dripping to the tile, every thick, liquid bead impaling itself into Dawn's chest, where it was so cold and still.

"Where . . . is . . . the . . . dragon?" she asked softly, shaking now with all the waning energy it took to keep attacking.

Blood seeped out from between Claudius's fingers, the red bathing his pale, naked body.

In response, Dawn's gaze turned to a deeper crimson, as if soaked. Breisi pushed at her, just like the Friend was trying to make her back off.

But why? This wasn't any time to be nice. Claudius would've killed Costin or any one of them.

The blood brother lifted his head to stare up at the slice in his stomach. Then, as he went limp, he smiled, like he was appreciating some sort of irony.

Did he know he was beaten?

He broke that illusion when he spoke. "There is no dragon."

"Bullshit!" Dawn yelled.

"No, truly."

He kept swinging, bleeding. And when he tried to use his charmed voice on her, she anticipated it, ripping at the vocal chords in his already damaged throat.

She just damaged it a little more is all.

The room plunged into an even deeper silence, but she wasn't done.

He was barely able to talk at all now, just in a grating wheeze. "There's only my community of girls who live with me. You already met them. Sweet little vampire *bitches* who would have the both of us for breakfast."

Dawn wanted to take him apart bit by bit for being so damned smug. "You're lying. We know there're two masters in your community. We saw it in your Awareness."

Claudius twitched, like he was surprised at the extent of what she could do.

"That's right," Dawn said. She was becoming more cognizant by the second that Kiko and Natalia were still covering Claudius with their own weapons, that the Friends were ready to attack if the vampire made another move. "We've got your number."

The vampire opened his mouth as his own blood trickled into it, then he laughed again, sputtering red, maybe because he knew he wasn't going to get out of this after all.

"Mihas," he whispered with a combination of yearning and sorrow. But he said it in a way that also made Dawn think for some reason that Claudius had all the power of the Underground in his hands right now.

Was there some sort of power play going on between the two joint masters?

Would Claudius betray this Mihas with the proper persuasion?

"What about Mihas?" Dawn asked. "You ought to tell me now before I decide to just go ahead and tear off that head of yours. And I can do it, too."

She didn't know if that was true, but right now, she felt powerful enough to try.

Claudius opened his mouth, as if to talk.

But then, with a pained sigh, he closed it again.

The darkness didn't react well to that: It swamped Dawn with the urgency of getting the information that was at their fingertips. It crashed inside her, then screamed outward, surrounding Claudius's head and squeezing—

His face looked like two giant, invisible fingers were squishing it, vising his skull, ready to pop him open like a grape.

"Dawn!"

It was Breisi, who'd returned to Dawn while the other Friends flared around the room. In Dawn's peripheral vision, she could see that some spirits were lifting Costin out of the tub, propping him up while he barely raised his head to watch what Dawn was doing. But his face was so serrated with wounds, her focus so limited, that she couldn't tell what he might be thinking.

She could also see that the Friends were urging Kiko toward Dawn, probably trying to get him to talk sense to her, but he was resisting, just as intent on getting the information from Claudius as she was; in fact, he, in turn, was holding Natalia back from Dawn.

"*What are you doing?*" Breisi asked again as Dawn squeezed even harder.

Harder.

But Breisi wasn't asking what Dawn was doing as much as how far she would go to get this information out of Claudius.

The darkness felt like blood pulsing through her now, a part of her body, her composition.

And she was good at this, she realized. She was so damned close to getting this master to talk, better than Costin even—

She exerted more pressure, her vision red-thick and almost impenetrable.

Squeezing . . .

Something seemed to explode on her cheek, a burst of heat and pain, a sparkler in the pitch of a summer night, but she ignored that and kept pressing. . . .

Breisi crashed against Dawn, jarring her, making her lose hold of Claudius, who clumped to the floor, where a rush of Friends held him down.

In the clarity of Dawn's restored vision, she saw that he wasn't moving. He was only staring at the ceiling, as if Dawn had mushed his brains.

Just as she started feeling relieved at that—she'd gotten Claudius before he'd gotten Costin—she saw Costin moving toward her, using some Friends as a crutch, and his gaze . . .

His gaze was sadder than she'd ever seen it.

The discovery brought her back like a hard wallop, and she looked at Claudius, then at Costin, who'd never taken a thrill out of hurting his quarry, even though he was supposed to be more of a monster than she was.

Shame heated her, and she became aware of the pain on her cheek. The mini explosion she'd felt.

She touched it. No wound. Just a slight tenderness.

Costin hovered above her, barely balanced, the injuries on his face and neck already starting to close.

She started to explain why she had done it, why she had been fighting for him so thoroughly with all she had in her, but he only turned away.

She wrapped her arms around her torso, sinking into herself.

Kiko and Natalia, who stayed near the door, were staring at

Dawn with even more fascination and . . . disgust? . . . than the other day when she'd puppeted the smoker in that pub. Slowly, she realized that there wasn't any more barking outside because she'd broken Claudius's hold on the animals.

As Costin spoke, she locked her gaze on the master vampire, whose eyes were still fixed on nothing.

"Now we transfer the master to headquarters," he said in the low voice that had never chilled her as much as it did at this second. "Afterward, Friends should inspect the area at Highgate where they first saw Claudius running."

Kiko blanched. "What about killing this thing?"

"No," Dawn said, startling even herself. "Claudius knows more than he's letting on."

Costin didn't acknowledge that. "I am going to use the security of our own territory to extract the information." He barely glanced at Dawn. "In my own way."

She didn't understand at all. Why be kind to the enemy that was keeping him from reclaiming his soul? Why handle the vampire with kid gloves when he had already tried to kill Costin and wouldn't hesitate to do it again if he had the chance?

But she had no high ground where she could throw down an argument. Not now, while everyone was avoiding even looking at her.

That is, everyone except Kiko.

"By bringing Claudius to headquarters," he said tightly, "you're inviting any vampire who's connected with him to pay a visit."

Using a Friend for balance, Costin walked toward the doorway. "If they choose to bring the fight above, we will be ready."

He left the room in stunned silence, because before now, he'd been adamant about keeping the war under the ground, refusing to risk revealing their presence to the world. Once society knew about vampires, they'd go after Costin, too, since in their view he was one of them.

Was he daring this Underground to come and get Claudius?

Was he using the vampire as bait just as he'd used Dawn in Hollywood?

There was no way to know, even if she and Costin were supposed to be connected.

As Costin left the room, the Friends bound themselves around the unmoving Claudius, restraining him in case he had more fight in him than it looked like. Then Kiko got out his crucifix, telling Natalia to do the same so they could also visually bind the vampire if it came down to it. The remaining spirits then pushed the master out of the bathroom; they'd have to discreetly get him to the car, where, together, all of them would transport their interviewee to headquarters.

Kiko glanced at Natalia. "He didn't get to you with his charmed voice like he did to us."

She looked puzzled as she left the room. "No, he didn't. Not very much. But don't ask me why, Kiko, because I have no answers for you." She started moving her face toward Dawn, but then stopped. "No answers at all."

She exited without completing that backward glance.

Kiko stood there for a second, just before the doorway.

"Dawn?" he asked.

She met his gaze, afraid to see what'd be hiding in his eyes, now that they were alone.

"You beat it tonight," he said, his eyes a clear blue. A gaze that wasn't wavering from hers.

He wasn't talking about beating a vampire, either.

"Remember that, okay?" he added. "You stopped whatever it was you can do with that head of yours. You ended up keeping it under control."

Then he left, and Dawn tried to feel good about what he'd said.

But, instead, she felt like she'd been locked in a dark room.

A room where a slant of light was the only thing creeping through the broken shutter of a window that had been pried halfway open, only to be slammed shut again.

TWENTY-EIGHT

The Beauty Mark

About an hour later, after they'd secured Claudius under a watch group of Friends and bound him with nearby crucifixes down in the lab at a fortified headquarters, Dawn peered in the mirror in her bathroom, her wig tossed to the side as she scrubbed her face for the fifth time.

The makeup had come off during the first cleaning, but after all the others, her face still wasn't clean.

There was still a mark above her left cheekbone in the exact place she'd felt that tiny explosion while she'd been squeezing Claudius's skull to the breaking point.

She backed away from her reflection.

Was this what was in store for her? A mark for every bad thing she did from now on?

The darkness taking over from the inside out?

A tremor ate away at her gut as she started to walk away, but then, like she couldn't stop staring at that mark, she was back at the sink again, leaning closer to the looking glass, her heart throttled by something like panic.

Every time she glanced at the spot on her face, she couldn't decide what it was. On initial inspection, she'd discerned a small, vague crescent that resembled a half-moon, just like the earring she used to wear before she became a real hunter. On the second look, she'd gotten the feeling that something on her skin was half smiling in one of those little grins a person wore when they'd done something wrong and they'd almost gotten away with it. On the third, she'd only seen something that resembled a gunpowder burn—a blemish she could scrub off if she tried hard enough. Then on the fourth, she'd told herself it was only a scar that had replaced the ones she'd lost when she'd become a vampire for a short time.

But now, as she kept looking, she thought that maybe the mark was a Rorschach test designed to make her crazy.

She felt someone—something—behind her before the mirror even showed Costin.

Was he here to tell her she'd be okay, like Kiko had done earlier?

But then she realized that his eyes were blue, and she glanced back at her mark.

"You doing okay?" Jonah asked.

She'd forgotten—he'd returned to his dominant position even before they'd exited that scummy apartment in Dalston. On the drive back, he'd told the team about how he and the boss had fought together, and she'd understood only then that Jonah had been helping Costin use his vampiric powers, encouraging him.

She had no idea just how Costin felt about that, now that he must've realized fighting with his new powers was necessary for him to survive out there.

"In what way do you think I'd be okay?" she asked Jonah. "In that yay-we-caught-a-master way? Or in a more of a wow-it-felt-great-to-almost-kill-another-master one?"

He took her wounded sarcasm in stride, leaning back against the door frame, his gaze on her facial mark, even though he didn't comment.

"Just thought I'd come up here to check on where you'd gone after we took care of Claudius in the lab," he said. "Thanks to security precautions and the Friends, this place is as good as a fortress, so if the Underground comes to us to stage an escape for Claudius, we're ready."

Were they?

He added, "Dawn, the sun's almost up, and you should get some sleep in before tomorrow night comes around and Costin emerges to question Claudius. After that, things could go pretty quickly, with us getting a location out of this master, then destroying him, then figuring out how we'll lay waste to this Underground and the co-master."

"There's no sign of Shadow Girl outside yet?" she asked, finally glancing away from the mirror and grabbing a hand towel to wipe down a marble counter that didn't really need it. "If anything like one of those shadows was tuned into what we were doing or saying back at that apartment building, they're going to follow us here."

"There's no sign of much right now. Really, Dawn, shut down, okay? I'm going to do it so Costin's rested and ready for Claudius. If there's an attack on the horizon, the Friends have got it covered. They'll alert us."

Shut down, he'd said. Just like a robot.

"Dawn," he continued, and he sounded the way he did when he'd almost bitten her and she'd been all too willing to let him.

She tossed the towel back on the counter. "Jonah, is it too much to ask to be left alone for even an hour?"

"No." Yet he didn't go anywhere. "But if you don't plan on sleeping, maybe it'd be a good idea to come and lounge with the others. They're winding down themselves."

The others. Why did she feel so far removed from them?

But even if that was the case, going downstairs to be with Kiko, Natalia, and her dad tempted her. Better yet, the thought of going into Eva's room, where her mom hadn't emerged from, seemed like perfect medicine for what Dawn was feeling. Sitting by her mother's bed while she slept sounded like a good way to be around someone who didn't insist that she talk about tonight.

Dawn made eye contact with Jonah in the mirror, and he seemed so understanding that she didn't want to look away. Not this time.

"I'm not sure what I'd do," she said, "if I went downstairs and they all stopped talking. I'd know exactly what the subject was, Jonah. I'd know what they were thinking while they looked at me, all awkward and embarrassed and judgmental."

"And what exactly would they be saying about you?"

Was he for real?

"Okay." He straightened from the door frame. "Maybe Natalia was taken aback—I'll be honest about that, but she hasn't been in this business long at all. She really has no idea what it's about on more than an ideal level. But Kiko's on your side through and through. So's Frank."

"He is?" She could barely get the words out.

Somehow, even though they hadn't been the closest throughout the years, her dad's approval mattered.

"He gets it," Jonah said softly. "He knows that it's easy to lose yourself in the fight sometimes."

She wanted to believe Jonah, but . . . God. It couldn't be this easy. "Breisi doesn't understand. And I know Costin sure doesn't."

Before Jonah could give her any platitudes about that, she looked down at the sink, away from the mirror, her voice wavering until heat rushed her eyes.

She fought it back. "I'm going to change. I'm not going to let it happen again. I'm going to . . ."

She gestured to the dark spot on her face, stopping short of saying that she was going to do everything within her power to avoid being marked every which way.

But Jonah's expression hardened: that face she had once likened to a broken saint's, back when he'd first come out of the shadows and become more than just a voice.

Yet that had been Costin coming out of the shadows in Hollywood, not Jonah.

"You are what you are," he said, his voice intense. "The worst thing you could ever do is deny it, Dawn."

She liked hearing that, but then again, she didn't like it, because she knew that it was one thing to use what she had for the greater good and another to use it because it *felt* good.

Besides, this was Jonah talking. When had she listened to anything he had to say, no matter how much she wanted to hear it right now?

Still . . .

She walked past him before he could persuade her any more, because what he had to say was too destructive. But as she headed downstairs to face her coworkers—she had to do it sometime, and it might as well be now—she sensed Jonah following.

Yet strangely, she didn't tell him to go away.

Instead, she headed for the lounge where everyone was sitting around, their voices strung out in murmurs that echoed off the old wood and paintings. And the second she stepped into the room—the one with the hunting tapestries on the wall—they all really did stop talking.

Dawn wanted to turn around and get out of there, but then Kiko stood.

Then Frank.

Natalia stayed in her chair, watching Dawn as if she was concerned about her breaking loose on her next.

Dawn swallowed, knowing she should say something but, for the life of her, she had no idea what it should be.

Frank extended an arm. "Why don't you just come here, Dawnie."

Hesitantly, she went to him, sitting next to her father as they both sank down to the sofa, his arm draped over her shoulders while he pulled her to the hard bulk of him.

For the first time in ages, she dropped all her defenses and leaned her head against her dad, just like she'd done a few times as a girl during the rare occasions they had actually been getting along. And when he hugged her closer, her eyes went hot and wet again.

She was still a girl, she realized. Still making her way in a world she didn't understand at all.

She glanced back to see where Jonah was, but he wasn't around anymore, so she turned back to the rest of them as they slipped into a conversation about vintage cars—a subject she knew they'd plucked out of thin air.

But as she listened to them make distracting talk—the only thing that was probably keeping them together right now—she kept resting her head against Frank.

Almost feeling like part of the family again.

Dear Reader,

Thank you so much for reading *The Path of Razors*. You won't have long to wait for Dawn and the team's business with this Underground to conclude—the next book in the London trilogy, *Deep in the Woods*, will be released March 2010, and I hope you'll keep your eye out for it. As you know, this series uses trilogies to complete mystery, character, and mythology arcs, so as with Books One through Three in the Hollywood trilogy, this London adventure will be resolved in the next installment.

Please stop by www.vampirebabylon.com for more news about future releases, and once again, I really appreciate all your support.

Happy hunting,
Chris Marie Green